"LET ME SHOW YOU HOW NICE I CAN BE.

Come—sit here next to me."

He sat down. She put her arms around him and kissed him on the neck. Then she began unbuttoning his shirt, at first with both hands and then with just one. The other caressed his face for a moment and then reached back and slipped under the pillow.

It was so easy. He was so busy enjoying himself that he didn't even see the knife until the blade was at his throat. And then it was too late. By the time he began to pull away she had already cut him. He tried to say something, but the first word died in a wheezy gasp as his windpipe was severed. Angel's hands were becoming slippery with blood as she struggled to hold him down.

Angel had the impression that he was looking at her face when the light went out in his eyes. He had taken only a few seconds to die. . . .

Angel

A Novel by

Nicholas Guild

A Dell Book

Published by
Dell Publishing
a division of Bantam Doubleday Dell Publishing Group, Inc.
1540 Broadway
New York, New York 10036

ISBN: 0-440-22285-0

Reprinted by arrangement with Carroll & Graf Publishers, Inc.

Printed in the United States of America

Published simultaneously in Canada

December 1996

10 9 8 7 6 5 4 3 2 1

OPM

Nel mezzo del cammin di nostra vita
mi ritrovai per una selva oscura
Dante, *Inferno* I, 1-2

This book is for
Susan Sheridan,
who helped me find my way back to the light.

chapter 1

The Indian Pines Motor Lodge was just beyond the Dayton city limits, outside the official jurisdiction of its police force, but its reputation was well established and no one would have imagined Lieutenant Pratt might need directions.

Interstate 675 was a good five miles away and the road, which was used mainly by farm trucks, led to nowhere in particular. There was no reason to stray out here among the apple orchards except that you could park your car behind one of the tiny clapboard cabins without anyone knowing you had ever been there. These days you wouldn't think people would take the trouble, but they did. So far as anyone knew the same elderly couple named Daniels had been running the place ever since the invention of sin.

Not that there hadn't been problems—there were always problems—but mainly it was just the odd jealous husband or, more often, the lovers' quarrel that led to lots of shouting and maybe a black eye. Once some college kids had staged a party and one of them had ended up falling off a roof. When things got out of hand Perry Daniels phoned the state troopers, who would drive out in one of their black-and-whites to send everybody home. At worst somebody might have to finish the night in the district lockup.

Usually, though, it didn't come to that and, when things had settled down again, old Mrs. Daniels would fix up the Officer-on-the-Scene with a cup of coffee and a slice of pecan pie and no hard feelings. That was how the place stayed in business, by accommodating everyone's needs, by preserving a certain drowsy calm in the midst of baser passions.

But not today. All the way out from town Pratt had been listening to the radio traffic on his two-way, and when he turned into the gravel drive that led past the office to the guest cabins he counted six patrol cars. More were coming, including the meat wagon from the county coroner's office. This was going to be very bad for trade.

It was a hot morning, even at 8:30, and when Pratt looked around the yard it was clear there was no shade. The only air conditioning that came out of the vents below his dashboard was like a dragon's breath.

The troopers were always very touchy about jurisdiction and Pratt had been up half the night on a particularly nasty case. He wasn't sure he could muster the patience to be diplomatic, so when he saw Josh Carlson, District Commander, standing in the doorway of one of the cabins and frowning under the brim of his Smoky-the-Bear hat, he almost turned around and drove back to town.

But he didn't do that. Instead, he nosed his car into a flower bed, got out, dropped his keys into his jacket pocket and smiled. The two men had quietly disliked each other for fifteen years, but business was business.

It was only then he noticed that the expression on Carlson's face had nothing to do with the arrival of a city cop on his turf—whatever was eating him, it wasn't that. In fact, he didn't even seem to notice Pratt until he was spoken to.

"How are you, Josh?"

When Carlson glanced up, recalled by a human voice from whatever was darkening his inner world, he seemed actually relieved. His manner for the next four or five seconds was by his own standards practically cordial.

"Better check a map, Pratt," he said as his eyes narrowed in a not-quite-convincing display of suspicion. "Looks like you're off your beat."

He stepped a little to one side and Pratt was able to read the number on the cabin door—lucky Seven.

With his right hand Lieutenant Pratt made a little circular

movement in the air, seeming to dismiss himself from all official attention, and smiled again.

"I only drove out here to ask a few questions, Josh. I promise not to put my foot into any of your shit." He took a few absentminded, sidewise steps away from his car and glanced around like a man trying to remember something. "You feel like telling me what you got here?"

Carlson was a big man, a bit paunchy in middle age but heavy with muscle through the arms, chest and neck. The creases in his face and his heavy black eyebrows gave him a look of sullen self-confidence, as if he had never in his life experienced a moment of doubt. Only his eyes betrayed him now, and only for an instant, until the shadow of anxiety steadied into something like triumph. He might have been about to enjoy some long-sought-after revenge.

"A homicide," he announced, as if the fact amounted to a personal vindication. "A white male probably in his late twenties or early thirties, but it's a little hard to tell."

"No chance the guy slipped in the bathtub or shot himself in remorse over an unpaid library fine?"

"No chance."

"He check in last night?"

"About a quarter after ten. It's in the office registry book. 'Mr. and Mrs. Smith.' "

"So there was a woman with him." Pratt raised his eyebrows. He didn't mind letting that much surprise show. "I don't suppose she's anywhere around."

Carlson shook his head.

"The car is gone too—and his wallet. Either she took them or they had a visitor."

"Who found the body?"

"Mrs. Daniels." Carlson let his gaze drift up to a spot about two feet above Pratt's head. It was his way of distancing himself from any suggestion of failure. "We haven't taken a formal statement yet. Perry and his wife were still both pretty rattled when we first got here. We've let 'em hole up in their apartment, give 'em a chance to settle down."

Pratt didn't say anything—it was a point he felt he could make better by not saying anything—but he knew, and probably Carlson knew, that leaving witnesses alone together was always a mistake, since they tended to check their stories against each other and smooth out all the little inconveniences. So for about two beats he let Carlson feel the weight of his silent disapproval, and then he managed a tight smile.

"How long have you been on the scene?"

Carlson made a show of checking his watch. "A little more than an hour."

"That's long enough. You mind if I sit in while you question them?"

He didn't like it, but Carlson agreed. He couldn't very well disagree without implying he thought he owned this case, and that wouldn't give him a chance to share the blame later. So he managed another of his ponderous nods.

"Sure—come on."

They found the Danielses sitting at their kitchen table, a massive wooden affair with a top at least five inches thick and polished as smooth as a butcher's block. Their chairs were drawn close together and they were holding hands.

Both of them were pale and delicate-looking and rather small, and age had bleached their hair to the same perfect whiteness. Perhaps their long marriage and the privacy afforded by the Indian Pine Motor Lodge had worn away a lot of differences, because they looked so much alike they could almost have been cloned.

With a slight tilt of her chin, Mrs. Daniels indicated the chairs on the other side of the table. She seemed relieved when the two policemen had sat down and she no longer had to look up at them.

"This is Lieutenant Pratt, Dayton Homicide," Carlson said. Pratt nodded acknowledgment and took a pen and notepad from his inside coat pocket, the message being that he was present as a mere observer. This seemed to satisfy Carlson, who, for the first time, took off his hat and set it on the table beside him.

"Now, the gentleman in Number Seven," he began, "which of you folks signed him in last night?"

The Danielses exchanged a worried glance, as if they feared that any response might somehow be incriminating.

"Perry did."

"I did."

The two replies followed each other so closely that they blurred together.

"And that was when?"

"It was just ten-fifteen." Mr. Daniels was the one who answered, but his missus nodded in confirmation. She might have been punctuating the sentence for him.

"You have any other guests staying with you?"

Mr. Daniels shook his head. "It's the slow season."

"And a weeknight," Mrs. Daniels added.

"That's right—Mildred's right. A weeknight."

"Did you hear the car drive off?"

"No. That would have been after we went to bed."

"On weeknights Perry turns the sign off at one."

"And before then, did you hear anything to indicate a disturbance?"

"No," they both said, this time in unison.

Carlson touched the brim of his hat with the tip of one finger. It was a perfectly unconscious movement but an admission nonetheless. He was not gifted at this sort of thing, which did not fall within his normal duties. He wished he were somewhere else.

"I notice you have a drop box in the front door," Pratt said, speaking for the first time. "Was the key to Number Seven in there this morning?"

"No. Hardly anybody uses that thing."

"Mostly we find the keys in the rooms."

"Or people carry 'em off for souvenirs."

"That's right. Souvenirs."

Pratt nodded, as if he had never expected anything else.

"So, Mrs. Daniels, you let yourself in this morning with a passkey?"

"Yes, of course."

"Why not? It's our place, isn't it?" Mr. Daniels seemed ready to take offense until Pratt smiled and opened his hands in a gesture of submissive agreement.

"Absolutely. Why not? And you saw that the car was gone, so you . . ."

"That's right—so I knew the room was vacant."

When Mrs. Daniels realized what she had said, tears started in her eyes. She and her husband exchanged an anguished glance.

"Was the key in the room?" Pratt continued, trying to make the question sound as insignificant as possible.

For a moment there was no answer. Mrs. Daniels didn't seem to understand what he was talking about.

"Did you find the key in the room?" he repeated. "Was it on the bed or the chest of drawers or anyplace like that? Do you remember? You could have let yourself in, seen the key and put it in your pocket. Then after you found the corpse you might have forgotten all about it."

"It didn't happen like that. The second I opened the door I seen his feet stickin' out from the other side of the bed. After that I didn't worry about any key."

Pratt wrote the words "no key" in large letters across the first page of his notebook, leaned back in his chair and smiled benignly. If he asked another question these people would turn against him, and Carlson was beginning to look like he remembered this was his case. It was time to shut up.

"I can understand that, Mrs. Daniels. Thank you."

"Did you see the woman?" Carlson asked, aiming the question like a weapon. Probably he was just angry at Pratt, but it didn't come out that way.

"She stayed in the car."

"Did you see her in the car?"

"No." Perry Daniels looked uncomfortable, almost embarrassed. "But where else would she have been?"

"So you can't even be sure he had a woman with him."

"Now why in hell would a man sign in 'Mr. & Mrs.' if he didn't have a woman with him? Can you tell me that?"

"Could've been another man."

This was too much for Perry. Almost from one second to the next he became very pink in the face. He leaned against the table as though he meant to stand up.

"I saw her," Mrs. Daniels said, putting a hand on her husband's arm. "I saw her through the back window—I always check."

"Why, Mildred . . ." Mr. Daniels could not have looked more surprised if his wife had admitted to theft, but the elderly woman, who seemed to have regained her self-possession, merely shook her head.

"Perry's too trusting, so it's up to me. If we rent to a couple, I like to know it is just a couple and not all the uncles and cousins for good measure."

She took a deep breath, making it seem as if the admission was a load off her conscience.

"I saw her just for an instant while he opened the door for her. A pretty woman. Small, fair-haired. Elegant. Not the usual sort at all."

Mrs. Daniels nodded to herself—apparently "the usual sort" was a clearly defined category for her. Then, for the second time, her eyes filled with tears.

"I suppose now you'll be finding her dead somewhere too."

In the uncomfortable silence that followed, Pratt took something out of his jacket pocket. It was a standard-sized color snapshot of a man in a blue polo shirt holding a little boy on his lap—both of them were smiling, the way people only do for the camera. The photograph had a couple of white crease lines at the corners to suggest that it had been in somebody's wallet for a long time. Pratt slid it across the table toward Mr. Daniels.

"You ever seen this man before?" he asked.

Mr. Daniels took his glasses out of the case in his shirt pocket and studied the picture.

"That's Mr. Smith," he said, clearly taken by surprise. "Is he a suspect in something?"

"Not anymore."

"You want to tell me about this?" Carlson asked, once he and Pratt were outside again.

"Everything, but it's a long story. I think I'd better have a look at your stiff first."

"Okay. It isn't very nice."

Pratt would have known that much blindfolded. He had been a cop for nearly twenty years, the last eight in Homicide, and he had long since learned to recognize the smell of stale blood.

It was not a large room, no more than ten feet by twelve, with a couple of closets with sliding doors in the far wall and a half-open door that led predictably to the bathroom. The wallpaper was yellow with age and its floral pattern had faded almost to invisibility. There were lines running down the wall where the paper didn't quite touch, as if someone had scored them with a knife. A double bed with the pale green coverlet wadded up and thrown onto the only chair; one night table on the side closest to the bathroom—the lamp was still on—a chest of drawers painted white, its top scarred with cigarette burns and the dark circles left by drinking glasses.

The room was already crowded. There were four evidence technicians in their white coveralls, all very busy, all seeming to ignore each other's existence and that of the corpse lying on the floor on the other side of the bed so that only his legs and one arm, the hand already encased in a plastic bag, were visible from the door.

"You boys want to give us a minute?" Carlson asked in the

growly whisper he used with subordinates. It worked, because in less than ten seconds the technicians had cleared out, without even a glance at the Commander and his fellow tourist. Somehow their departure seemed to take all the air out of the room.

Pratt stepped around the bed for a better look. The dead man was naked, lying on his back; his head was up against a leg of the night table. He looked like he had kept himself in pretty good shape and there was no gray in the hair on his chest and arms. Judging from the appearance of his hands and feet, Pratt would have put him a year or two under thirty, but it was difficult to be sure without seeing the face. There was no face. It was just gone, peeled off like the skin from a grape.

"Since you're here, I wouldn't mind an opinion," Carlson said. He was still standing by the doorway. He looked like he would have preferred to leave.

Pratt didn't answer at first. He was kneeling beside the body, telling himself that he had seen worse messes—hell, a lot of traffic accidents were worse—that he was long past being affected by such horrors. A murder victim with his face cut away was just a novelty, a little unexpected but nothing else.

There were other wounds at well. The guy's genitalia, the whole standard issue, had been neatly sliced away, making him as smooth between the legs as any woman. And his throat was cut, from one side to the other in one clean, careful stroke, right under the chin.

The carpet was soaked in blood and there was blood on the night table, on that corner of the bed, even on the wall. It was always a little astonishing how much people bled when the carotid artery was severed.

"He was lying on the bed when he got it," Pratt said quietly. "You can see that from the spray pattern—it's pretty evenly horizontal and there isn't any blood on the wall higher than about three feet. Our perpetrator did him from behind, cutting from left to right. A very neat piece of work.

"I'd guess the guy was too busy dying to put up any kind of

a struggle. His heart was still beating when he hit the floor, since that's where he did most of his bleeding, but there was no fight in him. He might have been still alive when he lost his dick. You find a weapon?"

Carlson shook his head.

"Well, look for a knife, not a straight razor—come around here and take a peek at this."

Commander Carlson finally did step away from the door, but he didn't come any nearer than the foot of the bed and you couldn't say he took a particularly close look. Except that cops weren't supposed to be so fastidious, you couldn't really blame him.

This murderer seemed to do wonderfully careful work. The incision followed the hairline precisely, right down to the sideburns where it angled back to the corner of the jaw and then ran straight down to the slash which had severed the victim's throat and, presumably, ended his life. Then the skin had been peeled away—eyelids, lips, everything, probably in one piece, like removing a mask—so that the muscles and bones beneath were exposed as if for anatomical inspection. It must have taken some time. The only hint of haste or carelessness was that one of the eyeballs had been pierced and was somewhat collapsed in its socket.

Pratt regarded the fleshless face without the slightest trace of pity, which surprised him. Even after all these years murder victims, with their terrible exposed vulnerability, almost always exercised some claim on his sympathy, but not this one. Possibly that meant he should take retirement when he was eligible in another month. When you can't feel anymore, it's time to get out. Or maybe it was just that his sympathy was all used up. It had been a bad night for a lot of people.

"See these scratches along the brow ridge?" he said at last. "And these nicks in the cheek muscles? I think our perpetrator was using some sort of knife, something with a point. It would be tough to get under the skin and cut it away from the supporting tissue with a straight razor. Maybe a surgeon's scalpel—something with a blade two or three inches long. I assume the detached portions of our friend here are nowhere around."

"We haven't found them." Carlson continued to stand there, staring at nothing. He wasn't having a good time.

"I don't suppose you will," Pratt answered, nodding to himself. "Why go to all this trouble if you didn't plan to keep a few souvenirs?"

He stood up, locking his knees and putting a hand out to steady himself against the wall. He was more tired than he realized.

"Have they done the bathroom yet?"

"Sure." Carlson looked him straight in the eyes while he answered, as if he felt the need to assert himself. "Lots of prints—Mrs. Daniels doesn't do much more than change the bed between guests. We sent the towels off to the state lab. Seems like somebody took a shower."

"Wouldn't you?"

Pratt checked his watch. It was just three minutes shy of 9:00 a.m.

"My guess is he's been dead about twelve hours. He smells like twelve hours."

"You finished in here?" Carlson asked, with evident distaste. "My boys'd like to finish up before the coroner arrives."

"Sure."

Outside the heat was building fast, but at least the air didn't carry the smell of death. Pratt took a couple of deep breaths to clear his lungs and decided he was thirsty. But he was a lot of other things too, and they would all have to wait.

Carlson let his gaze drift back to the cabin doorway as if he wondered whether he ought not to go have another look.

"You think that's the guy in your picture?" he asked.

"It's a working assumption." Pratt took the photograph out of his jacket pocket again, glanced at it and handed it to Carlson. "We've wired the FBI for his prints, so we'll know by this afternoon. I think it's him. His name is Billinger, Stephen W. Billinger. The 'W' stands for 'Wentworth.' The address is 2343 Standish Road—it's in one of those new developments up by Shiloh."

"Any family?"

"A wife and two small sons, all deceased as of about two-thirty this morning."

"Jesus."

Carlson returned the photograph to Pratt, who put it back in his pocket without looking at it.

"Somebody phoned, said they'd heard shots. We sent over a squad car and they found the front door wide open. Mrs. Billinger was at the foot of the stairs in her bathrobe. She must have heard something and come down to investigate— maybe she thought hubby'd finally found his way home. She got a hollow-point bullet in the face at close range. It damn near took her head off. The two boys were in their beds upstairs, each shot through the top of the skull. From their positions it was evident they had died in their sleep.

"It's one of those little box houses on a small lot, and as far as we can tell the neighbors slept right through everything," Pratt went on, looking at nothing as he spoke. "You know what? I don't think anybody heard anything. I think whoever did it got in with Billinger's house key and then used a silencer. I think the report was phoned in by our perpetrator. I think somebody wanted us to hurry up and find the key to bungalow Number Seven in Mrs. Billinger's dead hand."

"And that's why you're out here?"

"And that's why I'm out here."

"So somebody killed Billinger here, sliced him up, drove into Dayton to do his family, and then phoned the cops. And maybe if Billinger hadn't been catting around last night his wife and kids would still be alive."

"Maybe."

"Jesus."

Pratt turned to watch the county coroner's wagon pull into

the driveway and stop in front of cabin 7. The man who got out on the passenger's side was about sixty, ponderously heavy and dressed in a dark suit that was in obvious need of cleaning and looked half a size too small. He ran the palm of his hand across his bald head and wiped it on the lapels of his coat. Then he looked over toward Pratt and Carlson and executed a cheery little wave, the circular lenses of his eyeglasses twinkling in the sunlight. He had lost interest and turned away even before they had a chance to return the greeting.

"One of the worst things about getting murdered in this county would be having Big Jimmy Lipson handle your corpse," Carlson said under his breath. "I'll bet he's sorry Billinger's girlfriend isn't in there. I think he gets off on this sort of thing."

Lieutenant Pratt, Dayton Homicide, didn't say anything. Carlson worked for the state, but coroners were elected in Montgomery County and after six consecutive terms in office Jimmy Lipson, M.D., was a figure of some importance in local politics. Of course that didn't mean he wasn't a creep.

"Where do you guess we're gonna find her?"

"Well, wherever it is, I think she'll be safe enough from Big Jimmy."

"Huh?"

Pratt looked back toward the doorway of bungalow 7. How many bedrooms just like it had he seen over his career? In the thousands, probably. The cheap furniture and the worn nylon rugs, the cigarette burns and the faded wallpaper and the bloodstains—it was enough to make you think that nobody ever died in good hotels.

There was a room on Wayne Avenue, three flights of stairs above a Chinese restaurant, where five years ago a prostitute named Amelia Terlecki had tried to kill her pimp, one Georgie "Iron Dong" Davis, known for giving his women a bad time. She had waited for him to climb up on the bed with her and then, after offering enough of the preliminaries to get him good and up, she had reached under her pillow for a straight razor and sliced him right off at the root. The poor son-of-a-bitch had lived to press charges.

It was a woman's trick to shave a man off like that. It took a woman's deep sexual hatred. Pratt had seen a lot of homosexual homicides, and a lot of them had been pretty nasty, but he had never known of a case in which one man mutilated another in that particular way.

And Billinger had been lying on his side when his throat was cut, his back turned as the murderer either crouched or lay beside him. One imagined he was expecting something much more pleasant.

It all fit together. Probably by now someone had tracked down the telephone operator who had taken the call on the Billinger case, and it seemed a good bet she would report that the caller had been a woman, probably fairly young.

A pretty woman, Mrs. Daniels had said. *Small, fair-haired. Elegant. Not the usual sort at all.* That was for sure.

"I mean, if you find her it won't be half naked in some cornfield after the birds have been at her," Pratt answered finally. "None of us have to worry about that, because she did it. She's our murderer."

chapter 2

"You okay, Dad?"

As he stood in the bedroom doorway James Kinkaid's hand felt for the light switch. He would wait maybe ten seconds. If he didn't hear an answer or, failing that, the slight snore that would mean his father had fallen peacefully back to sleep, he would flip it on.

"Is that you, Jimmy?"

The lamp on the nightstand went on with a little ping, making it unnecessary to answer. The man in the bed was sitting up, with three massive pillows propped behind his back, the folded top of the sheet making a neat line just below the second button on his elegant striped silk pajamas. He would stay that way all night, awake or asleep, hardly moving. It was a habit he had fallen into since his heart began giving him trouble.

He did not look sick tonight. Sometimes, when his angina was acting up, his skin would turn as yellow as candle wax, but tonight he seemed fine. In daylight the perfect whiteness of his hair and his smooth, saddle-leather tan made him look like one of those youthful old men who play tennis for an hour every morning, seem to have learned nothing from life and still find it amusing to flirt with young women.

It was only around the eyes that he showed the strain—eyes, pale blue and restless, that peeked hopelessly out from beneath their puffy lids like an actor parting the curtain a little to count the house.

But that was not his heart condition. That was just life.

When James saw at once there was no immediate danger, that this was to be a purely social occasion, he took a chair from beside the wall and carried it over to the bed.

"Did I wake you, son?"

"No. I was reading." It was a lie. They both knew it was a lie, but it spared the old man from imagining himself a nuisance. He wasn't a nuisance. "Do you want one of your pills? I'll get some water."

Mr. Kinkaid Senior, whose first name was also "James," as had been his father's and grandfather's, smiled and shook his head. "I was having a bad dream," he said. "I don't remember anything about it, except that it was bad. Too much pot roast, I guess."

"We had pot roast last night," his son answered. "Tonight was vegetable lasagna, although with Julia's cooking it's not an unnatural mistake."

"We ought to fire her before she poisons us."

"On the contrary, I'm convinced that Julia's vegetable lasagna has remarkable preservative powers. I always finish dinner feeling like I've been embalmed."

The father allowed himself one syllable of laughter, a sound that came out as a restrained and judicious "hmmm." Their housekeeper's cooking had been a standing joke between them for thirty years, a joke to be enjoyed only in their most private moments because neither of them would have dreamed of offending her.

"What were you reading?"

James Kinkaid IV paused for just a fraction of a second and then remembered what he was supposed to have been doing when a sound from his father's room had awakened him.

"The Abelson brief," he said, with a slight shrug. The case folder was, in fact, open on his night table.

"The abuse of trust?"

"Yes. I go in to Karskadon and Henderson on Thursday."

"Are they buying the champagne?"

The son nodded. The question was his father's time-honored formula for inquiring if the opposition was prepared to settle.

"Oh yes. They know they'll get their brains beaten out if

we ever go to trial. I expect them to come down for eighty percent of the amount listed in the suit."

"Then you must have really thrown a scare into them." Mr. Kinkaid Senior swelled visibly. He could not, even if he had wanted to, disguise his pride in his son's growing reputation, now sufficient to strike terror into the hearts even of Karskadon and Henderson. "But the nabobs don't like to be reminded that they're only human. Maybe it wouldn't hurt you in the long run if you let them down lightly."

"Be a gentleman?"

"Something like that."

James the son raised one shoulder in an almost imperceptible shrug, a gesture he had painstakingly acquired from his father almost before he was in grade school.

"I remember somebody who used to tell me, never be a gentleman with the client's money," he said, smiling thinly. "Besides, Abelson was screwed over good. The man comes down with leukemia and while he's at home knowing that he's probably going to die, most of the time so nauseated from the chemotherapy he almost wishes that he would die, he gets his business liquidated out from under him because he was stupid enough to trust his good friend and partner."

"So you're going to strip the friend and partner naked."

"I'm going to make him give back most of what he stole. But don't worry. The condo in Redondo Beach is in his wife's name, so he won't have to sleep in the street. And a year from now he'll probably still be alive, which is more than Abelson can say."

James the father laughed again, this time allowing it to sound like laughter. "They should make you a judge, Jimmy— even better, a prosecuting attorney. How are you ever going to get ahead in this sleazy racket with all that moral fervor weighing you down?"

"You were never sleazy."

The sad eyes registered this assessment with a faint narrowing, as if trying to focus on some distant object.

"I was also never in your league." With the tip of his right middle finger, the old man smoothed down his moustache, which, like his hair, was bone white and perfectly trimmed. His son read this as a gesture of embarrassment. "A small-town lawyer isn't required to make so many unpleasant choices. In fact, very little is required of him except discretion."

"To be the keeper of everyone's secrets and yet never even to appear conscious that there are any secrets to be kept."

The father smiled at hearing himself quoted.

"It's good advice," he answered. "For four generations now we've practiced law in the same town. We have to live among these people, and it makes the client nervous to have you across the table from him at a friendly dinner party when you look as if you're remembering the property settlement his wife forced on him after catching him with the *au pair* girl or how he's cut his grandchildren out of his will. I've always found it best to cultivate amnesia. Don't remember anything until you have to.

"But by God, Jimmy, nobody ever had to remind you about discretion. You're uncharted territory, even to me."

For just a moment James Kinkaid IV regarded his father with that studied impenetrability which had seemed to grow on him with manhood, and he thought, *I am what you made me*.

But he did not for an instant dispute the criticism, if as such it had been intended. He merely wondered how he had wounded the old man's feelings, how he had tempted him into striking back thus. In the end he merely shrugged and looked away.

"I never meant to be," he said, instantly regretting that he had said anything at all.

"I wasn't faulting you for it."

Mr. Kinkaid Senior picked up his glasses from where they were resting on the night table beside his bed and put them on. It was a diversionary tactic, a piece of stage business, for they were the half-lense type, used only for reading, and he continued to study his son over the tops of the frames.

"Why should I lay claim to understanding you? You take after your mother—you're smarter than I am." He knitted his fingers together over the linen sheet that covered his belly and then let the pads of his thumbs separate and then drop back together, as if to forestall any quarreling with the obvious. "I just muddled through at NYU and you finished Yale at the top of your class and editor of the Law Review. I was glad to go in with my father—the practice suited me and, anyway, it saved a lot of embarrassment. But I think you've always looked upon it as something of a trap."

"Dad, what is this about?"

"It isn't *about* anything. I just didn't want you to imagine I hadn't noticed, that's all."

There followed an uncomfortable silence, lasting perhaps ten seconds, during which the two men carefully avoided meeting each other's eyes. James Kinkaid IV, known as "Jimmy" nowhere except within these four walls, ransacked his memory for something with which to distract his father, in whom these rare bouts of quarrelsomeness, whether as symptom or cause, were usually the harbinger of some further loosening of his tenuous hold on life—first an argument about nothing, then, when he was heated up sufficiently, stabbing chest pains that radiated down the left arm, then nitroglycerine tablets succeeded quickly by an Inderol chaser, all ending in a night under the oxygen tent at New Gilead Memorial as slowly, inexorably, the walls of his heart died.

"I never felt trapped," the son announced at last, trying to smile. "When I was little I used to sneak into your office and sit in your chair."

Mr. Kinkaid Senior appeared to consider this for a moment and then nodded.

"I know. That's the way you felt—when you were nine years old. Then you grew up and figured out there was more in heaven and earth than Kinkaid & Kinkaid. Would you have stayed in New Gilead doing real-estate contracts and setting up trust funds for debutantes if I hadn't gotten sick? You don't have to answer. I know the answer."

The old man regarded his son with a weary resignation, which, in its way, was something of a relief. There was not going to be a quarrel, so probably there was not going to be a trip to the hospital and tomorrow morning everyone would wake up feeling fine. Still, James Kinkaid IV did not like to think that his father was obliged to carry the burden of having stood in his way. It was strange how one could be made to feel guilty for having sacrificed something.

Then James Kinkaid III closed his eyes for a moment and ran both hands over his hair, as if to smooth it into place.

"I think I'm too tired to sleep," he said finally. "I think I'll follow your excellent example and read for a while. Have we got anything in the house more exciting than the Abelson brief?"

"You've got a pile of mail on your desk—you shouldn't have any trouble finding half a dozen scandals in there. Do you want me to go get it?"

"If you wouldn't mind."

Without turning on the light, James Kinkaid IV made his way down the darkened stairway. He knew without counting that the first landing was seventeen steps down and that the third step from the bottom would creak under his weight with a sound like a nail being pulled loose. He could have laid his hand upon the cedar balustrade and, without searching, found the small rounded dents he had left on the railing at age six, when someone had been foolish enough to make him a wooden sword out of some discarded builder's lath. He did not need his eyes to move with perfect confidence within these walls. He had lived in this house all his life so that he knew it as well as his own body. His grandfather had been born, and doubtless conceived, as he himself had been, on the very bed where his father now rested, waiting for something to read.

The stairway ended in a tiny waiting room—two wooden

chairs, an upholstered bench and a newspaper rack—just inside the great double doors that were the front entrance to the house. To the right, closed off behind an Oriental screen, was a parlor which was hardly ever used and to the right was an antechamber guarded during the day by an ancient secretary behind an oak desk but now standing dark and vacant. Beyond were the law offices themselves.

His father's was the larger of the two and occupied the front corner of the building. A collection of law books, the most recent of which dated from 1948, the year James Kinkaid III passed his bar exam, stood neatly arranged in cases the glass doors of which protected them not only from dust but from intrusion, as James Kinkaid IV had learned when, in his teens, he began to take an interest in them. The keys, it seemed, had long since disappeared.

The walls were wood-paneled and decorated with framed diplomas and photographs. There was also a photograph on the desk, of the late Mrs. Kinkaid, who had died when her son was only five and was thus a shadowy figure in his memory.

The day's mail was arranged in three neat stacks on the desk's green felt blotter. There were magazines, four of them, business correspondence and then personal correspondence. Without stopping to examine them he gathered up the personal letters and slipped them into the pocket of his bathrobe. The business stack contained but two items, both from a property development company in Stamford. James knew these would only bore and weary his father, so he left them. Tomorrow morning he would carry them into his own office, which was reached through a door almost hidden by the wood paneling.

He had been in and out of "the Front Office" as it was called probably three or four times a day almost every day of the five years since he had finished law school. Like the rest of the house, it had been familiar to him since childhood, so that for a long time he had hardly noticed it. Yet recently, in the seven months since his father had suffered his second heart attack, the room had begun to have a peculiar effect on him, leaving him depressed and inexplicably anxious.

The theory he had formed for himself was that it had become an emblem for the trap into which his father's illness had led him. The first heart attack had come a month before his graduation and he had entered the family practice, which was stiflingly routine, because he felt sure the old man would be dead in a year if he did not.

He could have taken a job in Manhattan and commuted— even Karskadon and Henderson had made him an offer—yet he understood enough about the workload expected of first-year lawyers in the big firms to know that, as far as his father was concerned, he might just as well pack his bags and move to Chicago. Compromise was impossible, would in fact have been betrayal. It had to be Kinkaid & Kinkaid.

So it had been Kinkaid & Kinkaid for five long, mind-numbing years—and after another five he probably wouldn't be fit for anything else.

Hence the dilemma: the only possible escape lay in his father's death, which gave even the desire for it a strong taste of disloyalty. There was no solace in the thought that he genuinely loved his father, that he scrupulously concealed his disappointment, that he had been a careful and attentive nurse. All he had to do was to go into the Front Office, look at the rows of out-of-date law books behind their glass doors, and the words *I hate this* would come unbidden into his mind, followed almost at once by a twinge of remorse, as if the thought itself had been a kind of murder.

That was how he explained to himself the effect his father's office had begun to have on him, and yet the explanation somehow did not entirely satisfy. It was perfectly true and yet it was not the whole truth. There was too much it left in shadow.

It did not explain, for instance, the sense of something hidden. James could not remember when he had begun to experience a certain feeling of exclusion—a sense that the room was keeping something back from him. Perhaps the feeling had always been there.

Yet there was a kind of justice even in this. Was he not keeping a secret of his own? Even if it was only that he had not found perfect contentment as the junior partner of Kinkaid & Kinkaid.

"Here's your fan mail," he said, handing his father the letters. "There's one in there from Gloria Steinem. She's seen the error of her ways and now only wants to be your slave."

James Kinkaid III held a brown, legal-sized envelope up to his nose and closed his eyes as he appeared to enjoy its perfume. The return address read *Field and Stream*.

"Perhaps she plots to kill me with kindness."

"You never know."

He would never know what woke him. His digital alarm clock on the dresser said 5:52 and no hint of dawn had yet filtered through the curtains. He sat up and threw his legs down over the edge of the bed, feeling his way into his slippers and listening, but there was nothing to hear. He took his bathrobe from the hook on the closet door and stepped out into the corridor. His father's door was closed, but there was a sliver of light showing beneath it. He understood what had happened even before he touched the knob.

"Dad?"

The lamp on the night table was lit, the three-way bulb on the lowest setting, exactly as it had been four hours earlier when James Kinkaid IV had left his father amusing himself with a letter from someone he had known in prep school. The figure on the bed was in the same posture, although the smile on his lips had vanished and his reading glasses were now lying on the floor. His right hand was concealed beneath the blankets and his eyes were half open; otherwise you might have imagined he was asleep. Kinkaid crouched beside him and, just to be sure, felt the side of his throat. The skin did not feel particularly cold, but there was no pulse.

"Oh, Dad . . ." Kinkaid murmured. If he had meant to say anything else it was lost in the deep sob that seemed to crack his breast.

It was several minutes before he was conscious of anything except his own grief, but in the end one remembers that death can never remain an isolated event. In half an hour the housekeeper would be moving around in their kitchen, preparing a breakfast of toast, stewed fruit and coffee for a man who was no longer alive to eat it. She would have to be told, of course, and then there would be the doctor and the undertaker and the whole rigmarole. Not only was his father dead, but very soon his corpse would be turned into an object of inspection. How James Kinkaid III, that private and patrician man who couldn't step outside his own door without adjusting his tie, would have hated it.

The last service his son could perform for him was to keep the intrusion to a tolerable minimum.

He picked the eyeglasses up from the floor and slipped them back into their case, which still rested on the night table. Then he closed his father's eyes.

It was impossible to tell, just looking at his face, whether he had died in much pain. Perhaps the final heart attack had come in one big wave that killed him before he knew what was happening to him. Certainly it must have been quick, because he hadn't had time even to open the drawer where he kept his pills. That was something, at least.

It occurred to Kinkaid that his father would not want anyone else to see him like this, sitting up like a stuffed monkey, so he pulled away the blanket, slipped his arms under the corpse's back and legs, and shifted it down in the bed until it was lying on its back. Then he brought the sheet up to cover the face.

An envelope drifted to the floor. Kinkaid picked it up and read the return address: "Four Star Clipping Service, 3rd Floor, 282 West 42nd Street, New York, NY 10036." The envelope was empty.

There were seven other envelopes on the bed. Four of them had been opened and the rest were still sealed.

James Kinkaid III had been a man of careful and unvarying habit, and mail was something to be treated with respect. He would read personal correspondence or a subscription notice from *Ladies Home Journal* with precisely the same attention and then slip the item back into its envelope and set it aside, even if it was destined for the wastepaper basket.

Thus it followed that, since the envelope was empty, he must have died almost immediately after seeing what it had contained.

So where was the clipping?

He found it, crumpled into a tight little ball, under the night table. It seemed that his father, in those last few seconds of life, had done his best to hide it.

The article, cut out of the *Dayton Tribune*, was two columns wide and dated from Wednesday of the week before. The headline was in the best tradition: "Motel Murder Linked to Shiloh Massacre."

chapter 3

The law offices of Karskadon and Henderson occupied the fifteenth and sixteenth floors of Building Number Three of the World Trade Center. The lobby was circular and full of maroon upholstered benches screened off from one another by forbidding-looking plants with leaves like saber blades growing out of unglazed pottery tubs that seemed scattered around at random. There were no magazines and no ashtrays—it was a room designed to be uncomfortable, to turn one's thoughts inward, to stimulate a sense of defenselessness.

James Kinkaid had been here before, so he decided to ignore it and read the copy of *The New Gilead Register* he had bought at the train station. He wondered if perhaps they didn't have another lobby for clients.

His appointment had been for ten in the morning, which is the New York Bar's equivalent of the crack of dawn, but it was already twenty past. This he knew was also simply more of the psychological gamesmanship that is part of every litigation. Both sides knew that this sort of thing would make no difference whatever to the outcome, but the forms had to be observed. He had been ten minutes late himself.

Thus it came as an actual surprise when the frosted glass double doors to the counsels' chambers opened and he saw Bob Festmacher marching toward him, his face already set in the obligatory lodge-brother smile.

"How are you, Jim?" he asked, taking his hand while simultaneously moving in to clap him on the upper arm. Festmacher, who was about Kinkaid's age and had played football for Dartmouth, was blessed with blond hair and a brick-red complexion, which made the elegant English tailoring of his black pinstriped suit look faintly like a disguise. "How was the train?"

Probably not much different from the one you took down from Greenwich, Kinkaid thought to himself, before mumbling something that sounded like "great."

The smile instantly collapsed. "Listen, I read about your father. . . ."

Kinkaid managed his own thin smile and a dismissive gesture. The funeral had been only two days before and already he was thoroughly sick of the condolences of strangers. He simply did not understand how everyone on the Eastern Seaboard seemed to know—and, worse yet, seemed to feel bound to express an opinion—about the death of James Kinkaid III.

"Well then. Shall we proceed to business?" Having apparently taken the hint, Festmacher, who had never surrendered his hold on Kinkaid's arm, adroitly wheeled him about and began steering him back through the frosted glass doors. "I hope you don't mind, but one of the partners asked if he could sit in on our little discussion. . . ."

The office was at the end of a wood-paneled corridor. One wall was all window from about the waist up, and the carpet was wine-red and thick enough to trip the unwary. The furniture was restrained modern—all dark wood but apparently designed for speed. Kinkaid was invited to take one end of a gigantic sofa upholstered in black leather.

"Coffee?"

Festmacher was poised beside his desk, and he seemed genuinely disappointed when the answer was a negative. He frowned and pressed the button on his intercom.

"Doris advise Mr. Tollison that Mr. Kinkaid is here."

The name was familiar, although Kinkaid could not immediately place it. Certainly it did not belong to anyone who had appeared so far in the paperwork. He wondered if perhaps they were trying to throw him off his stride right at the end by introducing a new player, but then he decided that was just paranoia.

Instead of occupying the other end of the sofa, which one might have expected, Festmacher dropped into a chair just opposite. He unbuttoned his jacket and smoothed down his tie with the flat of his hand. On the coffee table in front of him was a thick manila folder which presumably held his case papers on the Abelson suit, but he didn't open it or even glance at it. Instead, he subjected his wristwatch to a careful inspection, giving the impression he suspected it might have stopped running.

"I suppose I should make a note of the time," he said. "We're billing this client by the hour."

In what is usually called a significant glance, he turned his eyes to Kinkaid, who, without looking up from the open brief-case on his knees, acknowledged the point with a nod. As his father had never tired of reminding him, all litigation revolves around only one significant point, which is to discover a means by which all the lawyers get paid.

"I hope you haven't let him fall behind."

It took a split second for the other man to realize he was being guyed, but that was long enough. Before he could organize a reply his office door opened and he sprang to his feet, as if he had just received the signal he had been waiting for all his life.

The smile on Festmacher's face was positively radiant.

"Jim, I'd like you to meet Eric Tollison," he said, rushing past to take the hand of a spare man of about sixty in a medium-gray suit.

Kinkaid stood up. He remembered now. Six years ago, while he was in his last year at law school and before his father's first heart attack, he had applied to Karskadon and Henderson for a job. Eric Tollison had been present at the interview.

"We've met," Tollison announced, with the tone of someone covering an awkward fact. He was a commanding presence, with a rather pointed face that made you think of a predatory animal. He hadn't spoken three complete sentences at the interview, and yet Kinkaid had ended almost everything he said with a glance in his direction.

The two men shook hands, quickly and warily, like prizefighters touching gloves before the opening bell.

When everyone had sat down again it was Tollison who occupied the other end of the black leather sofa.

Bob Festmacher resumed his chair, leaned forward to open the manila folder on the coffee table, glanced at the first page and closed it again. Kinkaid's briefcase was already snapped shut. One had to give the impression that one had done one's homework.

"I have informed Mr. Abelson that he is in a position to file criminal charges against your client," Kinkaid began. "He liked hearing that. He liked hearing that a lot. I think, when you report to your client on the results of this discussion, you had better point out to him that having to give back the money isn't the worst thing that could happen to him. Ask him how he would enjoy prison."

Festmacher shook his head and laughed, as if he relished the joke.

"First of all, there isn't all that much money to give back . . ."

"I know—Gelson has stashed most of it in his wife's name." Kinkaid raised his eyebrows and smiled, if only to show that he could appreciate a good piece of villainy as much as the next man. "If she wants to keep him at home she'll just have to return the swag. And if she doesn't, there's always room for her name on the indictment."

"You aren't kidding, are you."

"No. I'm not kidding."

"You'll never get an indictment against the wife."

"I'll get an indictment. I may not get a conviction, but I have enough to insist on an indictment. Explain to Mrs. Gelson how much defending a criminal prosecution costs by the time a jury gets the case. When we reach the end of that road—and after she's flat broke—the best she can hope for is to have avoided joining her husband in the slammer."

An hour and a half later they had reached a settlement: within three weeks Mr. Joshua Abelson would receive a cashier's check for $200,000, to be followed before the end of the year by the balance. The total would come to precisely eighty-five percent of the $900,000 stipulated in the suit, which would leave Mr. Harry Gelson enough to pay his tab with Karskadon and Henderson and maybe bus fare back to Redondo Beach, where he and the Mrs. could try living on their social security.

The firm invited Kinkaid to lunch—or, rather, Eric Tollison, breaking the impenetrable silence he had maintained during the negotiations, invited him. Festmacher mumbled something about a prior commitment and mysteriously faded from sight somewhere on the way to the elevator.

Tollison took him by the arm and guided him out of the building and into a side street to one of those places that never advertise in the restaurant guides. It occupied a large upstairs room containing no more than a dozen or so tables with almost as many waiters. The linen was so white it hurt your eyes. The maître d' was as solemn as a funeral director and carried his tassled menus in the crook of his arm as if they were made of stone and he was afraid they might break.

"Six months ago I would have said you were wasting your time on this Abelson thing," Tollison announced while he watched his water goblet being filled. "I thought Gelson was home free, the nasty little crook. You really did your homework."

There was nothing Kinkaid could say without sounding like a pompous jerk, so he pretended he hadn't heard.

"How much, if one is permitted to ask, are you retaining as your fee?"

"Twenty percent."

At first Tollison didn't react. He observed as the waiter

drifted off with swanlike dignity and then he studied the walls, which were blank.

"Twenty percent? Is that the going rate in rural Connecticut?" He smiled languidly, as if to extinguish any possibility of offense. "In the civilized world the lawyer keeps a third."

"The Abelsons are family friends. What with his illness they've had heavy expenses and there are more to come—dying isn't cheap these days. As it is, I don't think Annette will be left with more than four hundred thousand."

Tollison executed an almost imperceptible shrug, as if he found such considerations unintelligible and, in any case, slightly vulgar. The two men observed a decorous silence for the minute or two until the waiter brought their salads.

"Your scruples do you credit, I suppose. But they would be out of place in a firm like ours." Tollison turned over a leaf of romaine lettuce with his fork as if he expected to find something unpleasant underneath. "Our overhead is killing and, besides, most of our clients don't tempt one to generosity. I was surprised when you turned down our offer five years ago."

"Maybe I decided you were out of my league."

"Our league as defined by Bob Festmacher?" He seemed to consider the possibility for an instant and then shook his head. "You beat his brains out."

"I had the stronger case."

"No—you *made* the stronger case. There's a difference."

Having decided, apparently, that his salad wasn't actually dangerous, Tollison seemed to lose interest and set his fork down.

"Festmacher is presently billing at a hundred and seventy-five dollars an hour. He was our second draft choice, right after you. I think if your father hadn't had that heart attack you'd be up to three-fifty today."

He smiled again. Nothing remained a mystery to this boy.

"We don't get stood up very often. When it happens we like to know why."

"And so you found out."

"And so we found out."

Once you stepped off the train, the air in the Times Square subway station was thick with noise and a peculiar humidity that smelled like motor oil. On the platform an emaciated black man wearing a knitted beret was playing a ragged, bluesy solo on a saxophone—entirely for his own pleasure it would seem, since he did not appear to be soliciting money and, in any case, the crowd of passengers swirled around him as indifferently as if he had been a support post.

At street level the sunlight was almost painful. Half the movie houses seemed to be closed and everyone looked angry, or perhaps only desperate, as if each of those hundreds of souls walked around enveloped in their own little cloud of misery. If, another time, Kinkaid had closed his eyes and thought of 42nd Street he would have imagined it at night, the way he had seen it as a college boy coming down from Yale for a razzle with his friends. Maybe it really did look more cheerful at night, but somehow that was hard to believe.

Did the big fish of Karskadon and Henderson ever come near Times Square? Did any of them take the subway to work? If they did, would they ever talk about it? That too was hard to believe.

Tollison had offered him a job, so maybe he would find out.

"We do a fair amount of billing in Connecticut, most of it involved with real estate. We can work out some sort of arrangement about continuing your present practice— perhaps, for a while, you could be in the city for half the week. It's not something you have to make a decision about right away."

He had listened very politely and said almost nothing, because Tollison's instinct was right. He didn't want to make a decision right away. Two days after his father's funeral he didn't even want to think about it, although it was impossible not to. He didn't want to complicate his feelings any more than they were already.

He could feel the outline of the empty envelope in his inside coat pocket just as if it were sewn to his skin. The clipping itself was safely locked away in his desk drawer, but he had been carrying the envelope around with him ever since he had found it. He had not been sure until this moment whether he really wanted to solve this puzzle.

"If I don't find out I will feel like I never knew him," he whispered to himself. "And then I will lose even his memory."

None of the buildings on the other side of six lanes of traffic seemed to bear a number, as if in this neighborhood it was considered prudent to keep even the addresses secret. When the light changed Kinkaid joined three or four other wary pedestrians hurrying across Broadway and found that the plateglass door of a coffee shop carried the numerals "86."

The Four Star Clipping Service was just east of Ninth Avenue. The first-floor storefronts housed a pizza place and a window full of video rentals, most of them pornographic. The building had no elevator. The only door on the second floor bore a small gilt sign, "Foxy Club"—it was slightly ajar and heavy metal music poured out onto the landing. On the third floor the door was emphatically locked and there was no sign. Kinkaid tapped with his knuckle, waited about thirty seconds and then knocked louder.

There was the sound of a bolt sliding back and a rattling of chains and the door opened about two inches.

"Yeah?"

The voice was so raspy it was impossible to be sure whether it belonged to a man or a woman, but it was a woman's face that peered out at Kinkaid with manifest suspicion, as if anyone who showed up here in a business suit was obviously up to no good. The hair, pulled straight back, was blond going to white, and the pale brown eyes rested in a fantastic network of wrinkles, although she did not otherwise appear to be particularly old. There was a cigarette hanging precariously from the corner of her mouth.

"Is this the newspaper service?"

"Who wants to know?"

He took out his wallet and produced a business card, which he then held up for her inspection.

"I'm not here to serve you with anything," he said, being careful not to smile—he sensed that she would not trust a smile. "I only want to make an inquiry."

"James Kinkaid IV," she read. "Attorney at Law. New Gilead, Connecticut."

She seemed to consider his credentials for a moment, and then she nodded.

"You're a subscriber. I recognize the name. Yeah—come on in."

The door closed, there was more rattling of chains, and then it reopened. The room was perhaps twenty feet by thirty and, except for a wall of filing cabinets and a single table and chair, unfurnished. There were stacks of newspapers everywhere, some of them almost up to the ceiling.

The woman walked over to the filing cabinets. She was tall enough to lean against them, resting her arm on the top. Beside her elbow was a glass ashtray the size of a soup bowl, into which she dropped her cigarette. It had plenty of company.

"Actually, I think my father was the subscriber," Kinkaid began, glancing around the room as if he might be interested in renting it himself. "You sent him a clipping . . ."

The woman's eyes narrowed.

"Then it ain't any of your business, is it."

"He died a few days ago."

If he had been appealing to her sympathy he realized at once that the attempt had failed. She said nothing and her eyes remained narrow, suspicious and calculating.

"He was not only my father but my law partner," Kinkaid went on. "I'll be taking over his clients, so I might or might not be interested in continuing the subscription. We'll have to see."

This elicited a flicker of interest. The woman took a half-empty pack of cigarettes out of the pocket of her shapeless trousers and lit one from a book of paper matches that rested beside the ashtray. She took a long drag, as if she had been perishing for a smoke all week.

"Our rates are a hundred and fifty a month."

She was trying to gouge him, but that was just as well. Kinkaid knew he stood a better chance of finding out what was going on if he let this woman think she was getting away with something.

"That sounds a little high," he said, looking at the newspaper lying open on the room's only table—it was a copy of the *Los Angeles Times*, dated three days back. "What were you checking up on for him?"

"I'll have to look into that."

She reached out and tugged on the handle of the top drawer of the filing cabinet closest to her. Without taking her eyes from Kinkaid's face she reached in with one hand and pulled out a folder, letting it drop open in her grasp.

"Just names," she announced, glancing at the single sheet of paper. "Nobody famous. We've only been able to find something on two of them—one a while back and the piece I sent out last week."

"Do you have a copy of the earlier clipping?"

"No."

"Do you happen to remember what it was about?"

"No." The woman shook her head the way she might have if he had asked to borrow ten dollars. "Why should I remember? It was nearly two years ago. You have any idea how much newsprint I've read since then?"

He must have looked very disappointed, because she glanced down at the sheet of paper again and then closed the folder with a snap.

"It was from the *Philadelphia Inquirer*, dated September

12, Section B, page 3. They'll have it on microfilm at the library."

Her cigarette dropped an ash on the top of the filing cabinet and she brushed it over the edge with the side of her hand.

"You gonna renew the subscription?" she asked. "It's only paid up until the fifteenth."

"If I can copy out that list of names I'll write you a check for three months."

Kinkaid just made the first peak hour train leaving Grand Central. He walked all the way to the front car to find a place by the window and hoped nobody would slide in next to him before the train pulled out. Nobody did, so he had the seat to himself. He had a morbid suspicion that it might be the last piece of luck he would ever enjoy in this life.

The woman had been right—they were just names. They might have been taken out of the phone book at random. None of them rang any bells.

But the clipping, which he had had photocopied at the 42nd Street library, was bizarre.

Up until the afternoon of August the 27th, 1992, Terry Vogel had been a demonstrator of computer software for a company in Princeton, New Jersey. He was divorced, lived alone, and traveled a good deal in connection with his job. He had money in the bank and no known bad habits. Nobody could understand what could have possessed him to go to a second-floor apartment in East Philadelphia, lie down on the bed, press the muzzle of a double-barreled shotgun against the underside of his chin, and pull both triggers. The whole front half of his head had been blown away.

It had taken exactly two weeks for the Philadelphia police to get a fingerprint report from Washington, and so the body hadn't been identified until the 11th of September. The next day the *Inquirer* had published the story and three days later the woman at the Four Star Clipping Service had posted a copy of the article to her client. Kinkaid knew from experience that mail from New York City generally took about two days to reach New Gilead.

On the 17th of September, 1992, James Kinkaid III had been unusually quiet and preoccupied during dinner, had excused himself before dessert, something he had never been known to do before, and had collapsed on the stairs while trying to reach his bedroom. He had nearly died before his son could get him to the emergency room at New Gilead Memorial.

chapter 4

George Tipton pulled into one of the re-
served slots in the employee parking area of the Peachtree
Shopping Center. It was only 8:30 in the morning, but he
hated to open the door and get out. The single ramp leading to
the underground garage took you down about twenty feet into
this concrete cavern where there was no ventilation and
hardly any light and you could taste the exhaust fumes every
time you opened your mouth. And it trapped the heat like the
inside of an oven.

His house had a wall unit in the bedroom and after a night
in his garage the car stayed tolerably cool as long as he didn't
open the windows, but the second he stepped outside he would
run smack into the humidity like it was a wall. The staff entrance was a hundred feet away and by the time he reached it,
and the safety of the shopping center's air-conditioning system that kept even the stockrooms feeling like they were re-
frigerated, he would already have sweated through his shirt.

Eight-thirty and he already knew what the day was going
to be like. Lucille had started chipping at him almost before
he stepped out of the shower and by breakfast they had been
shouting at each other loud enough to wake the baby, who
was only eleven weeks old but took after his mother and
could scream the house down.

Lucille wanted him to look for another job that paid a
higher salary. She said she also wanted to go live with her
mother and George had told her fine, go ahead, because lately
he never got anything for dinner except take-out food and,
besides, they hadn't fucked since three months before the

baby was born. Except for the quiet, which would be a relief, he wouldn't even notice she was gone.

But Lucille wasn't going anywhere. She couldn't stand to be in the same room with her mother for more than about half an hour at a time. All she wanted was for him to bring home more money to feed her credit cards with—Lucille couldn't even go to the laundromat without it costing fifty bucks.

Southern girls. He had moved down to Atlanta four years ago because one time somebody had told him it never snowed there—you grow up in Darkest Michigan and you learn to hate snow—and two weeks after he got off the bus he had met Lucille at a disco in the Underground. There she was, up against the wall with some girlfriend, wearing one of those white, off-the-shoulder blouses you can practically see through, all smiles and long black hair, just like she had been waiting for him all her life.

But it was the accent that got him, that sleepy, flirtatious southern drawl that makes a woman sound like she just can't wait to smother you with it even if she's just reading out the address on a mailing label. Don't listen to the words, Baby, because it's the tune that matters. God Almighty, if he hadn't gotten a hard-on just standing there under the colored lights listening to her talk about how if you weren't careful the bartender would short you on your change.

Well, not everything lives up to its advertising.

He opened the car door and stepped out, scraping the soles of his shoes on the gritty cement as he took a deep breath of the hot, sticky, gasoline-scented air. There was no point in putting it off. He took his sports jacket from the backseat and dropped his keys into the pocket. It was unnecessary to lock up. His car had been three years old when he bought it and thieves had better taste.

When he pushed open the employees' entrance the temperature seemed to drop about fifty degrees. He went to the men's room and washed his face in cold water, which made him feel better. It was still going to be a lousy day.

George sometimes wondered if in marrying Lucille he had gone through a civil ceremony or simply fallen under a curse, because that one misjudgment had seemed to taint his entire existence. Even when he was out of the house, out of reach, safe, Lucille seemed to dog him. If they had a fight over breakfast he could count on a string of disasters throughout the day—one time, when she had gotten mad enough to throw a bowl of Kellogg's Corn Flakes at his head, he hadn't been at work more than twenty minutes when Mr. Jenkins had told him, with obvious pleasure, that he was being passed over for the job of assistant manager at the downtown store. Over the lunch break a pickpocket had bumped into him and lifted his wallet.

But there hadn't been any actual violence this morning. It hadn't been anything more than a shouting match, so maybe he wouldn't actually get fired.

The Jock Shop was a regional sporting-goods chain with fifty-six stores stretching from Amarillo, Texas, to Spartanburg, South Carolina. There were three of them in Atlanta, but the one in the Peachtree Shopping Center, with a staff of eight, was the biggest.

George was in informal charge of the Running Gear and Cycling Departments; he knew the stock and read the magazines enough to have become fluent in the jargon and he was thin, so customers tended to assume he was an enthusiast, which was good for business. Actually, he hated exercise.

Like everyone else except the manager, he worked on straight salary—the store did not have a commission system—but like everyone else he had to move a weekly average of two thousand dollars in merchandise just to keep his job. Sometimes, and particularly now in the summer, when people just wanted to huddle in front of their air conditioners, making the quota was a squeeze.

He reached the store just as Mr. Jenkins finished cranking up the chain-link curtain that sealed off the entrance and the display windows after hours. Raising the curtain was a little ceremony, like running up the flag and, as one of his pet tyrannies, the store manager liked his staff to be there while he did it, witnesses to the start of a new workday as they stood at something like attention. If there had been a company song he would probably have insisted they all sing it.

They made an odd little group in the vast emptiness of the shopping center. Not even the security guards were around. George could hear the splash of water, which meant someone had turned on the fountain in the central plaza—that and the metallic creaking of Jenkins' crank handle as it turned in its slot were just about the only sounds.

Mr. Jenkins was almost bald and what little was left of his hair he plastered down against his glossy scalp as if he wanted to be quite sure it would still be there when next he checked. He was small, strengthless and round-shouldered. He was the sort of man whose childhood must have been a catalogue of athletic humiliations, an impression confirmed by the mean, bottle-brown eyes behind his heavy wire frame glasses. How he could possibly have ended up in the sporting-goods business was anybody's guess.

He merely glanced at George as he stepped over the store threshold and flipped on the overhead lights, but that glance was enough. A manager can turn your life into a misery if he feels like it.

"Um, um—better have a lawyer handy while you fill out your swindle sheets," Sally Bronowski murmured seductively up into George's ear. She was about twenty and red-haired and did a lot of swimming, so it was a great pity that she had only been married about three months and appeared to be still in love with her husband. "The Potato Bug's got it in for you today."

The name fit. They watched him disappear insectlike through the door to the stockroom. It was no insignificant mercy that Jenkins hardly ever showed himself on the sales floor.

"He's got it in for me any day. Why don't you go back

there and seduce him so I can catch the two of you together? No? Where's your team spirit?"

"No thank you. Not the Bug. Besides, I think there's something wrong with him. He doesn't even look."

"Well I look, so I must be healthy."

This made Sally laugh. She was a nice kind of girl. You could flirt with her.

One thing about sporting goods, they didn't much excite people's sense of urgency. No one rushed to the shopping mall first thing in the morning to buy a new pair of exercise shorts, so it would probably be another three-quarters of an hour before the Jock Shop saw its first customer.

George knew this and counted on it, just as he counted on Mr. Jenkins' morning immersion in the delights of the stockroom. Once he had put in an appearance he liked to take the escalator up to the sixth floor, get a can of diet ginger ale out of the machine and have a cigarette. The ginger ale he would carry back with him, hardly tasted, and secrete it in an empty bowling bag that had gone so long unsold everyone else had forgotten it was even there. Food and drink on the premises were strictly against the rules and the ginger ale would be room temperature and flat by ten o'clock, but there was a certain pleasure in getting away with this infraction, month after month. It was a secret victory and life had few enough of those.

The cigarette was another matter. A cigarette lasts exactly ten minutes and while he smoked it George could lean over the balustrade and look down at the first trickle of shoppers— at this season of the year usually teenage girls, hunting in packs—as they floated around on the walkways below like motes of dust. Those ten minutes were precious, a brief period of philosophical reflection, a reverie on the littleness of all human struggle which was somehow profoundly comforting. After ten minutes on the sixth floor he was ready to face anything.

Even Mr. Jenkins was uncharacteristically prowling around

the display area. George just had time to drop the ginger ale can in a trash can outside the store entrance.

"It's rather early to be away from your post," he announced blandly. "Or perhaps we've opened a branch in the staff lounge."

Away from your post. Lovely. He made it sound like guard duty during the siege of Vicksburg.

But George merely shrugged and allowed his eyes to drift over the deserted aisles that spread out from the cash registers.

"There's no one here. No one comes in here at nine o'clock in the morning."

"Of course not—doubtless because they know, from long experience, that there will be no one to wait on them."

Jenkins' face tightened in his prim version of triumph.

"And don't bring any more of your soda pop on the premises. You've ruined the lining of that bowling bag. It will be charged against your next paycheck."

He turned his back, refusing even the possibility of a denial, and almost skipped away through the door to the stockroom.

George checked his watch. Nine-thirteen and he already felt as if he might as well quit for the day and go home— except that home meant Lucille and the baby. On the whole, he preferred Mr. Jenkins.

Well, maybe things would pick up. Maybe there would be a fevered run on bicycle pumps.

But there wasn't. Trade was almost glacially slow. By eleven forty-five total sales in the Running Gear and Cycling Departments consisted of one paperback copy of *Aerobic Training Over Forty* and a pair of tube socks.

"You want to break for lunch?"

"Only if you come with me."

Sally Bronowski flashed him one of those quick smiles that make you think a woman is blushing even when she isn't, as if you have answered the most secret wish of her heart. So maybe it really wasn't all bliss between the newlyweds. A man was entitled to hope.

"Then it'll have to be the Mexican place," she said. "I'm tapped out this week."

"We'll go to the Baker's Basket, and it'll be my treat."

He half expected her to refuse—what the hell, it was a pretty naked pass—but she only smiled again, apparently pleased with the masculine attention. Life was once more luminous with promise.

Lunch was one of George's little indulgences. The store did not keep a refrigerator, so you were risking your life if you brought a sandwich, at least if you liked mayonnaise on your lettuce and bologna. And it was just too beastly to go across the street and stand there with the noonday sun beating down on you while you ate some greasy mess thrown into a taco. So that left Weinberg's Deli on the second floor or the Baker's Basket, and at Weinberg's, which was always crowded and was in fact owned and staffed entirely by Vietnamese refugees, the coleslaw tasted like they made it out of lawn clippings.

So at least three times out of five he went to the Baker's Basket, where the menu was Nouvelle California, they didn't automatically sweeten the iced tea and there were hanging plants all over the place and where, most important, you could sit down and eat in peace. Even if he didn't go overboard on the tipping he still dropped about forty dollars a week there, which was more than he could really afford but, hell, life has to be made worth living.

Today, George decided, he would throw caution to the winds and buy dessert. The desserts were terrific, especially the bread pudding, and Sally looked the kind of girl who might appreciate that sort of thing.

But almost the moment they sat down he lost interest in what Sally might or might not appreciate.

They were shown to a table next to the wall of plateglass windows that looked out onto the mall and Sally immediately buried herself in the menu. It was just as well.

Because three tables away a pair of elderly women were arguing over the list of daily specials as if it were a disputed inheritance, and the waitress was standing over them listening with serene and carefully perfected indifference.

Her back was to him, so George couldn't get a look at her face. He didn't need to. Her hair, which was a perfect white blond like no woman had a right to hope for, was gathered up in a roll so that he could see the back of her neck and the line of her cheek and jaw. On that basis alone, plus the way her body suggested itself beneath her dreadful mint-green uniform, he was sure she was the most beautiful creature he had ever beheld—even better than Joan Greenwood in *Kind Hearts and Coronets*.

"Is the chicken-in-a-basket any good? George?"

But George was not really in a position to answer, having entirely forgotten that they served food here. At that precise moment the waitress turned her head, seemed to look past him, and then met his gaze.

And she was more than beautiful. She was radiant. She was . . .

She even smiled—intimately, just for him, as if they had been lovers forever.

"George, what is the matter with you?"

When Sally's voice finally registered he found he was master of just enough self-control to tear his eyes away and look at her. She was annoyed, so he smiled.

"The service is slow here," he said. "You have to get their attention when you can."

"Is the chicken-in-a-basket any good?"

"God knows."

The waitress began to move toward them. Even her walk was beautiful. In a moment, he thought to himself, he would hear her voice. He could hardly wait.

She was an angel.

chapter 5

In the last few years before his death, James Kinkaid III had restricted his legal work to some dozen or so old clients, most of whom never bothered him except to come in once a year to review their wills. Thus James Kinkaid IV had very little to do to close out his father's practice. A week after the funeral he had cleared away all the paperwork, moved everything that was still active into his own files and sent the rest to the archives down in the basement. None of it had brought him any closer to understanding the little mystery represented by the Four Star Clipping Service.

There had been ten names on the list and none of them belonged to anyone who had done business with the firm of Kinkaid & Kinkaid anytime in the last five years. Of that James Kinkaid IV was quite certain, because for all practical purposes during that time he had been the firm. Anything earlier he would have to refer to Molly.

Every successful law firm has a Molly. Molly Scofield had already been behind her desk in the reception room for two years when the infant James Kinkaid was first carried in through the front door and, although she was not sentimental about such things, she probably remembered the color of the baby blanket. She seemed to remember everything, every case, every client, every appointment, every telephone number since her first day on the job. In fact, if she had ever forgotten anything no one had ever caught her at it.

"Just let me die before she reaches retirement age," James Kinkaid III was fond of saying. "A secretary that good breeds habits of dependence. *You* might be able to get along without Molly, but not me."

Well, at least he had been spared having to get along without Molly. The morning after his father's death Kinkaid had waited downstairs to tell her when she came in to work, and they had sat together on one of the sofas in the reception room while she spent about five minutes weeping into his shoulder. It was the only time he had ever seen her cry, and when she was over the first shock she had dried her eyes and resumed her duties. By lunchtime she had made all the arrangements for the funeral.

Her relations with her employers, both father and son, had always been an odd mixture of intimacy and reserve. Seven-year-old Jimmy had had a collection of baseball cards which for some reason excited his father's mild disapproval, and when he had gotten tired of being teased about them he had moved the whole lot to the bottom drawer of Molly's desk, which was the absolute best place to hide anything because Molly would never tell on him. Molly was on his side against all comers, even his dad. Yet when he graduated from college she had started calling him "Mr. Kinkaid"—had, in fact, insisted on it. "In September you'll start law school," was the way she put it. "You are no longer a boy."

For the rest she lived with her sister in Norwalk and, judging from her perfect willingness to work evenings and weekends, enjoyed no private life worth mentioning. A New England spinster and fairly typical of the breed. Her employment records gave her age as fifty-six but, slim and extremely well groomed, with hardly a trace of gray in her little cloud of brown hair, she looked about ten years younger. Perhaps, having submerged herself in her work, knowing herself to be both indispensable and completely trusted, she had come to such terms with life that it was no longer in any hurry to devour her. Or perhaps she was simply too proud to show her wounds.

In any case, Molly was the one to ask about matters of ancient history.

But it was necessary to put the inquiry in properly veiled

terms. Kinkaid just wasn't ready to tell anyone, not even Molly, about the Four Star Clipping Service since, after all, what were the odds that two men out of a random sampling of ten would finish up gruesomely murdered? It was possible this business could get no end of nasty and if he had to stir up the mud he preferred not to begin by noisily splashing around in it. Kinkaid had a lawyer's distaste for revealing secrets and, besides, no one had a better claim to his discretion than his own father.

So one morning, before the office was open, Kinkaid copied the ten names down on a nice anonymous three-by-five index card—the original list was on a sheet of the clipping service's letterhead—and waited with his office door slightly ajar so he would know when Molly came to work.

She had a key. Kinkaid could hear it turning in the lock of the front door at ten minutes to nine. He listened to the sound of her sensible mid-heeled shoes on the hardwood floor. Then there was an interval of silence as she straightened out the magazines on the waiting room table, then a faint creak from the top hinge of the door to the hall closet, where she hung up the jacket of her perfect suit, usually charcoal-gray wool in the winter but now, in the summer, almost anything was possible, such as, for instance, a fawn-colored linen. (No, that was Thursday.) Then a grinding noise from the rollers on her chair as she sat down at her desk and started going through the in-basket.

"Good morning, Mr. Kinkaid," she called, presumably just to let him know that his presence behind his office door had not gone undetected. "Don't forget to look at your calendar."

Instead, he came out and laid the three-by-five card down on her spotless green blotter.

"Do we know any of these people? I found their names in some notes of Dad's."

Molly picked up the card, checked the back to make sure that nothing else was written there, and then glanced at Kinkaid with the faintest of accusations. Of course she knew that he was lying, but the obviousness of the lie would caution her against asking any questions.

"We had a *Ted* Tilson once. You remember him—he owned the lamp store on Ridge Road. Your father did the probate work for his wife when he died in '86."

"But no George Tilson?"

"No."

"And none of the other names ring any bells?"

"Not a tinkle." She smiled—it was as close as Molly ever came to a joke. "Do you want me to check through the old files?"

"No. If they aren't in your memory they won't be in the files either. I don't suppose it goes back to my grandfather's time."

It was a quiet day.

At ten-fifteen Kinkaid met with a local builder anxious that he was about to be sued over the construction of a shopping center he had put up half a mile outside of town. The appointment lasted less than twenty minutes. Kinkaid listened politely and then informed the man that he could not possibly represent him because the case would involve a conflict of interest since one of the tenants had already discussed the case with him. He was not being strictly truthful—Jerry Seymour, a friend from high school, managed a stationery store in the center and had mentioned to him about a month before how last winter the facing on the walls had begun to crumble like stale cottage cheese—but Kinkaid thought that perhaps he wouldn't starve to death for want of this crook's business.

At twelve-thirty he had lunch with his accountant at the Carriage House Inn (three minutes' walk from his front door, erected in 1938, and enjoying no known associations with either carriages or inns). He ordered a chicken salad sandwich and listened to chapter and verse on the tax consequences of his father's death. There were no surprises.

He spent the rest of the afternoon working alone in his office, waiting for Molly to go home.

"Good night, Mr. Kinkaid."

He rose from his desk and helped Molly on with her jacket (pearl-gray, as it happened). They talked about the state of the front walkway, which had revealed a large crack after the spring thaw. Someone might trip and, in any case, what would the clients think? Kinkaid promised to call the handyman. It was a quarter after six before he closed the front door behind her.

He stood in the front hall listening. Julia was occupied in the kitchen. He could hear the gurgling of the ancient iron pipes as she ran water in the sink for the ritual cleaning of the lettuce. His salad dish would be on the table in another ten minutes and if he wasn't sitting in front of it in fifteen she would come into the office to tell him his dinner was ready. Fifteen minutes was surely plenty of time.

The basement was divided into two small, unfinished rooms, one of which was home to some old steamer trunks, a carpenter's workbench and various pieces of exercise equipment—Kinkaid's efforts at physical culture tended to proceed in fits and starts—while the other was a warren of filing cabinets containing the firm's archives, stretching back to the beginning of the century. Kinkaid found a thin folder marked "Tilson, Edward" in the bottom drawer of the cabinet marked "III\S - T." He took it back upstairs with him and put it on the desk in his office. It was time to eat.

The dining room, which was filled with heavy, dark furniture, all purchased before the First World War, was somber enough under the best of circumstances, but with the table set for one it was positively melancholy. There was a clock in the room, occupying a little wall shelf which faced the head of the table, but it had stopped running sometime during Kinkaid's boyhood and no one had ever thought to have it fixed. For years James Kinkaid III had always glanced up at the clock as if to check the time and always frowned and then sneaked a look at his watch. Kinkaid took his seat where he always had since he was first old enough to be admitted into the dining room, just to the left of his father's chair, with the clock and its ironies out of his line of sight.

For the first three evenings after the elder Kinkaid's death, Julia had continued to set his place for dinner—the plates, the oversize coffee cup, the cloth napkin held together in the middle by a wooden ring young Jimmy had carved in the Boy Scouts, even the water goblet half filled with crushed ice. This went on until after the funeral, when at last Kinkaid's own depression of spirits took a healthy turn toward anger and he told the housekeeper, very gently, that it would not do, that his father was gone and that they had to stop acting as if he was about to step into the room. Julia had taken the plate and cutlery back into her kitchen, weeping furiously, but the next night they did not reappear.

She was still in deep mourning, however. Kinkaid had only to consider the evidence of the salad, which was a very complicated affair, complete with corkscrew-shaped radish shavings and four different kinds of lettuce. Cooking was Julia's therapy, and recently the dinners had become markedly more elaborate as she buried her grief under a succession of excellent sauces which, had his father been alive to enjoy them, would certainly have ended by killing him.

Yet after the business with the plates Kinkaid was unwilling to say anything. He would just have to take his chances.

The situation would have amused his father. But it was a joke they would not be able to share. Sitting there, in the silent dining room, listening to Julia moving around behind the swinging door to the kitchen, Kinkaid experienced the most terrible feeling of solitude.

For years there had been a kind of veil between father and son. They shared the surface of their lives together, but nothing more. The relationship had consisted of inside jokes and the details of whatever might be happening at that moment, close but under a constraint that neither of them had felt able to remove. The past—the past that mattered—was simply never mentioned, as if, by unspoken consent, they each had agreed to remember it only in private.

But as he sat in his dining room, quite alone, it was the father of his childhood he missed, his hero and friend, with whom anything seemed possible.

And now even the hope of regaining that early intimacy had vanished forever.

He had no idea how he got through dinner. He had no appetite but simply ate mechanically, exchanging small talk with Julia as she carried things back and forth. When it was finally over, he went back to his office.

Within five minutes of opening Edward Tilson's file, Kinkaid had found the link he sought.

Clipped together with a Xerox copy of the lease agreement on the lighting store were three pages of notes, written out in longhand and dated August 1981, from a juvenile court hearing designated as *Tilson v. the State of Connecticut*. August was when Molly spent her annual two weeks of vacation rummaging through the antiques stores of southern New Hampshire, which explained why she didn't remember the case.

The defendant had been stopped for speeding on Route 106 and could not produce a driver's license. Hardly surprising, since he had been fifteen years old at the time. The arresting officer smelled marijuana smoke in the car and, upon making a search, discovered four joints in the glove compartment.

The presiding magistrate was designated simply as "Harry," which suggested that he was probably some old crony of Kinkaid's father, which was probably the only way Tilson *fils* had ended up with probation rather than a ticket to juvenile hall.

There were no other references to the young offender anywhere in the file, not even in his father's will. Perhaps Edward Tilson had suffered other disappointments in his son, whose name was George.

chapter 6

Kinkaid was already in his first year of law school before he discovered running. He liked it because it was challenging without being competitive and because it was solitary.

He was not athletic. He believed himself to be naturally awkward, which he was not, and shrank from displaying his imagined inadequacies. He had never tried out for a team, either in high school or college. At his father's insistence he had expended considerable effort to become merely average at tennis, but he did not enjoy the game and had not played since the elder Kinkaid suffered his first heart attack.

The truth was that, on a purely personal level, he lacked the necessary aggressiveness. In his professional life he could be ferocious enough, but that was because winning there mattered. The legal issues of a case were important as they supported the law itself as an idea—for Kinkaid believed in the law as a kind of secular religion—and his clients deserved his best because they had put their trust in him. But to triumph over an opponent in something as trivial as a tennis game struck him as almost rude.

Running, however, was another matter. At six in the morning, when he slipped out of the house and started down the street at a slow jog, New Gilead was still asleep, bathed in gray light and quiet enough that usually the only sound he heard was the soft clop, clop, clop of his Nike Airs against the asphalt. There were no cars and the traffic lights pulsed yellow and red like the slow beating of a heart. Sometimes he would meet another runner and they might wave at one another and smile and pass on, but for the rest he was alone and unobserved. His mind was free and he seemed to turn inward upon himself. It was a sustaining experience.

The nice part was when he got outside of town, away from the expensive, cookie-cutter houses that fed the commuter trains, on the road out to Silverbridge or some other narrow asphalt track that snaked along beside an open field or one of the endless stone walls that some 18th Century farmer had probably spent the best part of his life piling up. As he got into a rhythm, Kinkaid would begin to pick up a little speed, and after about half an hour it became effortless. He would begin to feel as if his legs were on automatic pilot and all he had to do was keep from falling over to go on running forever.

He would go out five or six miles and then loop back.

About half a mile outside the central business district he would begin to slow down, then he always walked the last three or four hundred yards through town so he would have stopped sweating by the time he got home and could take his shower. Besides, by a quarter to eight or so people were beginning to stir. Kinkaid didn't care to make a spectacle of himself streaking along Putnam Avenue, dodging in and out among the minivans rushing for the 7:48 to Grand Central.

At that hour the only reason for a business to be open was the commuter traffic. The antiques stores and the dress shops could stay dark for another few hours, but Mr. Wiseman's grocery, which somehow the new Food Emporium had failed to drive out of business, might sell a bottle of milk to a woman on her way home from dropping hubby at the train depot. And of course by 9:00 a.m. the service stations had all sold enough gas to meet half their daily running expenses.

The Exxon dealership across Cedar Road from the public library wasn't two hundred feet from Kinkaid's front door. It was where Charlie Flaxman worked. That particular morning he was outside, refilling an oil can rack.

For all that the census figures might show, New Gilead—the real New Gilead, not the town of the housing developers—was actually a small place. A lot of people lived there because their companies had transferred them from places like Cincinnati, but the natives were still essentially tribal in their outlook. They had all had the same kindergarten teachers, watched the same Fourth of July parades, learned to swim in the same YMCA pool and bought their first full-price tickets at the same movie theater. They all knew one another's personal histories, both real and imagined. They had watched each other grow up. Thus the personal relations among them involved a certain intimacy which existed alongside and in some ways transcended everything else. They might be friends or sworn enemies, but the one thing they could never be was strangers.

In school Charlie Flaxman had been two classes behind Kinkaid and they had not moved in the same circles, but their lives had overlapped enough that they could take each other for granted. Had Charlie been even two years younger he might have addressed the man who approached him in gym shorts and a sweat-soaked tee shirt as "Mr. Kinkaid," but he didn't. It wouldn't have occurred to him.

"Morning, Jim," he said instead. "Staying in shape?"

He smiled, not very benevolently. Charlie Flaxman was about three inches taller than Kinkaid and a good fifty pounds heavier and still carried himself like the eighteen-year-old kid who had been first-string guard on the high school football team. It was as if that one distinction had left him with nothing else to prove in this life.

Kinkaid walked over to the garage—the bay doors were still closed; no one else had come to work yet—and took a long drink of water from the hose that was used to fill radiators. When he was finished he let the water run over his face for a few seconds. It felt marvelous.

"I try," he answered, smiling a little wanly. He was pleasantly tired after his run and, besides, he didn't want to start trading insults. "How's business?"

"Not bad." Charlie looked around at the station, frowning as if it had somehow disappointed him. He had a one-third interest in the place, bought in part with money he had borrowed from his wife's parents, so he was entitled to care. "The tourist trade's been good this month—city people driving up for the day 'cause we're so quaint."

The remark was vintage Charlie. Bite the hand that feeds you, particularly if belongs to somebody who wasn't born here, or wasn't a high school sports hero, or—God forbid—might imagine he was as good or better than the one-third owner of New Gilead Exxon. With anyone else you might have said maybe he felt disappointed by life, but Charlie had been just the same at ten years old.

"How's the law, now you ain't got your daddy to do your thinking for you?"

Charlie's eyes narrowed as he waited for the thrust to hit home. He was a malignant bastard who was always goading people and got into one or another kind of serious trouble about every other year. Only last autumn Kinkaid had had to drive down to Stamford to bail him out of an aggravated assault charge, for which he was still on probation. Lots of people in town wouldn't have anything to do with him.

But he was disappointed this time. Kinkaid seemed not even to have heard the question.

"You happen to remember a kid named George Tipton?" The lawyer let his gaze rest on the front door of the library across the street. Somehow it had always reminded him of a bank vault. "He would have been a contemporary of yours, I think. Did you know him?"

"Yeah, I knew him. Yeah, he was a *contemporary*, I guess."

Charlie seemed to taste the word, rolling it around on his tongue, and then he shook his head. These dumb-ass, wimp college boys . . .

"Did you keep in touch with him? Do you know where he lives?"

"He doesn't *live* anywhere." When Kinkaid looked

puzzled, Charlie Flaxman grinned, as if that had been the idea all along. "Man, he's been dead three years."

The story, as Charlie told it, had a certain inevitability.

"George was always a crazy bastard that never cared about nothing but racking up touchdowns and pussy. That and getting high. Quit school in his senior year, as soon football season was over, but by then his old man was ready to throw him out anyway. Joined the Marines right after. Had an idea Reagan was gonna start World War III down in Guatemala or some damn place. Didn't want to miss it."

Leaning against one of the gas pumps, he let his gaze slide along Cedar Road toward the center of town as if estimating the probability that a car in need of a fill-up would pop out of the empty asphalt and pull in. Not today, it looked like.

"When he got out of the Corps he drifted around for a couple of years. He came back here for a while, about four years ago. We went out and had a few beers together, but by that time he wasn't much fun to be around. Finally he got into a big shindy with his family and disappeared again. The next thing I heard he'd piled up his car someplace over in Jersey. I drove over for the funeral—Jesus, the guy was twenty-five years old and looked about forty. So much for the fast life."

"So you saw the body?"

"Oh yeah." Charlie looked at him a trifle strangely, as if he considered the question not quite decent. "They'd laid on the paint pretty thick—seems like he was really messed up in the crash—but it was him."

At nine-fifteen that morning, sitting behind his desk with his hair combed and the jacket of his business suit hanging from a peg behind his chair, Kinkaid phoned the New Jersey State Police, Traffic Division, to see if they had a file on George Tipton.

"It's in reference to an estate settlement," he told the officer with whom he was eventually connected. "We'd like to be sure it is the same George Tipton and, assuming that it is, we'd appreciate any information you could provide concerning the circumstances of his death."

"And who might you be, sir?" The voice at the other end of the line sounded like it belonged to a man in late middle age—not suspicious precisely, but careful.

Kinkaid gave his name, address and telephone number. "I'm the attorney of record for Edward Tipton, now deceased. He was the father of George Tipton."

"I'll have to call you back on this, sir."

"Perhaps I could just give you my fax number. Since the case is only a few years old it should still be in your database. When you finish your inquiries could you send me the relevant information?"

"I could do that, sir."

It was a technique Kinkaid had used before with title companies, the Motor Vehicles Department and half a dozen different tax agencies, if not actually with the police. Your average clerk doesn't like to go sifting through a computer printout trying to decide what the "relevant information" might be—it is easier simply to push a button and send it all on its way. And a fax machine is a wonderfully impersonal device which somehow frees people from the natural bureaucratic suspicion that they might be giving away the keys to the kingdom. After all, they haven't actually said anything, and nothing has physically left the office. The result is that you tend to get more than you actually requested, sometimes a lot more.

Besides, this way Kinkaid didn't have to ask the New Jersey State Police if there was anything to suggest that George Tipton's death had not been just another accident statistic, and they didn't have to ask him why he wanted to know.

Two hours later the little icon appeared on his computer screen to let him know that something was coming over the wires. After about ten minutes he turned on his trusty Laser-Jet and slightly curled sheets of bond paper began to come out. He had hit paydirt. It looked as if they were sending him damn near the whole case file.

Fax transmissions take forever to print and paper was still staggering out when Kinkaid returned from lunch. He told Molly to hold his calls and started reading.

It was apparent that the police had also found George Tipton interesting, but not because they suspected he had met with foul play. By the time of his death he seemed to have been into drugs in a big way. His rap sheet showed four arrests on narcotics charges in the last six months before the accident. The officers at the scene had found a couple of vials of crack on the car floor and the autopsy report confirmed the presence of cocaine in his system. It was all perfectly straightforward: another doper cooks his brains in a louch pipe and the pink alligators on the back seat chase him into a bridge support at eighty miles an hour. There had been no murder investigation because there had been no murder. In a way it was kind of a relief—George Tipton had died of his own bad habits.

There was an interrogation report on a Helen Grier (age, 32; hair, brown; weight, 105; arrest record, extensive) who was listed primarily as Tipton's "live-in companion." The police believed that George had died on his way home from a drug buy and they wanted to know the name of his supplier. Helen couldn't tell them. Helen, one gathered, shared George's recreational tastes and probably had a lot of trouble remembering how to put her shoes on.

But, since there were no subsequent cross-references to other police reports, whatever future horrors might have awaited Helen Grier, at least she hadn't ended up with a hole in her face like Mrs. Billinger.

Kinkaid gathered up the hundred-some-odd sheets of paper, stuffed them into an unmarked manila envelope and dropped the envelope into the bottom drawer of his desk.

"Okay, Dad," he whispered to himself, "where does all this leave us?" Nowhere, apparently. Three out of the ten names had been accounted for by a mass murder, an apparent suicide and a traffic accident, but that didn't count for much in the way of progress.

"Mr. Kinkaid, I'll be leaving now."

He glanced up and saw Molly standing in his office doorway. He must have looked surprised.

"You'll remember I told you I had a dental appointment this afternoon."

"Right." He smiled encouragingly. "You go on ahead. I hope you have a good report."

"It's only a cleaning," she answered, with the tone of someone answering an accusation. "I left your phone messages on my desk."

After he had seen Molly to the door, Kinkaid went into his father's office and sat down behind the big desk. He had an idea—really more of an instinct, since it was hardly articulated as a rational proposition—that this was the place to come to terms with his father's secrets.

What is this about, Dad? A million years ago you defended a kid in juvenile court. How does any of this touch us?

After a few minutes he found himself staring at the glass case within which slumbered a handsomely bound collection of out-of-date law books. He had no idea what had attracted his attention to them, since he had never looked into any of them, had never even opened the case. The key . . .

It hit him just like that. He rose and went upstairs.

The bedroom had not been altered since the morning of his father's death. After the ambulance left Julia went upstairs, made up the bed with clean sheets, and closed the door behind her. No one had been inside since.

Kinkaid had not been present while the ambulance crew, with practiced efficiency, hoisted his father's corpse up by the wrists and ankles and dropped it into the black plastic body bag that lay open on a stretcher. He had witnessed the stretcher coming down the stairs and had noted its burden, but apparently he had not accepted the obvious inference because he was still surprised to find the bedroom empty.

But it was. The air was damp and lifeless, as if the room itself resented his intrusion.

He's dead, he thought to himself. *You saw him in his casket an hour before they put him into the ground. What were you expecting?*

He went over to the dresser, slid open the top drawer and took out a handkerchief box covered in scuffed brown leather. Inside he found what he had expected to find: his father's pocket watch.

Like the clock in the dining room it did not run, although a few drops of oil would probably have set it right. James Kinkaid III would not have felt himself fully dressed without his pocket watch, but the point lay more in the display of gold chain looped through the buttonhole of his vest than in any use he made of it as a timepiece. Sometimes, if he needed a few seconds to think—or he wished to call attention to the lateness of the hour—he would take the thing out, pop the cover and take a long look at the dial face, but he had been born just one generation too late for that to be anything more than a mannerism. So it didn't matter whether the watch kept time or not.

Still, he had always carried it, in case he needed it for a bit of stage business. "The little old ladies just love that sort of thing. It makes them think they're dealing with Oliver Wendell Holmes." And then he would smile, just to show that he wasn't joking. "You always have to remember, Jimmy, that about thirty percent of lawyering is pure theater. That's your one weakness—you seem to think you have to believe everything you say."

It was a beautiful watch, made in London before the turn of the century and acquired by the first James Kinkaid, according to family legend, as a gift from a grateful client rescued from a well-deserved prison sentence. But it was not the watch itself which interested his great-grandson.

The watch was attached to a massive flat-weave chain, also gold and purchased in 1922 by James Kinkaid Jr. from Honeyman & Lowe in New York—the receipt was among his private papers, in the basement. At the other end of the chain was a small, flat, folding cigar knife acquired at the same time and more for decoration than use. There was also a small key with a cylindrical shank and a hollow oval bow through which it was attached to the chain by a clip. The key was nickel-plated and altogether about an inch and a quarter long.

It was a puzzler. Kinkaid did not remember when he had first noticed it, or if it had ever occurred to him before to wonder why his father would carry it around with him. It was obviously not of recent manufacture, but there was nothing about it to excite a sentimental interest. Doubtless every old house in New England had accumulated drawers full of such keys.

The obvious inference was that there was a lock somewhere that James Kinkaid III had wished never to be opened by anyone except himself.

The elder Kinkaid had not been a man to lose the distinction between convenience and esthetics. In his office the books he actually used, such as *Webster's Pocket Dictionary*, an edition of Roget and *Bartlett's Guide to Contract Law*, were between a pair of marble blocks on a narrow table directly behind his desk. In the normal course of the day he had hardly had occasion to notice their existence, but if he wanted one of them all he had had to do was reach behind him and pick it up.

The bookcase on the opposite wall was another matter. It was dark oak and a beautiful piece of Victorian decorative art—the carving was all scrollwork and climbing vines—and the books in the upper section, behind beveled glass doors, were apparently valued for their bindings, which were stamped leather, rather than for their contents. To these Mr. Kinkaid Senior had merely to raise his eyes to receive whatever mysterious comfort they provided, for they were never read or even taken down from their shelves. They remained inviolate, for the key to the bookcase had been lost years ago.

Or had it? Mr. Kinkaid's son took from his pocket the key he had removed from his father's watch chain and inserted it into the lock. It fit perfectly. He turned it counterclockwise and heard the little square latch pull back with a snap. The bookcase door slipped open soundlessly on its hinges.

There was nothing inside except books, the same ones he had been admiring through the glass all his life. Kinkaid slid one of them off the shelf and opened it. The pages were divided into two columns of dense, black type. He read a few lines and discovered them to be a summary of the defense's closing argument in a mail fraud case, circa 1946. Whatever secret his father had been protecting, it wasn't here. He shut the book and put it back.

The covers of the volumes stuck slightly to one another, a sure sign no one had had them out in years. He picked up another, flipped through the pages, put it back, and then started going through them in order. There really was nothing.

For a moment he stood in front of the open bookcase feeling baffled and foolish, wondering what was the matter with him that he went around making mysteries out of every trifle. Then he remembered the bottom cabinet.

A gentleman does not always want the whole of his library on display. Only the upper part of the book case was enclosed in glass; underneath, to about halfway up one's thighs, the doors were heavy wood, so that any intruder would have needed an axe to break them open. They were closed in the middle by a lock that was the duplicate of the one above.

Inside Kinkaid found a metal file box about ten inches deep, the sort intended to protect its contents from fire but little else.

And inside the file box, along with some half-dozen antique keys bound together by a narrow black ribbon, were about thirty manila folders, each with its tab labeled and dated: Wyman-1960, Wyman-1961, and so on up to 1989.

It was a name he knew almost as well as his own. The Wymans, who had possessed a vast fortune derived from the textile industry, had been a power in this county and even beyond since the end of the last century, and the Kinkaids had been enjoying a share of their legal work for almost as long. The first James Kinkaid had even served a term in the state legislature under the patronage of the Wyman family. That patronage, in its many forms, had been granted early and was not forgotten by the generations that followed.

It gave Kinkaid an unpleasant turn to see the name. One of his earliest memories was of being taken out to be presented to Judge Wyman, the last of the male line, dead for twenty-five years now and as hard-faced an old sinner as he ever hoped to see. To a five-year-old boy the Wymans were the stuff of dreams and of nightmares. The family had never been lucky for him, and to this hour they occupied a back room of his soul which he visited rarely and only with vast reluctance.

But all of that was ancient history. It had been nearly six years since young James Kinkaid, still in law school, had accompanied his father to the funeral of Isabelle Wyman, the Dowager Empress who had died at the age of seventy-nine without leaving an heir. The estate had been parceled out among a few distant relatives, living far away, and a handful of eccentric charities. The real family, the family that had mattered so much for so long, was extinct. Beyond the files, which should have been gathering dust down in the basement, and a great white elephant of a house about two miles outside of town, there was hardly anything left to mark their passage through the world.

Thus there were now two things that James Kinkaid III had died leaving unexplained: a list of names and the reason he had kept the records of this long-concluded business locked up in his office. It remained to be proved that there was any connection between the two. A man's life may have many shadows thrown across it. He may have many separate sins to conceal.

Or perhaps concealment had not been the point. After all, the office was equipped with a shredder—if the Wyman files contained something he had wanted to keep hidden forever, what would have prevented him from simply destroying them?

Did you mean for me to find this stuff, Dad?

Then he remembered the time. If he wasn't in the dining room when Julia brought in his salad plate she would come looking for him, and he didn't want her to find him in his father's office. That would only bring on another flood of tears.

After dinner he went upstairs to his room and waited until he was sure Julia had finished cleaning up the dishes and would be safely absorbed with her television programs—he had checked the newspaper and there was a Richard Widmark movie on Channel 11, so she would not be heard from again tonight. Then he went downstairs to the office.

On the way he passed by Molly's desk and picked up his telephone messages. One of them was from a real estate company in Stamford.

They had a buyer for the Wyman house.

chapter 7

For two whole days, forty-eight consecutive hours, Lucille had somehow managed to avoid goading her husband into an argument. They had even made love, for the first time in what felt like months, and on her initiative. It wasn't half bad either.

Lucille had probably been faking—she really wasn't much of an animal in bed and, anyway, it's only in the movies people make that much noise coming—but the remarkable thing was that she had gone to the trouble. George wondered if she wasn't beginning to suspect something.

But what could she suspect, after all? Four lunches in a row at the Baker's Basket don't constitute proof of anything, even if Lucille knew—even if the waitress was starting to look at him like he was the main course. So far things hadn't gotten further than unsatisfied lust and a little conversational foreplay.

God, she was a piece of work. Blonde, firm-fleshed, and so pretty she didn't look quite real. Too good to be true.

And that was the problem.

Her nametag said "Annie," which was the sort of name you'd expect a waitress to have, but waitresses were usually either high-school girls or frumpy divorcees. Annie wore her uniform like a disguise.

She lived in an apartment building eight blocks from work. George knew because on the afternoon of his day off he had gone over to the shopping center about a half-hour before it closed and then followed her home.

Except for employees, the place was deserted when she came out of the restaurant, a blue, soft-sided duffle bag hanging from her shoulder by a strap. From the other side of the plaza and careful to stay behind her, George watched her as she took the escalator down to the third floor and then ducked into a ladies' rest room.

That was where she almost got past him because when she came out she had changed out of her uniform and was wearing a crisp, bone-white suit that looked like it had probably cost about $600 off the rack at Nieman Marcus. She had even let her hair down so that it reached to the small of her back. He had seen her come out and was staring in something close to awe before he even realized it was the same woman.

She had walked home. Atlanta wasn't a very safe place for a woman after dark, but she didn't seem the least little bit skittish. God damn, she was ready for anything.

The apartment building had a plateglass front door and a marble lobby the size of a tennis court—not the sort of address you can afford out of the earnings from waiting on tables.

She didn't wear any rings, but George began to worry that she might have a sugar daddy or something. After all, somebody had to be paying for all that.

Then he had gone home to get the vamp treatment from Lucille, who caught him in just the right mood. He had damn near bounced her off the ceiling.

But Lucille's Theda Bara act didn't wear well and by the time she headed for the bathroom he was already tired of it. She was her old bitchy self again at breakfast, so he was glad he had a job to go to.

"You want to hear about the daily special?"

It was about a quarter to two and the lunch crowd was starting to thin out. George had taken a booth in the corner, away from the windows that faced out into the shopping center.

Annie was standing so close that the hem of her dress was brushing against his knee. He was beginning to get a hard-on.

"You mean to tell me all the good stuff's not on the menu?"

"I just thought you'd like something special," she answered, with a knowing little smile that tugged at the corners of her beautiful mouth.

That afternoon George had an incredible run of luck. Along with a half-dozen pairs of running shoes and a couple of sweatbands, he actually sold five bicycles, one of them a Trek 8000 which, even on special, went for $699. There was also a brisk trade in women's exercise tights.

It was a sign from above. Tonight, before he went home, he would make his move on Annie.

He was actually rather slight of build, not at all like his original. There was no real physical resemblance. But he had the same athletic gestures. It was the way he had of rolling his shoulders and throwing out his chest, as if expecting you to admire his physique, that had doomed him.

The woman who was listed on the restaurant employment records as "Anna Dexter" was on her long break after the lunch-hour rush, which in fact lasted from noon to a little after two-thirty. Most of the other waitresses used the opportunity to get something to eat themselves, and the tiny cloakroom where they retreated to rest their feet or puff some tobacco through their lungs was crowded with women precariously balancing plates of food on their knees.

"Is that how you keep your figure, Anna?"

Patsy Barledge, the baby among them, who at eighteen was as chubby as a cupid and would weigh a hundred and sixty pounds before she was out of her twenties, gestured with a dirty fork toward the glass of iced tea the other woman was holding by the rim.

"It helps. Besides, I get sick of the smell."

"That's right," Clara Price joined in, through a cloud of cigarette smoke. "It's bad enough to serve this shit all day—you don't have to eat it!"

She laughed at this, hard enough to send her into a coughing fit. The gurgling in her lungs sounded like tar was being

boiled inside them. At fifty, and so thin she looked dessi-
cated, Clara had given up on food and a lot of other things.

"I wish I could feel that way."

Patsy smiled at "Annie." That name would do, although
Anna Dexter had not existed four weeks ago and would
soon vanish forever. She knew that Patsy admired her and
yearned to be her friend, yet she felt nothing for the girl, not
sympathy nor kindness nor even distaste. Patsy Barledge had
no more reality for her than if she were an image projected on
the wall.

Yet Anna returned the smile. It would not do to seem at all
out of the ordinary. She did not wish to leave any vivid memories behind her.

This seemed to satisfy Patsy. "Well then, maybe I just
won't have dessert." She stood up, holding her by now empty
plate almost at arm's length, as if to emphasize her resolve.

"You'll disappoint Julio. You know how vain he is about
his bread pudding."

Patsy blushed deeply and was pursued out of the room by
Clara's wheezing laughter.

"I caught them in the supply locker again this morning,"
she said, shaking another cigarette out of the pack she carried
in the pocket of her uniform, where the bulge it made was
concealed behind an apron. "That girl'd better watch out or
she'll get him fired. The boss likes to think he got there first."

There was no reply, but apparently no reply was expected
since Clara seemed absorbed in the ritual of lighting up—first
the pungent sulphur flare of the match and then that first deep
breath of smoke, as if her lungs had been deprived of nicotine
for days. The silence was perfectly comfortable.

It would be a relief to leave this place. No more living eight
hours a day with the smell of food, no more jokes about
Patsy's romances, no more Anna Dexter, whose taste in men
ran to sporting goods salesmen. After tonight, no more George
Tipton. She was quite sure it would be tonight. George didn't
seem the patient type.

Her apartment was a sublet, contracted through an agency and paid for in advance. It was in a big building, full of young executive types who were always away, so there was no one who would think anything odd if her little studio remained vacant for the month before the regular tenant came home from his summer in Europe. The few personal items still there would fit comfortably into a shoulder bag. Her suitcase had been in a locker at the Atlanta airport for the last three days. All that remained was to see to George.

He had followed her home last night. He had been so obvious about it that it was difficult to keep up the pretense that she hadn't seen him. And at lunch today he was really primed. She was quite sure he would hang around the mall this evening until her shift ended. It wouldn't take very much encouragement to get him to make a move.

"I guess we better be getting back to it."

"Look at that," Clara said, glaring out at the empty tables with evident disgust. "Not a soul. Some days it hardly pays to come to work."

The early shift lasted until five-thirty in the evening, or whenever your last order was out the door. The girls who did the dinner crowd were already working their tables. It had been a slow day, so there was nothing to linger for.

As she walked out of the restaurant, her shoulder bag riding beneath her left elbow, she allowed herself one quick scan over the runway crowd. He wasn't anywhere in sight. That was all right, though. It was better, in fact, because she didn't want anyone who knew her to see them together. The farther away from the Baker's Basket the better.

Still, she could feel her stomach tightening—what if she had been wrong about him? What if he was just a guy who liked to flirt with waitresses, another harmless tourist without the nerve?

Deliberately repeating her routine of the day before, she took the escalator down to the ladies' room on the third floor to change out of her uniform. She went into a toilet stall, locked the door behind her, and pulled a red rayon dress out of her bag. It wasn't really her color, but men who wore white patent leather belts generally were not afflicted with much fashion sense and she wanted to stand out. Besides, clingy fabrics and shoulder pads would be right up George Tipton's street.

She took her time, combing out her hair and applying eyeliner, which she hardly ever used. She wanted to give George a chance to show up, and she wanted time to think.

Because there was always the chance that he wouldn't show. It might mean nothing—he might have had a dental appointment, or his car might have broken down—but it might also mean that he simply wasn't ready. And once she had made contact every day was a risk. As the game went on it became more and more dangerous.

She had to decide if George Tipton was worth it.

She could always settle on another. She would locate him the way she had found this one. The phone books were full of them.

But it might be months before she found someone as nearly perfect and, besides, in her mind this one had become *the* George Tipton, overlapping the original in so many ways that now she could hardly distinguish between them. The need was too strong. She would never be able to leave him behind.

Thus, no matter what the risks, she would have to wait until this one fell into her net.

As she smoothed on lip gloss with the tip of her middle finger she studied herself in the mirror to estimate the effect. She knew she was beautiful, but the knowledge was impersonal, without pride or pleasure. She considered the matter in purely tactical terms. She might have been trying to gauge the precise range of a weapon.

All she needed was a few seconds. A word or two and a smile, and George Tipton would follow her anywhere, do anything she asked, never think of reasons or consequences. He wouldn't be able to help himself. It would be so easy.

If she just got the chance.

And as she came back out and the door to the ladies' room swung closed behind her, there he was, standing next to the down escalator. This time he wasn't being coy. When he saw her he stepped out into the middle of the aisle, deliberately trying to attract her notice. He even managed a little wave.

She stood quite still. Relief flooded through her, and the temptation to run over and capture him was almost overpowering, but she knew it was better to force him to come to her. So she waited.

She did smile—she would give him that much.

And it was all he needed. With the quick, ratlike glance to either side that is the talisman of the guilty husband, he scurried across the mall walkway to her as if closing in on a piece of decayed meat. He even grinned like a rat.

"Well, hello," he said, near enough now that she could almost feel his breath on her face. "I'm surprised. . . ."

"You are? Somehow I had the impression you were waiting for me."

"Did you?" He rolled his shoulders and started to throw out his chest, only catching himself when he saw she was smiling again. The smile gave him back his confidence. "Well, maybe I was."

He made a little gesture with his left hand, as if dismissing the matter, and she noticed that he had taken off his wedding ring.

"Then maybe you'd like to be a gentleman and take me out for a drink. I'd invite you up to my place except . . . I live with someone."

That struck a chord. He liked that—they were both out on the sly. He touched her then for the first time, sliding his finger around the inside of her elbow to take her arm, really enjoying himself. He was in the noose.

Predictably, he raised the stakes to dinner. For one thing he was stalling. He needed time to nerve himself up to an out-and-out proposition and, in any case, taking a lady to a motel in the early evening was bound to be a little awkward. Besides, he had to feel he had paid for the privilege. So he took her to a restaurant, well on the other side of town naturally. That sort of place where there was no risk he would run into anyone he knew.

It was clear that on a certain primitive level he had given the matter some thought. The restaurant was a steak place with a railroad theme—probably George's idea of really elegant dining. And it was just right for present purposes. The building was actually constructed using three or four old Pullman cars welded together, so the dining areas were narrow passages with booths on either side, which afforded lots of privacy. And the parking lot was in the back, so you couldn't be seen from the street. The parking lot was a bonus she hadn't counted on.

Inside he recommended the roast beef and ordered a pitcher of sangria before they made their pilgrimage to the salad bar. The salads came on dinner plates and there was warm French bread. She had known it was going to be like this and had starved herself all day to be able to do justice to the food—a certain kind of man always thought of eating as foreplay and therefore liked a girl with a good appetite. Conversation was a little slow until George got around to the subject that really interested him.

"So," he began, as if to signal the end of some logical progression, "you're not alone?"

"Now?" She made a show of looking around her. "I hope not."

"No, I mean . . ."

"I know what you mean."

For a moment she let the silence hang like a threat, and then she smiled. "He's quite a bit older," she went on, allowing herself a slight shrug. "He's very good to me, but sometimes that isn't enough."

"Is now one of those times?"

"Looks like it," she answered, smiling as provocatively as she felt she could get away with.

She kept him going for the rest of the meal. Once she stepped out of her shoe and ran her toes up his leg. He was so easy it was almost embarrassing.

"You want some dessert?" he asked finally.

"Not here."

After that he couldn't get her out of there fast enough.

There was no one in the parking lot, which was convenient. While they walked back to his car she reached inside her shoulder bag and took out a small hypodermic syringe, clutching it in her hand so that only the tip was exposed. The syringe contained two ccs of ketamine. Using her thumbnail she pushed the protective cap from the needle, letting it drop to the pavement. He never noticed a thing.

"Hey, I think someone creased your fender," she said.

"Where?"

"Back there. See it?"

When he bent over to look she shoved the needle into the seat of his pants—he probably thought she was goosing him. He turned around and started to say something and then simply collapsed. She took the car keys from his hand, opened the trunk and hoisted him inside.

Easy come, easy go. The ketamine acted almost at once, but it would wear off quickly and she needed at least six hours. For this she had pentobarbitol—all you needed was a pharmacist with a gambling problem and you could get anything, no questions asked. She took an ampule from her purse, refilled the syringe and gave him an injection in the leg. She closed the trunk and got into the car.

They hadn't been out of the restaurant more than three minutes.

It was tempting just to get the thing over with, but she didn't want to go blundering in on George's wife at eight o'clock in the evening. There were neighbors to think about and, although she didn't plan to make a lot of noise, you never knew.

What had George planned? Dinner, a quick fuck, and then home by ten? What had he planned to tell his wife? Maybe he knew his wife wouldn't be home to miss him. That would be inconvenient.

There was plenty of time. Half an hour later she drove by the house and established that the lights were on, which didn't prove that anyone was inside but was at least encouraging. She would just have to wait to find out.

She drove back to her apartment, leaving the car for the moment in the basement garage. She made herself a cup of coffee and changed out of her tart's uniform. It was ten minutes after nine. She would give it another three hours. To pass the time, she turned on the television.

Waterloo Bridge with Vivian Leigh had been on since eight. She had seen it before. She watched it for twenty minutes before she realized she was sobbing.

At a quarter after midnight George's garage door went up. The opener had been in his glove compartment. It wasn't the ideal arrangement, since his wife would be able to hear the car coming in, but that was better than leaving it out on the street with George still in the trunk. Besides, the outside doors would probably have deadbolts whereas the door from the garage wouldn't. She would just have to take her chances with Mrs. Tipton.

She drove in and let the garage door go all the way back down before she got out. She had a Walther PPK/S automatic with a clip full of .22-caliber hollow points, which would do the job nicely at close range and had enough frame weight to keep the noise low—outside the house you probably wouldn't even be able to hear it.

She let herself in with George's keys.

"All right, George, where the hell have you . . ."

Mrs. Tipton was coming out of the bedroom when she died. She turned left into the hall, heading toward the kitchen, which connected with the garage, when a single shot entered her left eye. She dropped to the floor, probably without even seeing who had killed her, and did not move. The bullet fragmented in her brain without making an exit wound, so there was very little mess.

She was wearing a filmy white negligee which normally reached all the way to the floor but was now bunched up around her thighs. Had she had plans of her own for this evening? Her murderess now crouched beside the body, the tips of her fingers pressed against the throat. For a second or two she fancied she could still detect a pulse, but very quickly there was nothing.

There was a workbench in the garage and in a drawer she found a roll of duct tape. When she opened the trunk of the car George was beginning to stir. Okay. Another twenty ccs of pentobarbitol and he was quiet again. She rolled him over and bound his wrists together behind his back with the duct tape.

She had just finished when she heard a thin wail coming from inside the house. Her heart almost stopped until she realized it was the baby. A timely reminder—there was still that to be taken care of.

George Tipton's first conscious sensation was the nasty taste in his mouth. It was bad enough that he felt a strong inclination to vomit, but he was distracted from this when a strong, white light shone on him, making his eyeballs feel as if they had dried up in their sockets. The light was exquisitely painful. When he tried to raise an arm to shield his face he discovered that his hands were tied behind his back.

It was only then that it occurred to him there was something wrong. He had been on a date, and now . . .

"Sit up, George," a voice said. "Just throw your legs over the edge there. You can do it."

It was a woman's voice, but not one he recognized. He couldn't see anyone behind the blinding glare of the light.

He tried to do as he was told. Only on the third attempt was he able to pull himself up, and then he hit his head. He was sitting in the trunk of a car and the edge of the lid had grazed him above his left eyebrow. Christ, it hurt. It felt like it was bleeding.

The light was only a flashlight. He figured that out when the woman set it down on the ground, apparently so he could see her.

She was Annie.

"I've been waiting a long time for you to come around," she said. "It's almost four-thirty in the morning. Another half-hour and we wouldn't have had a chance to talk."

They were outside somewhere—in the woods it seemed like. It was very quiet. He thought he could smell water.

He tried to pull his hands free, but they were really tied tight. He couldn't feel his fingers at all.

"Where are we?" he asked. It was a stupid question, but just then it was all he was up to.

"We're on the shores of Lake Hartwell, in South Carolina. The lake is just behind you, but you can't see it from here. There's a little bluff that drops right off into the water. It's about twenty-five feet deep just there."

"How did we get here?"

"We drove. What did you think?"

She had a delicious, sexy laugh. Any other time it would have thrilled him, but just then the sound hurt his head.

"We made a stop along the way," she went on, "but we weren't more than an hour and a half from your front door."

She was crouched on the ground about fifteen feet in front of him. That allowed him to see her whole in the narrow arc of the flashlight, which was probably the point. It also allowed him to see the pistol she held in her hand.

His mind, as it cleared, was capable of grasping the logic of the situation: they were somewhere deep in the boondocks, his hands were tied behind his back, and she had a gun. She had brought him here to kill him. Oddly, the only emotion he could bring to that conclusion was astonishment.

"My front door . . ." he repeated. Somehow the phrase made him uneasy. "What's going on? Annie, what's going on?"

She shook her head, and her perfect blond hair moved as with its own life. Even at this extremity he could not help but be struck yet again by her beauty.

When she smiled at him it was like a promise of forgiveness.

"You don't remember my real name? You don't remember me at all?"

"What are you talking about?"

"Ten years ago, in Connecticut. You used to climb over the wall to come to me."

"I've never been near Connecticut."

"It doesn't matter." She stood up, which had the effect of making her invisible above the waist. When he couldn't see her face anymore he was stabbed through with fear, as if she had abandoned him to death. "Nothing about you matters anymore, George. All your little sins will be erased."

"You're crazy."

"So I've heard."

She laughed again, only this time it sounded like no human laughter. Yes, absolutely—she was going to kill him.

She raised the pistol and pointed it at his head—he could just see her white forearm, and then the hand, and then the gun, as if she had lowered them into a pool of light for his inspection—and then she seemed to think better of it and let her arm drop. Perhaps she had only meant to frighten him, to make him realize how precarious his hold on life had become. It worked.

"Oh Jesus," he sobbed. "Oh Jesus, oh Jesus . . ."

"You can forget about Him too, George. He won't be interested. You've been a bad boy."

"Oh God, don't. Don't . . ."

"I'd be doing you a favor, George," she said, her voice perfectly even, as though none of this mattered to her. As though he himself were no more real than an image on the television screen. "If they ever catch you, it's over anyway. Do they still have the electric chair around here? I forget. You murdered your wife and her little baby, George. You drove home in your car—if anyone saw anything, that was all they saw—and then you shot them both dead. With this gun. They'll strap you down and cook you crisp as bacon, George. The best thing for you is to just disappear. The water of this lake is as cloudy as clam chowder—they'll never find you."

He just sat there, his legs dangling over the back bumper, weeping quietly. He was so filled with grief and fear he couldn't sort one out from the other. Knowing that Lucille and the baby were dead only made him feel the more hopeless. Nothing could save him. He was dead.

She just stood there. She seemed to be waiting for him to compose himself. She had to wait a long time.

"Why are you doing this?" he asked finally.

"I have my reasons. Does it matter?"

He shook his head. He was quite simply too terrified to do anything else.

"Please . . ."

"Shut up, George. Get back in the trunk." She raised the pistol again. "Or, if you like, I can kill you first and then put you inside. I don't really care. You choose."

He didn't want to die. Not this very second, he didn't. So he let himself fall backwards into the trunk.

"Get your legs in, unless you want a bullet through the kneecap. That would hurt."

He pulled his legs inside and huddled here. It was almost as if he were taking refuge.

"Goodbye, George."

She stepped forward and brought down the lid of the trunk with a slam. He heard the lock turn and then click shut. After a long silence, he heard the engine turn over and kick into life.

The car jolted forward so that he lurched to one side until he was almost on his knees. Then, for a few seconds, he could sense the front end sinking, as if it were following a downward arc through the air.

The impact came first and then he heard the splash. Then everything was still.

He did not start to scream until he could feel the water beginning to trickle over his face.

chapter 8

The bid on the Wyman estate was an even
$6,000,000, which struck Kinkaid as a little high, especially
since it had been over three years since the last serious offer,
amounting to $3,700,000 from an out-of-state developer who
had wanted to tear the house down and build condos. The
heirs, speaking through a law firm in San Francisco, had re-
fused even to counter.

It had been six years since Mrs. Wyman's death and the
property ate up a lot in maintenance costs and real estate
taxes. Besides, $6,000,000 was $6,000,000. It might be a
long time before that kind of money was on the table again.

But when Kinkaid placed his call to San Francisco he had
no idea what the reaction would be. He had never met the
heirs to the Wyman fortune. He did not even know their
names or how many of them there were. They existed for him
only as the beneficiaries of a trust administered in California,
and so far at least they had displayed very little interest in the
great white elephant of a house that was costing the estate
some thirty thousand dollars every year it went unsold.

Getting someone on the line at a big out-of-state law office
where nobody knows you—and, after three years, nobody
would—was often a time-consuming business. A lawyer was
not a client, and people were in no particular hurry to talk to
you when they didn't know if the time was going to be bill-
able. Yet in what was virtually a breach of etiquette the
switchboard girl didn't even place him on hold but he found
himself connected to someone named Grayson almost as
soon as he gave his name.

"Good afternoon, Mr. Kinkaid. It's a pleasure to hear from

you again," Mr. Grayson said, in the intimidating baritone of a man who has made full partner. "Or perhaps I should say 'Good evening.' What is it, about seven-thirty out there? You're working late."

Kinkaid glanced out his one and only window and saw that the light was already on above his neighbor's back porch. From his office in some huge glass skyscraper Mr. Grayson, to whom Kinkaid was quite sure he had never before spoken, could probably see the late afternoon sun lighting up the towers of the Golden Gate Bridge—at least, it was agreeable to think he might.

"It's one of the advantages of living above the shop," he answered, careful to put just the shadow of a chuckle in his voice. "You of course remember the Wyman property. We've had another offer."

"That's good to hear," Grayson answered, just a split second too quickly. "How much?"

"Six million."

"Then I think we should accept. Don't you agree?"

"Yes. Of course. As soon as your principals have approved . . ."

"Oh, I think you can just go ahead. You have power of attorney, if I remember correctly. I'll consult with the heirs, of course, but I don't anticipate any problems there. You'll hear from me in a day or two."

That was it. There wasn't anymore. And it simply didn't smell right. By the time Kinkaid hung up his receiver he was reasonably certain that Grayson had been expecting the offer and had probably already cleared it with his clients, whoever they were. There were just too many questions he hadn't asked.

For instance, there had been no mention of the terms of purchase—the date of closing, whether there were any contingencies, whether the buyer was likely to have any trouble with the banks about a loan.

And, come to think on it, why was the buyer paying list

when the property had been on the market forever? He might reasonably have assumed that the sellers were hungry and there would be some give on the price—probably a lot of give—and that he could save himself at least half a million by coming in at, say, four and then allowing himself to be screwed up to five five. Kinkaid did a fair amount of realty work and he couldn't remember the last time a property in New Gilead had sold for list.

Still, it wouldn't do to become too curious. A list sale meant not only a higher commission for the broker but more money for the heirs, and that was where his primary responsibility lay. Once this deal went through there would be no more business pending on the estate. An association between his family and the Wymans which reached back nearly a century would at last be ended and he could close the book on it.

That would be a relief.

He told himself that it was part of the job, that until the Wyman property was claimed by its new owners it remained his responsibility and he ought to go out there one last time to inspect the premises, to make sure everything was as it should be and there was nothing which could possibly queer the sale. That was what he told himself and it was all perfectly true, but he knew it was not the whole reason and that the account he hoped to settle within himself had nothing to do with land values.

So the morning after his conversation with Mr. Grayson he phoned the real estate company and told them he wanted the keys to the Wyman property.

"We can drop the keys off at your office," said a woman, presumably young, with an attractive, sweetly tremulous voice. "As a matter of fact, would you mind if I went with you? I've been the listed agent for nearly a year and I've never seen the place."

Yes, he minded. But he could hardly make an issue of it.

After all, what possible legitimate reason could he give for wanting to go alone?

"I'm not sure when I'll be able to get out there, and I'd hate to inconvenience you. . . ."

"Not to worry," she answered brightly. "I've got lots of free time. I can be there on twenty minutes notice. You have no idea how slow business has been."

Okay. So maybe she had him trapped. But he would make one last try.

"Then shall we say, tentatively, tomorrow morning? About eight?"

"That would be great!"

Just his luck, she had to be an early riser. Kinkaid decided he disliked her already.

He was watching from his bedroom window when, at exactly two minutes before eight, she pulled up in front of his house in a dusty, pale blue Fiat that was at least ten years old. She got out and slammed the car door vehemently enough to give the impression she meant it as a kind of wake-up call, in case he had overslept.

There is a limit to how much you can tell about a person when you are looking down at them from about a sixty-degree angle. He couldn't see her face at all, but she had shiny black hair, cut short enough that it hardly reached her collar, and above a dark, full skirt she was wearing a forest-green jacket that somehow managed to suggest the Austrian Alps. This on a morning that had already reached seventy degrees before the sun was up. Her gait, what he saw of it, was rapid and angry—her shoulders rocked a little as she walked, as if she looked forward to slamming his front door too, just for good measure.

He was already on the stairs when he heard the bell. He passed Julia in the hallway and told her not to trouble herself about seeing who it was.

"It's only business," he told her, with something like relief. "She won't be coming in."

So Kinkaid wasn't at all prepared for what he found when he opened the door.

"Good morning!"

She stood there smiling at him with that cheerful prettiness that goes with a slightly turned-up nose and freckles, except that there weren't any freckles. Her eyes were large and amused. With her little cap of black hair, she looked like a pixie.

Normally, pixies were not much to his taste.

"Mr. Kinkaid?" she asked. "I'm Lisa Milano—from Prestige Properties?"

She thrust out her hand and he took it, realizing with embarrassment that he hadn't answered her.

"I'm Jim Kinkaid," he said quickly, returning her smile. "Good morning."

For a long moment he stood there staring at her, struggling to find something more to say. Her hand, he noticed, was small and exquisite. She was not what he had expected—she had startled him, that was all.

Finally, he managed to suggest that they take his car, since he knew the way.

Well, it wasn't precisely *his* car. In real life Kinkaid drove a dark blue Honda with a dented right rear fender and bad shocks—the Mercedes had belonged to his father.

It was a 400SE, five years old but with less than 15,000 miles on the odometer. James Kinkaid III had bought it just a few months before his first heart attack and for the remainder of his life he had hardly driven it anywhere except around town. It was a metallic green and the paintwork was like new. Mr. Kinkaid Senior had taken it for a wash and polish two days before he died and it hadn't been out of the garage since.

His son, who had been raised to be a gentleman, opened the car door for the lady and, when he was behind the wheel, switched on the air conditioning.

"It's really nice," she said, looking at the instrument panel with admiration.

"My dad's," he answered, a little perversely. Still, he could not stifle a certain pride of ownership. It pleased him that she liked his father's car.

The Wyman place was far enough away from town that even the housing developers hadn't encroached on it, and as a result the drive there was a pleasant ten minutes along a road hardly wide enough for a farm cart. At one point they even had to slow down for a couple of teenage girls on horseback.

"I've never been out here." Lisa Milano gazed at the riders as if she had just discovered what horses were for. Then she looked embarrassed. "You can live in Stamford and think the whole of Connecticut is just like Philadelphia."

"Is that where you're from?"

She nodded, giving the impression she thought there was something a little shameful about Philadelphia. "You?"

"I was born here," he said. "Unless you count New Haven, I've never lived anywhere else."

"You must like it then."

Kinkaid shrugged. "I console myself with the thought that at least it isn't New York."

"Or Philadelphia."

He had to check to make sure she was joking before he allowed himself to laugh. Where he wondered had he learned to be so cautious?

He slipped the car back into gear and they were on their way again.

Three minutes later they turned into an even narrower road which, after about a quarter of a mile, ran through a patch of woods and up to a gate of wrought-iron bars, the two sides held together by a chain and padlock and each side displaying a florid letter "W" enclosed in a circle. The spaces between the bars were narrow enough that not even a small child could have slipped through them and the gate was the only opening in a wall of rough stone that stood about eight feet high.

"I gather they liked their privacy," she said, with what amounted to a kind of awe.

This time he didn't risk sneaking a look at her.

"When you have that kind of money, and that kind of power, you like to think you can keep the world at bay," he answered. "At least you did if your name was Wyman. But there were always chinks in the armor—about fifty feet from here, down there where the ground begins to slope, the wall slants in a few degrees and you can climb it if you know where to look for the handholds."

"Did you ever do it?"

He didn't reply but instead took the set of keys from her hand and got out to unfasten the chain. When he returned to the car they drove on to the house in silence.

The Wyman mansion dated from 1904. Preston Wyman, old Judge Wyman's grandfather, had had it built as a wedding present for his son and had given the commission to the architectural firm of Peabody and Sterns, who had designed Cornelius Vanderbilt's summer home at Newport. The house, called "Five Miles" because that was the length of the stone wall enclosing the property, was in the Palladian style, neoclassical and grand, with four great white columns and a thirty-foot-wide stairway marking the entrance. Preston Wyman had meant his new home to command the world's envy and respect, and he had succeeded. Judge Wyman had been born here and, at the end of a long life, he had died here, leaving a widow but no descendants. The line was broken forever.

The law firm of Kinkaid & Kinkaid regularly issued checks to landscape gardeners and painters. The gutters were kept clear and the roof was checked every spring. But the Wymans were gone now and the house had remained unoccupied. For six years no one had eaten a meal or slept within its walls. White paint and well-trimmed grass could not dissipate the sense of lifelessness. Its windows were as lightless and empty as the eye sockets of a skull.

Mrs. Wyman had been a very old woman when her heart

finally stopped beating. She had died just at sunset in the middle of a February snowfall, and her body had been carried out through the front door at night. That had been her exit from the world, in the muffled darkness, attended by a few old servants and the ambulance crew. Somehow it was as if the atmosphere of that last night had never been dispelled.

But for Jim Kinkaid the house had been dead longer than the six years since old Mrs. Wyman had relinquished her ferocious hold on existence. He had not set eyes on this place in over a decade, but it haunted his memory. He would have been glad if some accident had burned it to the ground.

"It looks like a hotel," Lisa said, favoring him with the full impact of her smile as he held the car door open for her. She seemed amused—after all, he hadn't been quite quick enough to bestow this old-fashioned courtesy before she was already halfway out. Perhaps she thought he was stuffy. He wondered when he had begun thinking of her as Lisa.

Maybe he was stuffy. Probably.

"Maybe it will be." He turned to look at the colonnaded entrance, which just then was easier to look at than Lisa Milano. "Maybe the new owners will convert it into a conference center, or maybe a nursing home."

"And thus the mighty are brought low." It was a simple declarative sentence that somehow had the force of a question, or perhaps even a reproof.

"Do I sound as if I'm avenging a social slight?" he asked, knowing even as he spoke the words that that was exactly how he sounded. And, yes, he would like to see the Wyman mansion turned into something like a hideaway for wealthy alcoholics. "Sorry."

She didn't answer, but only smiled at him again.

The house seemed to lead a charmed life. The landscaping people came every two weeks or so during the summer, so any damage would have been reported, but in six years the firm of Kinkaid & Kinkaid had never been called upon to pay for any repairs. Perhaps the place was too far out of the way to attract the notice of tramps or high-school kids looking for someplace to vandalize, or perhaps the prestige of the Wyman family had outlived its members long enough to keep people away. In either case, a quick tour of the perimeter revealed not so much as a broken pane of glass.

"It's even bigger than it looks from the front," Lisa said as they turned the last corner and found themselves stepping back onto the gravel driveway. "How many bedrooms, do you suppose?"

"No idea." Kinkaid shook his head, suggesting it was one of those unanswerable questions, like the weight of the planet Jupiter. "I've never been upstairs."

"Well, now's your chance."

The front of the house consisted of three huge rooms joined by arches wide enough to have comfortably straddled the driveway. The middle room was the foyer, a vast empty square with a double stairway at the back. The room on the left was the library and it was full of books which, had one opened them, would have revealed underlinings and marginal notes in several different hands, for the Wymans had always been men and women of high intelligence and vast cultural ambition. On the right was the sitting room, its chairs, tables and sofas exactly where Kinkaid remembered them but covered with sheets that had grown gray with six years of accumulated dust. Even the table lamps and chandeliers were thus shrouded, giving the place an odd, morguelike appearance.

The carpets and hardwood floors were also covered with a patina of dust that revealed no footprints. No one had been within these walls in a very long time.

Lisa peeked into the library as if she were afraid someone might catch her at it.

"Where's the dining room?"

"No idea," Kinkaid announced with a shrug. When she looked at him quizzically he smiled. "I've only been in this house half a dozen or so times," he said. "We weren't shown in through the servants' entrance, but we didn't move in the same circles as the Wymans. As far as I can recollect, not even my father was ever invited here to dinner."

"Were they such snobs?"

He didn't reply, since no answer could convey how inadequately a word like "snob" described the Wymans. Besides, he was forced to admit to himself, for some reason he felt uncomfortable criticizing the family in front of a stranger. Lisa Milano could make what she liked of his silence.

"I'm surprised all this furniture is still here," she said. She really was a remarkably nice girl to be so forgiving of his rudeness, and by way of apology he frowned.

"The heirs don't seem to want it."

To give himself something to do he picked up one corner of the dustcloth that covered a massive chair standing beside the fireplace. He recognized it at once—Judge Wyman had been sitting in it during their one and only interview, when Kinkaid was about seven years old. He let the cloth drop back into place as if it concealed some dreadful secret.

"I once suggested it could be put up for auction," he went on, "but I never got an answer. The books alone would bring in a fortune."

"Maybe they don't need it. You said they were rich."

"Did I say that?" He turned and saw that she was smiling at him. Maybe she was the cheerful type, or maybe the thought of somebody, anybody, having all that money made her happy. Or maybe she just liked him. In any case, the pressure of that smile made him avert his eyes. "Besides, there's rich and there's rich. And the estate was a lot smaller than expected—at least, than *I* expected. I can remember my father saying that Judge Wyman was one of the five or six wealthiest men in the state but, apart from this house and two hundred thousand set aside to maintain it until it's sold, there was only about five million."

"That sounds like plenty to me," she said almost gleefully, finally teasing a smile out of him.

"But not enough to make you indifferent to another couple

of million," he went on, forcing himself to resume a proper, lawyerlike sobriety. "Especially when you don't know how many other pockets it's got to fill."

"Maybe your father was wrong. Maybe the Wymans just kept up a good front."

"He wasn't wrong."

With a sense of having something to prove to himself, Kinkaid gave a yank to the dustcover on the Judge's chair and let it slip quietly to the floor. It was a wingback, dating from the end of the 19th Century and covered in black glove leather, slightly smaller than he remembered it but still giving the impression of great weight and dignity, like a throne carved out of marble. He had no trouble remembering the awe with which he had approached it all those years ago, and the man in the charcoal-gray suit, the oldest man Jimmy Kinkaid had ever seen, who beckoned to him with a slow waving motion of his fingers, as if testing to see that the joints still worked.

"Your father tells me you're a clever boy. Do you fancy yourself a lawyer like him?"

At this distance of time Kinkaid couldn't remember his answer, but he remembered the way Judge Wyman had nodded, with just the faintest shading of contempt, as if to say "Just so, perhaps the most that one could expect."

And then he had raised one bony shoulder in a dismissive shrug. "Well, I won't live to see it. You'll have to scratch around for other clients besides the Wymans, boy, because I'm the last."

His dry, lifeless laughter still seemed to tremble in the air.

And then it was dispelled in a sudden explosion—someone had sneezed. Kinkaid turned around to see Lisa Milano half doubled over, her face buried in a white handkerchief.

"It's the dust," she said, wiping her nose. And then she sneezed again, even more violently if that was possible. "These old houses . . . I should be in another line of work."

"Why don't you wait outside then? I'll just poke around a

little more here to make sure there aren't any gopher snakes under the beds—I'll only be a few minutes. Behind the house there's a garden as big as Central Park. Go sit under the shade trees."

She looked at him for a moment as if he had said something unaccountably odd, and then nodded.

"All right," she said. "You'll know where to find me."

"Yes. I'll know."

chapter 9

Until he heard the door close behind her, he hadn't realized how desperately he had wanted to be alone. The house filled him with a mingling of melancholy and dread, but these were feelings which, by himself, he was at least able to confront. With the girl there he had to hide them away, even from himself.

And yet he wasn't quite alone.

Kinkaid was not even a little superstitious—it was not the dead whose presence he felt but the living, the reverberation of their spent lives coming back to him like an echo. He felt himself like a ghost, a shade from the unreal future who wanders into a place where time has lost all meaning.

Except for one brief period when he was not quite twenty, Kinkaid had been an infrequent guest at Five Miles, and yet he had seen it so often in imagination, like a landscape reflected in a pool of water, that sometimes he felt it was the most solidly familiar place on earth. So much about his life had been decided here.

The stairway behind the reception hall was an elaborate affair. Like part of a double helix its two halves crossed in a kind of minstrel's gallery and then divided again to lead up to the left and right wings of the house. Kinkaid had never been upstairs, had never seen the rooms where the Wymans had lived their merely private lives. His footsteps were soundless on the dust-laden runner, and yet he felt certain his approach was heard and resented.

At first the second-floor landing seemed like a perfect square. One was able to look across an empty space, two stories high and capped with a skylight, to a balustrade of heavy,

dark wood and, beyond that, the entrances to the two principal bedrooms, facing the front of the house. These were assumed to have been occupied by the Judge and his wife. In
one or the other, doubtless, Old Mrs. Wyman had died.
Kinkaid felt no curiosity about them.

No other doors were immediately visible, but the side land-
ings stretched backwards into hallways where there were
other rooms and, in the rear, another two sets of stairs leading
up to the third floor.

There were three rooms along the right-hand corridor.
They had the anonymous look of guest accommodations and,
judging from the furniture and wallpaper, hadn't been used in
decades.

Along the left wing of the building were two more rooms.
The door to one of them was locked, requiring Kinkaid to use
one of his fistful of keys, and had a spare, masculine quality
suggesting that its last occupant had lived through his boyhood sometime before the First World War—sure enough, in
a desk drawer Kinkaid found a worn copy of *Liddell's Greek
Essentials*, dated "September 20, 1916" above the initials
"C.W." Judge Wyman's elder brother, named Christopher,
had drowned in a boating accident before he was twenty. His
bedroom, apparently, had been kept all these years as a kind
of shrine.

Kinkaid replaced the Greek grammar, closed the drawer
and left.

In the other room the curtains were ruffled and the single
bed had a canopy. There were four or five stuffed animals on
the dresser—not teddy bears, not the souvenirs of childhood.
A bright red gorilla with a potbelly and a black flannel face.
A blue dog with a lolling tongue and button eyes that
swiveled around in plastic saucers. These were the trophies of
adolescence, the sort of thing won in the arcades of amusement parks and county fairs. The sort of prize you gave to a
date after impressing her with your prowess at the ring toss.
For this was a teenage girl's room.

For a moment Kinkaid could feel the wild beating of his heart, and then he realized his mistake. There was a portable record player on a table, with a stack of 45s beside it. He took a few out to look at: The Everly Brothers, Buddy Holly, Elvis Presley singing "Heartbreak Hotel"—nothing pressed within the last thirty years. He opened the drawer of a night table and found an ashtray. This room must have belonged to the Wymans' daughter Blanche, their only child, who had gone to live abroad as soon as she flunked out of her last private school and, like her uncle, had died young. Angel had hated cigarettes.

"Angel," he whispered—he simply couldn't help himself. Even here in her house, even as he searched for some trace of her, he had tried to refuse her memory. But memories will take their revenge. It was the first time in years he had allowed her name to pass his lips and the emotion he felt at hearing it squeezed his throat shut, so that he felt physical pain.

"Angela, you've heard me speak of the Kinkaid boy," Mrs. Wyman had said, turning to a slender, perfect, flamelike girl with hair so blond it was almost white. The girl caught his eye and smiled without seeming to, as if she had already mastered the art of being unapproachable. "Angela is a relation of my late husband's. She will likely be staying with me for some time."

These last remarks were addressed not to Jim Kinkaid, who was home for the summer after his freshman year at Yale, but to his father, or perhaps to no one at all. Mrs. Wyman had a habit of not speaking to one directly, as if she found the familiarity distasteful. This was the only time Kinkaid remembered seeing her on the premises of Kinkaid & Kinkaid.

"Jimmy, perhaps you'd be good enough to offer Miss Wyman a glass of lemonade?"

Then, with a courtly sweep of his hand, Mr. Kinkaid Senior offered to show the Judge's widow to his private office, glancing back at his son to favor him with a significant but indecipherable look.

Young Jim, for his part, was almost speechless.

"Would you *like* some lemonade?" he asked, rather stupidly—it was literally the only sentence he could call up.

And then she really did smile at him, until he thought perhaps he couldn't stand it much longer.

"Anything," she answered. With the pink tips of her fingers she combed a strand of hair out of her face. She couldn't have been more than fifteen, but she was the most beautiful creature he had ever seen. "Is it always this hot here?"

For half an hour they sat together on a porch swing on the back veranda, drinking actual lemonade. They talked about school, which at least had the virtue of safety. She had never heard of Yale. She told him about the "Academy for Young Ladies" she had attended in Paris, although she did not seem particularly European. She spoke English with a certain crispness, as if she had just taken it out of the package and it was still in perfect shape.

"Will you go back at the end of the summer?"

"Oh no." She shook her head. Her gesture betrayed nothing, not the slightest hint of regret or pleasure. Paris, one gathered, was a place of completely neutral impressions. "There isn't any reason. I'm to interview next week at some school in Greenwich—where is that, by the way?"

"About fifteen minutes away. It's like New Gilead, only more so."

His little joke, if that was what it had been, went unnoticed.

That was all they were to have for the rest of that summer, a perfectly amiable conversation lasting thirty minutes. Then Mrs. Wyman's legal business was over and her car was summoned.

"Who is she?" Jim asked that night at dinner, after Julia had cleared off to the kitchen. His father, apparently busy with teasing the bones out of a salmon steak, regarded him out of the corner of his eye and smiled, as if enjoying some secret.

"I take it you mean the girl? A relative—Mrs. Wyman's description is quite adequate. You find her interesting?"

"She's . . ."

"Yes, she is that." Having completed the dissection, Mr. Kinkaid Senior stabbed a slice of lemon with his fork and began squeezing the juice out over the scattered remains of his fish. "But a little young for you, wouldn't you say?"

"I only asked who she was."

"Well, to the degree I'm able without breaching the lawyer-client relationship, I'll oblige you with an answer."

The answer was tantalizingly incomplete. Mrs. Wyman had recently returned from Europe with Miss Angela as part of her baggage. Mrs. Wyman hadn't even known of her existence before her trip—a call on some distant connection of the Judge's had found that person lately deceased and the daughter walled up in a Parisian convent school that seemed really to be a kind of orphanage for the inconvenient children of the rich. The inference was that the young lady had led an unsettled, nomadic life, but Mrs. Wyman intended to put a stop to that.

" 'One is obliged to do something for one's family' was the way she put it. It's a little out of character, but perhaps the old darling is lonely."

"Will Angela live at Five Miles?"

Mr. Kinkaid nodded sagely. "So I gather."

That summer Jim Kinkaid had a job at a textbook warehouse in Stamford. He spent the first three weeks packaging orders and then graduated to working the forklift. It wasn't very exciting work, but he earned a little more than six dollars an hour, enough to keep him in pocket money during the school year. He was on scholarship at Yale, so pocket money was all he needed.

On weekends and those evenings when he could summon the energy he would hang out with the young men who had been his friends in high school. They spent a lot of time at the public beaches in Westport, which were supposed to be *the* place for picking up girls although nobody ever seemed to have any luck. They also cruised around in cars, went to the movies and ate ice cream at the local Baskin Robbins. Kinkaid never saw Angela at any of these places, which didn't surprise him. The Wymans were not as a rule very gregarious. Probably none of them had ever been to a beach they didn't own.

By the time he went back to college he had almost forgotten about Angela Wyman—or, to put it more accurately, if he had had a little more personal vanity he would long since have concluded that she had forgotten about him. Why not? He doubted he had made a very dazzling impression. From time to time the memory of their half-hour on the porch swing would float pleasantly through his mind, but he didn't long for her. Neither did he long for Bo Derek, whom he regarded as not quite as beautiful and no less unattainable. He was not of a disposition to willfully break his heart.

Thus he was more than a little astonished, in the middle of the spring term, to find a letter in his campus mailbox. There was no return address on the envelope, the flap was decorated with some sort of school crest—he could just make out the name.

"They tell me you have a car. Why don't you pick me up after school on Friday?"

It was signed "Angel."

Angel. That was Tuesday morning. For three days he carried the little scrap of notepaper around in his pocket, taking it out from time to time just to reassure himself of its reality. He admired the handwriting, which was fluid, clear, and perfectly spaced. He even admired the color of the ink. He had an English class at two o'clock on Friday afternoon, but he wanted to be in Greenwich by three and, in any case, he wouldn't have had any attention for the niceties of Elizabethan verse. He decided to cut it.

Her sources of information were correct. Kinkaid had owned a car since the middle of his senior year in high school. It was a '76 Toyota which had cost him most of the twelve hundred dollars he had saved from the summer before. Two years later it had a fresh paint job—lemon-yellow—new seat covers and a rebuilt starter. Before much longer it would also need a fresh set of tires, but for the moment it was in good repair and running fine. That Friday afternoon, from about three-fifteen on, it was parked across the street from the front entrance to the Greenwich Academy. Somehow Kinkaid didn't quite have the nerve to just drive up onto the campus.

He waited for nearly two hours. Once a patrol car drove slowly by and the policeman inside gave him a hard look, as if considering whether to run him off, but Kinkaid nodded at him and smiled his inoffensive college-boy smile and that was that.

At ten minutes before five traffic into the entrance started to pick up. Women who drove elegant little British sports cars and looked like they were on their way to the polo matches started disappearing up the long driveway to wait in the parking lot for their daughters to be dismissed for the day. About fifteen minutes later most of them were gone again and girls in brown sweaters and dark tartan skirts started emerging onto the sidewalks. Angela was one of the last of these.

She looked odd in her uniform, with her books in a little canvas satchel she carried slung over her shoulder. There was nothing cynical or experienced about her, but the awkwardness of adolescence had vanished and her whole carriage suggested the self-mastery of adulthood. It was as if she wore her schoolgirl clothes as a kind of disguise—or a penance. The others, hanging together in little clusters, their laughter like the screams of birds, seemed like children. Perhaps they too sensed the difference because there were no companions about her as she walked.

Kinkaid got out and stood beside his car, where she would be sure to see him. Wishing passionately that this part of it could be quickly over, he even ventured a tentative little wave. He hadn't succeeded in attracting her attention—she had known all along that he was there. The only difference was that now she chose to acknowledge him. As she stepped off the curb toward him, her smile could have meant no more than "Oh, my ride is here."

"Have you been waiting long?" she asked as he held the car door open for her.

"No." He grinned at her, convinced she knew he was lying. "What time do you have to be home?"

"There's no hurry about that. Mrs. Wyman is in New York and won't be home until after dinner."

She said it quite casually, not even troubling to look at him, but for Kinkaid she seemed to be defining the precise character of their relationship. It was to be their secret. If Mrs. Wyman had been at home this meeting would not have been possible.

"Then maybe you'd like a soda?"

At first, from the sudden way she turned her eyes toward him, he felt such a fool he was ready to blush to the roots of his hair. Life wasn't an Andy Hardy movie, and who the hell did you take out for a soda anymore? The Yale girls would have laughed in his face. And Angela—Angel—for all that she was still in high school . . .

Or maybe not. Just then she gave him the sweetest smile, as if she were amused and pleased all at once.

"I would," she answered. "Yes, I would very much."

It was late at night when they finally made it back to New Gilead. They had their sodas on Greenwich Avenue, at possibly the last drugstore fountain in the civilized world, and then simply drove around. Around 6:15, when the light began to fail, they found a diner in Stamford and had coffee and dessert in a booth in the back.

They didn't talk much. It didn't seem necessary. It would have broken the spell of their perfect intimacy. Until the very end, he never even touched her. It was enough just to be there.

When the headlights of his car nosed up against the gates at the entrance to Five Miles, they were closed. They were like the doors of a prison, except that it was impossible to tell on which side lay captivity.

"I have a key," she said. She took it from her purse and showed it to him. "It's best if I go up to the house alone."

"Will you be all right?"

"Yes. Mrs. Wyman won't know or care."

When he turned to her he discovered that she had slid over toward him, so that their legs were almost touching.

"When can I see you again?"

She didn't answer. Instead, she threw herself into his arms and kissed him with an almost savage hunger. The second he began to respond he could feel her tongue sliding between his lips.

There was a girl in New Haven whom Kinkaid sometimes took to the movies and then, if he was lucky and his roommate had left for the weekend, back to his dormitory for an hour or two of breathless, exhausting sex. She went out with lots of other men and probably slept with them as well. She was of an athletic disposition and always eager for something new. She just liked it, she said. She certainly seemed to.

But nothing that had happened on Kinkaid's narrow dormitory bed could remotely compare with the passion of that kiss. Angel's breath came in ragged little pants and she seemed to want to crawl inside him, as if that one moment had to answer for a lifetime of longing.

When they came apart it was because they simply had to. Kinkaid's hands were resting lightly on the tops of her shoulders, and he longed to bring them down to cover her breasts. She wouldn't resist. She wanted him to—he knew that—and yet somehow he didn't dare.

"When can I see you again?" he repeated. "I have to see you again. . . ."

"Tomorrow night." She kissed him again, this time taking little nips from his mouth. "Mrs. Wyman goes to her room after dinner and doesn't come out. Come to the garden after dark."

Then, quite suddenly, she was gone. He heard the sound of the gate lock snapping open and saw her disappear behind that curtain of wrought iron. She vanished so completely that he almost couldn't bring himself to believe she had ever been with him at all.

He drove home. It was after eleven when he got in and the house was already asleep. At breakfast the next morning his father was more than usually roguish behind a copy of the *New York Times*, but he had long since stopped asking questions about his son's love life or his hours.

The hardest part was simply getting through the day. Kinkaid spent the morning and half the afternoon in his grandfather's old office attempting to put together a term paper on the political poetry of Andrew Marvell, but it wasn't a success. Usually he was able to lose himself in work, but today he just couldn't seem to find anything worth writing about. He would read the verses and they sounded in his ear like the tinkling of a wind chime. He didn't give a damn. All he could think about was Mrs. Wyman's garden in the shadows of night.

In the end he gave it up and drove out to Five Miles. He parked in a little patch of trees, pulling his car off the road where it would not be seen, and walked to the wall. The gates, of course, were closed, but after twenty minutes of searching he had found a spot he was reasonably sure he would be able to climb. Then he went back to his car.

While he waited he amused himself by wondering how he would explain himself if he got caught, especially since he couldn't possibly tell the truth. The idea that anyone might think he had come to steal something he found particularly tormenting, but it would be better to let them think that than to involve Angela.

There was a groundskeeper who lived in a cottage behind the garage, and the Wymans were not the type of people to be very tolerant of trespassers. He wondered if the grounds-keeper had a gun. He decided he was probably not destined for a life of crime—burglars had to be made of sterner stuff.

Finally, around six, it got dark. He tore the knee of his trousers getting over the wall, but he made it. He wondered how he would get back.

There was a gazebo in the center of the garden and he waited inside. The moon was very bright and at least there he didn't feel as if he were under a spotlight. It was almost eight o'clock before he saw a white shape moving up the path toward him.

"Have you been waiting long?"

The moonlight lent her beauty a touch of the unearthly, so that she seemed almost translucent. It was only with a deliberate effort that Kinkaid could answer her.

"Yes," he said, not as a complaint but as a kind of tribute. She smiled, as if she understood that. "How long can you stay?"

"As long as I like."

Perhaps he had voiced a doubt—at this distance of time he honestly couldn't remember—but she shook her head.

"Yes, all night if I feel like it. Mrs. Wyman won't be heard from again until morning, and the servants are forbidden the garden."

"What about the groundskeeper?"

"Dominic?" She laughed. It was the most delicious sound he had ever heard. "Dominic spends his evenings watching television and drinking bourbon. The drunker he gets the more he turns the volume up. We don't have to worry about him."

It didn't occur to him to wonder how she would know that, because by now she was standing directly in front of him, close enough that he could feel the hem of her skirt brushing against his trouser legs. She put her arms around his neck.

"Don't you want to kiss me?"

That was how it began, all those years ago. It didn't last very long, and then she disappeared like smoke.

He was in love. He was so desperately in love that he had to tell someone, so he told his father. He didn't expect anything to come of that—he had a right to be in love if he wanted to be.

But his father had looked very grave.

"When have you been meeting her?" he asked. "I take it that Mrs. Wyman knows nothing about this."

"I guess not."

"Well, she shall have to know before you see this girl again."

"Isn't that between her and Angel?"

The name caused something to change in Mr. Kinkaid's face—it was faint, but it was there. Suddenly he was almost angry.

"She's only sixteen, Jimmy. And she's a Wyman. She isn't pregnant, is she?"

"No, of course not!" He felt his face go hot. "We haven't . . . I mean, it hasn't come to that yet."

And now he felt like a fool. What had he expected? Why couldn't he have kept his mouth shut?"

Because he had always trusted his father, that was why. But now the man before him seemed almost a stranger.

"Well, in any case we can't have you sneaking around. I'll speak to Mrs. Wyman and we'll see what can be done."

"Why does anything have to be done, for Christ's sake?"

He never got an answer, and he never saw Angel again. His father went up to see Mrs. Wyman, and Mrs. Wyman packed her off.

And ten years later Kinkaid could find no trace of her. He looked through the whole house, from which after that night she had simply vanished, but he found nothing to suggest that she had ever lived there, that indeed she had ever lived anywhere except in his memory. Mrs. Wyman was dead, and her daughter was dead and buried somewhere in Europe. Old Judge Wyman's brother had been dead for seventy-five years. And Angel, it seemed, was a less real presence here than any of them.

He retraced his steps to the entrance and let himself out, locking the door behind him. Outside the raw summer sunlight hit him like a blow, making him wince, and all at once he felt a clutching pain in his chest. At any other time he might have wondered if he was having a heart attack, but he knew it wasn't that. It was those ten years having their revenge. He should never have come back here.

Finally, when the impression had passed off a little and he no longer felt in any danger of losing control, he followed the flagstone walkway around to the back of the house. There was the garden, which he suddenly realized he had never seen in daylight, and in its center the little gazebo.

As he approached it he saw someone, a girl, waiting inside. She turned her head—had she had been waiting all this time . . .

She was Lisa Milano, from the real estate office. She was dark and pixyish, not anything like Angel. The confusion had lasted no more than an instant. It was a trick of the light, and of his own longings, nothing more.

Then she smiled at him and Kinkaid felt as if he had never really noticed her before.

"I wonder," he said, a little surprised at the sound of his own voice, "if you might care to have some dinner with me tonight."

chapter 10

Dinner was a big success. They drove to Pound Ridge, which was in the middle of nowhere, and ate at an obscenely expensive French restaurant where the floors were uneven and the lighting dim but the desserts were beyond praise.

Lisa Milano wore a sleeveless, green silk dress. It was a good color for her, particularly by candlelight, and she had very pretty, well-formed arms. She listened with amusement to all his stories and then, when the meal was over, invited him back to her apartment, where she proceeded to seduce him. It had been a long time for Kinkaid, and the morning's visit to Five Miles had put him in a susceptible frame of mind, so he didn't put up too much of a struggle.

The apartment was in a huge, uncouth modern building directly across the street from the Stamford Hospital. She stood very close to him in the elevator. She never spoke a word. She just let her nearness work on his frazzled nervous system. Once she glanced up at him and smiled, but that was just before the bell sounded for her floor so he had no opportunity to put any interpretation on it.

She disappeared into the kitchen. The living room, where he had been left marooned, was small and haphazardly furnished, as if the life lived here was something that had had to be assembled on the run, but the overall impression was individual and pleasing. Miss Milano liked dark, lavish colors. The purple of the sofa was almost orgiastic.

After a few minutes she brought back a tray with two cups and a china tea service, complete with silver tongs for the tiny cubes of sugar. When she set the tray on the table, the same table he had been trying to keep from banging his shins against, and sat down beside him, she was close enough that if he moved at all he could hardly avoid touching her.

"I can't drink coffee this late," she said, in the manner of someone admitting to a serious weakness of character. "I hope you don't mind tea."

"Tea's fine. I've never been a coffee drinker."

"That's lucky then."

She turned to him and smiled, and as she turned her bare shoulder brushed against his coat sleeve, which made him feel as if he had been jolted awake. Were they really having this conversation? She wore her short black hair swept back, revealing that she had cute ears. Kinkaid wondered if the fact that he liked her ears so much meant there was anything odd about him.

She poured a few drops of milk into his tea, no sugar, and handed him the cup. She didn't ask. She just did it. Had she remembered from the restaurant, or was he just manifestly the type? And was that good or bad?

She took two lumps of sugar and no milk. It was suddenly obvious that that was precisely how every woman should have her tea. She stirred slowly. Just watching her move was an almost sensual pleasure.

Their conversation was the usual nonsense. Little Known Tea Facts. Adventures in Dining Out, Volume II. Pros and Cons of Life in Philadelphia. They weren't really talking about any of these things. The verbal dance wasn't patterned around its words.

Finally she put her teacup down and turned toward him. One of her small breasts brushed against his arm. She didn't say anything. She didn't even smile. But her face was so close to his, and the invitation so clear, that it would have been ungentlemanly not to respond.

So he responded. He let his hand caress the back of her head and then drew her in for a kiss. Which is when the fireworks started.

Kinkaid was never sure quite how it happened, but suddenly they were all over each other. It was pretty disorderly. There seemed to be no time to take their clothes off. They were flat out on the sofa and he was fumbling with the back of Lisa's dress while she was busy unhooking his belt and running down his zipper. When they came together it was rather like having a heart attack—very sudden and furious and completely out of control. Except that it was marvelous. Nothing, absolutely nothing, could have prepared him for this.

When it was over, and he was lying on top of her with her legs locked around his waist, he felt like he should be exhausted except that he wasn't. He felt great.

She was looking up at him with an astonished expression, exactly as if she were about to burst out laughing from pure exultation. Her cheeks were burning and, Lord love her, she was flushed pink right down to her nipples.

"There's a bed in my bedroom," she said.

"Is that why you call it your bedroom?"

"Yes. You want to go there?"

"Yes."

He kissed her and felt her tongue slide between his lips. It was a few minutes before he could summon the discipline to climb off her, and then he had to wriggle out of his trousers, which were bunched up somewhere around his knees. Finally he was able to reach down and cradle her in his arms. He carried her down the hall to the bedroom. She kept kissing him as if she were starving.

The second time, in bed, in the dark, with all their clothes off, was even better. Now they had the leisure to enjoy it.

It was odd, but he never seemed to get tired.

About three-thirty in the morning he started to hunt around for his shoes.

"I was hoping you'd . . ."

He was sitting on the edge of the bed, and when he turned around to look at her he saw how she reflexively pulled the sheet up to cover herself. He had to be careful or he would spoil everything.

"I really don't want to go."

"Then don't."

She reached out and switched on the little reading lamp on her night table. The harsh white light made everything very stark.

"This is going to sound stupid," he said. "I have a house-keeper who thinks I'm still nine years old."

"You're right. That does sound stupid." Yet there was that in her voice which suggested she might be prepared not to hold it against him. "Will she be waiting up for you?"

"It isn't that bad."

He forgot about his shoes and crawled back into the bed. Her arms went around his neck. Their lips just touched. This time it wasn't sex, it was something else.

"If I'm not there for breakfast, she'll worry," he went on. "She won't say anything, but she'll worry. She's been in a bad way since my father's death."

"Was she in love with him?"

"I don't think so—at least, not that way. She's in love with the family."

"And now you're all that's left."

"I'm it."

"Okay." She let go of him suddenly enough that it felt almost as if she were pushing him away. "I understand. You have to go home."

She was angry. Maybe she didn't want to be, but she was.

"Can I see you again?" he asked.

"Why?"

"What do you mean, 'why?' Isn't it obvious?"

"I don't do this all the time, you know."

She rolled over, turning her back on him. Okay, he couldn't blame her. She had given him everything she had, and now he was making her feel cheap.

He put his arms around her and kissed her on the shoulder. She didn't respond, but she also didn't resist.

"I don't do this all the time either. So what do you suppose that means?"

He kissed her again, this time on the neck, and this time she felt a little more pliant.

"So can I see you again?" he asked a second time. "You set the rules. I just want to be with you. How about dinner tomorrow night? How about lunch first and then dinner? We can have dinner and go to a movie, and I'll bring you straight home and kiss you chastely at your front door. I'll never touch you below the collarbone."

She turned back toward him and she was smiling. Everything was all right again.

"Now what would be the fun of that?" she asked.

That morning he skipped his run and slept until seven-thirty. When he caught himself whistling in the shower he burst out laughing from pure exultation of spirit. It seemed he had a girlfriend. What a surprise.

He kept smiling all during breakfast. Julia looked at him as if she thought he had gone mad.

Out of self-defense he hid himself in his office. After a while work sobered him up.

At ten minutes after ten he received a phone call from Eric Tollison.

"I wonder if you could manage a little something for us," he said. "It's a routine matter, but the billing will be substantial. Can you be in Denver Monday afternoon?"

Kinkaid glanced at his desk calendar to remind himself of what he already knew—that today was Thursday, which meant he would have a maximum of three days to prep.

"How routine and how substantial?"

"Dissolution of a partnership. A touch acrimonious, which is why I thought of you. It's worth a good two hundred and fifty an hour, but we need to clean this up quickly."

"So what do you want me to do, break somebody's legs?"

"It'll be enough if you just scare the shit out of him. I'll fax you a copy of the paperwork."

Kinkaid hung up the phone, wondering if he shouldn't feel insulted. Tollison made him sound like a kind of judicial thug. Was that how they thought of him, this gun for hire? He found the idea rather distasteful.

Of course his apparent standing with Karskadon and Henderson didn't depress him nearly as much as the fact that now he would have to spend Sunday afternoon on a plane rather than tucked in with Lisa Milano.

Twenty minutes later pages of a brief entitled *Fox v. Palmer* began pouring out of his laser printer. They seemed endless.

He met Lisa for lunch at a Chinese place in Stamford called The Golden Cod. It didn't sound very hopeful.

"You look beautiful," he said when he met her outside the restaurant. And she really did. She seemed to glow. He felt like a man saying goodbye to all earthly happiness.

They went inside and were seated against the wall, with just a decorative screen separating them from the kitchen. It was Kinkaid's fate in life never to be given a good table. Maître d's seemed to hate him on sight. The dining room was nearly empty.

"What's the matter?" she asked. "You're glaring at the menu. If you don't like Chinese, all you had to do was say so."

"I like Chinese."

"Then what is it."

"I have to go to Denver on Monday."

"So? What have you got against Denver?"

"There's a telephone book of stuff I have to get through before I leave—it all just dropped out of the sky this morning."

"So you'll be pretty busy."

"Looks like it." He risked a glance at her, wondering if he wasn't making a big mistake. "I'll be back Wednesday or Thursday."

"I'm not your keeper," she answered, without actually looking at him.

"No, but the timing is terrible. We seem to have a promising little romance here. I just hope it'll keep for a week."

"I suppose so." There was just a touch of mischief in her voice. "In the meantime, let me know if you need a study break."

The mail was waiting when he got back to the office. It was in a pile on his desk. After the death of the elder Kinkaid, Molly had stopped sorting it. Among the letters was a plain white envelope with "Four Star Clipping Service" rubber-stamped in the upper left-hand corner.

Kinkaid stared at it for about a second and a half before he remembered. It had been days since he had even thought about this little mystery. He didn't want to think about it now.

He opened the envelope and found a clipping from the *Atlanta Register* dated five days earlier and headlined "Local Man Missing After Family Murdered."

It was about George Tipton. Not *the* George Tipton, of course—he was safely dead and buried in New Jersey. This one was only missing, along with his car. His wife and six-month-old daughter had been found dead in their home by Mrs. Tipton's mother. Most of the story, in fact, consisted of an interview with the mother, which meant that the police weren't giving out very much information. George was wanted for questioning.

As he read through the story, which went on for two columns, Kinkaid experienced a mingling of grief and horror that was almost indistinguishable from nausea. He felt as if somehow he had as good as murdered these people— that George Tipton would never be found, that he was dead somewhere, it never occurred to him to doubt—yet he was unable to identify anything he could have done to prevent their deaths. He had informed the police. They had not been interested.

"All you've got is a list of names," they had said. "That doesn't help us. We would need some common denominator. A pattern somewhere. Call us again if you find one."

They probably thought he was a nut.

And maybe they were right. After all, maybe the clipping referred to the wrong George Tipton—how many George Tiptons were there in the wide world? Probably hundreds. Maybe the whole thing was just random, some kind of statistical quirk. . . .

No, that didn't make any sense. Besides, having a George Tipton in the files was just too big a coincidence to swallow whole.

And then there was the evidence of James Kinkaid III, senior partner in the firm, who had died of cardiac arrest after reading about Stephen Billinger's murder. *He* had seen a pattern in all this.

So it all came back to the same three things: a list of names, a small-town law practice, and a string of murders. The first two were keys to the third.

And, unlike Karskadon and Henderson, a small-town law practice doesn't specialize. It covers everything—probates, divorces, trust agreements, real-estate sales, commercial law, civil damages, even the odd penny-ante criminal case.

Which meant that the next step was obvious.

New Gilead had a police force of about twenty, most of whom were assigned to traffic or administration. They were presided over by the town marshal, Bill Cheffins, who had held the job for as long as anyone could remember. It was his day off, so Kinkaid phoned him at home.

"Am I interrupting anything?"

"I'm painting the kitchen," Cheffins answered. "Basic training for retirement. So don't worry, Jim Boy, I don't mind a little distraction."

"Under those circumstances, could you do me a favor?"

"Does it need doing today?"

"No."

"Damn. What is it, then?"

"Could you look up the juvenile records of one George Tipton?"

"*Our* George Tipton?" There was a pause at the other end of the line, as if Marshall Cheffins had the rap sheets right there on the kitchen counter with him. "He beat up my youngest boy Jerry in the fifth grade. *That* George Tipton?"

"Sounds like him."

"Juvenile records are sealed—you know that, Counsellor."

"Not to worry, Bill. The guy junked himself in a car crash a couple of years ago and is now occupying real estate in a New Jersey cemetery."

"Glad to hear it. Sure, then. Come by the station anytime tomorrow and we'll tour the cellars together."

Kinkaid replaced the telephone receiver, feeling dissatisfied that tomorrow was not today. His glance fell on the stack of brief pages that had come over the wire that morning.

"Screw it," he said, out loud to the empty office.

He wasn't done yet. There was still one more place he could look.

New Gilead High was a boxlike modern structure dating from the late 1960s, when the suburban population growth had at last reached this far north into Fairfield County. Kinkaid could remember spending summer evenings playing cowboys and Indians on the construction site, where a network of ditches and the cement foundation blocks had offered excellent concealment from The Enemy.

The school was still relatively new when he entered as a freshman. Everything about the place seemed newly minted, from the amberlike polish of the gymnasium floor to the student body, so many of whom had arrived with the real estate developments on the outskirts of town that at dinner there were witty references to "Carpetbagger High" and even some talk of sending an application to Choate.

The transfer never came about, but young Kinkaid did not imagine he would have gained much from it. His father sometimes said he lacked self-confidence, which was only a rough shorthand for the truth, which was that he was too shy and unathletic for great social success. Choate would not cure anything. He would just have to muddle along as best he could.

And in the end he did achieve a measure of success. He became an academic star, the school's very first graduate to win a scholarship to Yale. It didn't stack up to much with the girls—he would have to wait until college to lose his virginity—but his father was satisfied. And so were his teachers. Even at this distance of time the staff remembered him with a certain sense of shared triumph. He was counting on that.

"Jimmy! Jimmy Kinkaid—how are you?"

A woman in her late fifties, her hair a mess of gray-brown curls, looked over her glasses from behind a typewriter and then bolted up and toward him as if she had been startled awake. Kinkaid smiled and took both her hands in his—they ran into each other probably once a month in the Grand Union, but apparently his return to actual school precincts somehow transformed this into a reunion.

"Fine, Mrs. Sherl. How are you? How is summer session?"

Summer session was all remedials and typing classes. Mrs. Sherl had no use for summer session, a subject on which she became almost philosophical as Kinkaid smiled and nodded.

But at last she got around to asking what brought him by.

"I wonder if I could have a peek at the old files," he said, precisely as if he were asking if he could use the men's room. "It's an estate matter. You remember George Tipton?"

"I ought to, he was in here often enough. Don't tell me somebody's left him a fortune."

"No—it's his estate that's an issue."

"Oh . . ." Mrs. Sherl frowned, sticking one hand in the pocket of a emerald-green polyester vest that reached almost to her knees. "So he's dead, huh?"

Kinkaid nodded. "Traffic accident, a couple of years ago."

"Well, I'm not surprised. He was always a wild kid."

The two of them stood there, divided by the low construction-board counter that was the office staff's version of Hadrian's Wall, according to George Tipton his moment of silence. And then Mrs. Sherl looked up into Kinkaid's face and smiled.

"So what do you need to see, Jimmy?"

Jimmy Kinkaid, hometown boy, made a vague gesture with his left hand that trailed off into a shrug.

"Anything you've got," he said, the perfect picture of workhorse boredom. "It's just a question of picking up all the pins."

This explanation, deliberately unspecific as it was, seemed to be enough, because five minutes later Kinkaid found himself in possession of a thick manila envelope.

"Can I keep it for a day or two?"

What he was asking was doubtless in violation of school rules, and probably of state law as well, but Mrs. Sherl's brief consideration of the matter suggested that it did not deeply touch her conscience.

"Sure," she said, after about two and a half seconds of staring at the slight fur of dust along the envelope's top edge. "I don't suppose there's going to be much demand for it."

The class bell had already rung as he left the office, so the hallways were nearly empty. Like a knot of conspirators, a few teenage girls clustered around the main entrance, clutching clipboards and books to their bosoms. One of them, a skinny little dishwater blonde who was lucky to be fifteen, favored Kinkaid with a long sidewise look and, at last, her own version of The Enigmatic Smile. Apparently it never hurt to get in some practice.

"They're only babies," he thought to himself. He was

amused—that, and nothing more. The girl seemed to sense as much and glanced away.

Kinkaid hoped he had not inflicted a failure on her, the poor little kid.

And it occurred to him, with something like relief, that they had been no less little kids all those years ago. The unrequited passions of his own teenage years had been just the same, serving their apprenticeship in these same corridors. Perhaps for everyone adolescence was one long ordeal by humiliation.

He looked about him, at the display cases and the bulletin boards and the painted cinderblock walls, at once so familiar and so strange, and became conscious of a curious affection for this place, which he had hated so when he had belonged to it. Maybe that was why—he was only a visitor now, a tourist in a museum.

Had anything changed, or was it just the same? He read a notice, four months out of date, announcing tryouts for the senior class play. *Guys and Dolls.* Very appropriate.

Artifacts from an even more remote past were kept behind glass. A series of oak and brass plaques recorded class honors for each semester since 1976. The name "James Kinkaid IV" appeared five times, twice in the senior year.

But the really spectacular laurels—silver cups the size of coffee urns and trophies that might have been mistaken for coat racks—were reserved for athletics. Varsity Basketball Champions, 1990. All Conferences Swimming Champions, 1988. And the immortal football team of that glorious year 1986 . . .

Kinkaid's mouth went completely dry, and for several seconds he seemed to have forgotten how to breathe. They were all there.

A framed photograph stood beside the golden trophy, and their names were on a neat typewritten list, along with their positions and their years. Terry Vogel, Stephen Billinger, Andrew Castlesmith, George Tipton.

They were all there, every last one of them.

"Jesus, Jimmy, you don't want a girl like that," his father had told him, on the night the world ended. "From what I hear, she's been fucked by every guy on the football team."

chapter 11

Frank Rizza hated the drive up to Muir Beach. The road wound around like linguini and all those trees gave him the creeps. He liked the city, where he knew his way around, and he particularly liked the area south of Market Street because he owned it. That was nice. That was really having a life—not like this shit. You got out of your own territory and you never knew what might happen. Up here in fucking Marin County even the cops were strangers. One time some dickhead on a motorcycle had even written him a ticket.

Why couldn't the bitch live in San Francisco, where all that money could at least buy her a good time, instead of out here in the piney woods with not another living thing around except the fucking sea otters? A gorgeous piece like that, it was a waste.

Not that she seemed to care—or maybe she did, and that was the idea. She was weird. Frank didn't have the faintest idea what went on in her mind, which was the main reason she scared him so much.

That, and the fact she could put him in the gas chamber anytime she felt the need.

He would start thinking about it the minute he saw the Golden Gate Bridge. He would turn the corner and get a look at those spires and think to himself, this is the road to San Quentin. This is the way they take you when the end of the line is Death Row. And then, after about five miles, you would take the turnoff and the fucking trees just swallowed you up. It was spooky as shit.

The time he made his bones, when he was still a kid not

more than eighteen or nineteen years old, Frank stole a car, a blue '66 Dodge, and then went out looking for a small-time dealer named Patsy Trevi—the guy was a coon, so what the hell was he doing with a name like that?—who was snorting most of his product and selling baking powder on his patch. That kind of thing is very bad for trade. He was also into Frank's boss for four big ones, which there wasn't a chance in hell he was going to pay back, so Sal Gracchus, who ran South of Market in those days, decided it would set a better example if they took care of Patsy before some dissatisfied customer blew him away and they had to deal with that.

It was Frank's first chance to put himself a little forward, so he wanted to do the thing right. Patsy, who thought he was getting a quarter of a kilo of nose candy on consignment, met him in a bar on Clementina Street, so stoned he probably would have believed the stuff came straight from Santa Claus's big bag. They went out to Frank's car, which was parked in the back, and Frank conked him with a tire iron, stuffed him in the trunk and then, just to be on the safe side, cut his throat. He had thought the job through and there was even a plastic tarp spread out in the trunk so Patsy wouldn't mess up the carpeting.

Then Frank got into the car and drove up to the Muir woods to get rid of the body. Patsy Trevi was just going to disappear.

Except that when he found a good spot for the grave, off a dirt road that seemed to go nowhere, he opened the trunk and found that apparently he hadn't cut deep enough. He opened the trunk and held up a lantern and there was Patsy, staring at him with these big saucer eyes. It was a shock. Then the stupid fuck started screaming—a real high-pitched scream, like a woman—and climbing out of the trunk like he planned to run all the way back to Clementina Street. Frank was a little excited himself and went to work with the tire iron until you couldn't tell which side of Patsy Trevi's head had been the face. So much for keeping the upholstery clean.

The ground was soft under those big redwood trees and he was able to dig a nice deep hole. All the time he was digging it some god damn bird was up there in the branches, screeching its fucking head off—it sounded for all the world like Patsy's screams. By the time he got back to San Francisco, Frank Rizza was a nervous wreck. How he managed to drive home without piling up the car was a miracle, and when he got there he climbed into bed and didn't come out for three days.

No—no way he was ever going to get to like these woods.

And the broad had to live right here, in the middle of the fucking haunted forest, and she had to have his balls in a noose. Life was a motherfucker.

Well, maybe not in the middle. More like at the edge.

Eventually the road hit the coast again and followed it for three or four miles. Then there was a private driveway that slid off to the left and seemed to go on forever. It ended in front of the beach house, which was very modern, with lots of unpainted wood and huge windows everywhere. The house was maybe thirty feet above the ocean. From where you parked you couldn't hear the traffic up on the road anymore. All you could hear was the surf pounding on the rocks down below. The isolation was almost total.

Frank had never been inside the house. He had no idea what kind of life was lived there and he had more or less accepted the idea that he was never going to find out.

Not that he hadn't tried. One time, about two years back, he had even sent a man to nose around, to find out the usual details, like if there was a housekeeper or maybe even a boyfriend around, or when and by whom the groceries got delivered. That kind of stuff. Charlie Accardo was a good man, trusted and careful, the sort that could follow you around for a month and you'd never know he was there.

"Just go have a look through the trees," Frank had told him. "Take a few days, don't spook nobody, and let me know what you find out."

A routine piece of work for a guy like Charlie. But Charlie never came back. It was like he fell off the face of the Earth.

Frank never mentioned it to Miss Preston—that was her name, Miss Alicia Preston, and that was almost everything Frank Rizza knew about her, except that she seemed to be rich—and he never sent anyone else to check up on her. He never dared, because if Charlie had been alive he would have come back. Some people really cared about their privacy.

There were no other cars on the gravel turning circle in front of the house. There never were. Frank parked about twenty feet beyond the front door, beside the beginning of a little path that sloped downward toward the ocean, eventually becoming steep enough to turn into a wooden stairway that led to a deck shaded by a couple of huge trees. On the other side the path picked up again and went down to the water, but Frank stopped at the deck. There was a glass-topped table and a couple of lawn chairs. Miss Preston was sitting on one of them.

She didn't look at him as he approached. Her attention seemed focused on some object on the beach, although there was nothing to be seen down there. A tall glass full of ice and what was probably club soda rested on the table beside her.

She wore a white one-piece bathing suit, very sleek and cut high on the hip but leaving her ass pretty much to your imagination. It was sexy as hell without showing much. It just made clear the lithe animal perfection of the body that it concealed. Her hair was pale blond and tied back in a pony tail. Her skin looked as if it would be cool to the touch.

He sat down on the other lawn chair and waited. It was a pleasure just to be allowed to look at her. She was the most unapproachably beautiful woman he had ever seen.

After what was probably only a minute or so but seemed much longer, she turned her head a few inches and her gaze fell on him. Frank Rizza felt his breath catch, whether from fear or desire or something closer to astonishment he couldn't have said. She smiled at him. The smile meant nothing, as he had come to understand, but it still had its effect.

"I see you're still out of jail," she said, in a perfectly neutral voice. "Haven't they handed down an indictment yet?"

"It'll never come to that." Frank shrugged and allowed himself a slight smile, as if to reassure a friend that he was fine in spite of everything. The IRS had been all over him for more than a year. "It's just the usual harassment. They haven't got a case and they never will."

"I'm sure of it."

Before directing her attention back to the shoreline, she let her eyes rest on his face for just a second or two. Her expression never changed, but somehow she managed to make her point.

"Yes, of course," those few seconds whispered into Frank Rizza's soul. *"You are quite safe from everyone except me."*

Then she seemed to forget his existence. She turned her head away and left him alone with the consciousness that everything he had in this world, including his very life, was hers to take away.

"Where did you get the tape?" he asked suddenly, hardly able to recognize the sound of his own voice—he had never, never meant to speak those words. Now, somehow, he couldn't help himself.

"Who gave it to you?"

"What makes you think anyone *gave* it to me?"

She didn't even look at him. He was a dangerous man, a killer with a bad temper, a man known for getting even, but there was no crisis as far as she was concerned. She sounded merely bored.

In that moment he hated her, more than he had ever hated anyone. Had there been a gun in his pocket he would have taken it out and shot her. He wouldn't have been able to help himself.

That was why his gun was in his desk drawer at home—he could not trust himself in the presence of this woman.

"Everything is arranged," she had told him once. "If anything ever happens to me the police will receive everything they need. The tape, the girl's dental records, the location of the grave, everything. You know you can't even get into a cab without their knowing about it—how far do you think you'd be able to run? You'll be in prison before dinner, and the only way you'll ever get out is in the back of a hearse. So don't be rash, Frank. California has the death penalty."

God how he hated her. It would almost be worth it to kill her. Almost, but not quite.

It had been the one completely stupid act of his life. He couldn't explain it, except that Velma, the little bitch, had started teasing him about his wife. The next thing he knew she was lying across her king-size bed with the handle of a pair of scissors sticking out of her throat.

They hadn't known each other long. He had found her working in a topless bar a couple of blocks south of Union Square and had set her up in an apartment. She had a great pair of jugs, but she had a bad mouth. Sooner or later, somebody was going to kill her.

So there she was, the late Velma Gray, stretched across the mattress with her eyes wide open and her best nightie ruined. She still looked pretty sexy except that she was dead. At least she had shut up.

Frank tore down the bathroom shower curtain and wrapped her in that to keep her from leaking blood all over everything. Then he phoned Charlie Accardo.

The hard part was getting her out of the building. They had to wait until the middle of the night and then take her down to the garage in a blanket. Charlie got rid of the body and the next day they went through the apartment and collected all of Velma's stuff to make it look like she had moved out.

Looking back on it, Frank was always a little surprised they hadn't found any trace of the camera.

But one was there. Two weeks later he got a call from his lawyer.

"Come down here. I've got something to show you."

"What—now? Sid, the timing is terrible. . . ."

"Now, if you want to stay out of court."

The minute he walked into his office Sid Lubash put a tape cassette in the VCR and Frank got to watch himself arguing with Velma Gray. When she started to scream Sid turned the sound down.

"Where did you get this?"

"It came Federal Express this morning. The return address listed is the county lockup."

"Very funny."

By the time the tape was finished Sid was mopping his bald head with a handkerchief. You'd think it was him up there wiping the blood from his fingers.

"It was in the closet," Frank announced. The whole thing had revealed itself to him in that instant. "She had a closet in her bedroom, with a full-length mirror on the door. That's where the camera was hidden—you can tell from the angle. The bitch set me up."

"Too bad you didn't give her time enough to say something."

Frank glared at his lawyer, until he realized the dumb fuck wasn't kidding. Sid was really in a bad way. He just didn't have the nerves for this kind of thing.

The film was a good half-hour long and included everything—the shower curtain, the call to Charlie, everything. Finally the sound broke off and the television screen went grainy.

"Was there anything else?"

Sid pulled the cassette out of the VCR and handed it to

him. Written across the label, in a tight woman's hand, was "I'll be in touch."

"I don't have to tell you what happens if the cops get this."

"They won't get it," Frank said. "Somebody wants to deal."

An hour later Frank was in his car, in a parking lot along Fisherman's Wharf, talking to Charlie Accardo.

"What did you do with Velma?"

Charlie was the placid type, for whom life held few surprises. So he didn't ask any of the obvious questions. He just sat there with his huge hands folded over his belly seeming to consider the question, as if making a choice among possible answers.

"She's fertilizing a field of brussels sprouts down the coast."

"Well, maybe you better go down there and dig her up. Maybe you could take her fishing and use her for bait."

Then Frank told him about the film.

"What are you gonna do about it?"

"First we find out who, then we decide. In the meantime, you take care of Velma."

But it was too late. That evening Charlie called from a gas station in Half Moon Bay. "She ain't there."

"Okay." Frank glanced over at the living-room sofa, where his wife was watching a rerun of *L.A. Law*. But it wasn't because of her that he decided he wouldn't pursue this interesting subject. He was having a lot of trouble with the Feds just then and there was at least a fair chance that his phone was tapped. "We'll talk tomorrow."

He hung up the phone and sat down on the sofa. When the station break was over, Stella Brittletits was involved in a class-action suit against a crooked cupcake manufacturer.

"You shoulda been a lawyer, Frank," his wife said. "They lead such interesting lives."

The next morning Charlie was waiting for him in the office of the building supply company he used as a front.

"She's gone—that's all there is to it," he said, shrugging his shoulders as if this sort of thing was bound to happen.

"Maybe you dug up the wrong hole."

"Not likely. Besides I found the shower curtain."

"Then somebody must've spotted you."

"Come on."

"Well, Velma didn't just climb out and walk away."

Charlie Accardo looked on the verge of taking serious offense, and he had a point. Charlie just wasn't the careless type.

"Nobody saw me, Frank. Nobody came anywhere near. I even replanted the brussel sprouts. You could look right at the spot in broad daylight and never think there was a body down there."

Except maybe if somebody knew that Velma was dead, knew that Frank Rizza would have to get the body out of her apartment and planted in a field somewhere, and then just tagged along at a discreet distance while Charlie drove out to Half Moon Bay.

And that, apparently, was what somebody did—the somebody who was sitting across the patio table from Frank, smiling at him tauntingly.

"What makes you think anyone *gave* it to me?"

That smile. If a leopard could smile, it would smile just like that. It seemed to measure the possibilities. What were the chances that Frank Rizza might be amusing in the sack? Maybe someday, the smile suggested, maybe just before I put him on Death Row, I'll find out.

The first time he had met Miss Alicia Preston, when she had given him the word that from now on his life was something she carried around with her like the loose change in her purse, she had smiled at him like that. And after she dismissed him he had driven down to a whorehouse on Filmore Street, found himself a blonde with big hooters, and fucked himself silly. Until there wasn't anything left inside him but fear.

Somehow just the fear alone was easier to take than the fear mixed with a cringing, humiliating lust.

The glass of club soda on the table beside her was sweating heavily. There were no lipstick smears on the rim. It looked as if it hadn't been touched. Frank wondered if she even knew it was there. He would have liked to see her take a sip, just to prove she was human.

"You mean you were the one who set me up?"

"With a little help from Miss Gray," she answered, after an almost indetectable pause. "I had a use for a reliable thug. We were only looking for some hold—just something to make you afraid of going to prison for a few years. It worked out better than I could have hoped, although not of course for Miss Gray."

"What did she want out of it?"

"Money. And probably revenge."

The smile never changed. Still, he could see that she was someone who knew all about revenge.

A reliable thug. The half dozen or so times she had asked him to do something for her she had always insisted on paying him. Fifteen thousand bucks once just to hire an out-of-state detective and find out if some guy up in Spokane had any bad habits. She could have had his chain pulled for five— Frank did lots of little favors like that for people who needed a reliable thug.

So why go to all this trouble? Maybe she felt she couldn't trust any man she didn't own.

"Money and revenge, was it?" He had to agree, that sounded just like Velma. "Well, she didn't get either, did she."

But Miss Preston had turned away again, had become absorbed once more in that mysterious object out on the shore which only she could see. Had switched him off as if he were a light.

After a moment she reached into a wicker bag that was resting on the ground beside her chair and took out a white, legal-sized envelope with a rubber band around it to keep it closed. It was almost an inch and a half thick. She tossed it across the table to Frank, who stuffed it into the inside pocket of his coat.

"Who do you want me to kill?" he asked, without actually joking.

chapter 12

Angel knew it was folly. She should wait until Rizza was finished with his little job—she knew better than anyone the dangers of yielding to impulse, but as she approached the end of her long exile, the pull of old associations became stronger and stronger.

She had planned a trip, scouting a location for the meeting with her next old acquaintance. She had her bag packed, and the ticket in her purse listed Florida as the destination. Even in her car, crossing over the Golden Gate Bridge, she really believed that was where she was going.

At the San Francisco airport she cancelled her reservation with Delta and bought a first-class ticket on Pan Am Flight 423 to New York, leaving in twenty minutes—that was the wonderful thing about first class; there were nearly always seats.

She wasn't sure when she realized that was what she would do. It was as if the decision had made itself.

The plane landed at Kennedy just before two in the afternoon and she rented a car. At that hour traffic was light, so the drive to Connecticut took only slightly more than an hour.

She drove straight to Five Miles.

The gate was padlocked. Somehow she hadn't expected that. It came as a mild shock to be thus reminded that the house was empty.

The lock wasn't the sort you could pick, so she parked the car in a grove of trees a few hundred yards away and walked around the wall until she found the spot where it could be climbed. George Tilson had come over the wall just here—and Steve Billinger and Charlie Flaxman. All of them. Even Jim.

Her shoes were flimsy little things with one-inch heels, so she took them off and threw them over the wall. She would ruin her nylons on the stones, but at least she was wearing trousers.

In patches the lawn was infested with rye grass, which was lighter in color than ordinary grass, had a broader leaf and grew faster. It was almost impossible to control and would eventually require that the whole lawn be killed off and re-seeded, but in Grandmother's time the grass had been an un-blemished dark green. Angel walked through it now, carrying her shoes, feeling the ankle-deep stubble brushing against her feet, resenting it as she might have the intrusion of some stranger.

Pieces of mulch clung to her laddered stockings, as if bear-ing witness that the lawn had been cut recently. Somehow she had imagined herself wading through waist-high fields of weeds to reach a derelict house, but she was disappointed. Rye grass notwithstanding, the firm of Kinkaid & Kinkaid had scrupulously fulfilled its trust.

The front of the house faced slightly away from the gate, as if disdaining any approach. While keeping well beyond it, Angel's path followed the general curve of the driveway, so that the house seemed to turn to meet her.

Had her mind been capable of that sort of speculation, the last of the Wymans probably would have believed that houses had as much claim as people to being thought of as endowed with souls. Certainly the house at Five Miles seemed to her an animate object. It was her grandmother's house and embod-ied, as she had, all that had been thought and felt by all the Wymans for all the history of the world, which had begun and would end with them. And so now the windows seemed to stare down at her, watching her with silent disapproval. *You have been away too long,* they said to her. *And now you claim an inheritance that is yours only because it is no one else's.*

But the reproach was somehow more cruel because the house was now warmed by no life except memory. Angel stood for a long moment on the gravel in front of the main entrance, waiting for the house to speak again, yet it would not. She knew where there was a key hidden in the base of one of the wooden pillars, but she found she was reluctant to fetch it. She did not want to step within the house's shadow until she felt herself becoming once more a part of it.

So she went around to the back, where, among other things, there was a garden.

Grandmother had been fond of roses. Angel had a theory that it was not the color or the scent or the shape of the flower that had attracted the old woman, but the thorns. Even if it was not true, the theory had a certain appropriateness. As you walked down the straight, symmetrical paths of the garden you had to be careful that the rose bushes didn't catch you.

Some distance off, as the ground began to slope away, was what looked at first like a fragment of ruined wall but was in fact the gardener's cottage, deliberately allowed to become so overgrown with vines that its real identity was obscured. The Wymans did not like to admit that they shared their premises with anyone.

There was a padlock on the door and the windows were caked over with years of dust, so that they might as well have been made out of sheet metal. Angel had no particular curiosity about the inside. She doubted the cottage had been occupied since her time—Grandmother would have been very careful about that—and her memories were perfectly clear as to its contents. She would have liked to know what became of Dominic, however. Doubtless he was somewhere no one would ever, ever find him.

She turned away and strolled over to the garden, where she sat down on one of the benches and studied the smooth carpet of lawn at her feet. Even the rose beds were grass. Most of the rose gardens Angel had seen, even the ones in Paris, had gravel around the plants, but Grandmother had believed gravel was the invention of the devil—a rose garden required grass. Perhaps the garden was still under her special protection because the rye infestation had not reached its precincts.

The garden had been designed as a retreat, both from the oppressive Connecticut summers and from the propriety of the house. There were wide marble benches beneath arbors covered over with flowering vines that provided plenty of shade and a good measure of privacy. It was a perfect place for lovers' trysts, as Angel had good reason to know. A stranger might have called it a romantic place, except that romance was not something one associated with the Wymans.

Had she felt romantic when she brought Jim here? She couldn't remember. She remembered everything about Jim and the time she had spent in his company except the way it had made her feel. She suspected she had felt very little, and she couldn't bring herself to regret this. She had the impression that strong feelings were for the most part painful and she regarded her own immunity from them as an asset.

But love did not have to be passionate to be real. Angel believed rather than felt that she had loved Jim Kinkaid. She had no idea whether she still loved him—this was something she would have to wait to find out.

It would be useful to love him. She was a Wyman and there was the preservation of the line to be thought of. She wanted to have a child, sooner or later, and Jim would do very well for that.

If everything worked out they could live at Five Miles together and she would help him to make a figure in the world, as befitted a Wyman. But if it didn't he could join the others.

Angel thought it would be her little joke that all the boys would end up here in the rose garden, where they had entered and left her life. She had been collecting souvenirs, bits and pieces, and they could all go towards nourishing Grandmother's rose bushes.

There was room for Jim if he turned out to present a problem.

When she grew tired of amusing herself with the idea she got up and decided it was time to face the house.

Sure enough, even after ten years, the spare key that nobody had known about but she and Grandmother was still behind the little piece of wood that fitted so precisely into the end pillar that you would never have guessed it slipped out—as a matter of fact Angel had to use her little pocketknife to work it loose because it had acquired a couple of coats of paint without anyone noticing its existence.

Inside, what she noticed first were the footprints on the dusty carpet. This too she had not expected.

They were fairly fresh, still sharp in their outlines, and there were two sets: a woman in narrow heels and a man. The man's footprints were large and revealed a long stride. Since the door had not been forced, Angel concluded that the man was probably Jim—as the family lawyer and the executor of the estate he would have a key. Who then was the woman?

The footprints clustered in the middle of the foyer and then led off into the main reception room. She followed them, keeping well away to avoid crossing their trail with her own. At no time did the two sets parallel each other closely enough that it seemed likely the man and woman were touching. And then the woman appeared to have broken off to the left and gone back outside.

She was nobody—a realtor maybe. Angel couldn't disguise from herself the fact that she was relieved. She didn't like the idea that Jim might have brought a woman to this house for any personal reason.

And he had been here, standing in this very room, probably only a few weeks ago. Perhaps even in the last few days.

Angel glanced at the sheet over Grandfather's chair and noticed that the evenness of the dust coating had been disturbed. Jim must have raised it to look underneath. It had to have been him. No one would come into a deserted house and lift up the dustcloth over a chair unless he had personal memories of the place.

She also observed that the woman's footprints appeared nowhere except in the foyer and this room, and her smaller tracks leading to the front door were unaccompanied. She must have come in, looked around a bit, and then gone back outside, leaving Jim here alone.

He didn't seem to have stayed long in the reception room—at least he hadn't moved around much. His footprints led to the stairway and then up to the second floor. He had stopped for a moment on a landing, apparently looking to the front, toward Grandmother's room, but he had not approached it. Apparently there was nothing there which interested him.

Then what did he do? It was not difficult to follow his progress. He stopped and opened the doors to three bedrooms along the left-hand corridor, but there were no footprints more than a yard beyond the thresholds. This was not surprising. The rooms were impersonally furnished, fitted out for the guests who, in Angel's brief experience of the house, were never invited and therefore did not come.

One of these had been her own, and she observed with no small bitterness that all trace of her occupancy had been removed.

The fourth room along that corridor had belonged to her Uncle Christopher, and it was with no slight surprise that she found the door slightly ajar. It had always been locked in her time.

She went inside. On one of the drawers of the desk she saw a set of finger marks. She looked inside and found nothing except some old books. There was no other trace of Jim's presence.

In the last room along that corridor, the one that occupied a corner of the building and therefore had more light than any of the others, the one that had belonged to Angel's mother, she felt sure she understood what he had been looking for.

He had spent some time in this room. Here finger marks were on several items of furniture and near one corner of the bed his footprints were close together, suggesting that he had sat down there. Angel had always regarded her mother as a stupid, shallow woman and the room offered some evidence to support that view, but it was a girl's room. The canopied bed, the records and the stuffed animals suggested a teenager—like the teenager Angel had been ten years ago, when she had lived in this house. Could Jim have imagined it was her room?

He had come upstairs alone, driven by memory, seeking some connection with the past. As he sat here, on her mother's bed, had he whispered her name?

The idea stirred an unfamiliar emotion in her breast. If Angel had been capable of pity she might have called it that, although it was closer to triumph. Instead, she called it love.

chapter 13

The next morning, sitting on the bed in her room at the Stamford Marriott, Angel stared at the Yellow Pages that lay open on the pillow. There was a small, three-line ad for "Kinkaid & Kinkaid."

She had had some idea about phoning and decoying him away from his office.

I wonder if I might speak to Mr. Kinkaid. I'd like his advice concerning a personal matter.

Then, when she had him on neutral ground, possibly in the darkness of some hotel bar, they could have a drink together and she could explain why everything had gone so wrong. After that, anything was possible.

It was a bad idea. She hadn't an inkling what she would have said to him. She might even have told him the truth.

And there were practical considerations. What if he recognized her voice? Ten years was a long time, but he might. He was intelligent and perceptive and had a lawyer's memory. He might hang up the phone, thinking that something wasn't quite right, and then it would come to him. What then?

What she ought to do was drive back to Kennedy and get on a plane to Florida, but she knew she wouldn't do that. Not yet.

She couldn't explain even to herself why all at once it was so important to see Jim. It might be enough just to set eyes on him—then she could walk away and go on with things as she had planned—but she wasn't sure. A dangerous reckless-ness had taken hold of her, making her feel as if she had sud-denly become two people, the one unable to stop the other from yielding to a whole series of destructive impulses the consequences of which she would have to deal with as best she could.

But between the two antagonistic sides of her nature there was just enough caution left to realize she couldn't very well drive up to New Gilead and park in front of Jim's front door to wait for him to come out. And she couldn't talk to him on the phone either. It was too risky. She would have to think of something else.

The problem was Jim had become almost a stranger. Angel would have known how to deal with the college boy, but the man was someone else entirely.

She didn't know what he did with his day. She didn't know his routines. How old was he now? Maybe thirty. At thirty even Jim would have learned to be suspicious.

And that was the answer. A lawyer learns how to screen himself off. He has a secretary, or at least an answering machine. She wouldn't have to risk speaking to Jim.

Had there been a secretary the one time Grandmother had taken her to the offices of Kinkaid & Kinkaid? She couldn't remember. All she could remember was Jim, and the taste of the lemonade.

She called the number listed in the Yellow Pages and, yes, there was a secretary. Angel gave one of her names to the woman with a middle-aged voice and explained that she wished to seek advice about obtaining a divorce.

"Mr. Kinkaid hardly ever takes domestic cases," the woman answered, with obvious distaste. "But if you'll leave a number where you can be reached . . ."

"I can't do that—I'm sure you understand. My husband and everything . . . I wonder if he couldn't see me, if only for a few minutes?"

"I *am* sorry, but his schedule is particularly heavy just now and he'll be away for the next several days. However, I'll raise the matter with him before he leaves and perhaps he'll see you when he returns to the office. You might phone again tomorrow."

"Isn't there any way I could see him today?" Angel inquired, seeing her chance. "I could be there in twenty minutes."

"I'm sorry, but that won't be possible. His flight leaves at one-fifteen.

"Perhaps I could drive him to the airport, and we could talk on the way. . . ."

"No, I'm sorry," the woman said, in a tone she probably reserved for naughty children and lunatics. "The limousine has already been booked."

"Then I'll call tomorrow. Thank you."

After she had hung up, Angel looked at her watch. There were eleven pages of listings in the Classifieds.

Actually, it wasn't that bad. Unless age had corrupted him, Jim was the Basic Transportation type, so companies advertising Mercedes and stretch Lincolns were probably out. And he would probably use someone local. Start in New Gilead and widen the circle.

She gave them the same story each time, delivered in her best ingenue voice: she was a temp working in Mr. Kinkaid's office and she wanted to make sure she hadn't messed up on the time the limo was expected. The first six companies she phoned had never heard of a Mr. Kinkaid, but lucky seven seemed to know all about him.

"Yeah, sure. Continental out of LaGuardia, right? We'll be there at a quarter to twelve."

"Oh thanks—you've saved my life."

A call to a travel agent revealed that Continental Flight 710 to Denver, leaving at one-fifteen, was booked solid, right up through first class. There was even a waiting list. Okay, every rule has its exception.

Angel had toyed with the notion of buying a ticket and then casually running into Jim in the passenger lounge, but now that was impossible.

And until Frank Rizza took care of his errand there were still too many dangers involved in a direct approach. A few days would make everything right, but for the time being she had to be careful not to do anything to make Jim conscious of her existence. It might prompt him to ask some awkward questions.

But she could at least arrange something that would allow her to have a look at him, to see if he had changed any in ten years. She could allow herself at least that much.

In her suitcase was a small, flat automatic pistol, made for her out of a special plastic by a gunsmith in California and hardly larger than the palm of her hand. The equipment used to scan passenger luggage on domestic flights had never detected it, and she didn't imagine the authorities would have given her much trouble about it even if they had—a woman traveling alone is entitled to feel a trifle insecure and the gun was duly registered under the name on her current driver's license and credit cards. Probably the worst they would do was to confiscate it.

She would take it with her tomorrow. She hadn't made up her mind about Jim and, in any case, if he recognized her it might be necessary to kill him. It would only mean that she would have to find someone else to father the next generation of the Wyman family.

The next morning she slept late and then took a long shower before breakfast. She wanted to enjoy each separate moment as if it were part of her last day on earth.

Eleven o'clock found her in New Gilead, driving slowly past Jim's front door. There was no sign of him, but there wouldn't be. He would be inside, finishing his packing or going through the contents of his briefcase. The limousine wouldn't show up for another forty-five minutes.

She drove back through town and down the Norwalk Road until she reached the Merritt Parkway. Then she turned back. It was eleven thirty-five by the time she passed by Jim's front door again.

She parked across the street, about a block away, but she was only teasing herself. It would be stupid to wait. She would only get a glimpse of him as he came down his walkway and got into the limousine. And she wouldn't dare come any closer and she wanted to be near enough to see the expression on his face, because then she would know what she wanted from him.

At twenty-five to twelve she turned the key in the ignition and drove off. Route 106 was only three blocks away, and that would take her straight to Interstate 95. There was no more direct route, so she would have about a ten-minute head start to LaGuardia.

At that hour there were no delays, at least until she hit the approach to the Whitestone Bridge where traffic narrowed down to one lane because of highway construction. By the time Angel got to the toll booth she figured she had lost almost twenty minutes—if Jim's driver knew about the bottleneck and decided to go over the Throg's Neck Bridge it would cut into her lead. They might be in a dead heat for the airport.

And she had to park. She would lose another five minutes hunting for a space and walking to the terminal.

As soon as she was on the bridge itself she let her foot sink down on the accelerator until, by the time she reached the Long Island side, the speedometer was clocking at over eighty. She encountered no police along the expressway, which was just as well. It would have gone very hard with any cop who tried to pull her over.

Even at the off-ramp to the airport there were no sirens wailing behind her. She parked in the short-term lot and ran for the terminal.

At the Continental information desk she was told the one-fifteen flight for Denver would begin its boarding process in a few minutes.

She had to see if he was in the passenger lounge. She was perhaps a hundred feet down the terminal corridor, within sight of the security gates, when she remembered the gun in her purse.

Fortunately there was a ladies' room just there. She went inside and washed her hands while she waited for the woman who was standing in front of the mirror to finish with her fucking lipstick. Then, when she was alone, she rolled out about two feet of paper towel, dried her hands with one end and then wrapped the automatic in the other. It made no sound when she dropped the parcel in the trash.

The security guards acted like they meant it. One of them was going over a man with something that looked like a loop of refrigerator tubing—"It's your belt buckle," he announced finally, in a tone that suggested this established proof of guilt. Angel dropped her purse on the conveyer belt for the X-ray machine and walked through the metal detector without setting it off.

No one asked to see her ticket.

She was cautious in her approach. Although it didn't amount to much of a disguise, she took a pair of dark glasses out of her purse and put them on. She stayed close to the corridor wall as it began opening out into the passenger waiting area.

He wasn't there. She scanned the little clusters of seats carefully, but he wasn't there. The one-fifteen to Denver was listed over Gate 4, but the door to the boarding ramp was still closed. He wasn't on the plane. Perhaps he was in the men's room.

She went into the ladies' and, just to give herself something to do, tied a scarf over her hair. She washed her hands, then she took off her sunglasses and checked her lipstick.

A man can be in and out of the can in two minutes, so she gave herself five and went back outside.

He still wasn't there. The purser was just announcing that Flight 710 was now ready for boarding. If she stayed any longer she was bound to arouse suspicion.

She started back down the corridor toward the main terminal.

At the security gate passengers coming in were separated

by a barrier from those leaving. A plastic screen had been set up beside the right-hand wall, making a passage narrow enough that two people couldn't have walked through abreast. The upper half was a kind of latticework to admit some light from the overhead fixtures. When Angel looked through it she could see a guard working his portable metal detector up and down between Jim's legs.

He appeared embarrassed. He didn't quite seem to know if he should raise his arms for a full frisk, and he was smiling and talking to the guard, who went about his work as if he were inspecting a block of wood. Angel could just catch the murmur of Jim's voice, without being able to make out the words. Even wearing a suit, he hardly seemed any older.

He was such a nice guy. Always polite, always ready to be human with anyone in the world, even some stupid son-of-a-bitch trying to goose him with a cattle prod. All you had to do was look at Jim to know he was a sweetie, without a bad thought for a living soul. He just made you love him. If she had had her gun along, Angel wouldn't have been able to help herself. She would have blown the guard's head off.

The search had come to an end and, yet once more, it seemed to be a belt buckle that was causing the problem. Jim was collecting the contents of his pockets from a small plastic tray and retrieving his briefcase. He was busy and preoccupied, but they were only about fifteen feet apart and if she didn't start moving in the next few seconds he was sure to notice her, even though the latticework—people don't stand still in airport corridors without becoming conspicuous.

She took one step and then another, and then it got a little easier as she settled into something like a quick march. She didn't allow herself to look back.

She had already pulled abreast of the ladies' room door when she remembered the pistol. No one was inside. She pulled the lid off the trash barrel, reached down inside and felt around for anything more substantial than paper towels. It didn't take much of a search.

As she slipped the gun back into her purse she went all over cold again, as if coming awake to find her pleasant dream was only that. Jim was not her lover because she could love no one. Even if they got back together somehow, she would always be staring hungrily at him through a screen, always afraid he would suddenly turn his head and see her, really see her. For her life was just this, walking through an airport terminal with nowhere to go. She felt cheated.

She should have stayed away. She should have waited for the plan to come to its fruition and then come back. Whatever she had expected to find here had eluded her.

And now Jim was on a plane to Denver.

Outside, the sun was a painful glare. Her head ached and she hated the very air she breathed. She knew she was in a dangerous mood.

"Hi, honey!"

In the parking lot, in a wilderness of empty cars, a salesman type, a little under average height, about forty and wearing a snappy light gray suit, with a grin as big as Christmas—the sort of jerk who gets a thrill out of making a nuisance of himself.

What the hell. He had it coming.

Angel stopped and favored him with a coy smile. The guy obviously couldn't believe his luck.

"Have you got your car with you?" she asked.

"Right here, sweetheart."

"Then get in."

Which he did, with almost indecent haste. But Angel surprised him by coming around to the driver's side.

She opened the door and took her pistol out of her purse.

"Lie down on the floor, sweetheart."

"Now wait just a minute, just . . ."

"Do it."

He did it. He really scrambled. Angel straightened her arm and took careful aim.

"Please . . ."

She shot him four times, very carefully. In the enclosed space of the car each one sounded amazingly loud, but thirty feet away they were just ambient noise.

Angel crawled over the seat to have a look at his face. Good—he was still alive. But the slow, random movements of the arms and legs indicated he was a goner. One of the bullets had probably got him in the spine. She hoped so.

He just stared at her with astonished, uncomprehending eyes. She reached down and patted him on the cheek.

chapter 14

      Denver was easy. It was that rare instance in which the lawyer had both the law and the facts on his side and which should never have gone to litigation at all except that Mr. Adrian Winslow was used to bullying his partner and thought he could continue doing so right up through the end of the relationship. He was one of those beautifully groomed tough guys, all ego and insecurity, who are common enough in the upper echelons of business. Kinkaid only had to look at him to know there was nothing inside the thousand-dollar suit. Mr. Winslow will fold, he thought to himself as he shook that well-manicured hand. The negotiations were over in two hours.

So he went back to the hotel where he had checked his luggage, cancelled his reservation and took a cab back to the airport, where he caught the 1:45 flight to Columbus, Ohio. It was a two and a half hour flight and it crossed a time zone, so by the time he hired a car and drove to Dayton it was already evening.

He parked across the street from the downtown police station, went to the front desk and asked for Lieutenant Warren Pratt.

"You cut it pretty fine," the duty sergeant told him. "His retirement party's tomorrow night. You want to give me your name?"

"My name is James Kinkaid. I'm an attorney and I'm here about the Billinger homicide."

The sergeant, who was probably used to fielding kooks, picked up a telephone and spoke a few sentences in a murmur that was almost drowned out by the air conditioning.

"You're lucky," he said, putting the phone down. "He's in the building. Why don't you have a seat over there."

Five minutes later a small, spare, middle-aged man in a gray suit came out through the frosted glass doors that had *Official Personnel Only* stenciled across them. He stopped in the precise center of the reception area.

"You Kinkaid?" he asked, without smiling.

By way of answer, Kinkaid stood up.

"Lieutenant Pratt?" He received the barest trace of a nod.

"Come along this way."

Pratt's office was a trifle cramped. There was room for a desk, three chairs and a couple of filing cabinets. That was it. One didn't get the impression he spent a lot of time there.

"You the one who phoned me from Connecticut last month?" he asked, in a way that implied he had already confirmed this information for himself. "Your dad had some kind of list with Billinger's name on it?"

"That's right. And since we spoke someone else on that list has disappeared."

Pratt leaned forward in his chair. He wore rimless glasses that caught the light, making it difficult to read his expression.

"I'm listening," he said.

Kinkaid took out his wallet and removed the newspaper clipping about George Tipton, unfolding it carefully and laying it on the desk where Pratt could read it.

"The police have a fugitive warrant out for him, but he's disappeared without a trace. So has the car."

"How do you know?"

"I was in New York City last night and bought an Atlanta paper. There was a follow-up piece buried on page twelve."

Pratt read the clipping through and then refolded it, holding it up between two fingers.

"Can I keep this?" And then, before Kinkaid had a chance to reply, "Do you think he killed his wife and kid?"

"Did Billinger?"

Pratt did not answer. Instead, he read the clipping through

again and then turned it over so that it was facedown on his desk. He kept his hand over it, as if afraid it might blow away. He didn't look happy.

"It doesn't necessarily mean anything," he said at last. "You have a list with eight names on it. Three get crossed off. I've seen murder cases with weirder coincidences."

"Then why are you even talking to me, Lieutenant?" Kinkaid's voice had dropped to little more than a whisper, as it always did when he wanted to command someone's attention. "Is it because Billinger wasn't a local boy?"

"No, he wasn't."

"No, he wasn't," Kinkaid repeated. "He was born in New Gilead, Connecticut, my hometown. And he played football at the high school. So did Terry Vogel, who blew his head off in Philadelphia on August 27, 1992."

"And what about our missing husband?" Pratt picked up a corner of the clipping with the tips of two fingers and glanced at it—probably for effect, since he looked like the sort of man who had never forgotten a name in his life. "George Tipton. Did he play football too?"

"Not at New Gilead High. But another George Tipton did. He died in a traffic accident some years ago and thus rendered himself unavailable."

It was as close as Kinkaid had ever come to a simple declaration of the idea that had been haunting him ever since he had first discovered his father's list, and even now he could not quite bring himself to say it. He would leave that to Detective Lieutenant Pratt.

But even Pratt seemed reluctant. He turned over the clipping again and stared at the headline for what seemed like a full minute but was probably only a few seconds. Then he looked up at Kinkaid and raised his eyebrows, not necessarily disbelieving, merely preserving a certain professional skepticism.

"So you think all three of these men were murdered," he said, more stating a fact than asking a question.

Kinkaid felt strangely exhilarated, as if the burden had at last been lifted. It was out now.

"Yes."

"And you think the same person killed them?"

"I think their deaths are related. I don't know if that's necessarily the same thing."

Pratt appeared to consider the point, then shook his head.

"Let's assume they are related," he began. "Then it would follow that our Atlanta victim was some kind of stand-in. Your George Tipton was dead, but the killer wasn't accepting any excuses. Somebody had to take his place. I don't see a murder like that coming out of a committee."

He turned the clipping facedown again and then, after the briefest possible hesitation, slipped it into an unmarked manila folder that was lying next to his telephone.

"So we're left with a choice between a statistical quirk and a nutcase who goes around wiping out whole families, sometimes just because the husband has the wrong name. On the whole I think I'd sleep better at night believing in the statistical quirk."

"Will you at least get in touch with the Atlanta police?" Kinkaid asked, trying to keep the eagerness out of his voice—he knew from experience that the more you sound like you want something the less willing people are to give it to you. "With respect to the murders of the families, you have two very similar cases here. If you reviewed the physical evidence couldn't you at the very least get an idea if you were dealing with the same killer?"

"Mr. Kinkaid . . ." Pratt took off his glasses and pinched the bridge of his nose with thumb and first finger. He looked tired, or perhaps only bored. "The Billinger homicide is a month old, and the crime scene—in fact, both crime scenes—were remarkably clean. Believe me, we've worked the case, and we aren't any closer to an arrest than we were on Day One. Serial killers that smart are very difficult to catch, especially if they don't stay in a particular locale. Yes, certainly I'll phone Atlanta, but I can't claim to be very hopeful."

"Then are you going to let a murderer just walk away? Seven people are dead, probably eight."

Kinkaid was on the verge of apologizing when he heard Pratt's joyless laughter.

"Lots of murderers just walk away. This isn't the movies."

"I know. I'm sorry."

"I don't like it either, Mr. Kinkaid." He shook his head. "I've seen a lot of bad things in twenty years, but a case like this . . ."

And he didn't like it. Kinkaid could see it in his eyes. It gave him the beginnings of an idea.

"Mr. Pratt, they tell me you're about to retire."

"Yes, finally." He smiled, and made a little gesture with his left hand that was roughly equivalent to a shrug.

"Any plans?"

Suddenly cautious, Pratt stopped smiling. He looked afraid that Kinkaid might offer him a great deal on some Florida vacation property, but he also betrayed himself. He had no plans. Whatever his reasons for getting out, he wasn't looking forward to it.

"I want answers, Mr. Pratt," Kinkaid went on, when he had let a decent interval pass. "I want the truth—or at least as much of it as I can get. But I'm not a criminal lawyer. I don't know very much about things like this, but you do. Maybe this is one case you'd like to follow through."

Pratt didn't say anything, but at least he was listening. That was encouragement enough.

"Could you look into this Atlanta thing for me? If there's nothing to it, then fine. At least I'll know. I'll pay you whatever you consider reasonable and I'll cover your expenses, in advance. I can write you a check right now."

For a moment Pratt remained silent. And then he allowed himself a short, astonished syllable of laughter.

"You're really serious about this, aren't you."

"I'm really serious. Will you do it?"

"I'll think about it. But first I'd like to know why it matters so much to you."

"Because it mattered so much to my father that it killed him. I have to know why."

"And the killer?"

"I have no idea who he could be."

Something in Pratt's face changed. He was silent for a moment, as if collecting himself, and then he cleaned his glasses with a pocket handkerchief and put them back on, making a little ceremony of it. The glasses somehow rendered his face masklike and unreadable, which was perhaps the point.

"There isn't any way you could have known," he began, with a shade of regret in his voice. "We kept it out of the newspapers. Billinger checked into that motel with a woman. She was blond and very beautiful, according to the manager's wife, and we haven't heard from her since. Either she's dead or she did it. We think she did it."

With an effort that was almost physically painful, Kinkaid tried to keep from letting the thought enter his brain. But it would come—it could not be kept out.

"Oh Jesus," he whispered. "It can't be. It isn't possible."

"Sir? Sir, are you all right?"

Her voice seemed to come from somewhere far away. When he turned his head he was surprised to see the stewardess, her face only a few inches from his own. She looked worried.

Kinkaid tried to smile.

"I'm fine," he said, lying. "I'm always a little motion sick on planes."

"Would you like something?"

"I'd like a good stiff drink."

It was clear that the stewardess didn't think that was such a terrific idea, but she took his order for a double vodka martini.

And she was right. He tossed the drink back in a couple of quick swallows, so that he could feel the precise instant in which the alcohol went into his bloodstream, but it didn't help. Because it wasn't the movement of the plane that was giving him a hard time, it was life.

He had no proof. He had nothing to direct him but the gathering sense of dread that tore at his bowels like splinters of ice. A woman glimpsed in the doorway of a seedy motel room—the world was full of blondes and probably half of them fit somebody's idea of beautiful. She didn't have to be the killer and she sure as hell didn't have to be Angel. The girl he had been in love with ten years ago wasn't a murderess.

Pratt had shown him the photographs. The skin stripped off Billinger's face like old wallpaper. His wife a crumpled mound on the stairway, half her head gone from a hollow-point bullet that caught her just under the right eye. The two boys, shot to death as they slept in their upstairs bedroom. Who could do such things? Not the girl he had known ten years ago.

But had he really known her at all? *From what I hear, she's been fucked by every guy on the football team.* He hadn't been able to believe that either.

He had made his confession to his father on a Sunday evening, just before driving back to Yale. The following Friday he came home and was invited into his father's office, where he was told that Mrs. Wyman had rendered her decision. It was impossible. Angel was forbidden ever to see him again, for his own sake.

"We'll see about that," he had shouted, getting up out of the chair his father called the Inquisition Seat and clawing his way back into his coat. "We'll just see. Who the hell does she think I am anyway, the Boston Strangler?"

"Don't go up there, Jimmy. Just don't."

"Fuck that, Dad—and fuck you."

He slammed out of the house and took off in his car. Six minutes later, having broken every speed law known to man, he was in front of the entrance to Five Miles, bellowing at the intercom.

"The family is not at home," he was told.

"I'm coming up to see for myself. You can open the gates or I can drive over them, you please yourself."

He slid in behind the wheel and waited. He would give them thirty seconds and then his car would probably need a new front end—he was as close to crazy as he would ever come. But apparently Mrs. Wyman wasn't crazy because after about fifteen seconds there was a loud click as the electric motor snapped on and the gates slid quietly open.

The old woman was waiting for him at the front door, which seemed odd. She was using a stick and she looked ancient. She gave no indication of being either surprised or angry that he should have forced his way into her home.

"You'd better come this way."

She turned to her left, apparently expecting him to trot along behind her.

"Where's Angela?"

"You won't see her," she said, without stopping to glance back at him. "She isn't here."

"I don't believe you."

"It makes little difference what you believe, young man. Nevertheless, Angela is not here. At my age one does not often take the trouble to lie. Now come along."

Mrs. Wyman's progress toward the principal drawing room was rather slow and she really seemed to need her stick. She took her place on a sofa and did not invite him to sit down.

"I will not resent this intrusion," she began, looking down at her lap as she smoothed out the folds of her dress. "Since it is so obvious that you have no thought of ingratiating yourself, I must assume that you fancy yourself in love. You may actually be in love. If that is the case, then I pity you."

"Where is Angela?"

She lifted her gaze to his face and seemed for a moment to consider whether he warranted an answer.

"I have sent her away," she said at last. "I can see now that it was folly to bring her here. She will not be coming back."

"Did you think me so little worthy of her, Mrs. Wyman?"

He remembered how humiliated he felt that his voice shook with emotion as he asked the question. Yet he could not help himself. If he had been alone he might have wept.

"Was the thought that she could love someone like me so very distasteful to you?"

He would always remember the way she looked at him in that moment. For years he had believed that she was mocking him, but now he began to understand that expression in her eyes might have been one of pain rather than contempt, and that the wound had been to more than simply family pride, that its sources would probably be hidden from him forever but that her suffering might indeed have made his own seem less than nothing.

"I know you will not believe me, young man," she had answered, "but I have acted more for your sake than for hers."

Ten years after their conversation, alone with his double vodka martini on the flight from Columbus, Ohio, to New York, with Mrs. Wyman long in her grave, James Kinkaid IV, no longer quite so young, was prepared to believe it possible she had been telling the truth.

chapter 15

"**What's the matter?** Don't you feel well?"

"I'm fine. Well—tired maybe. Maybe it's jet lag. I don't like air travel."

He was lying. And even if he wasn't lying he wasn't telling the truth. Whatever was wrong with him had nothing to do with airplanes.

But Lisa decided she wasn't going to get insulted. After all, whatever it was it hadn't diminished his ardor, which had about it a certain flattering desperation. He even stayed the night, and to hell with his housekeeper.

She woke up once in the small hours of the morning. Jim was asleep but restless. He seemed in the thrall of some terrible dream. She put her arm over him and pressed herself against his back, and after a while he quieted down.

So what happened in Denver, she wondered. She couldn't very well ask him, so she probably wasn't going to find out any time soon. Maybe it didn't matter.

Maybe it did.

Lying there with him in the darkness, comforting him in a way he would never know anything about, Lisa Milano recognized that she had fallen in love. She had had a few casual lovers—okay, to be perfectly honest, more than a few—but none of them had ever touched her soul. Jim Kinkaid was different. He was the smartest man she had ever known and the most vulnerable. It was the vulnerability that appealed to her. It was an unusual experience to really matter to someone.

After a while she fell asleep again, protecting him from the terrors of the night.

"I think it's the same shooter. The locals still want to go with the husband."

Warren Pratt, now a private citizen, was calling from a hotel room in Atlanta. He had flown down the morning after his retirement party.

"So where are we?" Kinkaid asked, sitting in his office in New Gilead, doodling on a yellow legal pad and wondering why he felt relieved. "There's no way to be sure, one way or the other?"

"Not yet—if two months from now we find Tipton's Honda sitting in a used car lot in Newark it'll probably mean that they're right and I'm wrong. I can understand why they like him as a suspect. It wasn't a very harmonious marriage. In the meantime, though, I think our blonde did it."

Kinkaid restrained the impulse to point out that *our* blonde might not be *his* blonde, that the fair-haired, elegant woman seen by Mrs. Daniels might not be, probably was not, the elegant, fair-haired Angela Wyman he had known ten years before. He wanted to, but he did not. Instead, he asked for an explanation. Why the blonde?

"It's a question of pattern," Pratt answered. "I don't have any hard evidence. The bullets that killed Mrs. Tipton and her little girl don't match up with the ones we took out of the Billinger family, and I didn't expect them to. Our killer is much too clever to use the same weapon twice. Both guns were about the same caliber, but that doesn't mean anything.

"What strikes me about both crimes is their sheer efficiency. In Dayton there was no forced entry, so we presume our perpetrator used Billinger's keys to come in the back door, since the front had a dead bolt. Then she went through the kitchen and dining room to the hallway, where she caught Mrs. Billinger on the stairs. Then she went up the stairs past the body, being careful not to step in any blood, and topped the two boys. Three shots, three corpses. Nothing was disturbed, nothing was touched, nothing was left behind. I think she was in and out in less than five minutes. Atlanta was exactly the same way.

"These murders were meticulous. As crimes they were works of art. Someone gave a lot of thought to the details and then just went through and did it like it was ballet. Domestic murders aren't like that. They're generally spontaneous explosions. Husbands who go berserk and wipe out their significant others just aren't that cool about it. If our blonde did both families she's a real ice queen.

"What do you want me to do now?"

It was a good question. In the end Pratt had simply not been able to relinquish the Billinger murders. "This is one of those cases that are always remembered," he had said. "I don't want to be remembered as the cop who came up empty. I'll clear this one, and then I can spend my twilight years chasing butterflies. If you're prepared to pay the tab I'll go on hunting."

But what now?

"Are you finished in Atlanta?" Kinkaid asked.

"I could use another day. I want to find out a little more about Tipton, and I'd like to have a look at the crime scene."

"Take whatever time you need. When you're done, go up to Philadelphia and see what you can find out about Terry Vogel's suicide. When you're done you can take the train up here. I'll meet you in New York."

When he had put down the phone, Kinkaid looked out his office window and noticed a gleam of light reflected off the board fence his neighbors had put around their backyard to keep the dog at home. That meant the streetlamps had been turned on, which in turn meant it was after 8:00 p.m. It was Julia's day off and he had forgotten to do anything about dinner. He wondered where he had put Lisa Milano's telephone number.

"Have you eaten?"

"Just finished," she answered. "Budget Gourmet Lasagna and a diet cream soda."

"I'm sorry I missed it."

"No you're not. But if you come over now I can provide you with scrambled eggs and various other physical comforts."

"I'll be there in twenty minutes. No, make it fifteen."

George Tipton, deceased, had led a troubled youth. The New Gilead Police Department's file on him was half an inch thick and concerned only juvenile offenses, since by his eighteenth birthday he had already left town forever.

The record started when he was thirteen years old and was arrested for trespassing and malicious mischief after throwing a brick through Mrs. Vivian Thompson's plateglass window on Halloween. The charge had been dropped the next afternoon, so probably George's father had paid to have the window replaced.

At fifteen he was found drunk and disorderly during a Sunday afternoon matinee at the Palace movie theater and received three months probation.

Then came the traffic tickets, eight within a single year, half of them for speeding. He had finally had his license suspended, but was cited twice more for driving without it.

But from James Kinkaid's perspective, ten years after the fact, the only item of real interest was the last. It was another arrest for trespassing, this time in company with Andrew Castlesmith, with the complainant listed as Mrs. Isabelle Wyman.

The two boys had been apprehended coming back over the wall at Five Miles, and the arresting officer had been Marshall Cheffins himself. The matter had been serious, especially since Castlesmith was eighteen and thus could be charged as an adult.

Three days later charges were again dropped, which was a little strange—old Mrs. Wyman had not been the type to be bought off at the price of a plateglass window. It was more than a little strange.

But George Tipton and Mrs. Wyman were both dead, and Andrew Castlesmith could be anywhere—certainly he wasn't in New Gilead—so there was only one person left who might know something about this particular piece of ancient history, even if it was only that there was nothing to know.

Every day he was on duty, and some when he was not, Marshall Cheffins ate lunch at the diner across the street from the police station. Many evenings he was there for dinner as well. It was a habit that dated from his wife's death, some fifteen years ago, and everyone in town knew about it. If you wanted a quiet off-the-record word with the marshall, you went to Curly's at one o'clock.

Curly's was a dark tunnel of a place, its walls lined with ten or twelve booths of the old-fashioned kind that were like little wooden rooms. It had changed hands several times over the years and was now owned and run by a Vietnamese couple named Ng. Mr. Ng, who had appeared in the late '80s, was now universally referred to as "Curly" and his wife was "Mrs. Curly," but the name was purely honorific, as Mr. Ng's hair was thin, straight and carefully plastered to his skull. If you owned Curly's, you were Curly. In fact no one seemed to remember the first Curly, but he seemed to have left his mark. Nothing about the place ever varied, not even the menu.

The marshall always occupied the back booth, nearest the kitchen. When Kinkaid sat down across the table from him he was just finishing a dessert which had probably been some sort of cobbler.

"How are you, Jim Boy? I see you brought young Tipton back. You want some coffee?"

"No thanks, Bill," Kinkaid answered, smiling and pushing the manila folder across the table. Bill Cheffins was a good deal more than twice his age, but he liked to be called by his first name for the same reason he liked eating at Curly's. He liked being an institution. "I just wondered if there was any-thing you could tell me that isn't in here."

The marshall raised his eyebrows in something that seemed like a mingling of astonishment and disapproval. He was a large man, with a deeply creased face and grizzled hair. He knew how to look intimidating, even if you had known him all your life—perhaps especially then.

"Like what exactly?"

"Like the time you busted him up at Five Miles. What was that about?"

Cheffins' suspicion evaporated instantly. He threw back his head and laughed, as if someone had reminded him of a favorite joke.

"Sure, I remember that," he said, shaking his head and laughing all over again. "The stupid little squirt had left his old Chevy in the trees—I'd tagged that car so many times I knew right away it was George's. All I had to do was pull in behind and wait. I watched him and his buddy climb back over the wall. They were laughing and making jokes, as pleased with themselves as jaybirds with a picnic basket. They practically walked into my arms."

"Did Mrs. Wyman call you?"

"Her very own self. Called me in the middle of the night, said there were intruders—'intruders,' that was what she called 'em. Said I should come out right away. She was pissed as hell."

"But you didn't go up to the house?"

"Nah. As soon as I saw that damn Chevy I knew there wasn't nothing to worry about. George Tipton had a little too much hell in him, but he wasn't gonna burn the place down. I called Mrs. Wyman from my car and said not to worry, that it was only kids and that she should tell her gardener to chase 'em out, that I'd be there waiting for 'em."

"Why did she drop charges, do you think?"

"Oh, Jimmy, I don't think. I know." The marshal's voice dropped and he leaned a little forward, lighting a cigarette.

"You ever meet that young girl Mrs. Wyman had kicking around the house for a while? Those boys was invited."

He slumped back, his head wrapped in a cloud of cigarette smoke, in a state of purely physical satisfaction that appeared to make him forgetful of anything else. He smiled faintly and to himself, but not in recollection. It was as if he had forgotten there was any past to remember, or anyone to share it with if there was.

Perhaps, or perhaps not. It was just possible that somehow he knew that young Jimmy Kinkaid had also climbed the wall at Five Miles, or perhaps no one knew.

"Yes, I met her once," Kinkaid said, keeping his voice empty of emotion. "I wonder what ever became of her."

"Do you?"

Cheffins shook himself out of whatever dream had enveloped him. He flicked an ash onto his empty dessert dish and, seeming just then to have noticed Kinkaid's presence, frowned slightly.

"I would've thought your Daddy'd told you," he said, making it sound like a reproach. "Now why do you suppose he didn't?"

It was the sort of story one reads in the newspapers every day, the story of a young life gone suddenly and inexplicably smash. Except, of course, that this particular story never made it into the newspapers. There had been a crime, and there had been punishment, but because it was Wyman family business it was not deemed the proper concern of the press—or, for that matter, even the law. And thus for ten years it had remained the exclusive possession of some half-dozen people.

"I got the call on a Thursday evening," Marshall Cheffins explained. "I know it was a Thursday because that used to be my lodge night and I got fined a bottle of Jack Daniel's because I missed the meeting. I'd just finished my dinner when the phone rang. It was your daddy."

The marshal was instructed—*instructed*, that was the word

he used—to come to Five Miles, alone and driving an un-marked car. And because it was Mrs. Wyman's lawyer who was calling, and because Bill Cheffins would never have become town marshal without the help of old Judge Wyman, he did as he was told.

"Mrs. Wyman wasn't anywhere to be seen when I got there," he went on. "Your daddy met me at the door. We didn't even go inside. He just led me around to the back. The gardener's cottage was behind the garage, and the door was open. There weren't any lights on inside, but the door was standing wide open. It seemed peculiar.

"The cottage was just a little two-room stone hut, not much bigger than a tool shed, and the bedroom was in the back. That's where he was.

"You probably never met Dominic Franco, did you, Jimmy?" The marshal smiled, not very nicely. "Not exactly the type who ends up going to Yale. A nice-looking kid, though, when he wasn't shit-faced drunk. And a perfect terror with the girls. I'd had a run-in or two with him. The sort you just know is gonna die young.

"And he did. He was lying on the bed, his face smashed in so bad his own mother wouldn't have recognized him. There was a shovel on the floor, the short kind with a hand grip, but a good heavy blade, enough to do the job. It was smeared with blood, so I didn't have to think too hard about what had been the murder weapon.

"He'd been drinking—there was a half-empty whiskey bottle on his night table—and he must have been out cold. He didn't look like he'd put up any kind of a struggle. I figure he'd probably been dead about two hours.

" 'She killed him,' your daddy said. 'Angela. She just went wild.'

" 'Any idea why?' I asked him, but he just shook his head. 'Where is she now?'

" 'Up in her room. She hasn't said a word—it's like she's in some sort of trance. Mrs. Wyman is with her.'

"He was pretty upset and I couldn't blame him. It wasn't like I'd never seen a killing before, 'cause even in New Gilead we get a killing every once in a while. But this wasn't like some guy goes ballistic and plugs his honey. Young Dom was a real mess. The whole front of his skull was crushed in so bad his head looked like a plate full of strawberry preserves.

"We went back to the house and had a look at the young lady who had done all this, and she really was in a trance. She was wearing a white, sleeveless dress that was spattered with blood, and she sat on her bed, her legs drawn up beneath her, her head a little bowed, staring at nothing. I remember thinking how pretty she was, as if that could matter anymore. Mrs. Wyman was on a chair beside the door, as if to guard the way out, and I remember there were tears in her eyes. They were both perfectly silent.

"Your daddy and I went down to the old Judge's study, where we both knew there was a bar behind one of the bookcases, and I made us each a stiff drink.

" 'Her mind has snapped,' he said to me. 'No matter what you decide to do about this, the end result will be the same— Angela's going into the nuthouse for the rest of her life.'

"I must not have been thinking too clearly, because it was only then that I realized what they wanted from me. I was having a quiet drink with the family lawyer while the old lady's granddaughter was crouched upstairs, out of her head, and never coming back, and there was a dead body in the gardener's hut, and I was supposed to clean up the mess.

"Well, it wasn't something I had to study real hard. In this county, when the Wymans want something done it gets done. The Judge had put me in this job and his Missus could take me out of it anytime she felt so inclined. If I wanted to stay marshal I had to solve this little problem for her.

" 'You'd better call a doctor for the girl,' I answered. 'But get her cleaned up first, and burn that dress.'

"I finished my drink and went back out to the gardener's cottage, where I wrapped Dominic Franco up in a plastic tarp and put him and everything I could find that he had bled on in the trunk of my police car.

"There's an old farm off of Route 6 the town picked up for delinquent property taxes back in the Seventies and then, when even the developers weren't interested, just forgot about. It seemed as good a place as any. I put Dom to rest in an abandoned well shaft and he hasn't caused any trouble since."

Marshal Cheffins crushed out his cigarette in one of the heavy glass ashtrays that showed as conclusively as anything could how far behind the times Curly's diner had remained. He sighed heavily, not in remembrance of past sins but out of an animal contentment—from the remaining evidence it had been a heavy lunch.

"And I've never said a word about any of this to a living soul," he went on. "Not in ten years. Now just you and I know, Jimmy."

Somehow James Kinkaid IV made it back to his car, which, thank God, was parked out of sight of the street. He climbed inside, but he couldn't have driven it anywhere. He kept dropping the keys. Finally he just left them where they had fallen on the floor and began pounding on the dashboard with his fist.

"Damn, damn, damn, damn!" he found himself shouting within the enclosed space of the car. His eyes were burning with unspent tears and he felt as if his chest were being crushed beneath someone's foot. "Oh God damn . . ."

It was all so horribly clear now. Marshal Cheffins was out a bottle of Jack Daniel's because it was a Thursday evening that Dominic Franco died, which meant he had only been dead about twenty-four hours when young Jimmy went storming up to Five Miles to have it out with Mrs. Wyman.

"You may actually be in love," she had told him. *"If that is the case, then I pity you."*

And she had said it with the full authority of her patrician

New England disdain for emotional excess, and her granddaughter by then would have been spending the first night of the rest of her life in a mental ward. The old woman must have been made of iron.

Her granddaughter. Miss Wyman, the mysterious young relative from a convent school in Paris, was her granddaughter, a fact Bill Cheffins mentioned so casually that he obviously supposed Young Jimmy knew as much already. Obviously Young Jimmy was and always had been pretty dense.

But not dense enough not to understand why the marshal had no qualms about telling him such a chronicle of indictable offenses—simply because he had known he could get away with it. Just as he had known he could get away with dropping Dominic Franco down a well shaft. Because he knew he had nothing to fear from anybody except Mrs. Wyman, who was safely dead now. Because he knew there was nothing Jimmy Kinkaid could or would do about conspiracy, misprision of a felony, and accessory to murder. Because if Bill Cheffins was guilty so was James Kinkaid Senior.

And his father would never have been party to such a thing, not even for the Wymans, if Mrs. Wyman hadn't had just the right weapon to use against him.

She had been in her grave for years, but he could hear her voice as clearly as if she were there in the car with him: "Don't imagine you have nothing to lose. You have your son to lose—your son, so full of promise. My granddaughter's life may be over, but if you insist on dragging our family's name through the mud I'll see that at least some of it sticks to your boy. If everything comes out, who will believe in his innocence? Who will want to believe in it?"

From what I hear, she's been fucked by every guy on the football team.

And in all the years since, to the very hour of his death, he had said nothing. He had kept his secret, letting its poison slowly seep into their relationship.

But all of this, his father's complicity, his even more terrible silence, was as nothing against the image of Angela Wyman, her white dress spattered with blood, her mind mute, broken and unreachable. It was like losing her all over again—only worse this time, because now he had lost even the idea of her.

What had made her kill the gardener? *The whole front of his skull was crushed in.* Had he been her lover too, like George Tipton and Andrew Castlesmith? *Those boys was invited.*

The chronology was clear. On Sunday evening Kinkaid had talked to his father before going back to New Haven. Sometime between Sunday and Thursday his father talked to Mrs. Wyman. On Thursday Angela beat Dominic Franco to death and almost immediately thereafter slipped into madness. By Friday, when Kinkaid drove to Five Miles, she was gone, as if she had stepped off the face of the Earth. *You won't see her,* Mrs. Wyman had said. *She isn't here.*

She isn't here.

Mrs. Wyman had implied, without perhaps actually saying so, that she had sent Angela away because of him. *I know you will not believe me, young man, but I have acted more for your sake than for hers.* Clearly this was not true in any literal sense, but it was somehow impossible to believe that on some level the old woman had not been telling the truth.

Then she must have spoken to her granddaughter about the purpose of his father's visit. Was that what had pushed Angela over into the abyss? Was it really possible to believe anything else?

It was as if he had just discovered that he had destroyed her. He had fallen in love—that was his only offense. And yet he felt the burden of his inadvertent guilt. One can be innocent and still feel the despair of shame.

What had become of Angela? It became suddenly necessary to know, yet how would he ever know?

The keys in his father's strongbox, the strongbox that contained thirty years of Wyman family files—files through which he had searched and searched and found nothing. Perhaps the point had never been the files themselves, but the keys.

Five Miles stood undisturbed. Except for the dust cloths over the furniture, everything was still exactly the way it had been the night of Mrs. Wyman's death.

The keys. That was his father's secret bequest to him, access to the truth.

Half an hour later he was standing in front of the massive front door, trying to keep his hands steady as he inserted the key into the lock. By now he even knew where to look.

Mrs. Wyman's room, the room in which she had died, would contain a writing desk such as a woman of her generation and class would have considered as necessary as her bed. Everything that really mattered to her, any scrap of paper that touched upon her inner life, would be in that desk.

As he walked across the empty reception hall, as he mounted the stairway to the second floor, he felt the dead as a real presence. It was almost as if he could hear the old woman's ghost screaming at him to turn back.

They are not your secrets. They are mine—all that I have loved and suffered for and lost is mine.

Not quite. Not now. Not anymore.

The master bedroom was at once vast and tomblike. The windows faced out towards the front of the house and it was not much more than one in the afternoon, but so impenetrable were the heavy curtains that Kinkaid had to switch on the overhead light to reveal anything beyond the sense of empty space.

Even the light, when it came on, seemed to struggle against a gloom so thick it was almost palpable.

The massive canopied bed was the only piece of furniture in the room which was not covered with a dustcloth, but everything was clear enough in outline. A vanity with a tall mirror stood beside the closet door. Against the front window was a low circular table and two chairs, and in the center of the room was another table, this one a blocky rectangle.

The bathroom door, which was on the left, stood slightly open, enough to provide a glimpse of pale green tile. The bed was against the opposite wall, on the other side of which was another door. It would not have been a convenient place to put a second closet and in fact the door led to a small sitting room, hardly large enough to hold a chair and an old rolltop desk. It was locked, but the lock yielded easily to one of the keys Kinkaid had brought with him.

Inside the desk was a mass of pigeonholes, all of them filled with envelopes and bits of paper. Kinkaid did not have to search very long to find what he was looking for.

Several of the envelopes were embossed with a return address for Sherman's Crest Private Hospital, Route 23, Vermont. One of them contained the committment papers for Angela Preston Wyman, diagnosed as suffering from catatonic schizophrenia. Another contained a death certificate, the date was filled in as "approx. November 8," almost seven years back. The cause of death was listed as hypothermia.

chapter 16

The train from Philadelphia was only about five minutes late and Warren Pratt had taken a seat in the lead car, so he was one of the first people to come through the double doors from Track 23. Kinkaid was sitting on a little circular bench in the middle of the concourse floor, looking as if he had been waiting for hours.

"Did you have a good trip?" he asked, smiling tensely as he relieved Pratt of his suitcase after they shook hands.

"It was short, at least. I got on at Princeton."

A good cop will always notice that flicker of uncertainty, but James Kinkaid's face didn't register a thing. He was smart without being a smartass, which was rare in college boys, and he didn't need to be reminded that Terry Vogel had worked for a company based in Princeton.

"Have you had lunch?"

Pratt shook his head, thinking to himself that Kinkaid had nice manners, which was rare in anybody. He could be polite before he was curious. Pratt decided that he liked him.

"I know a good seafood place on the way out of town. Of course maybe you'd . . ."

"Sounds fine," Pratt interrupted. "It's not something you get a lot of in Ohio."

"Fine, then. I'm parked just across the street."

They walked to the main exit together and might not have exchanged another word if Pratt hadn't decided to take pity on the kid.

"I don't think Terry Vogel committed suicide," he said, as if he were announcing a perfectly neutral fact. "He had booked a flight to Austin, Texas, just twelve hours before he died. He was supposed to make a big pitch to some computer company down there, an account his firm had been trying to get for months. It looked like he'd probably get it. Then he drives off to some flophouse in East Philly and goes to bed with a shotgun. That's not the way people kill themselves when they do it on the spur of the moment.

"There's also the fact that Vogel's corpse was found nude."

They were descending the ramp of a basement garage, and as he walked Kinkaid had been fishing around in his jacket pocket for the parking stub. He found it at the last possible moment and handed it to an attendant, who snatched it away as if he were reclaiming stolen property.

"You find that significant?"

"Yes." Pratt nodded, to no one in particular since Kinkaid was watching the attendant as he disappeared into an elevator the size of a phone booth. "Suicides are fairly predictable. The ones who worry about making a mess usually leave their clothes in a neat little pile somewhere and then kill themselves in the bathroom—it's easier to clean up. Our boy's things were lying around on the floor and, besides, why would anybody get undressed if he planned to spatter his brains all over the wallpaper?"

Kinkaid appeared not to be listening. He waited for his car to be brought up—a Mercedes in a particularly unappealing shade of green—tipped the attendant two dollars and then climbed in behind the wheel. In all it was probably about five minutes before Pratt heard his voice again.

"Then why did the Philadelphia police list it as a suicide?"

It was an intelligent question, but it showed that James Kinkaid, Esq., hadn't done a lot of criminal work. Pratt caught himself just in time to keep the note of condescension out of his voice.

"I probably would have done the same thing," he answered. "Homicide has a heavy case load in that town and they had no physical evidence. As a suicide the Vogel case is closed. As a murder it would stay open on their books for-ever. I'm sorry, Counsellor, but that's the way it works."

As if he were negotiating some sort of urban slalom run, Kinkaid drove down a side street that had been reduced to one lane by a broken pattern of double-parked trucks. The Dayton traffic squad would have written enough paper to cover the city's budget for a year, but things must be different in New York.

"Did he check into the hotel alone?"

"Yes. And nobody saw anything. But it's a place that caters to the trade, so nobody would."

"What about Princeton?"

"Just one thing."

Pratt held his breath for a moment as they slipped through an intersection, only just avoiding a cab that had jumped the light. It would be nice to get back to Dayton.

"I talked to a friend of Vogel's from work," he went on. "The friend said Vogel had mentioned something about an old flame."

"When was this?"

"The friend thought it was maybe a day or two before Vo-gel died. He had wondered at the time if maybe there wasn't some connection."

"Did he tell the police?"

"No. The Philly police never sent anyone to Princeton and the locals didn't care. It wasn't their case."

"I guess it isn't a good idea to die away from home."

"It isn't a good idea to die anywhere."

Eddie's was on Second Avenue near 86th, and there was a parking lot across the street. It was the sort of place where the napkins were the size of bed sheets, the waiters wore aprons that hung to within six inches of the floor, and there was a big gray crockery bowl full of oyster crackers in the center of the table. The bartender knew his business but the desserts were terrible, which after all is the defining test of a good seafood restaurant.

"What's a scallop when it's at home?" Pratt asked, staring at the menu as if he just couldn't quite believe it.

"Damned if I know, but they come in little medallions about the size of a poker chip. They cook them with a garlic sauce here."

That, it seemed, was sufficient recommendation. The former homicide lieutenant closed his menu with a snap and laid it flat on the table.

"You've found something out," Pratt said, after the waiter had come and gone, leaving a vodka gimlet next to his water glass. "But you'd be happier if you could keep it to yourself. Probably it would be best if you just told me."

It pleased him that just for an instant Kinkaid let his composure slip. It meant he had been right.

"Is it that obvious?"

"You're paying me a lot of money, Counsellor, and you barely show more than a polite interest. I have to ask myself, what soured you?"

"You can strike Angela Wyman off your list of suspects," Kinkaid said, tearing the corner off a dinner roll as if all he wanted was a look inside. "She's been dead for seven years."

Now it was Pratt's turn to be surprised, but he had the feeling Kinkaid wasn't paying attention.

"You know this for a fact?"

"I have her death certificate in my desk drawer."

"What did she die of?"

"She froze to death."

"Where?"

"In some private loony bin up in Vermont."

"Were you in love with her?"

Kinkaid made a slight gesture with his left hand. It could have meant almost anything. It could even have meant no. But it didn't.

"I was twenty years old and she was the most beautiful creature I'd ever seen," he answered, with the tone of one dismissing his own feelings as beside the point. "I think I was probably responsible for pushing her over the edge, but I'll never know for sure. She killed a man."

"How did she do that?"

"She beat him to death with a shovel."

"She didn't happen to beat his face in, did she?"

Kinkaid actually changed color—he was very far from being a fool and he saw the significance of the question at once. Very slowly, and with obvious reluctance, he managed a slight nod.

"It's just amazing how many people in this case end up that way," Pratt said, with studied casualness. He was careful not to look at Kinkaid. "Billinger had his face sliced off. The whole front half of Terry Vogel's skull was blown away. George Tipton disappeared altogether."

"She couldn't have done it if she's dead," Kinkaid said, with something like real anger in his voice.

He kept it hidden, probably even from himself, but somewhere down there he was still in love with Miss Angela Wyman. Poor sod.

"That she could not." Pratt took a sip of his drink, which was so cold it didn't matter whether it was any good or not. "But somebody ought to check."

It was probably just as well the waiter chose that moment to come back with two dinner salads in wooden bowls. "Now—who has the blue cheese?" he asked, smiling broadly from behind his walrus moustache. "Ground pepper?"

For a long time after he had gone again the two men ate in silence.

"I want to know what happened to all the other members of that football team," Kinkaid said at last. "Will that be difficult?"

"You're talking about twenty-two men, not counting the second stringers."

"My father's list only included the first team offense, and five of them we know about."

"Five? I thought the body count was only up to four."

"One runs a filling station in town—I see him every day. That leaves six names."

"Then if none of them are actually in hiding, I shouldn't have much trouble."

"Good."

"What about Angela Wyman? Do you want me to confirm the death certificate?"

For several seconds Kinkaid appeared not to have heard—appeared not even to be conscious of the other man's presence—but, as Detective Pratt was beginning to figure out, these vacant silences were merely a series of curtains pulled down to screen the man's inner life, a little trick he had picked up somewhere and used whenever he needed a moment to think, or perhaps to reassure himself that his self-mastery remained in place. Finally he shook his head.

"That's something I prefer to see to myself."

"With some people it's like an aura—they were born to serve as raw material for the murderer's art. All you have to do is glance at them and you find yourself imagining how they'll look in the crime-scene photos."

"Is murder an art?"

"In the hands of a true virtuoso, like our killer? Oh, yes." Detective Pratt nodded gravely. "But can't you see your neighbor over there as a natural victim?"

Jim Kinkaid couldn't see him at all, since he was facing away and at a slight angle so Pratt would be able to get a good look without seeming obvious about it. They were standing just in front of the public library, across the street from the Exxon station where Charlie Flaxman was filling somebody's Voyager from the Supreme pump.

"Either that or in the jug for a good twenty-to-life. Charlie's what you might call an authentic bad boy."

"Has he got a record? Any chance I could see it?"

Kinkaid shook his head. "As his lawyer I'd have to object." This made Pratt laugh, so that he seemed to lose interest in

Charlie Flaxman, and the two men continued down the sidewalk and away from the library, where they had been looking at old high-school yearbooks.

"I didn't see your girlfriend in there," he said, conscious that he was needling Kinkaid and not quite sure why.

"She went to a private school in Greenwich. I've never seen a photograph of her."

"Isn't that a little surprising? After all, you'd think her grandmother would have kept at least a snapshot or two."

Kinkaid didn't answer, but Pratt had grown used to having his leading questions ignored.

And yes it was surprising. They had spent part of the morning going through the contents of Mrs. Wyman's writing desk—Kinkaid had apparently cleaned it out, since he had a large cardboard box full of old letters, cancelled checks, photographs of deceased relatives and all the other customary detritus of a long life. Yet there was nothing relating to Angela Wyman except her death certificate and a couple of pieces of correspondence from the hospital where she was sent after flattening out the gardener.

"Are you on good terms with Flaxman?" he went on, deliberately changing the subject. "Do you think he keeps up with his old teammates?"

"I'm his lawyer—or, more correctly, I'm his father-in-law's lawyer—but that isn't the same as being on good terms with him."

"He told you about George Tipton."

"It's a safe bet he wouldn't have if George hadn't been dead. I think I've probably exhausted his fund of confidence."

"Then maybe I could have a word with him."

"Not a chance."

Kinkaid laughed, gently kicking a neighbor child's basketball back up on his front lawn, where it came to rest in a tangle of garden hose.

"You'd be surprised how few people take me for a cop."

"You're an outsider," Kinkaid explained, as if afraid he

had somehow given offense. "Guys like Charlie Flaxman live in a very narrow world, and you weren't born in New Gilead. You also didn't play football with him."

"I'm just as happy about it, considering the fates of some of the ones who did."

They continued on in silence until they reached the wooden sign that announced the law offices of Kinkaid & Kinkaid. The surviving partner looked up and studied the front windows of his house with what seemed to Pratt a peculiar mingling of affection and regret.

"Do you speak any French?" Kinkaid asked unexpectedly.

"Not a word."

"Neither do I." He smiled, expressing the comradeship of a shared affliction. "I wonder if you'd care to go to Paris for me sometime or other."

"Does it relate to this case?"

"Possibly—probably not. I don't know."

They walked up the stone steps to the front door. There were no clients in the waiting room, which was hardly surprising on a Saturday, and the chair behind the receptionist's desk was empty.

Kinkaid's office was small and rather dark, possessed of but a single window that looked out on a narrow strip of lawn and a white board fence. Except for the computer on the desk, it looked like a room out of the last century. There was a very comfortable leather sofa against one wall, and Pratt took his position there while Kinkaid rummaged around in the bottom drawer of his desk.

"How did you happen to put your office in here?"

The question evoked a look of faint surprise, so Pratt smiled.

"I'm just curious. It's the vice of my profession."

Kinkaid glanced about the room as if noticing it for the first time. "It was my grandfather's office," he said.

"Were you particularly fond of him or something?"

"He'd been dead ten years before I was born, so it was

available. I guess it's just inertia. I started doing my homework in here when I was a kid."

At last he found what he was looking for. He pulled out a large manila envelope and undid the clasp, letting the contents spill out over his desk.

"The Wymans had only one child," he explained, as if they had been the topic of discussion all along. "A daughter, Blanche. Hence, if Angela is the granddaughter, Blanche must have been her mother. Angela grew up in Paris, presumably living with her mother, since that is where Blanche died. I have everything here—death certificate, passport, a handful of singularly uninformative letters postmarked over a fifteen-year period, even the rent receipts for her apartment."

"Let me see the passport."

The photo was of a woman in her middle thirties, still girlishly pretty but beginning to show some wear. It was a color photo, so you could see that Blanche Wyman—that was the name under which the passport had been issued—had pale blond hair and used too much makeup.

"This is in her maiden name," Pratt said. "Did she ever marry?"

"There's no record of it."

"Is that what you want me to find out in Paris? Who Angela Wyman's father was?"

"I doubt you will." Kinkaid registered the faintest possible shrug. "If you can find out, great. But what I really want to know is why Blanche Wyman's daughter ended up in a mental hospital."

"Do you want this before or after I find out what happened to your football players?"

"After, but not by much."

chapter 17

There was no town of Sherman's Crest. The nearest town was Guilford, some five or six miles to the east, where the man at the Chevron station couldn't identify the spot in terms of local landmarks.

"That's the nuthouse, ain't it?" he asked, and then, after a second's reflection, looked embarrassed. "Sorry—you got anybody up there?"

"No. It's strictly business."

"Well, I hear it's a nice place."

"That's what I hear too."

Indeed, it lacked nothing on the point of location. As he drove along the winding, single-lane road that was Route 23, with its quaint covered bridges over streams that flowed fast through rock-walled gorges, Kinkaid had to think that, if you had to build a private mental hospital, this was the place to build it. The scenery was pretty, which could be thought to have some therapeutic value, and the patients, with whatever bad habits that rendered them intolerable at home, were safely out of the way. Some people, it appeared, were better loved at a distance.

The hospital occupied about forty acres and nothing could be seen from the road except what nature and the landscapers had put there. The property was fenced with chain-link, but there were plenty of trees around to render the few strands of angled barbed wire both partially invisible and completely useless. The gatehouse was manned by a single guard armed only with his uniform. There were girls' schools with better security.

Kinkaid gave his name and waited to be checked through.

He was expected. The guard told him that Reception was straight ahead.

The road rose for about a hundred yards, crested the top of a slight hill, and then dropped back down, with the effect that the hospital buildings themselves seemed to pop up in front of you like cutouts in a children's book. A couple of the outlying structures were of brick and reasonably nondescript, their function betrayed only by the fact that the windows were set so high up in the walls, but the main unit, which dated back to the Civil War, was entirely of limestone and about as cheerful as a Norman fortress. This was where the public relations stopped. This was not Club Med, but a prison.

Since it was a weekday, there was plenty of room in the guest parking lot. Kinkaid nosed into a space, locked the car and walked up the broad stone steps to the main entrance.

The interior of the building gave a completely different impression. The lobby was comfortably, even expensively furnished and bathed in natural light that came in through windows which were by no means obvious from the outside. As he was looking around, a woman of about fifty wearing an incongruously pretty dress came out of nowhere and asked in the sweetest voice if there was anything with which she could help him.

"I have an appointment with Dr. Crossman," he answered, smiling in spite of himself. "My name is Kinkaid—James Kinkaid."

A moment later a hearty, white-haired man in a blue suit, who somehow reminded one of a college president, came out and seized him by the hand.

"Mr. Kinkaid, it's a pleasure. If you'll just come this way. I'm Crossman."

The hospital director had a large, cluttered office with built-in cherry-wood bookcases. He motioned Kinkaid to a large chair upholstered in crushed purple velvet and then sat down himself behind a desk the size of a billiard table. For a moment he said nothing, merely smiled beatifically, and then the woman with the sweet voice appeared once more as if she could materialize out of thin air.

"Coffee?" Crossman asked, without taking his eyes from Kinkaid's face. "Or perhaps you would prefer tea."

"Tea, thanks."

"Mrs. Linden?"

It took Mrs. Linden no more than thirty seconds to return with a small silver tray bearing two cups, one of which she put on the director's desk and the other on a small table at Kinkaid's right hand. Then she vanished soundlessly.

Crossman took a sip from his cup, seemed to approve it, and then put the cup back down with a ceremoniousness that just missed seeming ludicrous.

"You've come about the Wyman case," he said, as if to remind Kinkaid of the fact. "It was a little before my time—I came here four years ago—but I've read the case history. A sad business. I take it you represent the family."

In the center of the ink blotter on his desk was a Cross pen, one of the gold, thin-barreled kind that work perfectly well as pens but are essentially symbolic. Crossman was rolling it back and forth under the tips of his fingers, as if he enjoyed the feel of it. Possibly he just wanted his visitor to notice it was there.

"The Kinkaids have represented the Wymans for four generations."

Kinkaid allowed himself a slight nod and waited. Yes, the good doctor swallowed it. He even liked it, the way he liked expensive pens and rich patients with Anglo-Saxon names. And he was sufficiently impressed that he didn't notice the evasion.

"Then what can I do for you?"

As a small test of a compliance that came just a shade too quickly, Kinkaid let his response hang fire for three or four seconds. He did not reply, he did not shuffle in his briefcase for papers. He did nothing.

It was an old lawyer's trick, one to which a psychiatrist with decades of experience should have been impervious, but it worked.

The eyes were what betrayed him, their almost imperceptible waver, even as Dr. Crossman continued to smile. They betrayed an anxiety, a protective reflex, a desire to conceal something. They betrayed the fact that there was something to conceal.

"Before my time . . ." Yes, he wanted to shield the hospital, but he couldn't resist the impulse to distance himself from any blame. That made sense now.

So there was a secret about the Wyman case—a small scandal.

Kinkaid now had his edge.

"Doctor," he began, with a kind of ponderous gravity that he knew from experience guilty souls found unsettling, "there are points about the death of Angela Wyman—indeed, about the whole of her time at Sherman's Crest—which need to be clarified."

He smiled, knitting his fingers together over his chest, conveying the impression that, really, nothing needed clarifying because everything was known in advance, that he, James Kinkaid, Esq., had both the hospital and Dr. Edmund L. Crossman firmly in his grasp but that he was prepared, under the right circumstances, to show mercy. On the whole, he thought it one of his better performances.

"It was, as you say, a sad business, Doctor, but we live in an imperfect world. Everyone recognizes that, and no one wishes to be vindictive. All anyone wants is to arrive at something like the truth."

"The truth?" Crossman shook his head and allowed himself one brief, voiceless syllable of laughter. "I'm under the impression that the truth was pretty well established at the time. No one saw fit to question the coroner's verdict. . . ."

"No one questions it now."

"Then what . . . ?"

He looked genuinely bewildered and Kinkaid could hardly blame him. The lawyer of the family of a long-dead patient arrives and, as the administrative head of a hospital, Crossman is certainly prepared for the possibility of a malpractice suit. Yet at once the threat of litigation is withdrawn. Not absent, since it would not do to make anyone too comfortable, but certainly placed at a distance. Of course the doctor is surprised. Perhaps, since everyone loves a little excitement, and since the implied malpractice did not take place on his watch, he is even a trifle disappointed.

Well, just maybe another kind of melodrama can supply its place.

"I take it, Doctor, that you never met Mrs. Wyman." Kinkaid smiled, as if on the verge of sharing a professional confidence.

"You mean the mother?"

"No, the grandmother." He spread his hands, seeming to measure the distance between them. "The mother died in Paris the year of Angela's admission—we know nothing of any father. Mrs. Wyman took the girl in, but she never publicly acknowledged the true character of the relationship. Tell me, do you have any record that she ever visited her granddaughter here?"

There was a table against the wall directly behind Dr. Crossman's desk. Kinkaid had noticed it when he first entered the room because it was littered with thick manila file folders, and, as he had hoped, the doctor now swiveled around in his chair and picked up one of them. Without thinking about it, without ever realizing the crucial significance of his act, he had entered into the conspiracy. He was now sharing information.

He placed the folder in the middle of his desk blotter and opened it. Kinkaid's heart nearly stopped when he saw the photograph of Angela stapled to the inside cover.

"No, there is no record of the grandmother on any of our lists." He paused, and flipped back to the first page. "Now here's something interesting. The commitment forms were signed by a lawyer—a James Kinkaid."

Kinkaid smiled. He felt a sickening giddiness spreading through his chest, but he smiled.

"My late father," he said. "The third of four generations."

"Yes, well . . . it appears that our patient was better served by her lawyer than by her own family, since he seems to have been her sole contact with the outside world. We have him down for three visits, spaced at yearly intervals."

"It is probable that, aside from Mrs. Wyman herself, he was the only person who even realized Angela was here."

It was too much. It was simply too much. Although he continued to smile blandly, Kinkaid could feel the sweat beginning to break out on his face. He felt as if he were about to fall out of his chair.

And yet he went on. Somehow, he contrived to go on.

"In fact it has only been quite recently, since Mrs. Wyman's own death, that what happened to Angela has come to light. I didn't go into partnership with my father until a few years ago, so I myself knew nothing of it until I began to review Mrs. Wyman's papers. . . ."

There was a look that floated briefly across Dr. Crossman's face, something almost like suspicion, to which Kinkaid responded with a faint shrug.

"I was still in college when Angela first came here, Doctor, and by the time I took my law degree she had already been dead for a year. Wyman family business is important to us. And Wyman family secrets are protected. On a matter as sensitive as this my father wouldn't have told me any more than I needed to know, which, as it happened, was nothing."

"Why?" Crossman smiled with a certain faint malice. "Are you indiscreet?"

"No—and neither was my father."

The doctor seemed to consider this for a moment, as if unsure whether to feel rebuffed or reassured. The issue was still in doubt when he spoke again.

"And now you serve another Wyman," he said. "One with presumably different interests?"

"All Wymans are interested in discretion," Kinkaid answered, having chosen to interpret the question as something different. "I am here for no other purpose than to clarify the history of Angela's last few years of life. I have no desire to achieve that end by turning this into a court case, and if I have your cooperation I will gladly provide you with written assurance that nothing I learn here will find its way into any civil action taken against Sherman's Crest, by the Wyman family or by anyone else. That amounts to as comprehensive a guarantee as I am legally entitled to give you."

That was it. He had shot his bolt, and now all he could do was to sit back and see if his promise of immunity—and the implied threat that it contained—would be enough.

Crossman began rolling the gold ballpoint pen beneath his fingers again, which presumably meant that he was thinking the offer through. Then suddenly he picked up the pen and slipped it into his inside jacket pocket.

"There is, of course, the question of patient confidentiality," he said at last.

Kinkaid forced himself to keep from smiling, because he knew now that he had won.

"If I speak to Angela's doctor I'll abide by any restrictions he puts on the conversation." He shook his head, seeming to dismiss the very idea that he would intrude further. "You can remove whatever you think proper from her records before you show them to me. Beyond that, it might be useful if I talked to some of your hospital personnel. The last thing I want, Doctor, is to cause any awkwardness, either for you or for your hospital."

"Well, in that case . . ." Crossman reached over to his telephone and pressed a button. Almost at once Mrs. Linden came soundlessly back into the room, and he turned to her with his college president's smile.

"I wonder if you'd be good enough to take Mr. Kinkaid in charge? See to it that he has everything he wants."

chapter 18

      Marshal Cheffins must have driven straight on through the night, because Angela Wyman was admitted at five-ten on the morning of Friday, May the 11th. He let a couple of orderlies deal with the patient. He didn't come inside, so no one remembered him except as a man sitting in a dark car. No one could remember whether or not he had been wearing a policeman's uniform. Somebody brought him a cup of coffee and eventually somebody had to be sent out to fetch the keys to the handcuffs Angela was wearing, but it was raining heavily that morning so no one was inclined to be especially curious.

Mrs. Linden, however, remembered the lawyer quite well.

"Your father struck me as a very refined sort of person," she told Kinkaid, ten years after the event. "He seemed genuinely distressed about the girl."

"What did he say had happened?"

"I've no idea, but it'll be in the admitting physician's notes. Angela never said and, of course, I never asked."

The case file, which was about an inch and a half thick, was resting on the table between them. They were sitting in the Records Room, where the walls were lined with similar thick manila folders, hundreds of them. They were quite alone, and the sense of isolation was heightened by the presence of so many chronicles of misery.

"You got to know her then?"

"Oh yes! Quite well." Mrs. Linden, whose beautiful voice was capable of the most subtle shades of emphasis, seemed surprised by the question. "She worked for me, here in Records, for two years. She was such a perfect young lady. . . ."

But it was a very different Angela Wyman who arrived in the driving rain that May morning. "Subject unresponsive" was the laconic note on the admission form. "Vital signs normal. No restraints required."

She was sitting on the back seat of Marshal Cheffins' car, wrapped in a blanket, and she had to be carried inside. It wasn't until the beginning of the physical examination that anyone noticed she was handcuffed.

"Responsible party (J. Kinkaid, Esq., family attorney) states that subject violently attacked her grandmother, lapsing into present catatonic state almost immediately afterward."

The signature on the report was indecipherable, but when Kinkaid showed it to Mrs. Linden she recognized it at once.

"That would be Dr. Meckler," she said. "He was on the night shift here until he got his practice established over in Rutland."

"Was he a psychiatrist?"

Mrs. Linden shook her head. "No—I believe he was a dermatologist."

There was no further notation in the case file for nearly two weeks.

"Is that usual?"

"Oh yes. She was on the wards. Unless there's something urgent, the doctors like to give a patient some time just at first."

"Is that policy?"

"It's the general practice."

"On what sort of ward?"

At first Mrs. Linden seemed puzzled by the question, and then unsure if perhaps she shouldn't be offended.

"I mean," Kinkaid went on, when he perceived the danger, "do you have a particular ward to which you assign new patients?"

"Oh no! Why ever would we do that?" She laughed faintly, having decided at last to be amused. "We always have a number of patients in Angela's condition."

Angela's condition, as defined by a specialist in cold sores sometime in the small hours of the morning, just as he was finishing his shift and beginning to look forward to a twenty-mile drive through the rain. If the diagnosis was correct it would have been purely by accident, but it was enough to get her shipped off to some gulag full of wallflowers where, if she wasn't crazy already, she would have learned her trade fast enough. The goods were labeled and put away, warehouse style. This was how you ran a hospital from which nobody was ever expected to come home.

But eventually, one assumed, a less preliminary diagnosis would have been attempted. Kinkaid flipped through the case file, finding the same signature, large and easy to read, on page after page: M. L. Werther.

"Dr. Werther treated her?"

"Yes—I believe for the entire time she was here."

"Would it be possible to speak to him this afternoon?"

"I'm sorry." Mrs. Linden shook her head, as if she were breaking the news of someone's death. "Dr. Werther is retired."

"To Florida?"

"Good heavens, no!" Once again she offered a specimen of her breathless laughter. "I saw him just the other day at the Food Mart."

Careful to try no one's patience, Kinkaid left the hospital at five and drove the half-dozen or so miles back to Quincy, the nearest settlement, which consisted of a single main street and, if the road atlas was to be believed, some six hundred souls.

Once in his room at the Whisper Quiet Motel, he covered about three pages of a yellow legal pad with notes—people get nervous watching a lawyer take notes and, besides, you miss too much of the unspoken side of a conversation if you're busy writing it down, so Kinkaid had trained himself to listen and wait. When he was finished he decided he was hungry.

The motel only had a Coke machine, but the manager directed him to a restaurant called the Surf 'N Turf. "You drive straight through town, take the bridge over the river, and it's just about the last building on your left. The steaks are pretty good, but stay away from the seafood."

"How far is it?"

"Maybe half a mile."

Kinkaid decided to leave his car in the parking lot and walk.

It was depressing to eat alone. Once you had read the menu, which came with a tassel but consisted of only two pages, one for meat and one for fish—and on the principle that it is always wise to follow local advice Kinkaid didn't even glance at the fish side—there was nothing to do except eat. The restaurant was surprisingly large, which somehow made it worse.

To cheer himself up he ordered a glass of white wine, to which the waitress, who was about sixteen and looked as if she had never in her life drunk anything stronger than milk, took exception. "You sure you wouldn't rather have red? It goes better with the prime rib." In the end the wine tasted like paint thinner and left him feeling no more cheerful.

But it was foolish to blame the restaurant, or even his solitude—he wanted to be alone. There was even a sense in which he wanted to be depressed, since there was a certain propriety in the emotion. After all, he was in this tiny hamlet to visit the gravesite of his youth's great illusion, and perhaps if he allowed himself to mourn for it he could at last put it behind him and get on with his life.

Which was why he didn't allow himself to think about Lisa Milano, who gave him her body whenever he wanted it and who he was perfectly aware only waited for permission to offer him the grownup version of everything he thought he had missed with Angela Wyman. Everything which, he now realized, had never been there in the first place.

When he returned from this journey, of which the trip to Sherman's Crest was no more than an emblem, he wanted to do Lisa justice, to be the sweetheart she deserved. He was looking forward to giving it his very best effort. But in the meantime he had to find a way to put ten years of transcendentalized puppy love to rest.

He declined dessert and, as a kind of penance, ended dinner with a cup of strong black coffee, which normally he never touched. It was as bitter as death, but a few swallows were enough to bring reality back into focus.

It was about six-thirty when he came out of the restaurant, and there was only just a hint of twilight. A couple of boys wearing their baseball caps backwards whizzed down the main street on bicycles. There seemed to be no other traffic. On the other side of the bridge was a shopping center with a grocery store, a post office, a laundromat and a pizzeria, but at this hour the parking lot was not even a quarter full. In New Gilead the commuter trains would be disgorging passengers for at least another hour and the roads would be jammed, but it seemed that existence here followed a somewhat different rhythm. For the most part, people were already safe inside the walls of their houses, living their purely private lives.

Feeling a stranger here, Kinkaid speeded up his pace. He was back in his motel room within five minutes.

A swim would have been nice but he hadn't brought any trunks and there was no pool anyway, so he settled for a cold shower. He came out gasping and refreshed and no longer quite so cozily sorry for himself. He dropped into a chair and began studying his notes. After all, that was what he was here for.

M. L. Werther. Kinkaid sat staring at the name for what seemed like forever before he realized that the next move was obvious.

Werther was retired. *"I saw him just the other day at the Food Mart."* The grocery store on the way back had been a Food Mart. The guy was right here in Quincy.

The phone book, which was no more than half an inch thick, confirmed that there was a Morris Werther, M.D., residing at 62 Jasmine Road. His number was 355-3115.

Kinkaid dialed the number and a man's voice answered.

"Hello?"

"Dr. Werther?"

"Yes, speaking."

"Dr. Werther, I would very much like to talk to you about one of your patients. Her name was Angela Wyman."

There was a pause lasting perhaps five or six seconds, and then, "Did you know Angela?"

Not *"Who are you?"* or *"What do you want to talk about?"* or any of the dozens of other things he might have said while he considered what might be the wise or prudent or even the professionally ethical response, but *"Did you know Angela?"* And spoken with a certain longing eagerness. This was our man.

"Yes, I knew her," Kinkaid answered, for once not finding it necessary to hide his feelings. "I knew her when she first came to this country, and then she disappeared. It was only a few days ago that I found out what happened to her."

"And you wish to know more," the doctor said, with a slightly liquid trilling of the 'r' that suggested his first language had not been English. The sentence was phrased not as a question but as a statement of fact.

"Yes. That's why I've come up here."

"Where is 'here'? Where are you now?"

"I'm at the motel here in town. I've come a long way, Doctor, and it would mean a great deal to me if you could spare me just a little of your time."

This time Werther didn't hesitate at all.

"Perhaps I'd better give you directions. . . ."

The house had a screened-in porch around the front and side, and the lights from the windows filled the space with a patchy, yellowish light. Doctor Werther was standing in this enclosure, near the front door, which was open. He looked as if he had been waiting there ever since he had hung up the phone.

As he got out of the car, Kinkaid could hear insects pinging against the screen. There was a certain desperation to the sound.

Werther said nothing as Kinkaid came up the flagstone walkway that looked as if it had been dribbled over the lawn while the rock was still molten. He was waiting to be acknowledged.

"Thank you for seeing me, Doctor," Kinkaid said as he stood just beyond the arc of the screen door, waiting for it to be opened. "It was good of you to take the time."

Angela's psychiatrist seemed to consider this for a moment and at last apparently decided that, yes, it was good of him and opened the door. He stepped back a little as Kinkaid entered and then offered his hand in a gesture that involved only his right arm. He did not smile.

Was he having second thoughts? No, Kinkaid decided. He was merely proud, after the fashion of wounded men, and perhaps a little frightened.

He was small, even a bit dainty, and he wore dark trousers and a sleeveless sweater over a white shirt. He was not bald, but his hair was thinning badly. His eyes were the only thing about his face that anyone would ever remember. They were a clear, cold blue and made him look desperately unhappy.

The sweater was odd, considering the time of year, but it might have been intended to give his appearance a touch of formality.

"Come in, Mr. Kinkaid." He made a gesture toward the open front door. "You must forgive the untidiness of things. I'm not accustomed to visitors."

In fact there was nothing particularly untidy about the inside of the house—at least as much of it as Kinkaid was able to see from the foyer, which opened directly into the living room. Instead, what one noticed was a certain barrenness, a lack of ornament or color, the absence of anything to suggest that there had ever been a woman within these walls. The furniture looked as if no one had ever sat on it and there were no pictures.

"Perhaps we would be more comfortable in my study."

The entrance to Doctor Werther's study was toward the back of the living room and there was another door that probably led to a backyard of some kind, although the curtains over the only window were drawn, so it was impossible to know. There was a rolltop desk against the wall, with a wooden chair. In the center of the room there was another chair, upholstered in worn green leather, and a reading lamp.

There were books everywhere. The walls were covered with an eccentric collection of bookcases, into which books and the small-format magazines that Kinkaid recognized as academic journals were stuffed at all angles. There were piles of books on the floor. Werther even had to clear a stack off the reading chair in order to offer his guest a place to sit down.

There were also several ashtrays, most of them filled with cigarette butts. It was obvious as soon as they came in that this room was the real center of Doctor Werther's house and probably of his life and there was no difficulty in imagining the character of that life.

"As you can see, I am a great reader," he said, giving his 'r's a faintly liquid pronunciation which suggested an origin somewhere in Central Europe. He glanced around the room with just a hint of smug pride. "My profession is one which demands a wide background of information, and the habit has remained with me in retirement. When one loses interest in the things of the mind one is as good as dead, don't you think?"

He did not wait for an answer but reached into the pocket of his trousers for a pack of cigarettes, which turned out to be unfiltered and foreign. He shook one out and lit it with a quick, impatient gesture that suggested long-ingrained habit.

"I trust you do not object. It is my only vice."

Kinkaid shook his head and grinned. "Mine is vanilla ice cream, which is probably worse."

Doctor Werther appeared not to have heard. His unhappy eyes wandered about as if he was already bored and searching for a means of escape. When he spoke again it was with the air of having cleared away all the preliminary nonsense of the conversation.

"So—how well did you know Angela?"

"Well enough to have been in love with her," Kinkaid answered. It was no more than the truth but, stated as such, it was also a deliberate provocation.

And it worked. For just an instant a shadow of pain seemed to move across Werther's face, a hint of something like jealousy. He took a drag from his cigarette, looking as if the stuff made his lungs ache.

"Was she in love with you?" he asked, his voice a little too even.

"There wasn't time to find out." Kinkaid decided it was time to relent. "You were her doctor, so if you have to ask I guess the answer is probably no."

Werther smiled. It was the benign smile of the Father Confessor, for whom there are no sins which are not forgiven in advance.

"She never mentioned your name," he said. "But for the first year she never mentioned anyone's name—she never spoke. And after . . ." He shrugged his thin shoulders. "Love is not a particularly resilient emotion. In the sea of troubles that flooded across Angela's young life just then, it might easily have been overwhelmed."

"What was the matter with her?"

The question seemed to amuse Doctor Werther. "Catatonia—will that do as a label? In psychiatry diagnostic terms are often next to useless because they describe the behavior an illness produces rather than the illness itself. It is thus rather circular, like saying that a patient is unconscious because he is in a coma. But let us by all means agree that Angela was catatonic when she first came to Sherman's Crest."

"Did you cure her?"

"Oh yes." The doctor shrugged again, as if the matter was of only peripheral interest. "I cured her of catatonia, and of other things. She responded very well to drugs and finally, when her mind became more accessible, to psychotherapy. She was, in many ways, the triumph of my career. And then, of course, they murdered her."

chapter 19

"**I shall always blame** them," Dr. Werther continued, as he moved toward describing his first encounters with Angela Wyman. "Her family and the institution both were more than eager to bury her alive in that place. And they did so without the slightest inkling of what they so casually destroyed. It was a tragic waste. I suspect that in all the world I was the only one who understood what she suffered. . . ."

Morris Werther would have been nearing sixty on the day Angela was admitted to Sherman's Crest. He had graduated without particular distinction from one of the New York State medical schools and turned to psychiatry in his forties, after nearly fifteen years of general practice in upstate New York. Instead of the teaching position he had hoped for, his career had led him to a number of large public mental hospitals, at each of which he would stay for a few years before moving on. In every profession it was a typical pattern for disappointed men.

Sherman's Crest had been his last refuge, and he stayed until he qualified for a pension. He had been there not quite two years when Angela arrived.

"There are many types of catatonia, Mr. Kinkaid. Not all of them are the rigid marble statues of popular fiction. Some repeat a particular action endlessly, like this. . . ." Dr. Werther put his two hands together so that only the palms and fingers were nearly touching. Then he let them bounce together in silent, mechanical clapping. "Some are as malleable as wax, allowing you to pose their limbs in any position you wish, only to droop slowly in a kind of slow-motion swoon. Some can walk if they are led, as if they must derive the will to motion from another person. It depends on the nature of the psychosis.

"True catatonia is considered a subcategory of schizophrenia, which is probably chemical in origin. Thus it is treatable with drugs, but traditional psychotherapy, what has come to be known as 'the talking cure,' yields little in the way of clinical results. I never believed that Angela was a true catatonic."

He was working on his third cigarette by then, and he had grown sufficiently relaxed around his guest that he no longer troubled to brush the fragments of fallen ash from his sweater. From time to time a slight and no doubt completely unconscious smile played across his face. It was almost as if he had fallen into a trance of recollection.

"In those early months Angela never spoke. She seemed oblivious to the presence of others. Yet if someone brought a spoonful of food to her lips she would accept it. If she was brought to a toilet and made to sit down upon the commode, she would empty her bowels. Once at night, while one of the nurses was putting her to bed, I heard her reciting 'Now I lay me down to sleep' to herself—very softly, as though having been reminded of something. One gradually developed the sense that she needed reminding that she was alive.

"A true catatonic, you see, is perfectly aware of his or her surroundings. Their behavior is not retreat; it is, rather, a rational response to an irrational crisis. For instance, I once had a patient who, while in remission, told me that she had believed that the Battle of Armageddon was being fought inside her body and that she was personally so evil that any movement she made could only aid the forces of darkness. Thus for eighteen months she did not move a muscle—a reasonable, even an heroic response once one accepts her premises.

"Angela was nothing like that," he said, making a dismissive little gesture with his right hand, a motion which stirred the cigarette smoke as if he were trying to find something in it. "Angela had simply chosen to go away somewhere inside herself. And sometimes she could be briefly summoned back. After a time, she was summoned back to stay."

"Then what was the matter with her? Was it depression?"

At first Werther appeared to be merely annoyed by Kinkaid's interruption, but after a moment or two he seemed actually to be turning the suggestion over in his mind.

"It was very like depression," he answered finally. "But then so many things are *very like* and yet not. Was she unhappy in her private place? Was she anything at all? When she came out of it, she was never able to tell me.

"And she did come out of it. About six months after she was admitted, the nurses found her one night sitting up in bed, her face buried in her hands, sobbing like a frightened child. She didn't know where she was, she had no memory of attacking her grandmother, she had no notion of what had happened to her. It was as if she had been asleep for half a year and the time in between was nothing more than a confused dream."

"And she had no relapses?"

"No, none. It was as complete a remission from a psychotic episode as I have ever witnessed."

"Did she ever remember the incident with her grandmother?"

"No."

"Did you ever speak to Mrs. Wyman about it?"

For just an instant Werther seemed not to know whom he was talking about, and then he remembered.

"She was not a particularly sympathetic character, was she," he said, smiling through the blue haze of his cigarette smoke. "Strong-willed, but a stranger to herself. I never met her, although I spoke to her three or four times over the telephone. I only asked her general questions. I find that is best. Specifics do not reveal so much about the inner life.

"She made only one glancing allusion, if that was what it was. 'It is not to be lost sight of that my granddaughter is a most dangerous person.' Angela must have thrown a scare into the old woman, which I don't imagine was easy."

For just an instant Werther seemed to be waiting for this assumption to be affirmed or denied. When it was neither he apparently lost interest.

"She was not dangerous," he went on. "If she were she would have killed her grandmother because she possessed both a systematic intelligence and considerable strength of character. Combine these with rage and you have a genuinely formidable lunatic. I am inclined to think that the attack, if there really was one, was probably more rhetorical than real."

Kinkaid found himself wondering what Dr. Werther would say if he knew that Angela Wyman had not attacked her grandmother, rhetorically or any other way, but had beaten a man's face in until it was no longer even recognizably human. Sixteen years old, and she had conned her doctor so well that the con had lasted from that day to this.

It made you wonder what else he had missed along the way.

"And what happened then?" Kinkaid asked. "I mean, once she had come out of her trance."

"She returned to normal life—or as normal a life as is possible within the confines of a madhouse."

Werther made a vague circular gesture with his right hand, leaving a trail of cigarette smoke in the air and somehow implying, doubtless without intending to, that the madhouse was this very room.

"She undertook a course of psychiatric treatment, which was still in progress at the time of her death. After a year it was judged no longer necessary to continue her medication and after two years she was given a clerical job, simply in order that she would have something with which to occupy her time."

"What did Angela talk about during her treatment?"

If the question was an intrusion of anyone's privacy, living or dead, Werther never gave any sign.

"She talked about Paris, her childhood—her mother," he

replied, with that same touch of wistful longing Kinkaid had noted over the phone. "She loved her mother intensely, the way children tend to love a wayward parent. But that is blindness, not insanity. It soon became clear to me that there was no compelling reason why she could not have been released."

"So why wasn't she?"

The doctor frowned, as if annoyed. "That is a question most appropriately addressed to Mrs. Wyman."

"But since she is not alive to answer it, I'm asking you."

"Because Angela was an embarrassment," Werther replied, even more annoyed. "Because, in certain families, people who go into mental hospitals do not come out. Because Angela could not bring herself to defy that dreadful old woman."

"Did Angela ever ask to be released?"

"No, she never asked. So in the end, when she could bear it no longer, she ran away. And that was how she died."

As he spoke the misery in his eyes clarified into what perhaps it had always been—a grieving love that could never be acknowledged, even to himself.

It was December, on the last Friday before Christmas, and the weather reports were full of storm warnings. The last time anyone on the staff saw her alive was at five o'clock when Angela walked Mrs. Linden out to the parking lot, as she did every Friday afternoon, and told her to have a nice weekend. She waved goodbye, smiling. Mrs. Linden didn't notice anything out of the ordinary.

Angela did not show up for dinner, but there was nothing unusual about her skipping a meal. She had her own room in the main building and, although she was subject to bed checks, no one looked in on her that night. No one looked in on her most nights. She had been so quiet for so long that most of the staff treated her as one of themselves. It was simply difficult to remember she was a patient.

She might not have been missed before Monday morning, when Mrs. Linden returned, if she hadn't received a package in the Saturday mail. Someone took it up to her room and noticed that the window had been left open. By the middle of the afternoon they knew she was gone. She had gone over the wall Friday night, a fact confirmed more than a week later by one of the inmates, who had seen her from his second-floor balcony, walking away into the darkness, bundled in a tan shearling coat that reached almost to the ground.

"Are you quite sure it was her?" he was asked.

"Oh yes. I saw her face when she turned to look back at the building. She knew I was there. She meant for me to see her."

"How do you know?"

"Because I'm there most nights at about that time, and she knew it. What doesn't she know, our Angela? If she hadn't meant to be seen, why else would she have come that way? You'll never bring her back here."

And they never did. By late Saturday afternoon a furious snowstorm had developed, the worst anyone could remember that early in the winter—twelve inches in as many hours, and more to come. It was days before anything like an organized search could be mounted. And by then they were pretty sure she was dead.

It stood to reason. There were no reports of any stolen cars, even presuming Angela knew how to drive. The bus only came through Quincy once every three days. You bought your ticket at the drugstore, where Mr. Mayfield the pharmacist didn't recognize her picture. Beyond that, Quincy was the sort of town where strangers were noticed, and there was nowhere else to hide.

That left the hills, which were under waist-high snow by Monday morning, and that was where a troop of cub scouts found her in the late spring.

She was at the base of a sixty-foot cliff, from which she must either have fallen or jumped because her face had been smashed in on the rocks below. Besides, by then the animals had been at her. On the basis of a general physical description, along with the shearling coat, the county coroner made a tentative identification, which was later confirmed by a forensic technician from the FBI, who had been able to take a few fingerprints from the tattered corpse.

"She had not mentioned going home in over a year," Dr. Werther said. "This alone should have alerted me. Yet I could not disguise my astonishment when she disappeared. She was not a fool, Mr. Kinkaid, and there was a clock radio on the night table in her room. She had heard the same weather reports as everyone else. I can only conclude that she meant to die."

"Where was she buried?"

"At Sherman's Crest—they have their own cemetery. She is buried there."

In a seemingly unconscious gesture, the doctor brought his right hand up to touch his chest, as if to say "And here, in my heart."

chapter 20

The next morning Kinkaid did look up the coroner who had performed the initial autopsy, but he wasn't very helpful.

"She was a mess. The fall just about pulverized her face. She was so broken up there was almost no chance of identifying her through dental records. And the badgers had been at her hands. The FBI man who did the fingerprint work was a genius—he injected the pads with water and managed to get two partials. But it was her, that I can guarantee you."

He was virtually the only person outside the hospital who had had any contact with Angela, living or dead.

And inside it was not much better. Perhaps it was the isolation, or perhaps it was the nature of the work, but Sherman's Crest had a high employee turnover. Thus in a mere six years Angela Wyman had faded into legend. Only a few members of the staff had more than heard of her, so Dr. Werther's version of her death had to stand as gospel.

It wasn't very long before Kinkaid had run out of people to interview.

"What about the patient who saw her the night she escaped?" he asked Mrs. Linden.

"Jimmy?" There was a certain note of incredulity in her lovely voice. "You want to talk to Jimmy Carfax?"

"Why? Isn't he here anymore?"

"Oh, he's here. He's one of our lifers." She glanced down and began smoothing away the creases in her skirt, as if conscious of having committed some indiscretion.

"Then can I talk to him?"

Yes, Kinkaid could talk to him, although no one was very

enthusiastic about the idea. Jimmy Carfax, it seemed, was one of those inmates who give mental institutions a bad name.

His room—or, rather, his suite of rooms, since he was very comfortably provided for—was in a locked wing of the main building. Dr. Crossman himself accompanied Kinkaid as far as the door, which he opened with his own key. They were met on the other side by a male orderly with a wrestler's build and crewcut-length blond hair who wore his hospital whites like a combat uniform.

"Vincent here will explain the procedures, Mr. Kinkaid. Be sure you pay attention and you won't have any problems. Vincent, Mr. Kinkaid would like a few words with Jimmy."

Vincent nodded and crossed his bulging arms over his chest. He didn't speak until Dr. Crossman had closed the door behind him, as if that were one of the rules.

"Do you smoke, Mr. Kinkaid?" he asked finally, without any preamble. When Kinkaid shook his head, Vincent seemed to approve. "Good. Then you won't be tempted into offering Jimmy a cigarette or accepting one of his. Keep your distance and you'll be fine. I'll be right outside the door if he gets frisky, but he won't. He's vicious, but you're a grown man and he's not a fool. He doesn't like to be hurt. Just remember, don't give him an opening. Did Dr. Crossman tell you what Jimmy did to get in here?"

"No."

"When he was fourteen years old he barricaded his sleeping parents into their bedroom and burned the house down around them. Keep it in mind."

Vincent then led Kinkaid through another door, behind which another muscular orderly was lounging behind a desk, reading a paperback copy of *Jane Eyre*.

"Everything quiet?"

The man looked up from his book and nodded. "Like in church," he said.

There was a steel folding chair leaning against the wall. Vincent picked it up and carried it under his arm like a newspaper as they walked down a corridor lined with doors painted a dreadful apple-green. Jimmy's was the last one.

He turned his key in the lock and opened the door a few inches. "Jimmy, you have a visitor," he shouted. Then he unfolded the chair and sat down.

"Go on in. And remember, I'll be right outside."

He smiled encouragingly.

The instant he touched it Kinkaid knew that the door was solid metal. It swung noiselessly on its hinges and revealed a room which, save for the metal bars on the outsides of the windows and the smell of cigarette smoke, might have been the bedroom of a twelve-year-old boy. The walls were covered with posters—Spiderman, various rock stars, an unidentified woman in a French-wrap swimsuit. On a small writing desk at the foot of the bed was a high-end Macintosh computer and several boxes of game software. From the ceiling were suspended by fishing leaders perhaps twenty model aircraft, each swaying and turning at a slightly different rate, depending on their relative size and their distance from the air-conditioning vent.

But the person who was seated at a polished teak worktable, putting together the pieces of an intricate-appearing replica of an antique plane, was not twelve, for all that the look on his face expressed an oblivious concentration that normally does not last very far into adolescence. This person was in late middle age, with gray, riverboat-gambler sideburns, rectangular eyeglasses with thick lenses and the build of a sumo wrestler gone to the bad.

He was immense. His face was so bloated with fat that the lobes of his ears were pushed out at nearly right angles. His eyes seemed lost in their sockets, so that it was difficult even to tell their color. He must have weighed more than three hundred pounds—he seemed half crushed by his own weight, so much so that even across the room one could hear his labored, wheezy breathing. His fingers were so thick that Kinkaid was astonished by the delicacy of his movements as he fitted the tiny landing gear to the underside of the right wing.

There was a cane, made of dark wood and at least an inch thick, leaning against the edge of the table. Clearly, moving around such a vast bulk required assistance.

"Mr. Carfax—Jimmy." Kinkaid waited eight, perhaps ten seconds, until he saw the man's head jerk up, as if he had been startled from a trance. "I wonder if I could speak with you."

"You're the lawyer," Jimmy answered in a lisping, child-like voice. "You're the one who's been nosing around about Angel."

Then he smiled. He tilted his head back slightly, so that the lenses of his glasses glared yellow from the overhead lights, and smiled in triumph. *That'll teach you,* the smile said.

"You've caused a lot of excitement," he went on. "I've heard all about you. I hear everything. But I'm forgetting my manners. Please, sit down."

Aside from the one taken up by Jimmy, which was really a sort of bench, there were two other chairs in the room, a matched pair with no armrests and a seat upholstered in red leatherette. One was beside the door and the other was across the table from Jimmy himself and therefore within reach of the cane, should he decide to pick it up and use it to crack his visitor's skull. The choice was important apparently, a test of sorts, since Jimmy had studiously avoided indicating which chair he meant Kinkaid to occupy.

Kinkaid took the one next to the table.

"You look nervous, Counsellor. Did they tell you that I bite?"

"They told me all kinds of things," Kinkaid answered, with a brief smile.

"Well, every word of it is true. I'm afraid I was always something of a problem child—at least before I turned into such a wreck. Have a chocolate?"

Jimmy picked up a rectangular box, about two inches deep,

and held it out to Kinkaid. Of the few remaining pieces most had already been chewed at and left for dead.

"I'll pass, thanks."

"You're sure?" He shook the box, making the empty paper doilies rustle dangerously. "See's. They're not available around here, but I have three pounds flown in from California every week—a friend of mine put me onto them. I like the caramels best. Oh well . . ."

He set the box down again and immediately reached down to open a drawer that was out of Kinkaid's line of sight. He came up again with a pack of cigarettes and a butane lighter. There were two large ashtrays on the table and they were both nearly full.

"I'm not supposed to have these," Jimmy said. "At first they were afraid I'd burn the place down, which was just a *little* unreasonable of them, but now they're only worried about the state of my lungs. So I'm forbidden to smoke. But, you know, it's a funny thing—you leave a twenty-dollar bill out in plain sight in the morning and by the afternoon there'll be a carton of Carlton menthols hiding under your pillow."

He smiled again, not very nicely. He wanted it understood that he was in control here.

"Did you know Miss Wyman well?"

The question seemed to amuse him. The eyeglasses began flashing again as he shook his head.

"It's a tough question, Counsellor. The answer is, not as well as I would have liked to but better than anyone else around here. Or maybe anywhere else, for that matter. Angel wasn't the confiding type, but I think we understood each other."

"Tell me about her?"

"Tell you what, Counsellor?"

"Anything you like, provided it's the truth. And my name is Kinkaid. James Kinkaid."

"Same as me—isn't that sweet." He laughed, making a

kind of gurgling sound deep in his chest, and then stopped short, as if he had just remembered something.

"But wait a minute. There was another lawyer named Kinkaid, if memory serves. Came around every few years to check on Our Lady of Transcendent Psychosis. Any relation?"

"The name of the firm is 'Kinkaid & Kinkaid.' We represented the Wyman family."

"Past tense? Did they fire you?"

"There aren't any left."

"Aren't there now. Then what are you doing here?"

The smile on Jimmy Carfax's broad, rubbery face seemed to stretch the skin so tight that he looked in danger of splitting straight across from ear to ear. Did he want an answer or was he just seizing an advantage?

"A little unfinished business," Kinkaid said, making it clear that that was all the information he was prepared to give.

But it seemed to be enough. Jimmy finally lit his cigarette, giving the impression he had lost interest in everything else.

"I sometimes wish I hadn't killed the folks," he breathed out with his first puff of smoke. "Then *I* could have been a lawyer. It would have been so gratifying to a nature as vicious as mine."

"When you saw Angela that last time, did you know what she intended to do?"

"To escape? Oh yes! I can't think why, though. This place is paradise."

"Apparently she didn't agree."

"Well, Angel's was a rather complicated nature. Not like me. I'm a simple soul who lives for pleasure. I get all my toys through the magazines, and UPS Ground will see to it that I don't perish from hunger. Cigarettes and sex I can get without leaving the room—the staff here is *very* obliging. What more could you ask for? Pure bliss. I knew it would be like this when I torched my parents."

"We were talking about Angela."

"Well, maybe *you* were. . . ."

Jimmy snorted with laughter and waggled his head from side to side, just to prove he was only having his little joke. His enjoyment of it was somehow a profoundly repulsive spectacle.

"Yes yes, all right. I'll be good," he went on at last, after his amusement had worn a bit thin. "Yes well, Angel, silly girl, wanted out."

"Did she ever tell you that?"

"Oh good heavens *no*! She wasn't the chatty sort. And, besides, she didn't like me."

He pretended to be hurt by this and stuck out his lower lip in a pout, causing his massive, bloated face to sag like bread dough hung over a stick. Kinkaid tried his best to ignore it.

"Then how do you know?" he asked.

"How do you know that Pee Wee Herman is queer? You just *know*. Besides, nobody is that goody goody unless they want to bolt."

Kinkaid raised his eyebrows, as if acknowledging the justice of the observation. It was, in fact, a good point, but that didn't really matter. What mattered was that Jimmy Carfax was more than a little vain about his insight into the Human Condition. What mattered was to keep him talking.

"Was she that? Goody goody, I mean . . ."

"Oh God, yes! She had them all fooled—listening to the staff around here, you'd have thought she was Mother Teresa and Grace Kelly, all rolled up into one. But inside, where they couldn't see, she was coiled like a spring."

"But she didn't have you fooled."

"Not me, the little precious. But it takes one to know one."

"One what?"

"I think you know what, Counsellor. That's why you're here."

The cigarette was nearly finished so Jimmy stubbed it out in the ashtray, somehow giving the impression that he had grown disappointed with it. Then he sagged ponderously to one side to retrieve his cane, which he then laid across the table, within easy reach. He sat quietly, his hands folded across his belly, his tiny eyes narrowed in speculation, as if interested to see how the implied threat would be received. When it was ignored he seemed to lose interest.

"You don't spook easily, Mr. Kinkaid," he went on at last, in the tone of someone making a perfectly neutral observation. "Would it surprise you to learn that most people are frightened of me?"

"No, that wouldn't surprise me."

"What frightens you? Death? Disgrace? The truth?"

"All three."

Jimmy Carfax seemed to consider this answer for a moment, and then he nodded.

"Let me tell you a story," he said, his gaze fixed on a point just above Kinkaid's right shoulder. "Once there was a delightful young lady named Angel who got a trifle excited one night and slammed her grandmother around a little—or so my snitches tell me. And for this offense they dumped her in the loony bin, not just for a while but for life. Do you like that story, Mr. Kinkaid? No? Neither do I. It seems a bit excessive, doesn't it. I mean, after all, whose grandmother could be that much of a bad sport? You know what I think our Angel did to get herself put away here? I think she whacked somebody."

He waited, his head cocked a little to one side, for his hypothesis to be confirmed or denied, but Kinkaid merely smiled.

"A little before my time," he said. "You might be right for all I know."

"You know, Mr. Kinkaid."

"Then tell me something I don't know. Tell me what you saw that last night."

His suitcase was in the trunk of his car and he had checked out of his motel room. In half an hour James Kinkaid would be on his way back to Connecticut, but he had one more call to make before he left Sherman's Crest.

"She passed directly underneath my window," Jimmy Carfax had said. "There are just two places she could have picked to go over the fence, both well the other side from the main entrance, and my room faces the front. I was rather flattered that she went so far out of her way for little old me. She even looked up, just to be sure I was there."

"Why would she do that?"

"Because she needed a credible witness—after all, I'm not crazy. And she knew I wouldn't be inconveniently eager to tattle on her."

Naturally not. After all, the escape would lose its entertainment value too quickly if Angel didn't get a good running start.

"So the next question is, why should she want a witness, credible or otherwise?"

"Because someone had to see the coat, dear boy."

And thus a mystery attached itself to the beginning of Angel's last journey, because Jimmy would say no more. He lapsed into an amused silence, leaving his visitor to figure the rest out for himself.

But it was the end of that journey with which Kinkaid felt he had now to come to terms, so his final stop was the hospital's cemetery.

"You won't have any trouble finding it," the grounds-keeper had told him. "All the graves have markers and we lay them out in order. If you know when she died you'll find her."

The cemetery was almost half a mile from the main building. You followed a narrow gravel road that led nowhere else and you came to a low stone wall surrounding an area about half the size of a football field but sloping gently downward. The grass had been cut recently but, judging from the length of the clippings that had been left scattered about, this was not something that happened more than three or four times in a summer.

The earliest graves, dating from the late 1870s and, in

some cases, marked with impressive granite headstones, were near the entrance and revealed no particular pattern. Order, it seemed, began with the new century. Thereafter it was possible to chart a rough history of Sherman's Crest.

In May of 1905 there had been a epidemic of some sort—Kinkaid found no less than twenty-two graves dating from that month. Judging from the number of burials, the '20s must have been a high tide in the hospital's fortunes, but the '30's were correspondingly lean. The '40s and '50s seemed to stretch on forever, but after about 1960 the cemetery population began thinning out. Perhaps the inmates' families started bringing their dead home for burial, or perhaps it was due to improvements in treatment. It was just as well, because the markers ran to within twenty or thirty feet of the far wall.

The graves of the last few decades were forlorn affairs, most of them consisting of no more than a low stone, no bigger than a brick, with a brass plate bolted to it. Angel's was one of these.

He knelt down beside the tiny marker and with his fingertips brushed away the grass clippings from its inscription. "Angela Wyman" it read—she would have been just twenty.

Except that Jimmy Carfax had been right. She had meant him to see the coat. She had intended it to be found, when they would need so broad a hint as that to help them identify the body buried here. Because, whoever she was who occupied this grave, she was not Angela Wyman.

chapter 21

Freddie Ju had eaten lunch at Curly's two days running, and he was afraid Cheffins was beginning to notice him. This town made him nervous. It was too small and full up with fucking Caucs, so that even in his Con Ed uniform, which in the city just about made him invisible, he stood out like a fucking hard-on. The shit you had to do to get a little ahead in this life.

It was a straightforward enough job—assuming there was ever anything straightforward about topping a bull—and he was almost home. Someone else had been here ahead of him to check out the mark's habits, so all Freddie had to do was a quick double-check, then whack the guy and then climb on the bus back to New York. It would be all over by rush hour, but he just didn't like the way this backwoods doughnut had eye-fucked him coming through the door.

I got you made, kid, that look had said. *I know all about you.* It wasn't anything new to get braced up by a cop. You just didn't expect to get made that fast out here in Frog Hollow. It was a little unsettling.

Or maybe Matt Dillon didn't much like Asians. Like there was some fucking line drawn through White Plains and the nice citizens of New Gilead expected to leave all that ethnic shit behind them when they got on the commuter train. Freddie thought he could deal with that. In a way it was safer if the guy was just your average bigot, and Freddie would have the pleasure of returning the compliment when he blew the fucker's head off.

Of course there was the owner. Curly was a gook in a white apron who brought his customers their food on a pewter tray and engaged them in light banter as he cleared away the dirty dishes. *That,* apparently, was okay. Gooks were supposed to be cooks, just like niggers could be musicians. Just sit on the wrong side of the counter, though, and you got funny looks from John Law.

Well, John Law was about to get his fucking toupee shot off.

It helped, Freddie had to admit. It helped that he could hate the guy, even if it was just a little. This would be the first time he had ever offed anybody and he was scared. Not scared that he wouldn't be able to do it, or even that he might get caught. He had a good plan and you could get away with anything if you had a good plan. He was just scared in general.

He figured it would pass off once he got going.

It would have to. This was a big career move. This would open a lot of doors if he didn't mess it up.

He had taken the call at his girlfriend's.

"It's for you," she had said, and then got out of bed and danced her round little ass into the bathroom so he could be alone with the phone—an unnecessary precaution as it turned out, because Connie wouldn't have understood a word. Connie was her stage name. She was a Korean hooker, and Freddie's friends didn't really approve. Even a Cauc would have been better.

"Do you know who this is?" the voice asked in Cantonese. Not your second-generation pidgen, but the real thing.

"Yes."

"Then if you can spare the time from your whore, come down here."

Three minutes later he was dressed and out on the street. He never even said goodbye to Connie.

He knew where to go, just like he knew the voice on the phone. It was showtime.

Mother Ting's was a tea shop down on Mott Street. The tea shop was cover for the gambling up on the second story, which in turn was cover for the narcotics business that was conducted one floor above that. People with the right connections still did a big business in crack, even if everyone said the future belonged to the designer drugs. Until now they had only used Freddie as a mule, but you didn't get a call from Mr. Quong if the only place you were going was the Eighth Avenue bus terminal.

Freddie did not know what he had expected when he climbed the stairs to the third floor, but what he found was a narrow corridor, the floor covered with green linoleum tiles, some of which were beginning to curl at the edges. All the doors along both sides were closed with that finality suggestive of heavy deadbolt locks—all of them except one, which was open about half an inch, just enough to throw a sliver of yellowish light across the wall.

"Come!" a voice commanded in response to his tentative knock. It was the same voice he had heard over the phone.

"Come in, God dammit," Mr. Quong said, in English, perhaps only to prove that he could. "Come in, and close the fucking door."

He was sitting behind his desk, a small, squat figure in his shirtsleeves, his tie undone, a pair of square-framed reading glasses pushed up into his slicked-back gray and black hair. He was probably about sixty, with a bulldog face and slightly protruding eyes that made him look like a Chinese J. Edgar Hoover. His hands, the nails of which glistened, were pressed palms down against the ink blotter, as if he were about to push himself up.

"You picked up bad habits running with the Dragons." He shook his head, which suddenly looked as big as a pumpkin. "You boys did some bad shit."

Freddie said nothing. He wouldn't have known what to say. The whir from the rotating fan on top of one of the filing cabinets seemed to fill the tiny room.

"You see those guys anymore?" Mr. Quong asked, a note of wariness having crept into his voice.

"Not for a while," Freddie was at last able to answer. "I see them around—you know. It was just kid stuff."

"Kid stuff. You bet." Mr. Quong nodded, as if he liked that answer. "Gouging protection money from the grocery stores down on Mulberry Street. Lots of rough stuff without much payoff. Kid stuff. And now you run crack for me. I guess maybe you're looking to move up in the world."

Freddie started to say something and then thought better of it—or, more accurately, he simply lost his nerve. This made Mr. Quong smile. If anything, his smile was even more terrible than his suspicion.

"That's okay, kid," he said. "Nothing wrong with a little ambition. I got a job for you if you feel up to it, something to oblige the friend of a friend. It's all been worked out in advance, so you'll just be in and out. . . ."

You didn't refuse a thing like that. You refuse Mr. Quong and he picks up the phone the minute you leave the office. Two blocks later something inconvenient happens.

A small-town cop, so there wouldn't be the heat you'd get if you dumped one of New York's Finest. Just push the button and leave. Nobody would care.

"You do this right and I'll remember it," Mr. Quong had said. "I been watching you. I can use somebody with guts and a few brains. And my friend's friend will have a little something for you when it's over.

"And get rid of that Korean bitch, or you'll end up behind the counter in a produce store. Find yourself a nice hometown girl to stick your dick in."

So Connie was yesterday's menu. He wouldn't even say goodbye—he wouldn't have to. Like the man said, he was looking to move up in the world.

But to do that he had to pull the plug on Wild Bill, the Law North of the Parkway.

Someone had done their homework. The marshall lived just south of town, and if you walked a hundred yards or so up a dirt road just past the second stop sign on Tunbridge Lane you had an unobstructed view of the back of his garage. Take a car, they had told him. If you park it just twenty feet back into the piney woods no one will spot it, and this is a town where people are suspicious of a man on foot.

Tuesday was Cheffin's poker night, so he always came home for dinner. All you had to do was wait.

The road apparently saw some use as a lovers' lane because there were a couple of used condoms lying around under the bushes. This spoke well of its privacy and Freddie planned to be long gone before it was dark enough for the teenagers to go into heat. He took a blue British Airways flight bag from the trunk of his car and set out back through the trees.

The garage was just as it had been described to him, a wooden shed at the back of the property. It had a set of double doors that looked like they had been left open for decades, and there were no windows. It was going to be almost too easy.

He was waiting at the back when he heard the marshal's car on the gravel driveway. He unzipped the flight bag and took out a .22 automatic fitted with a silencer. For close work a .22 was best and there were nine hollow-point bullets in the magazine. The pistol was guaranteed cold and untraceable.

Freddie edged nervously up the side of the garage. The car was in the garage now. He was nearly up to the entrance when he heard the motor cut off.

Then the car door opened. There were the sounds of someone clambering out, apparently with some difficulty, and then the car door slammed shut again. This was it.

Freddie stepped around to the garage entrance. He held the pistol in both hands. It was dark in there, but he could make out the outline of Cheffins' tan shirt.

"Who the fuck are you?" the marshal asked. His answer was four bullets in the chest. The distance was no more than fifteen feet, and each time the pistol went off with no more noise than the pop of a bubblegum balloon.

But he was tough. He just stood there, big dark stains on

his shirt front, looking surprised. So Freddie shot him once more in the throat, and then he went down.

Freddie snicked on the garage light. He was shaking all over. Very cautiously, he walked up on Cheffins and was a little surprised to discover the guy was still alive—not by much, but alive. Freddie pressed the muzzle of his pistol against Cheffins' head and pulled the trigger one last time. That settled that.

There was an oil rag on a little counter along the wall. Freddie picked it up and used it to wipe off the pistol, which he then dropped beside the body. Best to leave it behind rather than take the risk of being caught with it. Then he turned off the garage light and stepped outside. Standing in the doorway, he could just make out the soles of the marshal's shoes. It was six o'clock and the light was failing. No one was going to find anything before tomorrow morning.

Freddie walked back through the woods, forcing himself not to hurry. So far he had done everything right. He hadn't made a move that wasn't according to plan. All he had to do now was avoid getting picked up, and the best way to do that was to act natural and not lose his cool.

The walk did him good. By the time he got back to his car he had gotten over the jitters and was perfectly calm again.

The car was one he had rented with a stolen credit card. He dropped it off in Stamford and walked to the bus station. By eleven o'clock he was back in New York.

Now all he had to do was get paid.

His instructions were clear. He was to phone Mr. Quong's office with the message "birds fly south," simply to confirm that the job was done. Then he was to get back on a bus and go to Atlantic City, to the Oasis Hotel, where a reservation in the name of "Mr. Chan" would be waiting for him. The hotel was owned by associates of Mr. Quong, so he would be perfectly safe there. He was to wait in his room, seeing no one except the room service waiters, until Cheffins' death was confirmed in the newspapers. Then someone would contact him. He would get money and an airline ticket. It was thought best that he stayed out of the country for four or five months, so he figured that the money would have to be a comfortable chunk.

The only thing that bothered Freddie was the question he was probably never going to get answered: what made a small-town cop worth all this trouble? You could get a street hustler or a pimp done for five hundred, and the going rate on serious homicides was only four or five thousand. Cops were a little more because you had to bring in outside talent and that meant brokers' fees, but still it wasn't a fortune. Even a good hitter had to do eight or ten jobs a year just to earn a decent living.

But this thing with Cheffins was being treated like a real celebrity whack—four or five months was a long time to spend lying in a deck chair on somebody else's tab. It didn't make a lot of sense.

But Freddie was prepared to collect his money and keep his questions to himself. It was a good deal and he wasn't going to argue with it.

The hotel lobby looked very nice, the one time he passed through it, and his room even had a bar. That was about all he got to see of Atlantic City. One time he tried to go down to the casino, but he didn't even make it to the elevator. Some huge ginny in a blue suit appears out of nowhere, takes him by the arm and says, "Everything you need is in your room, Mr. Chan. If you're hungry we'll send you up a cheeseburger."

So Freddie waited, for three days. He watched the dirty movies on the Pay-Per-View. He made a pass at the Puerto Rican girl who did up his room. He made a serious dent in the bar stock. He waited.

On the third night he was awakened at three in the morning by the phone ringing.

"Take a walk, Mr. Chan. Leave the hotel through the kitchen exit. A car will be waiting for you."

The car was there, a dark Chevy. The door on the front

passenger side opened and Freddie got in. There was the driver and two men on the back seat.

"You did very well," the driver told him. "I like a man who can follow instructions."

Then he handed Freddie a plane ticket in a TWA folder and a wad of bills held together with a rubber band.

Freddie took them both and immediately began counting the money, which was probably the idea. At first he hardly seemed to notice when the man seated immediately behind him leaned forward and screwed an ice pick into the base of his skull.

All the time Sal was probing his brains, the Chink's legs jerked around a lot and his eyes rolled in their sockets. But a living man doesn't move like that. That was just his muscles twitching as they got the message: it's all over, Freddie Ju is no longer with us. Frank was pretty sure he never even had time to figure out he was being murdered. After all, it only took about ten seconds.

When he was absolutely satisfied the guy was dead, Sal yanked his ice pick out of Freddie's neck and covered his head with a plastic bag. It was an unnecessary precaution because there was hardly a drop of blood.

"You want him in the trunk, Mr. Rizza?"

Frank reached across and took back his money. Then he put the plane ticket into the late Freddie Ju's inside coat pocket—let the cops waste their time wondering what business this punk had in Dallas.

"Fine. Then drive to the Newark airport and leave the car in the long-term parking lot."

"Okay, Mr. Rizza. He'll be plenty ripe by the time they find him."

Both Sal and his companion, whose name Frank had heard but simply couldn't remember, thought this was very funny. The New Jersey families were full of such animals.

"You drive. You can drop me off right here."

Frank stayed long enough to watch them pull Freddie Ju out by his arms and then hoist him into the trunk, then he left. He was staying at the Trump, which was only five blocks away, and he could use the fresh air.

Not that he had any complaints. It was a good clean job and reasonably cheap. He had set up the hit himself and then paid Ed Quong $5,000 for a throwaway hitter—he had the impression that Quong, for reasons best known to himself, was more than happy to burn Freddie and might have taken less, but Frank didn't want to turn it into a question of prestige. The Chinese were funny about stuff like that.

The two goons who were presently on their way to Newark were on loan from Al DeCosta, who owed him a favor and was in control of Atlantic City, at least until the next car bombing.

So even after expenses there was a good ten or twelve thousand left over from the money the Preston bitch had given him for this job.

Frank had thought it over carefully and had decided to turn the rest of the wad over to Al. Al had good connections as far north as Boston. You never knew—he even might be able to find out what a country cop like this Cheffins had done to piss off a fine lady like Miss Alicia Preston.

And if he could find that out, maybe Frank could finally get her hooks out of him.

chapter 22

Warren Pratt took a cab straight from La Guardia Airport to Grand Central, where he caught the commuter train to New Gilead. He hadn't been on the ground more than two hours before he was standing in front of Jim Kinkaid's front door, which the housekeeper opened with apparent reluctance.

"Mr. Kinkaid isn't at home," she said, her thin face just visible behind the chain lock. "He's gone to a funeral."

"Is he out of town?"

"Mercy no!"

"Then where is it being held? The funeral, I mean."

"At the Second Congregational Church—just up the street," she added quickly, as if fending off a dangerous line of inquiry.

"Then I'll look for him there. Do you think it would be all right if I left my bag here?"

They both glanced down at the scuffed brown suitcase brushing against Pratt's trouser leg.

"Will you be staying?"

Julia—that was her name, he finally remembered—Julia looked as if she dreaded to hear the answer.

"That's up to Mr. Kinkaid. By the way, who died?"

"The marshal."

With that she closed the door in his face. He waited a few seconds, if only to see if she would reopen it, but when she didn't he started back down the walkway. About thirty feet down the sidewalk he turned around just in time to see his suitcase disappearing into the house.

The Second Congregational Church (Gathered in 1832),

was a wooden building painted glaringly white. The steeple rose like a needle over the front doors, which were standing open. Organ music percolated out onto the street, where only a few cars were parked. One of these Pratt recognized as Kinkaid's Mercedes.

Inside, the sanctuary was remarkably gloomy. The windows, of plain glass, were about twenty feet up on the walls and seemed to admit no useful light. As his eyes adjusted to the dark, Pratt could make out the casket, a large bronze affair, just this side of the altar rail, and the fact that the mourners seemed to consist of half a dozen uniformed policemen and only three men in civilian clothes, of whom Kinkaid was the one seated in the third pew back, on the left side.

Pratt went up and sat down beside him.

"The guy must not have had too many friends."

Kinkaid turned his head slightly and looked for just a moment as if he were about to utter a rebuke, but then he seemed to think better of it.

"The newspapers have been full of dark hints that he was crooked," he murmured. "He was shot to death last Tuesday evening."

"So the good citizens are staying away?" Pratt nodded, as if the scenario was perfectly familiar to him. "Where did it happen?"

Kinkaid raised his eyebrows slightly, which was probably intended to suggest that he found the question not unintelligent.

"At home. They phoned his house at ten o'clock Wednesday morning, when he didn't show up for work. Then they sent a deputy around. He noticed that the marshal's car was still in the garage, and when he went over to investigate he found the body. There were four bullet wounds to the chest and a coup de grâce in the head."

"What caliber?"

"Twenty-two."

"Very professional. What was the time of death?"

"The coroner hasn't taken me into his confidence, but it

must have been between five and eight in the evening—he missed his poker game that night. He was still in uniform, so I think he was probably killed as soon as he got home from work."

"Was he crooked?"

Kinkaid hesitated for just an instant, and thus even against his will revealed that he was privy to facts about the late marshal which he was not prepared to make known.

"Cheffins held an appointive office," he said finally. "And he held that office for a long time. Let's just say that he understood the limits of his authority."

Then he shook his head.

"But, no, he wasn't crooked in the way the newspapers have been suggesting. This is a small town, Warren. And in small towns the local lawyer gets to be something of an authority on local scandal. If Bill Cheffins had been dabbling in narcotics, I think I would have heard something."

"Was he your client?"

"No."

So who are you protecting? Pratt wondered. Then it occurred to him that this was probably the first time Kinkaid had ever called him by his first name.

The sermon was about fifteen minutes long but seemed much longer. Its one point of interest was the scrupulousness with which it avoided even the most passing reference to the deceased, as if that subject were even more painful than death itself. Clearly Marshal Cheffins' spiritual shepherd had been reading the crime pages.

When the funeral service was over, they went back outside into the sunlight. Across the street a smallish, Mediterranean-looking type in a dark suit was leaning against a shiny blue Ford, obviously a rental, and Pratt thought for a moment he might be some local hood come to pay his respects, but he didn't join the funeral cortege so apparently he was just a curious tourist.

Everybody else got into their cars and followed the hearse

to a cemetery about twenty minutes outside of town. As always, Pratt found the graveside rituals at once ludicrous and depressing. He was glad when it was all finished and they could leave.

For a long time on the drive back, Kinkaid was silent.

"Why did you go to the funeral?" Pratt asked finally. "Was he a friend of yours?"

"I've known him all my life."

"That isn't the same thing."

"No, it isn't."

"Then why? Do you *like* funerals?"

Just when Pratt had decided that his question was going to be ignored, Kinkaid shook his head.

"I keep wondering why the newspapers are going after him," he said, as if that constituted an answer—perhaps it even did. "Cheffins wasn't under investigation, or if he was there isn't a word of it in the stories. Where are they getting all this?"

"It isn't very difficult to sic the press on somebody once he's dead." Pratt searched through his pockets for the little cellophane packet of mints he had been given on the plane, and then he remembered he had already eaten them. He decided he was hungry. "Look at Robert Maxwell—look at Elvis."

"Bill Cheffins wasn't Elvis."

No, he wasn't. Pratt had to admit to the justice of the observation. Marshal Cheffins wasn't Elvis.

"You make it sound like you think his death had something to do with our little matter."

Kinkaid turned to him and smiled a trifle wearily. "Why should it?"

When they got back to the house, Pratt noticed that his suitcase had been left ostentatiously in the middle of the front hall.

"Let me take that upstairs for you," Kinkaid said, picking it up as if it were a pack of cards carelessly left out. "Julia will have made up the spare room."

"Don't be so sure. I don't think she likes me."

Kinkaid smiled, as if someone had made a lame joke.

At dinner the conversation was about movies, American foreign policy, the state of the airline industry, baseball—about which Kinkaid seemed to know next to nothing—celebrated criminal cases of the '30s and '40s, whether global warming was or was not a real threat to the world, and Madonna's singing ability. Every time Julia came into the room, Kinkaid followed her out with his eyes, which was warning enough to stay on neutral topics.

When they had finished their dessert, which consisted of little cubes of orange Jell-O, Kinkaid suggested they adjourn to his office.

"I can offer you a drink if you're like one," he said, as if providing a covering excuse. "And you can tell me about your trip."

The man's patience was really astonishing. In three hours it was the first reference he had made to the subject. And now he could wait until he had made his guest a large vodka gimlet and they were quite comfortably seated on either end of the big leather sofa.

"Andrew Castlesmith died three years ago in an explosion on his boat. The thing just blew up."

Pratt watched the skin tighten around Kinkaid's eyes, exactly as if the news caused him physical pain. Perhaps it even did.

"Was there any family?"

"No."

"Thank God for that. What about the others?"

"All the rest are alive. And from what one of them told me, I think they're safe enough."

Kinkaid had nothing except a glass of club soda—come to think of it, Pratt had never seen him drink anything stronger. But it was an unfortunate choice of virtue. He looked like he could have used a drink.

"I talked to Stu Geller," Pratt continued. He had very little inclination to prolong the suspense. "Remember him? He played right tackle. He's in the Army now, a first lieutenant stationed in San Diego, and he'd never heard of Angela Wyman. None of the other survivors had either. But he told me something interesting. Our four dead heroes and your good buddy at the gas station were a team within the team. They were like a club. If they'd had a good thing going, they would have kept it to themselves."

"So the loop closes with Charlie Flaxman."

"Or around him, depending on how you want to look at it." Pratt tasted his drink and tried not to make a face. Kinkaid was a nice guy, if perhaps a little too self-contained for his own good, but he was a lousy bartender. "She's such a logical suspect, I'm really sorry your little sweetheart is dead."

"But she isn't dead. And she is our killer."

It was the grave, apparently, that tipped it.

"You have to understand the Wymans," Kinkaid explained. He seemed to think the family had no more to do with ordinary humanity than if they had come from Mars. "For generations they've been like royalty in this part of the state, and that fact became part of how they defined themselves. You should go see their house sometime—it's huge and grand and imposing, and there's an eight-foot-high stone wall around it. They didn't build it to impress other people. They built it because it's the kind of house a Wyman should live in. There was no way Mrs. Wyman was going to let her granddaughter, the last of the line, spend eternity in some potter's field for loonies."

"So some other woman is buried there."

"That's right, and Angel killed her. When they found the corpse it had no face left. Does that bring back any memories?"

"Then what about the fingerprints?"

Kinkaid shrugged, using his left shoulder only, as if the matter were not even worth considering. "I've seen her file.

Her fingerprints are on a three-by-five card that's stapled to the inside cover. Hell, she worked in Records for two years. If we assume she set someone up to take her place, she could have switched the prints at any time."

"And is that what she did—set someone up to take her place?"

"Yes. The Wymans had the kind of money that makes anything possible."

"And you're quite sure she killed this nameless young woman? You're the one who was in love with her—she could do a thing like that?"

"It wouldn't have been the first time."

Then Kinkaid told him about the night Dominic Franco died.

He told the story slowly, with a lawyer's precision, as if it was somehow a psychological necessity to leave nothing out. He did not spare nor condemn his father—he merely reported. And when he was finished, you could almost hear the slam of Marshal Cheffins' car door as he and James Kinkaid III took Angela Wyman to what they must have imagined to be her final oblivion.

"When did Cheffins tell you all this?"

"About ten days ago. I knew by the time you came from Philadelphia, I even told you Angel was dead."

"You mind letting me know why you kept it to yourself until now?"

"I thought it might not matter. I thought I could conceal my dad's role in all this." With his left hand, Kinkaid managed a little movement strongly reminiscent of a fish struggling against the hook. "But we're well past all that now."

Pratt knew exactly what he meant but preferred not to acknowledge the suggestion.

"Do you think you could find this well where Cheffins said he dumped Dominic's body?" he asked instead.

"Sure." Kinkaid nodded. He might have been admitting to a knowledge of contract law. "I think he was talking about the Sinclair place—in fact, I know it. I checked the real estate records at Town Hall, and Mrs. Wyman acquired the property six months after Angel disappeared. My father handled the transaction for her. A couple of deserted farm buildings and forty acres of decaying apple orchard, and it's still part of the estate. The following year a construction company in Stamford filed for a permit to do some blasting on the site."

"So much for Mr. Franco's earthly remains. Three or four sticks of dynamite lowered down that shaft would have done for him nicely."

"Yes, I imagine so."

The two men sat silently for a long time, as if trying to wait each other out. If that was what was happening, Kinkaid lost.

"I think tomorrow we ought to pay a visit to the FBI office in Stamford," he said finally.

"If it will ease your conscience."

As Pratt could have predicted, the FBI field man who interviewed them thought the idea was hilarious.

His name was Wiggins—Special Agent Wiggins, as if you gave up all rights to a first name when you joined the Bureau. He was probably just shy of forty and was beginning to acquire the jowly, prosperous look of a desk cop. He wore a dark blue suit, beautifully shined shoes and, God help us, suspenders. Try as he might, Pratt found he could never quite bring himself to trust a man who wore suspenders.

Special Agent Wiggins listened carefully to everything that James Kinkaid IV, Attorney at Law, had to tell him, registering no reaction during the recital except, from time to time, a faint smile.

"Now let me see if I have this right," he said at last. "A woman named Angela Wyman is going around murdering her old lovers from the New Gilead High School football team. You have it on the authority of this Marshall . . ." He ostentatiously checked his notepad. "Marshal Cheffins, recently deceased, that she committed a similar crime ten years ago. The lady herself was declared dead—and the fingerprint identification was made by this Bureau—six years ago, but you believe her to be alive and the grave occupied by someone else, presumably another of her victims. Is that a fair summary?"

"As far as it goes, yes." Kinkaid nodded, his face grim. He knew perfectly well how it sounded.

"There is a strong circumstantial case . . ." Pratt started to say before Wiggins cut him off with a wave of his hand.

"Lieutenant, I have heard a strong circumstantial case made for the notion that President Kennedy is alive and living in a monastery in South Dakota. I'm not interested in circumstantial cases. The Bureau insists on something a bit more persuasive in the way of evidence, and I'm afraid evidence is precisely what you lack. You have no surviving witnesses to the murder of the gardener and no body—you don't even have a missing persons report. Of your four football players only one is convincingly a homicide. And your principal suspect has been declared dead. I'm sorry, gentlemen, but there are no grounds for opening an investigation into this matter."

And that was where they left it.

Kinkaid, to his credit, didn't rant and rave about how there was a maniac loose on the unsuspecting world—he didn't even raise his voice. Instead, he thanked Special Agent Wiggins for his time, shook the man's hand, and left. He was no fool. He knew when he was wasting his time.

Outside, in the glaring summer sunlight, which is never more intense than in front of a government building, he looked a trifle bewildered, as if he had forgotten where he was.

"There's a coffee shop across the street," Pratt said. "I could use some."

They took a booth and Pratt ordered for both of them. Kinkaid merely stared at the table. His coffee was no more than lukewarm before he at last broke his silence.

"Do you believe me?" he asked.

"That she's out there? I believe that you believe it. And I don't think you're some kind of hysteric. Let's say about sixty percent of me believes it. The rest thinks it's a lot of hooey."

James Kinkaid, Esq., did not seem terribly satisfied with this answer.

"You've got to admit, it sounds weird," Pratt went on, as if this constituted some sort of apology. "And you've got to remember that the one permanent ambition of every FBI agent is to avoid making the Bureau look stupid. I wasn't expecting any other reaction."

"Then what do we do now?"

"It's very simple, Counsellor. We find her, and then we catch her."

chapter 23

      Jimmy Carfax was growing bored with model airplanes. He had gone through the phase already once in his early adolescence, shortly after his commitment to Sherman's Crest, so in middle age he pursued the hobby with the sophistication of a connoisseur.

And that was part of the problem. The manual skills involved in assembling them were easily mastered and, considered abstractly, all balsa-wood models tended to be more or less the same. They were losing their challenge. Jimmy subscribed to some dozen magazines devoted to the subject, so he knew what was available and it had been some time since he had run across a kit he thought might be worth the trouble of sending for.

Because he did not build them as part of some fantasy about being an astronaut or a World War II bomber pilot, roles which, had he considered them at all, would have filled him with uncomprehending distaste. In fact, the 1:500-scale Concordes and the 1932 Silver Shadows he constructed with such painstaking attention to detail had for him almost no connection at all with external reality. If the genuine article had flown by overhead he would probably not have raised his eyes to look at it. The truth was that external reality was not a matter of very great interest to Jimmy. Life outside the institution—indeed, any life beyond the one he personally was living—hardly existed for him.

Still, that life was not without its pleasures. His lawyer had won for him access to some of the income from his maternal grandmother's estate, which had been left to him in its entirety when he was not quite four years old—and his mother's control over which had been the real if secret motive for murdering his parents—and money eased many constraints. He had his own phone line and his mail, while inspected, was generally not interfered with. Jerry, who had the night duty on the violent ward, was a compliant soul with an addiction to gambling, and he would supply any luxury for a price, even the services of a woman who normally worked in the kitchen but who once a week was smuggled into Jimmy's room and, once he had submitted to being handcuffed to his bed, would provide him with a measure of entertainment. She was not young and she was by no means pretty, but she would do.

But the greatest of his pleasures came from his notoriety. He enjoyed attention. He enjoyed being the center of other people's interest as he was the center of his own. In the four decades of his incarceration he had been interviewed by dozens of psychiatrists and eager young graduate students in Abnormal Psychology and even, once, some idiot from the *National Enquirer*. He had been the subject of numberless articles in professional journals, plus the odd squib in the popular press, reprints of which he collected. It was celebrity of a sort and he liked it. When he felt interest in his case beginning to wane he would grow depressed and slightly desperate. Once in his thirties he had even gone so far as to bite off another patient's ear simply because he felt the staff were beginning to take him for granted and he needed to reaffirm that he was still a dangerous head case. The attack had been a mistake, because ever since he had been kept more or less confined and the security precautions imposed were something of a nuisance. He would have found sex more amusing without the necessity of the handcuffs.

And, besides, he had eventually figured out that the real source of his popularity among mental health professionals and other assorted cranks was less the fear that he inspired than his impenetrability. All the shrinks who had examined him, all the psychologists who had given him Rorschach and random-association tests, and the article writers who had asked him impertinent questions about his childhood, none of them had an inkling about what was really going on inside his head.

Frankly, he lied. He was not a fool—he was doubtless a good deal more intelligent than most of his examiners—and he found it a relatively easy matter to lead them to false and even contradictory conclusions. He had been diagnosed as everything from an infantile schizophrenic to a full-blown sociopath, and it was all nonsense.

Because Jimmy knew exactly what was wrong with him. Or right with him, since he himself regarded it as an asset rather than a deficiency. He was not insane because insanity implied that his perceptions of concrete reality were somehow flawed, and this was not the case. He was not delusional. He was actually remarkably clearheaded. It was simply that pity, compassion, affection, all the things that bind one person to another, had no place in his inner reality. Except as they impinged on his own life, he genuinely did not care about other people. Somewhere in his dark, chilly little soul the thread of human sympathy lay severed.

But in his view that was not a pathology. It was, rather, a freedom from weakness. He wasn't a maniac. He was evil. There was an important distinction between the two, and the advantages were all on the side of evil.

It was actually rather restful not giving a damn about another living soul.

None of which, of course, implied a lack of discrimination in his dealings with his fellow mortals. He preferred some of them to others. For instance, he had enjoyed James Kinkaid enormously—just as he had enjoyed Angel Wyman.

At first he had been a little offended by Kinkaid, who had seemed neither afraid of him nor even particularly intrigued. True, the man had spent three days at a mental hospital, so perhaps some of the novelty had worn off, but it was just a little insulting to be regarded as apparently nothing more than an ordinary psychotic or, at most, an interesting witness. It was rather like having Angel back inside, and Jimmy had never enjoyed playing second fiddle.

But then he had realized two things. First, the man's composure was studied. No one who had not actually eviscerated half a dozen small children could possibly have that much ice water in his veins. It was a good act—Jimmy had tried several different ways to shake his composure and had failed utterly—but it was an act. Perhaps that was being excessively harsh. It was a technique that had acquired something of the character of a habit. Kinkaid was not the type to let anyone see inside to inquire how the wheels and levers moved.

Well, Jimmy couldn't fault him for that. He wasn't any different himself.

And, second, Kinkaid hadn't come up to this dark corner of the woods as any family lawyer. He had his own agenda.

"A little unfinished business," he had called it, and his eyes had gone dark as he said it. The poor baby was all knotted up inside.

Which was all right. Jimmy enjoyed other people's pain, and like a true gourmet he favored the soul's anguish over all the more obvious varieties. His favorite scenario was that Kinkaid had been in love with Angel—he would have been about the right age ten years ago, before Angel committed whatever indiscretion had landed her in Sherman's Crest, and heaven knew the girl was decorative enough.

Love, in Jimmy's opinion, was a rather ludicrous weakness, the stuff of farce rather than tragedy. Lust was another matter. Lust was simple biology. On that score Jimmy was decidedly attached to his Emily—that was her name, God help us, Emily—who took off her clothes for him once a week and was so very, very careful to keep out of the way of his hands and teeth while she attended to business, but it never would have occurred to him to go all tender and sentimental about her. Emily was quite right to stay out of reach.

Yes, decidedly, he favored the Grand Passion Theory over

all the other possibilities, perhaps because it made such an interesting contrast to Mr. Kinkaid's outward calm. Still waters run deep and all that. Oh it was a perfectly delicious idea.

It just went to show how much a pretty face and a nice set of tits can blind one, because he couldn't have had an inkling about what she was really like.

Jimmy loved gossip, and he had his sources. Sooner or later he found out about everything, but for a solid year Angela Wyman was nothing to him except a tantalizing rumor. There was this spectacularly gorgeous addition to the vegetable garden over in Ward D. She was as beautiful as a rose and about as sentient. Anyway, that was the story. Jimmy knew she was having everybody on.

In those days there was an orderly working at Sherman's Crest by the name of Gladys Cornman. And Ms. Cornman loved her job, particularly if she happened to pull the night shift, where there was usually only one person on duty. Because Ms. Cornman, you see, was as queer as a goat and loved having her way with the girls. And then one morning she was found at the bottom of a stairwell with her neck neatly broken. It was her first night on Ward D.

A terrible accident everyone said—except if the poor dumb dyke had tried getting into the wrong somebody's panties and that somebody had been sufficiently with it to take exception. It had always struck Jimmy as particularly significant that the pathologist had found so little bruising on the corpse. You would think that Ms. Cornman would have taken quite a beating on those concrete stairs, but there was hardly a mark on her.

And then, lo and behold, two weeks later Angel Wyman comes back to the Land of the Living. Dr. Werther practically had tears in his eyes. It was a miracle.

And then again, maybe not. Maybe Angel just got tired of pretending she belonged in a flower pot.

Seven or eight months passed before he got a peek at her, and well over two years before they had their first brief conversation—a suitably furtive business, achieved during one of his outdoor exercise periods.

Jimmy loathed the outdoors almost as much as he loathed even the thought of exercise. In his youth, when he was required to wear padded leg shackles to keep him from doing anything rash, it had been bad enough, but it was torture now. He was too old and too fat for this sort of thing. He was short of breath and his legs bothered him. Yet every afternoon it wasn't actually raining or snowing this martyrdom was required of him.

"Pedro, if I'm not allowed to sit down I'll stop your allowance. I mean it. I'm exhausted."

His warders, thank God, were all pragmatic types with small salaries. Pedro was even content to leave him alone for short stretches, knowing that a man who weighs over three hundred pounds isn't going to sprout wings and fly. He would go off and flirt with the nurses, taking Jimmy's cane with him to guarantee that his charge wouldn't wander from wherever he left him.

Thus it happened that that particular afternoon Jimmy was quite alone, taking his ease on one of the little wrought-iron benches that were scattered about the grounds at convenient intervals, when he noticed a flutter of cotton dress behind one of the ancient oak trees of which the hospital was so unreasonably proud. Some young lady was sitting on the grass, her back against the tree trunk, not twenty feet away, blissfully unaware of his presence. It was very provoking.

He was just beginning to think that perhaps he had a duty to teach her a little decent caution when she leaned to her right, supporting herself with her arm, and he saw the back of her blond head. He knew who she was even before she turned back to look at him.

She had deliciously cold eyes, and by their expression he saw that she had known all along he was there. She smiled mockingly.

"Run along, little girl, or I'll bite your lips off."

All Angel did was laugh. It was a sound as heartless as the wind at night. As he listened to it Jimmy knew with perfect certainty it had been the last sound that Gladys Cornman had ever heard.

"All right," he went on petulantly, "be a spoilsport."

"You're James Carfax," she said. "I've read your file."

"And it isn't a novel, my dear—every word of it is true," Jimmy replied smugly. She had already stood up and was beginning to walk away before he realized the significance of what she had told him.

"Then you've got access to Records?" he shouted after her, but she never even turned around. In an instant she was gone, as if she had stepped behind a curtain.

That night as he lay in his bed, staring up through the darkness at the invisible ceiling, he found himself wondering what she wanted from him.

That she wanted *some*thing he did not trouble to doubt. It had taken him only a second or two to confirm his suspicions about her. She wasn't even twenty, yet the moment he had heard her laugh he had known she was as old as time itself. She was just like him, less a human being than a constant of nature. She was beyond pity or love or remorse or death.

They had understood each other immediately. She wanted something and she knew she would have to trade for it, so she had let him know that she had access to everyone's secrets. She had the one thing he really wanted.

But what was her price? He had to wait three months to find out.

"Can you get into employee files?" he asked her, having once more sent Pedro off to amuse himself.

"It's difficult, but not impossible."

She was sitting directly at his feet. She was even teasing him with the view down the front of her dress. She wasn't afraid to do anything.

"Then I want chapter and verse on one Vincent Tessio, the

keeper of my kingdom if you must know. Now what do you want?"

What she wanted was so simple and obvious he was surprised he hadn't guessed. She wanted a safe line to the outside.

Because a few years back Jimmy had gone through his computer phase, a fact which, like everything else unimportant about him, would be in his folder. He had bought himself a Macintosh with a color monitor and all the bells and whistles, but he had soon tired to it. Now he only used it to keep in touch with devotees of his many other hobbies.

And that was precisely the point—by implication, Angel had already told him something of the greatest interest. He knew that they kept records of his telephone calls, but since he never called anyone except his lawyer and various mail-order houses he didn't really care. But when he wanted all the latest on, for instance, the current prices for baseball cards of the '50s and '60s he had only to log onto CompuServe, which was a local number but could connect him by electronic mail with anyone in the world. This was a fact which apparently had never occurred to his watchers.

Otherwise Angel would have found another way.

"Send messages for me from time to time," she said. Then she slipped him a piece of paper.

He unfolded it and looked at what was written on it.

"Aren't you afraid I might tattle on you, my dear?"

"Oh no. I'm not afraid of that, Jimmy. Because then I'd tell them about Emily."

He never learned how she found out about that, and it didn't really matter. In any case he had only been teasing. He would not have betrayed her.

So perhaps three times a month he posted something to a Peter Grayson, address number 24355,1717. Once Grayson, whoever he was, picked up his messages they were erased from the bulletin board's memory, as if they had never existed. When Angel went over the wall there would be no way to trace her.

Because over the wall she meant to go—she didn't even bother to conceal the fact. What would have been the point of trying?

"When I'm out I'll send you a box of chocolates," she told Jimmy, almost the last time he ever saw her. "What kind do you like best?" And, sure enough, a month after she disappeared he received a five-pound box of See's nuts and chews, postmarked San Francisco.

Jimmy was not sentimental about Angel. Loyalty and affection were strangers to his nature; there were but two considerations that kept him from betraying her. The first was that while Angel was free she was not at Sherman's Crest, which meant he had the place to himself—he did not fancy the idea of sharing his little domain with another predator. The second was that he enjoyed making mischief.

Thus, even while his model airplanes were beginning to pale, it still gave him pleasure to think of what he had helped to turn loose upon the unsuspecting world. He could not follow her progress, since Angel was far too clever to make it into the newspapers, but he knew she was out there. And he knew she was busy.

Well, now it would be perhaps even a little more interesting. Kinkaid was not one of the meat eaters, but he had strong nerves and there was nothing wrong with the contents of his mind. Even without Jimmy's little hints he would have figured out for himself that the girl buried in the hospital graveyard wasn't Angel. He might even be smart enough to catch her—anything was possible.

Jimmy would enjoy this little battle of wits, even if he never heard another thing about it, but he also would like to be the one who decided how things turned out. And, on the whole, he preferred to leave Angel running around loose. It was fine if Kinkaid gave her a bit of a hard time, but he mustn't be allowed to win.

So now it was time to redress the balance a little. A few days after Kinkaid's visit, Jimmy fired up his Macintosh, logged onto CompuServe, and left the following text file in Peter Grayson's electronic post office box: "Message from Jimmy. JK4 is busy adding up 2 and 2. Watch your attractive little derrière, sweetheart."

Having finished, he turned the computer off and treated himself to half a pound of Gummy Bears. He had done his bit to make the world a little more dangerous—he only wished he could be there to see Angel's face when she found out.

chapter 24

"**I thought maybe** you'd gotten bored with me."

"Not bored—no, definitely not bored. Just busy and preoccupied."

"A problem with your private life?"

"You're my private life."

She seemed to like that answer. She snuggled a little deeper under the covers, until her face was touching his chest. It was a delicious sensation to feel the tip of a woman's tongue along your breastbone.

"Then what's been keeping you away? Business?"

"Not exactly."

"Then what?"

"Archeological research. Spelunking into the darkest reaches of . . . Hey, you keep that up and I'll lose my train of thought."

"Wouldn't that be dreadful."

Following which, it was a good twenty minutes before he could have recalled even his own name.

"You want to tell me about it?" she asked, once things had settled down.

"About what?"

"Your spelunking."

And suddenly he did want to tell her. He wanted to very much. He felt as if the only way to make the thing real to himself was to tell her everything.

"I've only been in love one other time in my life," he said, staring up at Lisa's bedroom ceiling. "I was twenty and she was about sixteen. It didn't come to much. One day she just disappeared."

"Tell me more about the *one other time* you were in love— *other* implying 'as distinct from *this* time.' "

"Why? Have I neglected to mention that detail?"

"Well, actually, yes you have. But tell me about the girl— your Lolita. Was she absolutely gorgeous? Were you nuts about her?"

"Yes, on both counts. She was the most beautiful creature I've ever seen in my life. And if I live to be three hundred I hope I never see another like her."

As he spoke, Kinkaid was conscious of nothing so much as the soft, warm weight of Lisa's arm as it lay across his chest and shoulder. In comparison with that, it seemed, Angel Wyman had been a troubling dream.

"Try to imagine what it's like to have loved someone," he went on, in an attempt to do justice to his old passion, "to have carried the memory of that love around with you for ten years, and then to discover that its object was a phantom. Or worse."

"How much worse?"

"As bad as it can get."

"How bad is that?"

"I think she's out there killing people, sweetheart. I think she's as crazy as a rabid fox. I think she's the devil in skirts."

"Are you putting me on?"

"No such luck."

For a long, thoughtful moment they were both perfectly silent. A dozen possibilities raced through Kinkaid's mind, but they all came to the same thing—he had no idea how Lisa would react to this particular truth.

And when she did react it was in the last way he might have expected. She sat up beside him in bed and with a certain deliberation wrapped herself in the sheet, as if announcing that the fun and games were over for this evening.

"I think you'd better tell me about this," she announced. "I think you'd better start at the beginning."

It took him the better part of two hours to get through the story, and he had a very attentive audience. Occasionally Lisa would venture a question about a matter of fact—a name, a relationship, the timing of some event—but for the most part she merely listened quietly, as if nothing else in her life mattered.

"And this man Pratt," she asked finally, when there seemed nothing more she could ask, "this policeman—is he still staying at your place?"

"No. He left this morning to fly back to Dayton. By the way, how would you feel about moving in with me?"

"Are you kidding? What about your housekeeper?"

"I have to grow up someday. How about it?"

"Okay. When is Pratt coming back?"

"No idea. He has a few things to clear up in Dayton and then he's going on to Paris. Lisa, we have the room."

"And if you find Angel, what will you do with her?"

"I don't know. Put a stop to her somehow."

"Will you kill her?"

"I don't kill people, Lisa."

This was not, it seemed, a very satisfactory answer.

"And what will you do while Pratt's in Paris?"

"Get used to living with you."

"You know what I mean."

"I'll try to piece together how Angel got away. Maybe that will lead me to where she is."

"How will you do that?"

"Follow the money."

Because he had discovered something, something which had been left hidden in plain sight.

There was a small collection of reference books on a shelf behind his father's desk and in one of them, as if the elder Kinkaid had wished to mark his place in *Webster's Pocket*

Dictionary, was a slip of paper. It was a receipt from Bill's LockUp in Norwalk, dated January 23, 1990.

Mrs. Wyman had died in January of that year. Kinkaid had driven home from Yale to attend the funeral.

A phone call discovered that the space was paid up through the end of December and nobody at Bill's was interested in any legal niceties. Kinkaid had the key and he had the receipt, so within five minutes he had everything in the trunk of his car. In all there were four cardboard cartons, sealed tight with plastic tape. It was quite a haul.

He put three of the cartons in his father's bedroom, which he knew Julia never entered, and carried the fourth into his office. It turned out to contain twelve thick binders, each labeled with the month and the year. They were Mrs. Wyman's financial records for 1988.

Kinkaid didn't have to search very far through these to figure out what had happened to the family's immense fortune—all during that year Mrs. Wyman had been transferring large sums, sometimes as much as a quarter of a million dollars a week, to a bank in the Bahamas. These deposits would hardly have time to clear before the account would be drawn against for an equal amount.

"My guess is the next stop was Panama," he told Lisa the first Saturday morning after she moved in, after they had padded down to his office in their pajamas. "Their banking regulations mesh with Bahamian law in peculiar ways. The money would go into a joint account, the co-signator would withdraw it and deposit it in another account, also joint, and then the next co-signator, identity unknown, would withdraw it again and the chain would be broken. Almost nine million dollars in a single year. It could be anywhere today and no one will ever be able to trace it."

Lisa sat on his leather couch with her feet tucked up underneath her, looking like a child listening to a bedtime story. The new domestic arrangement was a big success—even Julia seemed to approve.

"So you won't be able to find Angel?"

"Not a chance. I can't even find her bagman in here."

"Her what?"

"Someone had to set this up for her," Kinkaid said, his finger moving in a wavy line down the columns of figures. "It wasn't my father because I've got his passport and I know it hasn't been used since 1976. But someone made a nice living wearing his suits shiny on a succession of airline seats. All these deposit slips aren't cable traffic—she probably didn't want to leave a paper trail that the IRS could follow, so she had everything hand-carried."

"Then why didn't she destroy all this?"

"Because Mrs. Wyman was who she was, and it never would have occurred to her that anyone might have the effrontery to go through her private papers."

"Then if you want her bagman, why don't you look for him in her cancelled checks?"

It was a suggestion of such dazzling simplicity that Kinkaid was a moment taking it in.

"Jim, sometimes I think you're too clever for your own good."

It was a fair criticism. A legal education breeds a distaste for the obvious, Kinkaid told himself while, back in his office, he rummaged through the monthly bank statements which he had carried away with everything else in Mrs. Wyman's writing desk but until now had not troubled himself to look at.

And there he was. Almost every envelope contained a check made out in Mrs. Wyman's spidery hand to a "Lewis Olmstead," sometimes for amounts in excess of $10,000.

There was no Lewis Olmstead in the directory, but a search through the library's archive of out-of-date phone books revealed that, up until three years ago, there had been a private detective agency listed in the Stamford yellow pages as "Olmstead Investigations," no address given.

Without much hope, Kinkaid dialed the number.

"Yeah?"

"Mr. Olmstead?"

"Who wants to know?" the name answered, in a voice that sounded rusty with disuse. "You selling something?"

"Mr. Olmstead, I got your name from a former client. I wonder if you . . ."

"You a bill collector?"

"Mr. Olmstead, I'm a lawyer. Now are you still in the private detective business, or should I call someone else?"

This seemed to require a moment's reflection, for there was a longish pause during which Kinkaid could distinctly hear the man's breathing.

"You can't be too careful in my profession—and I'm damn good at it. You know Whitby Street?"

"I'm sure I can find it."

"You come to 127 Whitby Street. You park your car in front of the grocery store. Maybe I'm home and maybe I'm not."

Judging from the mingling of small storefront businesses with residential property, Whitby Street was not a neighborhood where the zoning codes were enforced with much vigor. The first block had a beauty parlor and, directly across from it, a coffee shop. The signs were in Spanish. The lawns in front of the tiny houses were well kept and, in some cases, enclosed in chain-link fences. After that, however, the process of urban decay was visible almost from building to building.

By the time Kinkaid found his grocery store, which looked permanently closed, he was beginning to regret that he had driven his father's car down here.

127 looked as if it hadn't been painted since the Carter Administration. The front yard boasted a collection of well-worn automobile tires and the lid on the mailbox, which was nailed to a porch pillar, was so twisted out of shape that no one would every close it again.

Kinkaid did not even have to knock, because Olmstead

had apparently reached the intended conclusion about the Mercedes and decided that his visitor was unlikely to be a bill collector. He was standing in the doorway, a man of about fifty dressed in a black tee shirt and walking shorts of indeterminate color. He looked ill and clearly had not shaved anytime in the last three days.

"Mr. Olmstead? I'm James Kinkaid."

"The guy on the phone," Olmstead answered, ignoring Kinkaid's offered hand as he stepped aside to let him in. Then he seemed to remember his manners. "You want a beer?"

"I'll pass, thanks."

Kinkaid smiled, as if excusing his own eccentricity, and looked about him. The front room was hardly larger than ten by ten. Beyond it was a stucco archway leading into a tiny kitchen, and somewhere there was probably a single bedroom. Yet small as it was the house was a shambles. The furniture, which probably came with the lease, was faded and torn, and there were open newspapers lying about on the floor. The single table was decorated with a full ashtray and several water stains. There was dust everywhere.

"It's a mess, I know," Olmstead announced, as if the condition of the house were some irrevocable calamity over which he had not the slightest control. "I've been busy."

It was a lie for which he couldn't have entertained much hope, because clearly he wasn't prospering.

"I've been sick," he continued, perhaps more accurately. "Prostate trouble—in and out of the hospital all year. Probably have to have the thing out before I'm done. Sit down."

Kinkaid chose the sofa, as probably the safest, and it groaned uneasily under his weight.

"Where did all the money go?" He smiled again, the soul of affability. "By my calculations you were pulling in close to a hundred thousand a year while Mrs. Wyman was alive, so you must have some pretty expensive weaknesses. Was it gambling or are you on something?"

"Fuck you, shyster. You can't talk to me like that. Get out of here."

"How much are you in the hole, Mr. Olmstead?" Kinkaid went on, as if he hadn't heard a thing. "I need some information about what you were doing to earn all that lovely money, and I have deep pockets. And you needn't worry about self-incrimination. If you like, we can regard this conversation as covered by lawyer-client confidentiality and, besides, if I wanted you behind bars you'd already be there."

By then the man was standing over him menacingly, but Kinkaid appeared not to notice. He took out his checkbook and, balancing it on his knee, wrote out a check for $500, payable to Lewis Olmstead, which he guessed was probably more money than that individual had seen in several months. When he was finished he tore the check out, folded it in half and stuck it in his shirt pocket.

"Sit down, Mr. Olmstead, and tell me the story of your life."

Two hours later they were like old friends. Kinkaid had even accepted a beer.

"I'm not stupid," Olmstead confided, as if it were some kind of secret. "I knew there was something fishy. I was getting paid too much for it to be anything except crooked."

"There's nothing illegal about transferring money to overseas banks. It can be fishy without being crooked."

Like someone who has received hints of a new reality, Olmstead seemed to consider this for a moment. At last he nodded, conceding the possibility.

"But it *was* fishy. Am I right?"

"Oh yes."

Olmstead nodded again. That was enough—they were both men of the world, and sometimes it isn't a good idea to go into detail.

"I liked the Bahamas," he said, a little wistfully. "Sometimes, if it was a Friday and my plane was delayed, I'd get to stay over for a weekend. You can get used to anything, even banana daiquiris under the palm trees."

"Did you ever travel anywhere else for Mrs. Wyman?"

"Like where?"

"Like maybe Panama."

"No."

"Anywhere else?"

"San Francisco one time—two hours, can you believe it? I was in San Francisco for two hours. Never even got to leave the airport."

"What did you do there?"

Apparently remembering was an effort. Olmstead frowned and took another pull on his beer. He had been working on the same bottle for two hours so, whatever his other vices, he was at least not a drunk.

"Met a guy in the coffee shop. Gave him an envelope. That was it."

"Would you know him if you saw him again?"

"No."

It didn't matter because the essential point was made. Sometimes it was better not to let a witness know when he has said something important. Kinkaid changed the subject.

"The account in the Bahamas was joint. Did you ever meet the co-signator?"

"No, but I knew who he was." He shrugged, the modest detective disclaiming any special gifts beyond those granted by experience. "The airport down there wasn't that big. You fly in and out all the time, the way I did, and you get to know the regulars—at least by sight. Then you see the same guy an hour later in the lobby of a bank and you draw some conclusions."

"What was he like?"

"Slight, slender, Latin. Carried a briefcase that was bigger than he was. Had a moustache, the way they all do. Favored white suits."

"Did you ever notice what airline he used?"

"Air Latinas."

Kinkaid wrote down the name and then closed his note-book. He smiled as blandly as he knew how.

"And now maybe you'd like to tell me where you found the girl."

chapter 25

The change in Olmstead was immediate. A man may cheerfully confess to fiddling the tax laws, but this was something different. Clearly, he didn't want to talk about the girl.

Which meant, of course, that there had been a girl.

"I don't know what you're talking about."

"Yes you do." Kinkaid crossed his hands over his notebook, now closed, and shrugged. "Why? Was it a big secret?"

"There was no girl."

"Wasn't there? About twenty, five five or a little over, slender, light blond hair—sound familiar?"

"That sounds like a lot of girls."

"Don't fuck with me, Lew. I can leave you out or I can leave you in. It's my choice. I don't think you'll enjoy prison."

"Listen, there wasn't any law against that. I just . . ."

"You just what, Lew?"

It was almost possible to feel sorry for him, because he was trapped and he knew it. He wouldn't dare lie now, which meant that he had to live through it all over again.

"Start at the beginning, Lew. Take it one step at a time."

But where was the beginning? How soon had he reached the point when Mrs. Wyman owned him the way someone owns the change in their pocket? Did she have something on him—was that the way it had started?—or was it simply the money? After a while, money gets to be like the air you breathe. . . .

"She told me, 'Find someone.' Everything you said—twenty, medium height, hair almost white. She was very specific. And someone nobody would ever miss. A stray. 'You can be sure no harm will come to her. She will do one thing for me and then neither of us will ever see her again.' I didn't want to know what it was about, but I'd learned by then. You didn't say no to that old bitch."

So he had begun prowling around. "Half the people in the world are women, but pick a type and then just try to find her. It took me the better part of three months. Girls with no strings attached are harder to come by than you think."

The search ended in New York City at two o'clock in the morning, the hour and the place where it probably should have begun. There are designated patrol areas on the West Side, much favored by middle-aged husbands from New Jersey who want to party, where all you need is a car and a handful of twenty-dollar bills. The whores march up and down the sidewalks in platoons.

And sometimes there are turf battles, an inevitable occurrence in such a highly competitive profession. A new girl, just breaking into the business, can set up shop on the wrong street corner and end the night in the emergency room.

"By the time I turned up the fight was as good as over. Jenny was bent back over the hood of a car, getting her face rearranged. All I could see was her hair, but I knew she was my girl. That was her name—Jenny."

Her attacker was a Puerto Rican hooker who was using her fist like a hammer. Olmstead had started out in life as a vice cop up in Albany, so he was neither sentimental about women nor particularly chivalrous, and he knew the odds were good that this one, who looked like she was getting a little old for the trade and was thus naturally protective of her territory, had a straight razor in her handbag. He came up behind her and kicked her feet right out from under her. She went down with a bang and, just for good measure, Olmstead gave her the point of his shoe square in the midsection. Problem solved.

Jenny was more frightened than hurt, and there were a

couple of red marks on her face that would certainly ripen into dark, ugly bruises. She was crying hysterically. Olmstead had to shake her vigorously for perhaps half a minute to get her to stop.

"You'll be needing some ice," he told her, once she was calm enough to listen. About half a block down the street there was an all-night arcade of the kind that appeals to sailors and other adolescents. He bought her a snow cone without the syrup, wrapped it in his handkerchief, and gave it to her to hold against her battered face.

"Are you hungry?"

"Are you a cop?"

"Not anymore."

"Then yes, I'm hungry. Can I have some pizza?"

He bought her two slices, sausage and mushrooms, and a large Coke. They were able to sit at a table since the place was almost empty. She did the pizza full justice.

"How long has it been since you've had a paying customer?"

"Four days," she answered, licking her fingers. "And then I got robbed."

"How long have you been on the streets?"

"About three months."

"You don't seem to have much of a flair for it."

"You want to fuck me? Fifty bucks. I owe you, so I'll make it real nice for you. You got your car near here?"

She wasn't bad. She might even have seemed pretty, except that she was half-starved and probably hadn't had a proper bath in two weeks. She looked like she'd been sleeping rough for a few nights. And then there was the fact that her face was like raw hamburger.

"I don't want to fuck you, and you haven't seen fifty bucks in living memory," he said, standing up. "But I might have a job for you. You can come with me now or you can stay here and finish your pizza. Then you can go back to your promising career."

She was out of her chair before he had finished speaking. "Can I take the rest of it with me?"

He drove her up to White Plains and bought her a motel room, paying a week in advance. Then he drove home and got some sleep.

When he showed up again the next afternoon, with a thermos of coffee and a sack full of roast beef sandwiches, she was in the shower. When she came out she looked better than she had the night before. She was clean, for one thing, and she'd had ten hours sleep. She sat on the edge of one of the twin beds, chewing on her sandwich, naked as dawn.

"I washed my underwear," she said. "It was getting really bad. My suitcase is in a locker at the bus terminal. . . ."

"We'll get you some clothes."

Olmstead was trying not to stare at her hard, pink little nipples. She must have noticed how difficult it was for him.

"Look, if you want to fuck me that's fine. Just let me finish my sandwich."

"All right, so I fucked her," he told Kinkaid, as if the confession had been extorted from him. "I mean, Jesus, who wouldn't? She really had the body. A guy my age doesn't get a chance like that every day."

And she made it very easy, then and later. She didn't pretend to think Lew Olmstead was the answer to her prayers, but she didn't hold it against him that he wanted to climb on her. Lust wasn't comical or ridiculous. It was inevitable, like hunger pangs. And she seemed to regard herself as having no rights in the matter.

So for three weeks, until Mrs. Wyman was ready for her, he availed himself. He fed her and bought her clothes, including a woolen coat against the gathering cold. He talked to her, which she took as a special kindness.

"I guess she had had a tough time at home," he said of the experience. "She didn't have much to say about it, but you could read between the lines. She wasn't a bad kid."

And then an expression of pain crossed his face.

"I liked her," he went on, making this too into a confession. "And it wasn't just that she let me screw her, although that was part of it. You can't spend three weeks with a woman and not care about her at all, not if you're human."

Kinkaid discovered that he really did not want to hear about Olmstead's finer feelings. He did not want to share the man's pain. So he took his revenge.

"What did you tell her about the job?"

Olmstead actually flinched, as if he had been struck in the face.

"Not much—I didn't know much. I asked her if she knew how to drive, and she did. Then she asked me if this thing I wanted her to do would get her put in jail, and I said no. 'Will it get me killed?' she asked, and I said no. 'Then I don't care what it is,' she said."

You could see it in his eyes. He knew she was dead and that he had delivered her to death. No one had ever told him, but he knew. That was his punishment.

"And then you delivered her to Mrs. Wyman."

"Yes, I did that. I drove her up to that house, in the middle of the night, and I waited in the car while she and Mrs. Wyman talked. It was maybe a week or ten days before Christmas and it was cold as hell. I remember how the wind blew. When Jenny came outside she was carrying an envelope.

" 'It's easy,' she said. 'I'm going to Canada.' I didn't ask her to explain. I just drove her to New Haven, where she took the train to Boston. I never saw her again."

"And that's all you can tell me?"

"That's all I know."

Kinkaid believed him. He took the check out of his shirt pocket and left it on the table.

And in that moment he had a kind of hallucination. He was standing on a railroad platform, watching as the train pulled away—watching as Jenny, whom he had never seen in life or in death, waved goodbye to him. She was smiling. She was ecstatic with happiness. Her face shone like a light. And it was Jenny's face, and Angel's, and Lisa's, all at once. And he was Olmstead, and the guilt was his, for he knew he was the harbinger of death.

"Do you know what happened to her?"

And then the face that he saw was Olmstead's, and he was himself again, James Kinkaid, Esq., of that name the fourth, and no one else. For the enchantment had been broken.

"No idea," he answered, lying.

"Well, if you ever find out, don't tell me."

chapter 26

The one person who knew for certain was just then staring out over the rocky California coastline and attempting to come to terms with the significance of Jimmy Carfax's warning.

It was neatly typed out on a sheet of her lawyer's stationery, with his apologetic note above it: "Came back from vacation to find this in my E-mail. You'll best know what it means. Sorry for the delay." The date stamp on the message was from the week before.

JK4 is busy adding up 2 and 2. Angel did not need to have the abbreviation interpreted for her.

She subscribed to the *Stamford Advocate* and had read the elder Kinkaid's obituary. Perhaps that event had unleashed Jim's curiosity, or perhaps merely freed him to begin his search. She was reasonably sure the father would never have revealed anything about her disappearance to his son. And yet he had made his way as far as Sherman's Crest.

Well, maybe he would think the search ended there. Except that that was not what the message said: . . . *busy adding up 2 and 2* . . . Jimmy Carfax might have given the game away just for the fun of it. She should have arranged something for the malignant little toad before she went over the wall.

Except that it no longer mattered. If Jim had been to Sherman's Crest he knew about the grave, so if he ever found out that she was still alive he would know she was responsible for at least one murder. Thus she could never return to New Gilead, never have him as the lover he had never quite managed to become. The door to the new life she had promised herself was slammed in her face.

For ten years she had worked to clear the path. Everything she had done, her every thought had been focused on that one goal. She had achieved miracles—she had died and been reborn, she had erased the past—and now, just when she was about to reclaim everything that was hers by right, she found her way barred at the last step.

Dominic Franco had been her one mistake. In ten years, her only mistake. Now, after all this time, she couldn't even remember why she had killed him. Yes she could. She had killed him because, in that one moment, she had had to kill someone to keep her sanity.

Grandmother had driven her to it.

"Do you imagine for a single moment that I am unaware of how you have been amusing yourself? Your mother was a whore and so are you. Do you honestly believe that boy, that pure boy who has the world spread out before him, is such a fool that he will still want you when he finds out?"

She had said a great deal more. She had held nothing back, nothing. And in the end Angel had run from the house, had escaped into the darkness, blinded by her own tears.

She could not remember why she had gone to the gardener's hut, except perhaps that Dominic's was the one name her grandmother had not thrown in her face—perhaps she did not know. Perhaps, if she had known, this connection was too degrading to allow her even to speak of it.

Dominic had been her first. She had lost her virginity on his narrow little bed and then quickly lost interest in him. He drank too much to be a satisfactory lover and she had grown to hate the way he ran his hands over her, as if she had become his property. She had not been in his hut for five months.

And then, suddenly, she was.

He was asleep. The whole room smelled of whiskey, and he was so deep into his alcoholic coma that nothing could have roused him. He lay there on his back, his mouth open, and as he breathed he made a gurgling sound in the back of his throat.

I gave myself to that, she thought. *I lay on this bed, with those arms around me.* The idea of having been touched by him was repellent beyond endurance.

With his mouth open he looked as if he were getting ready to announce to the whole world that *I, Dominic Franco, the gardener, usually too drunk to unbutton my fly, nevertheless fucked Angela Wyman of the "Five Mile" Wymans.*

That he might say such a thing—ever, to anyone—was suddenly intolerable.

"Don't laugh at me, Dom," she shouted. "Don't you dare laugh at me!"

The fact that he was in no condition to laugh, or even to hear her, was beside the point. In that instant she hated him more than she had thought it possible to hate anyone.

There was a shovel leaning against the wall. Why he had brought it inside with him was impossible to guess. Perhaps if he had not he would still be alive. Perhaps nothing could have saved him.

He never moved. The whole time, as she beat in his face with the shovel blade, as blood and splinters of bone spattered the bed, the floor, even the walls, he never stirred. Could a man die like that and know nothing of it?

At last, when she was calm again, she threw the shovel away and sat down on the floor to catch her breath. She would go to her room, she thought. She would take a shower and then go to bed. But first she would tell Grandmother what she had done.

It was only as she walked back toward the house, and her dress, wet with blood, was beginning to grow clammy against her skin, that she realized this could not be kept simply a Wyman matter. Dominic was lying on his bed with his face smashed in, and he would never get up again. This could not possibly remain just within the family. It was the only time in her life she could remember being afraid.

So she decided she would be mad.

Ten years later, she could not remember if, just at first, she had been faking or if her trance had somehow been real—it did not seem a particularly important distinction.

She remembered everything else. She could remember being terribly cold.

And then all those years at Sherman's Crest, pretending to be disconnected from life, seducing her psychiatrist through his professional vanity, making him her lover even though he never touched her. Making them all love and trust her until she was more free than any of them, except that they could leave and she could not.

Grandmother had arranged everything. Angela Wyman could not be allowed to die in an asylum, even if she had murdered fifty gardeners. Whether it was love or pride or some pitiless mingling of the two, she would do whatever needed doing.

"When the time comes, find me someone to take my place," Angel had told her. "When I am ready to leave, they must imagine they know what became of me."

Because Jim's father and that fat policeman would never let her come back. Dominic Franco's death meant something to them, so they would never let her come back. If she ever returned to Five Miles it would have to be as someone else.

And they would both have to be dead. Jim's father obliged by having a heart attack, but Marshall Cheffins, Grandmother's faithful watchdog, required some coaxing.

It had been Angel's experience that most people went to their deaths quite willingly, with only a little show of reluctance just at the end. There was something in every human soul that wanted to die. It was otherwise difficult to explain the willful stupidity with which murder victims rushed to embrace their fates. What was so wonderful about most people's lives?

Certainly, whatever Grandmother may have thought—and she made a great show of horrified remorse when she found out—the girl who in death became Angela Wyman seemed to have little enough to live for.

"Where do we nab the car?" she had asked. "Somewhere around here?"

If Angel ever knew her name she had long since forgotten it. She was just a girl waiting in a pale gray Toyota at a tourist rest stop about four miles down the road from Sherman's Crest, and at that moment she was so near to death that names no longer mattered.

At first Angel didn't know what she was talking about, and then she remembered. The Official Plan involved stealing a car in Quincy, so the authorities would draw the obvious conclusion, and then letting the girl drive it up to the Canadian border, where she would flirt with one of the inspectors or cause a scene, anything to attract attention to herself. She had the right color hair and she was already wearing Angel's coat—there was even a superficial resemblance. The car would clinch the identification. And meanwhile Angel was to take the Toyota and go off in another direction. It wasn't a bad plan. It might even have worked.

Angel, however, was not prepared to chance it.

"What will you do once you get to Montreal?" she asked, changing the subject.

"I don't know—dye my hair I guess. God, we really look a lot alike. It's a little spooky."

She laughed, as if she were embarrassed or perhaps only wanted to be friends. It didn't matter.

"Move over and let me drive. I need the practice."

And she did. One of her mother's boyfriends had once spent an afternoon teaching her how, but that had been five years ago. Now, as she started up the road back toward the hospital, she wasn't at all sure she remembered and it would be a great nuisance if she had to keep the girl alive just to act as chauffeur.

But it came back quickly. Within a few miles she knew it would be all right.

"Did you happen to bring anything to eat? I'm starving."

"I bought a couple of sandwiches in Manchester, just in case."

"Then let's pull over somewhere."

It was so easy. They ate the sandwiches, then Angel announced she had to pee. She took the flashlight that was in the glove compartment and headed out into the darkness. She gave it about a minute and a half and then she screamed. The girl bolted out of the car and started running straight for the narrow circle of yellow light where the flashlight was lying on the ground. When she reached over to pick it up Angel stepped forward and kicked her in the face, breaking her nose and knocking her over onto her back. There was no fight left in her. All that remained was to select a rock of the proper size and use it to crush her skull.

By then it was already beginning to snow. There was a woman's raincoat lying on the back seat of the car and Angel used it to wrap up the corpse's head to keep it from bleeding all over the upholstery in the trunk, because by then she had pretty well obliterated the face. There were plenty of cliffs along the road and almost no traffic. No one would be out with a blizzard coming.

Once she had gotten rid of the body she headed south and east, away from the storm front. She was just inside Massachusetts when road conditions forced her into a motel. She was snowed in there for three days, living on the contents of the snack machine in the lobby, until the roads were cleared enough to let her go on to Boston, where she turned the car in at an Avis dealership and caught the train to New Haven.

During the trip she entertained herself by going through the suitcase the dead girl had intended to take to Canada. The suitcase was full of new clothes, some with the price tags still attached—the J. C. Penney Spring Collection. It had been an act of mercy to kill her. Otherwise she would surely have frozen to death.

As soon as the train arrived in New Haven she checked into Howard Johnson's near the station.

"Plenty of room," the woman behind the counter told her. "Plan to stay long?"

"I don't know. Is Yale far from here?"

"Only a few blocks, but there's nobody around. Place closes down over the term break. Why? You know somebody there?"

Angel didn't answer. Instead, she collected her key and went to her room.

Mrs. Wyman had a telephone on the night table in her bedroom. It was on a separate line and only half a dozen people on Earth knew the number. It was the only phone in the house which one could be reasonably certain would not be answered by a servant. The evening of her arrival in New Haven, Angel placed a call to that number from a pay phone in the hotel lobby.

She told her grandmother where she was.

"It will be impossible to come just now," Mrs. Wyman said.

"Don't come at all if you don't feel like it."

"Tonight is Christmas Eve. It would arouse suspicion if I were away from home just now. The day after tomorrow, take the train into New York City. I *want* to see you, child."

It was as close to a declaration of love as Angel had ever received from the old woman—from anyone, perhaps, except from Jim Kinkaid. They would meet on the ground floor of Sak's at one o'clock. They would have lunch together in the restaurant.

So the next day, which was Christmas, Angel was marooned in New Haven.

It was perhaps just as well that all the students were gone, or she might not have been able to keep away from Jim. He would be in law school now. Today he would be home, with his father. It was almost possible to hate him for that.

Except that she did not hate him. She had hated only a few people in her life, and then never for more than a second or two.

Love and hate struck her as unintelligible extravagances, like the passions of a child. She had been born with an immunity.

She wanted Jim Kinkaid because he loved her—or had loved her once. Other men had desired her, but she could sense that his emotions had a different texture from theirs. It had made her feel ... She was not quite sure what it had made her feel, but she knew she wanted to feel that way again. So she would have to have Jim back in her life. He was hers by right.

She spent Christmas day wandering around the Yale campus, wondering what Jim's life was like here. Her experience of the American educational system had been brief and unimpressive. Her notions of school had been formed by the convent in Paris, which she viewed, with some justice, as a sort of well-bred, academical prison. Even though her mother had lived in the same city, Angel had boarded at the convent, to be let out during vacations and for the odd weekend. It seemed to her that she had spent most of her life in one or another sort of prison.

Clearly this was something different. All of Yale's buildings seemed to exit directly onto the street—there was no "campus" as such and there were no walls. Where did people go after classes? Could it be, anywhere they wanted?

She wondered if Jim ever slept with any of the women students. He had never slept with her, had never even touched her breasts, so perhaps not. It hadn't even seemed to occur to him that such things were possible. Or perhaps he was simply afraid of her grandmother.

She didn't really think so. It was she herself he had been afraid of, the way men are always afraid of women.

The next morning she paid her hotel bill and boarded one of the commuter trains for New York.

Her grandmother was at her best during that interview. They had hardly sat down for lunch when the old woman took out of her handbag a manila envelope about the size and thickness of a brick and pushed it across the table to Angel.

"You will find ten thousand dollars in small used bills in there, along with a birth certificate, passbooks to two savings accounts taken out in San Francisco banks and a ticket on tonight's flight."

"You seem eager to get rid of me."

Her grandmother ignored the remark. "The money is all in place. All you need do is make yourself known to Mr. Grayson."

"Who am I, by the way?" Angel opened the clasp on the envelope and slipped out a passport. " 'Alicia Preston.' A relative perhaps?"

"Your grandfather's cousin, on his mother's side. She died in infancy. Now she will come into a considerable fortune. And she is in my will as the sole beneficiary. She will not have long to wait."

It was true. It had been not quite three years since Angel had seen her grandmother, but she looked as if she had aged ten. A waitress brought them coffee and the old woman's hands trembled slightly as she picked up the cup.

"There were no difficulties about the young woman, I trust. She is an excellent likeness, but persons of that type tend not to be very reliable."

"She will be perfectly reliable after five or six months under the snow."

The old woman's admirable self-possession hardly faltered. She was majestically silent, her lips a little compressed, as if in mild disapproval. Her real state of mind was betrayed only by the way her hands gripped at the edge of the table, as if she feared she might fall out of her chair.

"What did you expect?" Angel smiled sweetly. "Did you really think I was prepared to trust everything to some little street urchin? Why did you imagine I wanted the fingerprint card?"

Judge Wyman's widow shook her head slightly, the reproach seemingly aimed more at herself than anyone else.

"I sent that child to her death," she said at last. "She was meant only to play a brief part and then go on her way."

"Well, she'll play it all the better after the spring thaws her out and she's had a chance to weather a bit. Angela Wyman had to die, Grandmother—I should think you would see that. It isn't enough for her to just disappear. They won't stop looking for her until they know she's dead."

"You really are a monster."

"Yes. It runs in the family."

They never did get lunch. They simply got up from the table and left, taking the escalator down together and parting at the ground floor without a word being spoken.

For months afterwards Angel waited for some signal that her grandmother had lost her nerve and confessed everything, but it never came. And then, about three-quarters of a year later, her lawyer informed her that Mrs. Wyman was dead. The provisions of the will remained unchanged and no one came around with an arrest warrant, so in the end it seemed that family pride had won after all.

Unless, of course, Grandmother confessed to her lawyer, who would hardly be in a position to notify the police. Perhaps, in the end, that was how Jim came to be snooping around Sherman's Crest, busily adding up two and two.

But perhaps all was not lost. Perhaps he would have reasons of his own for keeping the secret, at least until he had served his purpose.

It would just be more interesting now. She had underestimated Jim—probably that was one of his strengths as a lawyer, that people tended to underestimate him.

She wouldn't make that mistake again.

chapter 27

    Warren Pratt had been in Paris since one o'clock that morning and so far he didn't much care for it. The coffee was terrible, there was no soap in his bathroom and none of the hotel staff seemed prepared to admit that they spoke a word of English. From the point of view of a homicide detective these were serious defects.

Worse was that he had no clear idea what he might be looking for and only one solid piece of information: the address of the apartment that Blanche Wyman had been renting at the time of her death. But it was difficult to imagine how that would help—a trail can grow very cold after ten years.

He showed the address to a taxi driver who wheeled him around town for about half an hour and then deposited him in front of an imposing gray building on a street lined with imposing gray buildings and demanded twenty-five francs. At least that was what his meter said. Pratt gave him three ten-franc notes and the man drove off as if he had been insulted.

There were fancy shops and restaurants all along both sides of the street. There were no signs on the buildings above the ground-floor level, which suggested the upper stories were given over to apartments. The sidewalks were clean. The plateglass windows were polished like mirrors. People were well dressed and there weren't too many of them. Clearly this was a wealthy neighborhood.

Pratt decided to look around a little, to get his bearings before he tried the address Jim Kinkaid had copied out for him from one of the letters in Mrs. Wyman's desk. He crossed the street to look at the building from the other side, and when he happened to glance to his left he noticed that he could see a corner of the Arc de Triomphe, about five blocks away.

"The guy stiffed me," he thought. This morning at breakfast he had had almost the same view through the dining room window. He was probably within walking distance of his hotel.

He scanned the street with a policeman's eye and noticed a doorway almost completely surrounded by magazine and newspaper racks. About half the magazines had naked women on their covers, but Pratt had been in the country long enough to understand that meant nothing about the respectability of the enterprise. Still, back in Dayton the neighborhood newsstand was always a good source for the local gossip.

He descended about three steps down to a small room containing still more newspaper racks and a glass counter displaying cartons of cigarettes and various other items. The woman behind it glanced at him and then seemed to forget his existence.

Pratt found a three-day-old copy of the *Observer*, took it to the counter and then pointed to a small box of licorice.

"That is four francs fifty," the woman said, in passable English. "The paper is a three francs."

"It's so obvious I'm a foreigner?"

The woman shrugged, registering that perfect indifference of which the French are masters. She wore a man's cardigan sweater over a starched white blouse. Although her hair was dyed a uniform bright yellow, Pratt would have put her age at about seventy.

"You buy an English-language paper and, besides, in those clothes you have to be an American. In this business you get to know the types. Do you want the licorice? It is from the Netherlands and not at all what you are used to."

"I'll try it, thanks." He was partial to licorice. "Do you see many Americans around here?"

"There are one or two who live nearby. Otherwise, here we are a little away from the tourist track."

From the way she looked at him it was clear she knew perfectly well he wasn't a tourist.

"You speak beautiful English," he said.

"I was married to an Englishman. I spent six years in Birmingham. That was shortly after the War. Have you ever been to Birmingham?"

"No."

"You haven't missed anything."

She watched with interest as he took another mint-condition ten-franc note out of his wallet. He was careful to let her see that it came from a big family.

"There was an American woman who lived just across the street a few years back. Her name was Wyman. Do you remember her?"

The woman might not have been listening. She ignored the ten-franc note that lay on her counter until Pratt put another one down beside it, then she swept them both up and stuffed them into the pocket of her sweater.

"She has been dead a long time," she said. "Why suddenly do you come all the way from America to ask questions about her?"

"Then you do remember her."

"Of course! How could I forget?" She shrugged again, this time punctuating it with a cynical little laugh. "This is not Chicago. It is not often such a thing happens in our placid little neighborhood."

"Oh yes, I remember her," Madame Augé told him, Augé being the name of her late second husband, the successor to the English soldier she had married in 1945. "She was a *client*. She bought those thin American cigarettes and British magazines. I got to know her quite well, as one does with some people—she was the sort who would talk to anyone. It was a shock when I heard she had been murdered, but not a surprise. Somebody was going to do it one day. She got on one's nerves."

"Who killed her?"

"Oh, some brute of a lover—she had a taste for the *louche*, so I have been told. They never caught him."

Pratt was a trifle disappointed but decided not to press the issue. It had been his experience that witnesses tend to supply more detail when they are allowed to tell a story in their own way.

"Did you know the daughter?"

"No. Madame Wyman was not particularly maternal, it seems. I did not know she had a child until after the poor woman was dead."

That was the pattern. The details of Blanche Wyman's life were hazy. Only the manner of its extinction stood out with perfect clarity.

Madame Augé remembered the day well. It was in early May some ten years back and it had rained that morning. She remembered the beads of rainwater on the polished black roofs of the police cars. She remembered how the *gendarmes* had kept everyone in the neighborhood under virtual house arrest until after lunchtime and how Madame Serif, a particular friend of hers and the *concierge* of the apartment building, had come running across the street to tell her everything as soon as she was allowed out.

"Her husband had found the body, you understand. Ernestine was chiefly affected by the novelty. She told me what Claude had told her, but she was very little touched by the tragedy of the thing."

"Could you help me get in contact with her?"

"I am not a *médium*, my dear. Poor Ernestine is no longer of this world, she and her husband both. They retired four years ago and moved to the South and *poof* . . . I think they died of boredom."

"What did she tell you?"

"That Claude had discovered the front door to the apartment

standing open. That he went inside, as anyone would—as was his duty—and he nearly stumbled over the corpse of Madame Wyman, sprawled across the entrance to her bedroom, where the shades were drawn and the room was still in twilight. That he would not describe to her the condition of the body, except to say that even after he had switched on the light he could hardly tell who it was."

Madame Augé seemed to lose interest in the story. Her attention turned to the stairway that led down from the sidewalk, as if she expected some particularly favored *client*.

"It is a hard life for a woman alone," she said, in what Pratt initially took to be an entirely personal observation. "Even if she is rich it is hard—sometimes particularly if she is rich. And Madame Wyman was a rich woman with a weakness for men from the criminal classes. It was an unfortunate combination."

With certain reservations, Chief Superintendent Daugard of the Sureté was of the same opinion.

"It was a characteristically French crime," he said, halfway through his third glass of wine—the Chief Superintendent had taken something of a shine to Pratt, like himself a student and philosopher of homicide, and, since he happened to be in the midst of one of his periodic separations from his wife, suggested that they adjourn their discussion to a local bistro, where they enjoyed a skimpy meal with appropriate lubrication. "In America murder is an extension of commerce and the typical victim is a small-time drug dealer who has become embroiled in some business dispute and is found with five or six bullet holes in his face and chest. The crime is impersonal, tidy and perfectly efficient, and most of the time no arrest is ever made."

He looked at his American colleague as if expecting a demur, but the appraisal struck Pratt as essentially accurate and, besides, he didn't want to deflect Daugard's attention from the death of Blanche Wyman.

In the teeth of this perhaps unwelcome concurrence Daugard tasted his wine again, made a face and seemed on the verge of complaining, but then dismissed it.

"In France," he continued, as if consoling himself, "in France murder is both intimate and ferocious and is generally the sort of dramatic gesture which disdains consequences. It is for this reason that usually within twenty-four hours we have the guilty party in our lockup and a lengthy signed confession filed with the examining magistrate. Justice has been rendered to everyone's satisfaction, including the perpetrator's. A French murderer is not only easier to catch, he has a better sense of theater."

"Was Blanche Wyman's murder good theater?"

Daugard glanced at him slyly, as if acknowledging the hit, and then indulged himself in a deep, operatic sigh—French policemen, it seemed, were also not without a sense of theater.

"You no doubt refer to the disappointing conduct of René Bec. He was a disgrace to French homicide, but alas, my friend, what can one expect from a failed pimp whose mother was half Algerian?"

"You never caught him?"

"No. But never fear that he has gone unpunished. Since we foolishly did away with the guillotine, the worst he faced would have been a stay in one of our luxurious prisons while he waited for the next general amnesty. As it is, by now surely someone has cut the little rodent's throat."

"Tell me about the crime scene."

At first the Chief Superintendent, who was impatiently gesturing at their waiter, appeared not to have heard him. It was only after his wine glass had been refilled that he was once more able to devote his attention to professional matters.

"Did I tell you it was one of the last cases I handled directly?" he said. "Shortly thereafter I was promoted and my work is now largely administrative. I have never regretted the change. One can grow weary of anything, even murder. It loses its power to shock."

You should have seen Stephen Billinger, Pratt thought to himself, but he said nothing. He merely nodded, one burnt-out homicide detective to another.

"I have always felt a certain sense of grievance against René Bec—what if he *had* been the last? One does not like to abandon a lifetime's work on a false note."

Daugard smiled with reassuring cheerfulness and raised his glass, as if offering a toast to some dimly remembered crime.

"Fortunately a bakery clerk in the Tenth *Arrondissement* saved me from that fate by beating his sister to death with a silver candlestick, part of their mother's estate over which they had been quarreling for months. The candlestick, by the way, turned out to be plate."

They laughed over this charming irony and then Pratt rephrased his request. "Tell me about the crime scene at the Wyman killing."

"Distasteful in the extreme," Daugard answered, shaking his head. "The weapon was a pair of bronze fireplace tongs, heavier than one would have thought. Madame Wyman's head was little more than pulp."

The food on the Chief Superintendent's plate was some sort of goulash. He pushed it away from him now as if the sight of it stirred unpleasant memories.

"There were no signs of a struggle and no signs of forced entry. The victim was found in her nightdress and an autopsy revealed traces of semen, indicating that she had had sexual intercourse within a few hours of her death, which the Medical Examiner put between one and three in the morning. What does one conclude from this? That shortly after entertaining her lover Madame Wyman is beaten to death by someone whom she had voluntarily admitted to her apartment or who had a key, and that that someone had sufficient strength—and, perhaps more important, sufficient rage—to inflict a great deal of damage on the corpse. The incident carries all the hallmarks of a romantic quarrel, wouldn't you agree?"

"So you are quite satisfied that Bec did it?"

"Oh yes. The *concierge* placed him in the apartment late that afternoon and four years earlier he had served eighteen months of a three-year sentence for stabbing a prostitute. There is also the fact of his disappearance."

"And you never traced him?"

"No. It is as if he stepped off into oblivion. I personally believe he returned to Algeria, which comes to much the same thing."

"Did you question the daughter?"

Daugard allowed himself a look of amused incredulity. "What do you take us for, Lieutenant? Of course we questioned the daughter, but she could furnish us with no useful information. She had not seen her mother in three months and had never even met Bec."

"So she was never a suspect?"

"No. At the time of the crime she was locked up in her convent—an alibi not to be trifled with, believe me. Besides, one only had to look at her to know she was incapable of such an act."

Incapable of such an act. The professional opinion of an experienced homicide detective—but, then, Pratt had never met Angela Wyman and therefore could not judge. It just went to show . . .

"Did you meet the mother?"

"You mean the victim's mother?" Daugard raised his eyebrows significantly. "A formidable woman. She manifested no interest whatever in our efforts to catch Bec. Without actually putting the thing into words—since that kind, you must know, says very little to the point—she managed to suggest that the murder was entirely her daughter's fault. One gathers that the women of that family are not strongly maternal."

He peered into his wine glass as if to confirm to himself the sad truth that it was in fact empty and then leaned back against his chair and sighed, pursing his lips in resignation. Apparently he had reached some self-imposed limit, because he did not recall the waiter.

"But she was not far wrong, you know, my friend? You, like I, have sifted through the lives of many murdered men and women, but how many have you found that were entirely blameless? There is usually a certain rough justice in the victim's fate. He or she deserves to die. Blanche Wyman surely did. If René Bec had not killed her, eventually someone else would have. She was a bad woman."

Pratt did not disagree. If pressed he would have said that no one deserves to be murdered, but it was also true that some people attract violence to them, as if somehow they could never be complete until their heads had been beaten into pulp.

The Chief Superintendent seemed in danger of losing his train of thought. Evil, like blood on the wallpaper, had apparently lost its shock value and was in danger of becoming a bore.

"Did you ever find a father for the girl?" Pratt asked, simply to pull Daugard back. "Was there any record of a marriage?"

"No, no marriage. There were many men, most of them like Bec; certainly none was in any hurry to claim paternity. There was no father and, for all practical purposes, there was no mother. Madame Wyman hardly ever saw her child. It is a mystery to me why she ever went through the pregnancy, since she seemed the type for which an all-seeing Providence put expensive Swiss abortion clinics on this earth. Narcotics, gangster boyfriends, all the usual vices of wealthy, bored women, these were her natural element. I am at a loss to imagine how even the briefest excursion into motherhood could have tempted her."

"I would have liked to talk to Bec," Pratt announced suddenly, as if the idea had just occurred to him.

"Why?" Daugard made a face, a mingling of horror and distaste. The waiter might have just offered him a peanut-butter sandwich. "Take my word for it, he was not an interesting conversationalist."

"I would have liked to speak with someone who knew her habits—who knew what her life was like."

"Well. If that is all . . ." Daugard made a small, dismissive gesture. "I suppose something of the sort can be arranged."

It was the smell, of course—that mingling of hopelessness and disinfectant. Prisons were the same everywhere. Pratt could have closed his eyes and imagined himself back in the Dayton city lockup.

But he was not. He was in Paris, enjoying celebrity status as an emissary of American police culture. Daugard placed a car and driver at his disposal, and the young constable with whom he went splashing through the rain puddles of suburban streets—and who had probably never even heard of Dayton—entertained him with questions about life on the homicide squad. Pratt decided not to be flattered. After all, policemen live on crime, so America is the Promised Land. Every cop in the world wants to be Kojak.

In any case, everyone had been wonderfully cooperative. Daugard even promised to look for one of Blanche's bad boys who spoke English. As it happened, just such an article happened to be doing twenty-to-life in the slammer at Corbeil-Essonnes for multiple counts of burglary and aggravated assault.

Jean-Pierre DuBoisseau was a rather seedy thug of about fifty who looked as if he had come to terms with the fact that he was going to die behind bars. Fifteen years ago he had probably been handsome in a brutal sort of way, but boredom and bad food had softened him. He hadn't shaved in three or four days and his black hair was shot through with gray and beginning to grow grizzled.

"Do you have a smoke?" he asked, in an accent he seemed to have picked up from Humphrey Bogart movies. His fingers rested against the heavy steel mesh that divided the visiting room in half. The spaces between were just wide enough to allow Pratt to push through one of the cigarettes with which he had been farsighted enough to provide himself. The guard, who was standing just behind and to the right of his chair, raised his eyebrows but made no objection—a fact which was not lost on DuBoisseau.

"Camels," he said, holding the cigarette under his nose with the appreciation of a connoisseur. "Delicious. They kill you all the faster, but who cares? Do you have a light?"

Pratt lit a paper match and held it through the grating. "You can have the rest of the pack," he said. But DuBoisseau only shook his head.

"There is no point." He glanced at the guard standing beside the door through which Pratt had come in. "*He* will only take them away the moment you leave. Let us have a long conversation, long enough to allow me to smoke five or six. Whom are you collecting evidence against?"

"Against no one. I want you to tell me about Blanche Wyman."

For a moment DuBoisseau seemed not to have understood, but then he smiled. It was a smile full of cruelty.

"That one," he said, and then took a deep drag on his cigarette. "She had plenty of money and she was a good fuck. What else is there to tell?"

"Where did you meet her?"

"Why? Are you an aggrieved relative?" The idea seemed to amuse DuBoisseau, or perhaps it was simply that the nicotine in his lungs was making him feel more relaxed. "Perhaps you are the husband Blanche left behind when she ran away from America."

"I never met the lady. Is that why she came to Europe, to escape her husband?"

DuBoisseau's face collapsed into an expression of droll melancholy, and he shook his head. "There was never any husband—if there had been she would have mentioned him. I don't believe she knew herself who was the father of her child."

With the guile born of scores of homicide interrogations, Pratt allowed his eyes to drop to the cement floor, as if he found the oblique reference to Angel slightly embarrassing. He did not want to talk about Angel just yet, because he did not want DuBoisseau guessing that Angel was the real subject of their conversation. DuBoisseau was a man with hardly any power left over the world, and Pratt did not want him to be aware that he had it in his power to deny him what he most wanted.

"Where did you meet her?" he repeated.

DuBoisseau shrugged. "I picked her up in a café, I think. I hardly remember. Why? What is it to you?"

"I've been hired to find out what I can." Pratt managed a faint smile—he was a mercenary, you see. He was in it for the money. He didn't really care. "Someone wants to know about the life Blanche Wyman lived in Paris. I didn't think it very tactful to ask him his reasons."

"Someone in America?"

"Yes."

"Oh, well. In that case it is all right. I shouldn't like anyone having trouble with the police, but America doesn't matter."

"I have the feeling the thing is entirely personal—the police don't come into it. Perhaps my client is the husband she ran away from."

DuBoisseau laughed loud enough at this that the guard pursed his lips in disapproval.

"Then perhaps you should tell him how she liked to have sex with a man's hands around her throat. She was a gasper, that one. She couldn't come unless you half killed her."

"Do you think that was how she died?"

After considering the matter for a few seconds, DuBoisseau shrugged once more. "I understand she was beaten to death, but it is possible her tastes in lovemaking had something to do with it. A woman like that can lead a man into bad habits."

"I gather you didn't like her very much."

"She had her uses. That is the most which can be said."

DuBoisseau took the cigarette out of his mouth and looked at it with an expression of evident distaste. It was only half consumed, but he dropped it on the cement floor and ground it out under his shoe. Pratt passed him another through the mesh.

"In prison one smokes them until they burn one's fingers," he said, "but I assume you are prepared to indulge me. There is no pleasure after the first few puffs—one is merely feeding an addiction."

"Did Blanche Wyman have any addictions?"

DuBoisseau blew smoke through the grating that divided the visiting room in two, simply to annoy the guard.

"You are not who you claim," he said. "You are police. Otherwise this fat monkey would have had me dragged back to my cell."

"I'm retired."

"Retired? From what? Narcotics?"

"Homicide."

"An American homicide detective—no wonder they are so tolerant. Even I am impressed."

"Then perhaps you'll answer the question. Did Blanche Wyman have any addictions?"

"Do you mean to something besides myself?" DuBoisseau smiled, as if uttering a boast, but when Pratt didn't respond he seemed to lose interest. "She had the usual vices. She liked men. She liked the fast life. Had she lived she would be a ruin today. Whoever killed her did her a favor."

"Is there any doubt?"

"About what? That she is better off dead?"

"No." Pratt shook his head. "About who killed her. The police seem quite certain it was her last lover."

"Bec? No—it was not he. I knew him. René did not have

the vitality to kill someone in so direct a manner. Blanche's murderer had to have been someone who really hated her."

"Then who?"

"Perhaps an old lover. Perhaps that pretty daughter of hers—there would at least have been a certain poetic justice to that. In any case it was not René."

"Did the daughter hate her mother, then?"

"Who said so?" DuBoisseau looked suddenly wary. "Is that it? Did you come here to question me about Angel?"

"Was that her name?"

"Yes. And I have no desire to cause her any trouble."

"She's beyond trouble. She's dead."

"Oh."

The middle-aged convict's face sagged and an expression of tenderness began to appear about his eyes, confirming yet again Pratt's theory that all petty criminals are at bottom sentimentalists.

"How did she die?"

"I don't know the circumstances, except that she died in a mental hospital."

"I don't believe it," DuBoisseau announced, without defiance. "Angel was not the fragile type."

"Then perhaps I'm lying."

"Do not mock me."

With an almost comical dignity, DuBoisseau threw his cigarette away so that it rolled along the floor, scattering sparks. A few minutes later, however, he was constrained to ask for another one.

"So she is dead, eh?" he said, almost as if to himself. "Alas—what a waste. What a beauty that child was!"

"Could she have killed her mother?"

"Do you mean, was she capable of it? Yes. She was capable of anything. To survive being Blanche's daughter she had to have had considerable resourcefulness. Beyond that you will have to consult the police, for I was in Lyon when the crime was committed. By then I had not seen Blanche Wyman in over a year."

"I wasn't suggesting you were involved—I don't care who was involved," Pratt said, in a tone of emphatic sincerity he only used when he was lying. "I'm not concerned with the legal consequences of Madame Wyman's murder. I only want to understand the kind of life she led that made such an end possible."

DuBoisseau shifted slightly on the metal prison chair and folded his arms as he tucked his head down in an attitude of concentration. The cigarette between his lips looked as if it had been nailed in place.

"Possible, no," he answered at last. "Inevitable."

"Then tell me."

Daugard's young constable had at least learned when to shut up. During the entire drive back from the prison, with Pratt sitting morosely beside him on the front seat, he never uttered a syllable.

This was wise. The last thing Pratt wanted was conversation. He wanted to think, and to remember.

"Men wandered in and out of Blanche's life as casually as if it were a metro station," DuBoisseau had said. "I myself lived with her on three separate occasions, once for nearly a year. I had other women as well—she did not care, so long as I did not bring them home."

"This was going on while she had her daughter with her?"

"Yes, of course. Have I shocked you?" DuBoisseau smiled with a kind of amused pity. "Well then, perhaps you are not precisely shocked, but you do not like hearing it. Nevertheless, Angel had nothing to fear from her mother's various lovers. Bec, for instance, was in awe of her."

"And you?"

"Angel was eight or nine years old when I first knew her. We were perfectly content to ignore each other."

"And later?"

"Later, her mother had much to be jealous of."

Jean-Pierre DuBoisseau, petty thief, minor league drug dealer, suspected murderer, smiled again, implicitly adding child abuse to his list of offenses.

"I thought you said Blanche wasn't the jealous type."

"She was jealous of Angel—why do you suppose she locked her away in that convent? To safeguard her virtue? Hah!"

His one syllable of laughter appeared to startle DuBoisseau, enough that he paused for a moment and then lapsed into a fit of coughing.

"Cigarettes are very bad for the health, but one must die of something, eh? Be kind enough to give me another."

"Fine." Pratt fished one more out of the pack and slipped it through the wire mesh that separated the prisoner from his visitor. He lit a match but held it away, cupping his hand around it as if to focus its light. "Now tell me about Angel."

For perhaps three or four seconds DuBoisseau was perfectly still, and then he moved his head closer to the mesh, inviting Pratt to light his cigarette.

"What is it you wish to know?" he asked.

What indeed? Why would anyone wish to hear such things?

"She was not a victim," DuBoisseau had said. "If humanity is truly divided between predators and prey, then she belonged among the former. I have had little experience of children, but I do not believe that Angel was ever a child. Once, when she was very young, I bought her a doll, a pretty, old-fashioned thing I found in a flea market near the University. I took it home to her, thinking she would be pleased. She took the doll by the legs and broke its face in against a radiator pipe. She was not even angry. She simply did it."

In his mind's eye Pratt could see the crime scene photos of Branche Wyman's corpse, her face beaten into an unrecognizable pulp. It would have taken a fair amount of time to inflict that amount of damage—more time than could be accounted for even by psychotic rage. And he remembered another corpse, found lying on a motel room floor, its face peeled carefully away.

"Did she hate her mother?"

"No more than she hated the doll," DuBoisseau answered, his eyes narrowing slightly to show that the parallel had not been lost on him either. "As I said, she was not a victim. At thirteen and fourteen she was all but seducing her mother's lovers—Angel had a heart that beat once an hour. It was Blanche who hated her. And with reason. Can you imagine what it must have been like in that apartment, the two of them alone together?"

"Did she kill Blanche?"

DuBoisseau, his faced clouded in cigarette smoke, merely shrugged.

"The police say René Bec killed Blanche. Who am I to challenge the wisdom of the police?"

Who indeed. Riding back through the streets of suburban Paris, trying not to listen to the buzz of his own mind, Pratt had no difficulty imagining how the crime could have been committed. In outline it was clear enough.

It was a maxim of police work: if you need to find your way around an apartment house, just find yourself a kid who lives there. A kid will know everything—all the forgotten doorways blocked up with old packing cases, all the dark, shadowy hiding places beneath the stairs, every inch. And Angel had lived in the same building all her life. There was nothing surprising in the idea that she could have gotten in and out of her mother's apartment without the concierge having any knowledge of it.

The convent, of course, was no problem. What boarding school brat hasn't gone over the wall once or twice?

And she knew the routines of her mother's life. She knew when Blanche would be entertaining René Bec and that Bec might then absent himself for a time, for a breath of fresh air or a nightcap or just to get away for an hour or two. Bec would return to an empty apartment, the air cold and stinking of blood, and find Blanche stretched out on her bedroom floor. He would know that he was the obvious suspect. He might have decided to disappear.

Or maybe Angel was waiting for him. DuBoisseau said Bec was afraid of her, if that was what he had meant, but maybe the canary had come under the cobra's spell—maybe Bec, against his better judgment, had fallen in love with her.

"We can run away together," she might have told him. "Otherwise, I'll say you did it."

In which case, René Bec was somewhere no one would ever find him. He probably hadn't outlived Blanche by more than a few hours.

It was not, however, a theory that recommended itself to Daugard. Daugard apparently had romantic notions about the innocence of childhood.

"Believe me," he said, as they sat together in his crowded little office. "I interrogated her myself—she was not involved."

"Then perhaps René Bec had a rival."

"No—it seems not." Daugard managed a Gallic shrug, as if to say, *what a delightful idea, but alas . . .* "We went over her apartment with great care, and it would appear that Bec's hold on her was perfectly secure. We found no fingerprints except those belonging to Madame Wyman, her daughter, Bec and the elderly woman who came in twice a week to clean. There was no one else."

In that instant Pratt felt as if he had been startled awake as the obvious hit him with all the force of revelation. Sweet Jesus, he thought, the French police had Angel Wyman's fingerprints.

chapter 29

The pilot had announced they would be on the ground in ten minutes. From the window beside his first-class seat Kinkaid could see the long thumbprint of San Francisco Bay glistening in the late afternoon sun. He could see into people's backyards now. In one of them he saw a woman on a riding mower, wearing a floppy straw hat. Her arms were bare beneath its shade, and her elbows flaired out to the sides as she moved over the bare, parched lawn. She seemed to be traveling faster than the plane.

"If I live through the landing the rest of my life will hold no terrors for me," Lisa murmured. She looked a trifle green. Lisa, as it turned out, was afraid of flying.

"I didn't think it was a good idea for you to come, if you'll remember."

"Let's not go through that again."

Kinkaid considered the matter for an instant and then nodded. No, there wasn't any point in going through that again.

"If you like we can go home by train," he said.

Lisa did not look particularly consoled. He had offered her the window seat, but she had declined. She wanted a clear field to the ladies' room, she said.

Kinkaid turned his attention back to the view. The world down there was becoming more real every second. Pretty soon they would be back in it. He wondered, for the millionth time, if he hadn't been criminally spineless to agree to bringing Lisa with him, and for the millionth time he decided that, yes, he had been.

Because Angel was down there somewhere. He was sure of

it, as sure as if he could see her tracks in the muddy shoreline of the bay. And Angel was the real reason he had come.

"It's a huge deal," Eric Tollison had said over the phone. "The developer is our client and he's been throwing up shopping malls all over the Northeast, but he's stretched too thin and he needs money. The California group has the money— we just have to make sure our client doesn't have to trade his balls for it."

"The biggest real-estate deal I've ever been involved in was the sale of a two-family house."

"That doesn't matter, Jim Boy. Our San Francisco affiliates are well versed in the subtleties. I just need you out there to put a little spine into them."

Tollison always called him "Jim Boy" when he wanted Kinkaid to play gunslinger. It was just part of the pep talk.

But spine had been a department in which Kinkaid had been rather conspicuously lacking just recently, as was evidenced by Lisa's presence here beside him on Flight 5 from Kennedy.

"What was that?" she asked tensely, clutching at his arm as they heard the shrill whine of the plane's hydraulics.

"They're just lowering the wheels."

"We'll probably crash on the runway."

"These big planes are so computerized you won't even realize it when we touch the ground."

"Of course not—I'll be dead from the impact."

Kinkaid smiled. If she was making jokes she was all right.

He should have said no. He realized that now. But it is hard to be firm about a thing like that when the woman in your life says the whole relationship is on the line.

"Don't shut me out now," she had told him. "You've kept this locked up inside you for so long—if you find her out there, and if I'm sitting back here in Connecticut, I think you'll be alone with it for the rest of your life. Don't do that to us."

And he had at last consented, thinking that, after all, there was probably no real danger. Angel was killing off her old lovers, among whom young James could not be numbered, so there was no reason to believe she would take any particular interest in him.

But now, with California only two minutes away, he couldn't help but remember that he really didn't have any clear idea what was going on in Angel's head, that her motives were probably intelligible to no one except herself, that he was putting Lisa within reach of a maniac who had killed at least seven people.

Once they had landed, and the airplane was rolling tentatively around the runway like an old woman in a wheelchair, Lisa jumped up and started wrestling a soft-sided overnight bag free from beneath her seat.

"I can't wait to get out of here," she said. "With a mob like this disembarking we'll have to hustle to get a cab."

"Not a problem. The first-class luggage always comes off first, so we'll have a head start, and anyway they're sending a limousine to meet us."

She sat down again with a thud, looking disappointed.

"I know it isn't very democratic . . ."

"That isn't the point. I was just thinking, a limousine makes it kind of official, doesn't it. It's not like we're sneaking off somewhere nobody knows us for a dirty weekend. I guess I'll have to get used to being pointed out as The Girlfriend."

"We're living together, remember? If Julia can accept it, so can the brethren at Gilhuly, Carp and Dunlap. Or maybe I could just put you out of your misery—Las Vegas is only an hour's flight away and there's no waiting period in Nevada. You could be Mrs. Kinkaid in time for bed."

"Thanks, no. If it means another plane ride I'll go on living in sin. Don't think I don't appreciate the thought."

"I wasn't kidding, you know."

She smiled at him with that mingling of tenderness and

gratitude that always made him understand with perfect clarity why he loved her.

And then the moment was lost when the cabin door opened and everyone began scrambling for their coats and their carry-ons. They drifted along with the current of departing passengers and suddenly found themselves in the terminal.

"What are you looking for?"

"Our driver," Kinkaid answered, lying. He hadn't been aware he was looking for anyone, but of course he was. It was idiotic, really—as if he had expected Angel to meet their plane.

"How will he know where to find us?"

"We'll find him, probably down by the luggage carousels. He'll be standing out in plain sight, probably wearing a black suit and holding up a piece of cardboard with 'Mr. Kinkaid' spelled out in block letters. That's the way it usually works."

And all the while he spoke his eyes darted about, searching for the face he had not seen in ten years yet which was as familiar to him as his own. She was not among the little knots of people turned expectantly toward the off-ramp, looking for someone they knew to pop out from among the disembarking passengers. She was not sitting in the departure lounge in an attitude of bored hopelessness. She was not one of the ground crew that clustered around the check-in counter. It was with a slight shock that he realized he was disappointed.

"Are you still in love with her?" Lisa had asked him, more than once.

He had always answered "no." The girl he had loved was an illusion, as spectral as a ghost. How could love survive the discoveries he had made about Angel Wyman? And yet he was disappointed not to see her face.

Because he felt her presence, like a stain in the very air. Perhaps he hoped that the sight of her would dispel it.

"How do you know she's in San Francisco?"

He had smiled at the question, because it was so faint a chance. "I don't, but if she isn't there I don't know where else to look. Lew Olmstead came to this airport to meet a man in a coffee shop and give him an envelope. Jimmy Carfax favors a brand of chocolates he has sent to him from California—he told me a *friend* of his told him about them."

"Are you saying you think she's out here because this is where a nutcase gets his goodies?" Lisa shook her head in disbelief. He couldn't blame her.

"Okay, it was the way he said it. He was such a coy bastard—he was throwing out a big hint, just for fun. Besides, how many friends do you suppose Jimmy Carfax has in the wide world?"

"That's it? That's all you're going on?"

"There's also the fact that the lawyer for the Wyman family heirs is in San Francisco. Personally, if you want to know the truth, I think there's only one heir."

"It still isn't very much."

"No kidding."

Yet he had only to set foot in California to know that he had been right. She was here.

The airport corridors were endless. Near the entrance to the main lobby he saw someone he thought might be their driver—perhaps because he looked somehow familiar—but the man turned and seemed to melt away almost as soon as Kinkaid's gaze touched him. Otherwise there was nothing.

She isn't here, he told himself. She probably isn't even in the state. Maybe I'm the one who's crazy and she really is buried back in Vermont.

He didn't believe it for a moment—she was there, watching him.

The impression stayed with him through the long walk to the carousels, where, sure enough, a man in a dark suit was holding up a sign with "Kinkaid" scribbled across it. It was with him while they waited for their luggage. It did not leave until they did. Only when the door closed on the black stretch limousine and they were on the highway leading north to San Francisco did he lose the sense that her eyes were on him.

But it was Frank Rizza who copied down the number of the limousine as it drove away with Kinkaid and the woman, who looked like she might be Italian—a nice little guinea broad to keep the sheets warm while he had to be away from home. The WASP college boy was slumming.

Rizza tried to work up some anger against this anonymous lawyer, whom he knew only by sight and through Al De-Costa's sketchy reports, because he knew he was probably going to have to be fairly hard on the guy and he wasn't very happy about it.

The problem was, you do a drug pusher or a pimp or even a customer and the cops treat it like it's a public service. You can do a whole family of Colombians in one of the housing projects and the investigation won't last any longer than the publicity. But Kinkaid just didn't belong to the whackable classes. He was a lawyer and, at least according to Al, he didn't have any dirt under his fingernails. Living or dead, the guy had clout. Kill him and it's not a statistic, it's a murder.

So Rizza knew he would be taking a chance, but he didn't see he had much choice. He had pretty much decided that Kinkaid was the only way he was going to get himself free from the Ice Queen.

Al DeCosta had turned up some very interesting information on Kinkaid, which Rizza was inclined to believe because Al hadn't ended up running Atlantic City simply because he was married to the old don's only daughter. He was no fool and Old Man Ricolli surely would have died in federal prison rather than in his own bed if it hadn't been for his son-in-law.

And according to Al for decades the law firm of Kinkaid & Kinkaid had had as their principal client an old Connecticut family named Wyman, so powerful they almost ran the state. Supposedly they were all dead now, but the house was about to be sold and it turned out that the money was going to the heirs, who were represented by a lawyer in—you guessed it—good old Frisco by the Bay.

Rizza had made the connection at once. He had known Kinkaid would be his ticket home, from the instant he saw him come out of the church after that hick marshall's funeral—except for one other guy, who turned out to be a retired cop from someplace in Ohio, Kinkaid was the only one there who wasn't in uniform. Miss Alicia Preston orders Marshall Cheffins chopped and then, even after the newspapers have had him for breakfast and all the decent citizens want to forget they ever heard of him, our lawyer friend turns up as the chief mourner.

Then it turns out that Kinkaid was the *consigliere* for the mandarins who put Cheffins in his job. Could it be that Miss Look-But-Don't-Touch is tied in with the all-powerful Wymans and she had the marshall killed because he knew something? And maybe Kinkaid is still her lawyer and is in on the secret too.

In any case, Rizza had decided he just had to have a talk with this guy.

But it was awkward. Short of sticking a gun up his nose, a lawyer was hard to intimidate. And their first instinct, after they've been pushed around a little, is to go to the police and tell them all about it. So Rizza knew he had to be prepared to kill James Kinkaid. He wasn't pleased about it, but there just wasn't any nice way to do these things. So what the fuck—it was an imperfect world.

chapter 30

The law offices of Gilhuly, Carp and Dunlap occupied the fourth floor of a triangular building in North Beach, an area which laid claim to a certain bohemian charm decades after the last beatnik had moved away and the coffeehouses had all closed down to be replaced by upscale topless bars that did a brisk tourist business. Kinkaid had been booked into the Saint Francis and his room faced out onto Union Square, which also wasn't turning away anyone's money but managed to be a little less obvious about it.

A car and driver had been put at his disposal, but after the first morning, when he figured out that North Beach was not even a mile from his hotel, he decided that he preferred to walk. He tried to vary his route a little each time, coming and going, but he liked Grant Avenue best because it ran through Chinatown. Sometimes he even walked back to Union Square to meet Lisa for lunch. By the end of four days he had decided that his walks were by far the most interesting part of his trip.

Because by then he was close to deciding that Eric Tollison had been less than candid with him about what he was supposed to be doing in San Francisco. Certainly there was nothing about this particular piece of business that required his special talents—the boys at Gilhuly, Carp and Dunlap gave the impression they were a pretty hard-nosed bunch who could look out for themselves. They set him up in a borrowed office with a nice view of the street and sent a fair amount of paper across his desk, but they were just being polite. They seemed to think he was there for some sort of crash course in real estate law.

So why? What was he doing that was worth the daily two thousand and change it was costing Karskadon and Henderson to keep him there? By the weekend he was about ready to phone New York and ask.

"So why don't you?"

They were sitting in a booth in a seafood restaurant down on Fisherman's Wharf and Lisa was wearing the huge paper bib that had come with her crab dinner—somehow it made her look about nine years old, which was enough to make Kinkaid feel all runny inside.

"Because if I do Tollison will either tell me to just go on billing at two fifty an hour and stop talking like a jerk or he'll say 'Okay then, come home.' And I don't want to go home. All I've found out about Angel Wyman so far is that she's not in the phone book."

"Then what are you going to do?" She had slipped out of her shoe and was running her stockinged foot up the inside of his trouser leg, which made it hard to concentrate.

"Go on billing at two fifty an hour and stop talking like a jerk. And, if you keep that up, we'll probably end the evening under arrest for lewd and indecent behavior."

"I didn't know that was illegal."

"It is in public, even in San Francisco."

"Then we'll make an early night of it, and stay out of jail."

At this point they were supposed to exchange intimate, knowing smiles, but Lisa's face had changed in a way that demonstrated that her attention was occupied elsewhere. She wasn't even looking at him, but over his shoulder and toward the entrance.

"What's the matter?" Kinkaid asked, touching her on the back of the hand to get her attention. "If you want the waiter you're looking in the wrong direction."

That seemed to break the spell. She laughed, although she must have known he wasn't making a joke, and then went back to pulling apart her crab as if nothing else in the world mattered.

"I hate to sound paranoid, but I think we're being followed."

Kinkaid glanced first at her and then at his dinner, in which he discovered he had completely lost interest, and then outside, where a seagull had landed on one of the pilings and was observing them both with insolent calm.

"Anyone I might know?"

"I don't think so. I saw him this afternoon, while I was shopping, and I think I might have seen him at the airport when we arrived."

"Where is he?"

"At the bar. But don't turn around—he's watching us."

"What does he look like?"

"Dark sports coat, yellow shirt. About forty. A little under average height if he isn't slouching. Dark hair. Southern Italian but not Sicilian."

"You're sure?"

"Take my word for it—where are you going?"

He was standing by then, and he smiled down at her. "To the gent's."

The restaurant was a long room built over a pier, with plateglass windows down either side so that the diners had a view of the bay, or at least of the fishing boats that were anchored just outside. The bar and the men's room were both in the front and in so narrow a space there was no way the two men were going to miss each other, no matter how hard they tried.

The man looked annoyed. He slipped outside as Kinkaid approached and, although he wasn't stupid enough to risk eye contact, there wasn't any doubt he was the one, yellow shirt and all.

"Did you see him?" Lisa asked when he came back.

"Yes. And you were right. He was at the airport."

By then, of course, Kinkaid remembered the first time he had seen him, leaning against the fender of a dark blue car after Marshal Cheffins' funeral. He had been across the street— Pratt had pointed him out.

But he said nothing of this. He merely sat down and went back to his bluefish.

"What should we do about it?"

"Do?"

Lisa, who was the positive type, looked impatient, as if he were being willfully stupid.

"He might be dangerous," she announced. "He might have a gun."

"Yes, he might. He might be a policeman or a private detective. He might also be nobody at all."

"You know that isn't true. You saw the way he ducked out."

Kinkaid shrugged, as if he couldn't see how it mattered. "What would you suggest I do about it? The police wouldn't be very impressed. Anyway, maybe he's after you—that at least I could understand."

"Don't be silly. Maybe you should think about protecting yourself."

"Now who's being silly?" Kinkaid managed a wan smile. "A gun? Is that what you have in mind? We haven't all had your advantages, my dear. I'm not the firearms type. I'd probably end up shooting my foot off."

Lisa extended the first two fingers of her right hand, aiming straight at his head, and made a little popping sound with her mouth. Then she laughed, just to show that she hadn't lost her sense of humor.

"I should get my dad to teach you how," she said. "He's really good. He'd turn you into Dead-Eye Dick."

"I don't think I'd care to take the chance. An Italian ex-Marine—he'd probably decide the family honor demanded my life."

"He'd like you."

"Thanks, but I'd rather not risk it until after the wedding."

The next morning was a Saturday. The original plan had been to take a boat ride around San Francisco Bay, but a thick fog had come in the night before, so there didn't seem to be much point. Instead they took a cab out to Golden Gate Park and went to the aquarium. The place was cavelike and the octopus was hiding. There was a big tank full of eels and in another tank was an alligator gar the size of a submarine. Lisa said she would probably never go swimming again.

They tried to have lunch at the Japanese Tea Garden but discovered that all they served was tea, so they settled for pizza at a stand. Directly across from the aquarium was a museum full of paintings by people neither of them had ever heard of—lots of 19th Century American local color and perfectly terrifying Spanish religious art, with here and there the odd student of a student of Poussin. They loved it. They spent all afternoon there.

They had dinner on Union Street, and when they got back to the hotel there was a message waiting. No name, just a telephone number with a 513 area code.

"Pratt must be back in Dayton," Kinkaid said, putting the note in his jacket pocket. "I guess they're about two hours ahead out there. It'll keep."

The next morning, before he went out for his run, he called from one of the lobby phones.

"Blanche Wyman was murdered," Pratt told him, with no preamble. "The French police think our little girlfriend is in the clear, but who knows. The point is they have her fingerprints in their files."

He paused, no doubt waiting for some reaction, but not for long.

"She's alive, Jim. She's loose in the world. I got them to have the FBI fax over the prints they took from the girl buried in your loony bin, and they don't match. She pulled a switch, just like you thought. How does it feel to be right?"

"Just at the moment, not so hot. What do we do now?"

"I've given everything to the feds. As soon as they get over the shock they'll issue a warrant for interstate flight. I've already talked to their behavioral science people and they're very interested. A lot of dead case files are going to come back to life."

You could hear it in Pratt's voice, a stifled joy. He was the hunter come within sight of his prey. He was a cop, a homicide detective, and this was the biggest case of his life. He couldn't help himself.

"She's in San Francisco, Warren."

"Is that what you're doing out there, looking for her?"

"I thought so until a few days ago. Remember what they say—a man chases a woman until she catches him."

"What are you getting at, Jim?"

"I think I've been set up. I think I'm here because she wants me to be here. Remember the guy who was outside after Cheffins' funeral?"

"What guy?"

"The guy you thought was probably a crook come to pay his respects. He was leaning up against his car."

"What about him?"

"He was at the airport when we arrived. I saw him again yesterday."

"I'll be on the next flight out."

chapter 31

Rizza didn't want to involve the girlfriend, so he decided the best time to do it was first thing in the morning. Five mornings in a row, the watchers had reported, Kinkaid comes out of his hotel in a tee shirt and pair of blue nylon shorts and goes loping off down Post Street and over to Market toward the Embarcadero. Then it's a long run along the waterfront, way the hell and gone past the Presidio and back, a good ten miles round-trip. The guy had to be nuts.

Okay, maybe he was good for Number Six. Anybody with half a brain spends Sunday morning sleeping it off while the wife and kids go to Mass, but Kinkaid didn't seem to be much of a one for nightlife. And Sunday was good for Rizza because the docks were pretty much deserted. A couple of the warehouses along Pier 17 were owned by friends who knew how to mind their own business, so he could invite the track star in for a chat.

Anyway, that was the plan. It was reason enough for Rizza to be sitting in a car at 6:15 in the fucking morning. He was going to be pissed as hell if Kinkaid didn't show up.

He sat on the front seat, on the passenger's side. Ralph Getz was in back and Terry Szorza—known as Terry the Ton or Two-Gun Terry, depending on which way you wanted to slam him—was driving. They were contract players, not family, but they were good at what they did and reliable. They had been partners for years.

"Ralph, gimme the thermos," Terry said. He was wedged in so tight behind the steering wheel he could barely turn to look over his shoulder. "I can't believe you forgot the dough-nuts, fer Chrissake." He unscrewed the cap and filled it nearly to overflowing, and then he remembered his manners. "You want some coffee, Frank?"

Rizza dismissed the idea with an annoyed wave of his hand—as if anybody could stand to drink Terry Szorza's coffee, mixed with about half a pint of heavy cream and enough sugar to make it taste like molasses.

"I don't ask much, just a little consideration, like you remember to bring the fuckin' doughnuts. And what d' you do? You forget, you fuckin' kike."

"I'm not a kike," Getz answered from the back seat, exactly as if he were responding to the most routine enquiry.

"Yeah, but your mother was."

Getz merely shrugged, the gesture suggesting that mothers didn't count.

"Jesus, we don't get this buttoned up by eight, eighty-thirty I'm gonna die. I'm gonna fuckin' starve to death."

He drained off the cup in what seemed like one gulp and then refilled it. When that was gone he screwed the cap back on the thermos and threw it into the back, where Getz deftly caught it. Then, with considerable effort, he reached down to scratch the inside of his left calf, revealing the lower part of a black leather holster. Apparently the straps were chafing him.

"Stupid goddam place to carry a gun, you ask me," Rizza said, still irritated about the coffee—he would have liked some if this fat slob hadn't turned it into maple syrup.

Getz leaned forward, resting his arms on the front seat, and laughed. "He's just showing off, Frank. Everybody's gotta know about the leg piece, and everybody does. We got busted down in Millbrae last year. The cops yank Terry out of the car and tell him to assume the position, first thing they frisk his leg. Fucking Millbrae they know about it."

"So what's the fucking point?"

This time Terry laughed. "Girls love it," he said. "They start playin' footsie and touch that with their little toes, they just about come on the bar stool."

Terry Szorza was old enough his hair was turning white,

and big as a bus while he was at it. A goddam fat, wheezing slob in a wrinkled suit, and he had the idea he was hell with the women. What broad was gonna touch him, on the leg or anyplace else, she wasn't paid to? Goddam creep—a good set of hands if you wanted somebody worked over, not the type to get carried away and crush the merchandise before you had what you wanted, but a creep just the same.

The car phone rang and Rizza picked it up. He had a man on the hotel's front desk, some fag who liked to play the horses. This guy was way overdue on his tab, which was inching up to twenty-seven grand, and he was really, really afraid of pain. So he did what he was told. If Kinkaid bought theater tickets, Rizza knew the seat numbers before they were delivered. Rizza got lists of his phone calls. He got everything. So it wasn't any problem to find out when Kinkaid began his morning run.

"He's on his way," Rizza announced, putting down the phone. "That means he'll be going by the Pier in less than ten minutes."

"Guy sounds like he's more dependable than the commuter trains," Terry said with a laugh as he eased the car into gear.

In two minutes they were in front of Pier 17. Rizza got out and, taking a large brass key from his pocket, unlocked one of the warehouse doors. He left it standing open and went inside, where he wouldn't be seen.

He knew Kinkaid was coming up fast when he saw Ralph Getz open the back door of the car and step nimbly out onto the sidewalk.

Like all beautiful things, it was very simple. Getz is just there on the sidewalk, an innocent pedestrian. When Kinkaid comes even with the warehouse door, Getz appears about to move out of his way and then steps right in front of him. The two men collide—Rizza can already hear Kinkaid beginning to offer an apology when Getz kicks his legs out from under him. Kinkaid goes down. Before he knows where he is, Szorza is out of the car, takes half a dozen steps and drop-kicks him right in the pit of the stomach. Kinkaid, suddenly all legs and arms, can't even remember how to breathe. Then Getz and Szorza pick him up by his hands and feet and carry him into the warehouse. It's all over in about ten seconds.

The warehouse was vast, with a cement floor and a ceiling that had to be forty feet up. There were crates stacked around everywhere, dividing the space into a series of eccentric little rooms. They tossed Kinkaid behind a wall of boxes with "Pacific Rim Garden Supply Company" stenciled on them. Then Szorza rolled him over and kicked him again, after which he turned expectantly to Rizza.

"You want us to soften him up a little?"

Rizza considered the matter for a few seconds and then nodded. "Just be careful of his head."

They were very careful. Kinkaid wouldn't have any broken bones, but it would probably be a week or two before he was any use to that girlfriend of his. Rizza was very happy he had hired Getz and Szorza for this job. It was a pleasure to watch a couple of artists at work.

"Okay, that's enough. Now go outside and wait in the car."

Like true professionals, the two men showed neither surprise nor curiosity. It was not their party—they were there merely to provide the entertainment. Rizza watched them leave. Until they had closed the warehouse door behind them, he did not turn to look at the limp, groaning figure on the floor.

"And now, Counsellor. Welcome to San Francisco."

Kinkaid could hardly hear him for the buzzing in his head. It hurt to breathe and it was impossible to think. He felt as if they had dropped him into a stone pulverizer filled with broken glass.

Finally he started to cough. It was agony, but he couldn't help himself. Something came loose in his chest and he spit it up—it was a clot of blood about the size of his thumb. After that he felt as if he might live through the next ten minutes, which was an improvement of sorts.

After several attempts, he managed to struggle into a sitting position. The man perched on a packing case ten or twelve feet away from him was wearing a wine-red shirt today, but Kinkaid didn't have any trouble recognizing him. He took a small, flat automatic pistol out of his jacket pocket and held it up for Kinkaid to see.

"If you were planning to kill me, I'm afraid your friends may have beaten you to it."

The man shook his head and smiled mirthlessly, as if acknowledging a joke he didn't think in very good taste. Then he put the gun back in his pocket.

"I'm not gonna kill you if I don't have to, Counsellor. I just want you to know that we're serious people here and you ain't goin' nowhere before we decide to let you."

Kinkaid found himself wondering why a certain type of person always called him "Counsellor" when they wanted to needle him. In this case it was a mistake, however, because he was supposed to be scared—that was surely the point of the exercise, after all—and now he was annoyed. He was still scared, just not as much.

"I probably could have figured that out for myself," he said. "You want to tell me what this is about?"

"No, you tell me, Counsellor. What do *you* think it's about?"

"The name is Kinkaid, as if you didn't know."

For some reason this struck the man as very funny, and he laughed in merry appreciation.

"Okay, Mr. Kinkaid. Have it your way. I like a guy who doesn't rattle easy."

"You were outside after Bill Cheffins' funeral. Did you kill him?"

"Everything considered, that's not a very smart question, Mr. Kinkaid. But no, I didn't kill him."

"You mean not personally, or not at all?"

"I mean you better let it lie. I saw you there too, and I'm not askin' you if you killed him."

"Since I live in New Gilead, I have an excuse. I'd known Marshall Cheffins all my life, so it isn't unreasonable that I should go to his funeral." Kinkaid put a hand inside his tee shirt to check for damage. It seemed to him that there should be several large, gaping holes under his rib cage, but surprisingly there were not. "What were you doing there?"

It was a trick he had picked up in his high-school debating society—put your antagonist on the defensive. Force him endlessly to explain himself and he never gets a chance to attack your position. In this case the tactic had a real, practical application because it was obvious that, regardless of what he said, this thug planned to kill him as soon as he had what he wanted, whatever that was, so Kinkaid wanted to keep him off his agenda.

And, within limits, it was working.

"How do you know I'm not from out there?" he asked, looking worried—which was a little silly, considering he was the one with the gun.

"Because to you it's *out there*. I'll bet that was the first time you'd ever been east of the Mississippi. You're a native son, aren't you. I could tell that much when I saw you in the bar night before last. You looked so at home.

"By the way, have you got a name you're not ashamed of?"

"No, I ain't ashamed of it. If you gotta know, I'm Frank Rizza. Around here everybody's heard of me."

"So what does that make you, a gangster?"

"Yeah. I'm a gangster."

He said it with almost touching pride. He was a gangster and he was famous, and it obviously hadn't occurred to him that, since all the famous gangsters ended up in prison, those two were conflicting career choices.

In a way it was a hopeful development. Frank Rizza appeared to be only moderately stupid, which meant that it might be possible to reach some arrangement.

"So what can I do for you, Frank?"

The question took Rizza by surprise, which was the whole idea. For a moment he looked merely puzzled and then he seemed to pull himself into focus.

"What you can do for me is tell me everything you know about Alicia Preston."

Figuring out who "Alicia Preston" was didn't require an act of divine revelation. All he had to do was listen to Rizza's description.

"She's something. Blond hair, almost white. The god damnedest woman I've ever seen. Like an angel."

The muscles of his chest and belly were stiffening with pain, so that he felt like one continuous bruise from groin to collarbone, but Kinkaid hardly noticed. He had the odd sense of being two entirely separate people, in different times and places. He was who he was, sitting on a cold concrete floor in San Francisco, and he was twenty years old, on the porch swing in his father's house, drinking lemonade with the most beautiful girl he had ever seen. *Like an angel.*

Then other memories intervened, and bridged the gap.

"What makes you think I would know anything about her?" he asked, once more the lawyer and prisoner.

"That's none of your fucking business, Counsellor."

Kinkaid shrugged, which turned out to be a difficult maneuver when your ribs hurt that much. He didn't really need to know and, anyway, he could guess.

"I'll tell you what, then. I'll ask you another question, and this time if you know what's good for you you'll tell me the truth. What is your involvement with this woman?"

"Why should I tell you that?" Rizza nearly shouted—the mingling of fear and anger in his voice was almost answer enough. "Maybe I'm just wasting my time with you. Maybe I should just pop you right now. Maybe you don't know shit."

"Then let me tell you something for free, and if I'm right you'll know why you should answer my question."

"So tell me."

" 'Alicia Preston' is the most dangerous woman you'll ever meet in your life."

And Rizza knew it. You could see it in his eyes. Save me from this, they said, and I'll give you anything you want. Even your life.

"She knows things about me," he said. "She has proof. She can put me on Death Row anytime she feels like it."

"And just killing her, I take it, does not happen to be the solution?"

"No. I touch her, everything goes to the cops."

"I see."

In the melancholy silence that followed, Kinkaid decided that he lost nothing by telling this frightened thug some small part of the truth. After all, the truth could sometimes be the basis for a successful bluff.

"Her real name is Angela Wyman," he began, noting the slight flash of recognition in Rizza's eyes. "On her mother's side she is the last surviving member of an old and wealthy Connecticut family—her father is unknown, even by name. Ten years ago in a fit of rage she killed the gardener on the Wyman estate, but her grandmother managed to hush it up and had her sent away to a mental hospital. She escaped, and a body was subsequently found which was identified as hers."

"So whose was it?" Rizza leaned forward, his elbows resting on his knees. "I mean, how could the cops make a mistake like that?"

"They didn't make a mistake, any more than you make a mistake if you step on a land mine. They were the victims of a carefully planned deception. So was the young woman who occupies Angela Wyman's grave—some innocent, chosen for the part. She was the second person known to have been murdered by Angela Wyman—there have been at least eight others since and probably more."

"Jesus."

Frank Rizza, the gangster, the bad guy of such impressive

local reputation, could only shake his head. It was impossible to avoid the impression that his astonishment was shaded with a certain awed respect.

At last he glanced at Kinkaid and his eyes narrowed.

"So what's your angle? What are you going to do about it if you find her?"

"I haven't got an angle. I just want to put her away, so that this time she never gets out. That's why I'm here."

"How? How will you do it?"

"She was fingerprinted in Paris when she was fifteen years old. If I can find her, I can prove she's alive. And if she's alive she's a murderess."

"That won't help me any," Rizza said with a kind of baffled disapproval, as if Kinkaid had suggested something he found morally distasteful.

"I know it won't. And if she finds out about me and spooks she's very likely to just disappear, in which case she'll probably burn you just for the fun of it."

"So maybe I oughta just take you out of the frame." Rizza's hand went into the pocket of his jacket. "What do you think?"

Kinkaid smiled pleasantly. "I'm not an idiot, Frank. The evidence that will do for Angel Wyman is in the hands of the police—they also know about you, by the way, so if I should just happen to go missing I'm sure they'll draw the obvious conclusion. What do you think—if I end up as an item in the tabloids and you get hauled in for questioning, how is Angela likely to react? And what do you think she's likely to do about it, just before she disappears down the rabbit hole?"

"Then I'm fucked. I'm really fucked." The hand came back into sight, empty, and lay helplessly in Rizza's lap. "I'm really fucked."

"Maybe not."

chapter 32

Angel left her car in a parking lot right at the foot of Lombard Street, almost as soon as she got off the Golden Gate Bridge. Then she called a cab to take her to the Saint Francis Hotel.

As "Agnes Wycott" she had made her reservation through a travel agent in Los Angeles. She had an American Express card in that name. It was a name she used a good deal. Agnes Wycott had a long credit history, if anyone was interested in checking.

So she arrived by cab, which furthered the desired impression of an anonymous business traveler. Her luggage consisted of a briefcase and one small, gray, soft-sided bag. She wore a gray suit. It was a color she knew did not become her.

The woman at the front desk looked her over carefully—people always looked; it was something to which Angel had long since become accustomed—but she would remember nothing unusual. Nothing she would ever think fit to mention to anyone.

Hopefully there wouldn't be any reason to remember anything. Angel only wanted a look. Anything else would require a great deal more planning and, in any case, she didn't want anything to happen to Jim Kinkaid while he was in San Francisco. She would prefer some neutral site. She would just have a look around and leave it at that.

The reservation was for two nights and was paid in advance. Angel didn't expect to occupy her room for more than a few hours.

Getting the hotel and the room number had been the easy part. All she had had to do was to phone Gilhuly, Carp and

Dunlap, pretending to be a secretary at Karskadon and Henderson who had misplaced the relevant file card—"Be a sweetie, would you? God, my boss is Genghis Khan and I could lose my job. . . ." The hard part had been getting her hands on a maid's uniform.

The hotel supplied them and they were sent out to be cleaned. There were less than half a dozen laundries that catered to the hotel business. Again she phoned, calling them one after the other. She was the assistant housekeeper and she wanted to know why the uniforms hadn't been starched properly. The first three had told her she was crazy, but the Sacramento Street Commercial Laundry had asked her for an invoice number.

A week ago she would have called Frank Rizza, who would have found out that one of the press operators was a heroin addict or was into a loan shark for ten thousand dollars, and she would have had the uniform by lunchtime. But she couldn't trust Rizza anymore. She had seen him at the airport the day Jim's plane came in. It hadn't been a coincidence. He had followed Jim down to the luggage pick-up. He might even have followed him into San Francisco.

It wasn't very difficult to hide in a crowd. Angel had learned a long time ago that her particular type of beauty found its source in a certain perceived fragility and that nothing was easier than to coarsen a delicate face with makeup. Her eyes were her only really striking feature and even they would yield to colored contacts and a lot of shadow—that was better even than dark glasses because less obviously concealing. Add a dark wig and she seemed a different person.

But with Jim, as she soon discovered, she had to be careful. She had waited at a magazine stand and then dropped in behind him in the surge of passengers from his flight, but she could tell quickly enough that he sensed something. He kept looking around, as if trying to identify what was out of place. He was too wary. She had had to break away after only a few seconds. If she hadn't, she was sure he would have spotted her.

In a way it was reassuring. Even after ten years, she apparently remained fresh in his memory. He could know everything about her, everything she had done, and he was still her lover.

Rizza had almost bumped into her and never noticed.

She was going to have to do something about Rizza. He was playing some game of his own—she was quite sure of that. Besides, he had almost outlived his usefulness.

And in the meantime, because of Rizza's apparent defection, she had had to deal with the Sacramento Street Commercial Laundry on her own.

So she took a chance. She walked straight in the front door Saturday morning and simply asked for what she wanted.

"Look, we're in something of a bind over at the hotel," she told the man at the counter—thank God it was a man; a woman would have been more suspicious. "Some idiot dropped the housekeepers' uniforms in a tub of bleach, and not one of them is fit to be seen in. I know they aren't due yet, but could we get a couple of dozen just to tide us over?"

She had smiled sweetly and pulled a wad of loose bills out of her purse. All the while the laundry clerk, who was about sixty with the neck of a walrus and a tongue that looked too big for his mouth, stared at her with an expression of vacant puzzlement.

"They'll be on the truck this afternoon, lady," he said, as if begging for mercy.

"Trouble is, we need them now." Angel started counting off twenty-dollar notes. "Just credit our account, okay?"

When she reached a hundred she looked up at him and let her smile change just a little, to suggest she might be about to turn nasty. The man climbed off his stool and went into the back.

He was gone for maybe five minutes. It seemed like an eternity—was he back there calling the hotel? The police? Finally he reappeared with a large parcel wrapped in brown paper.

He seemed to take forever filling out the receipt.

So she had the uniform. It was in her briefcase, which had

come up on the porter's cart. But her means of obtaining it imposed a time limit.

Because Sacramento Street Commercial, if they were to be believed, would have delivered the rest of the laundry Saturday afternoon. The sign in the window listed their business hours as nine to five, and they were closed all day Sunday, so it was unlikely that anyone at the hotel had had a chance to discover that the delivery was two dozen uniforms light and lodge a complaint about it in time to hear about how someone from Housekeeping had come by especially to pick them up. But by Monday morning everyone would realize that a theft had taken place. So by Monday morning Hotel Security would be looking for an unfamiliar face above a hotel uniform.

Angel was not happy with Sunday—people slept late on Sundays, especially when they were in a strange city and therefore perfectly at their leisure—but there was no other choice. She wanted a look through Jim's things, although she couldn't have said why exactly, and this was absolutely the only chance she was going to get.

It was nine-thirty in the morning by the time Angel had changed into the loose-fitting, heavily starched housekeeper's uniform. She used the telephone on her night table to dial the hotel operator.

"Room 521 please." She let it ring for a full minute before she hung up.

Her own room was two floors above. She took an armload of towels from her bathroom and went down the cavernous interior stairway that was used by the hotel's employees. She met no one.

On the fifth floor there was a housekeeping cart parked in front of Room 536—Angel could hear the toilet flushing through the open door. She figured she had a good forty-five minutes.

One of the many skills Angel had perfected during her time as a psychiatric patient was lock-picking. One of her mother's hoodlum lovers had taught her how when she was no more than twelve, and the convent had provided many opportunities for practice, but Sherman's Crest had been her postgraduate course. In a mental hospital everything is kept locked—the pharmaceutical closets, the filing cabinets, every door in every building, even the one to your own room, everything. As a medium of barter, narcotics are better than money. If you can get into the files you not only have access to information but you can rewrite your own history and identity. And when it is time to leave . . .

One learns to dispense with keys.

So the lock on Jim's door presented no difficulties. She was inside in less than ten seconds.

The room had two large windows through which hard, sharp blocks of sunlight seemed to force their way, to rest precariously against the carpeted floor. The light was the first thing she saw and for just an instant Angel felt a shudder of dread at the idea of moving out into that cold, white, dazzlingly impersonal space, where she might simply vanish like any other shadow.

Jim spends hours and hours in this room, she thought. *He isn't afraid of the light.*

It was only then that she noticed the double bed, and the second suitcase resting on a luggage rack beside the closet.

And then she became like two separate people, the one who experienced the rage and the one who observed the experience. It had simply never occurred to her that Jim might not be alone in the world, as she was alone. They had been apart for ten years, and yet she never thought of him forming any other attachment. She always imagined him as waiting, as she waited. They had moved far apart and now they were moving closer together, but always in her mind each had remained for the other as the only fixed point.

She felt wash over her a humiliated fury at his betrayal and in the same instant stood aside from it and knew that it was unrealistic, even ridiculous.

I really am mad, she thought. *Grandmother, the doctors,*

all of them—they misunderstood everything. I am madder than any of them ever guessed.

And then Angel was only herself again, and the rage was all that was left.

Every morning the pattern was the same. Jim, who seemed to be able to get by just fine on about six hours of sleep, was out of bed while it was still dark, and without switching on the light he would slip into the running outfit and do five or ten minutes of stretching exercises, all without making a sound. In the hotel she sometimes heard the room door closing behind him as he left, but usually she did not wake up until he had been gone for half an hour or so.

His run averaged about an hour during the week and perhaps an hour and a half on the weekends. She always tried to be showered and dressed by the time he came back—he was more fastidious than any man Lisa had ever known and he didn't like her around while he cleaned up. He never said anything; it was just something she sensed. Perhaps he thought she would find his sweaty body offensive, she didn't know.

So she would wait downstairs for him to be finished and then they would have breakfast together. At home Julia had the table laid by seven-thirty. Julia would serve and then disappear—her little contribution to their domestic happiness. Contrary to all expectations, Julia seemed to like having another woman in the house.

There was a coffee shop around the corner from the hotel. They would meet in the lobby and then go there. Jim had only ordered room service twice, and never for breakfast. He seemed to think room service was slightly immoral. So at about five minutes after seven she would see him sliding through the front doors of the hotel, glance around until he spotted her and then pass on to the elevators with a smile and a little waggle of his hand. Then she would know she had about twenty minutes to wait.

Except that this morning he didn't return. She didn't think

very much of it when he wasn't back by seven-thirty because, after all, this was the weekend and sometimes, when he felt strong, he would run for as long as two hours. Then it was eight o'clock. At eight-thirty she checked at the desk, just to see if Jim might have phoned. But the slip the clerk handed her was only a message from Warren Pratt, stating that his plane would be arriving at two-twenty that afternoon. Lisa hadn't even known he was coming.

By nine she was seriously worried.

And there wasn't anything she could do. Lisa did not have a highly developed sense of direction and after a week San Francisco was still a maze to her. Besides, she didn't have a clue where Jim went on his runs. She couldn't track him down and there was nothing useful she could tell the police.

By nine-thirty she was giving active consideration to phoning the hospitals.

But the possibility that he might have been sideswiped by a taxi wasn't what alarmed her. She kept remembering the man they had seen in the restaurant the night before last. She kept remembering Angel Wyman. Better an errant taxi than either of those—the taxi would only kill by accident.

At ten o'clock she decided to go back up to their room and wait, just in case he called. There was nothing else she could do.

The corridor on the fifth floor was shaped like a capital 'L' and their room was just at the angle, at the very corner of the building but with a view of Union Square.

The even-numbered rooms were along the interior side and odd-numbered ones faced out onto the street. When the elevator doors opened, Lisa saw the big stainless-steel housekeeper's cart in front of Room 530. In a split second, and merely to distract herself a little, she developed a theory that the housekeeper must work like a mail carrier, doing one side of the street and then the other, without crossing over, because their room was never done before the early afternoon.

So she was surprised a few seconds later to see the door to

their room open and the housekeeper come out with a set of towels over her arm.

And then it occurred to her than she could hear the vacuum cleaner running in Room 530.

When she saw the housekeeper's face—that exquisite face, framed with hair so blond it was almost white—she knew at once.

Lisa did not know where she found the courage to keep walking. The woman in the housekeeper's uniform clutched the towels to her as if they were struggling to escape. As they passed in the corridor she glanced at Lisa in a speculative, predatory way. Their eyes met for just an instant. Lisa kept right on going, past the woman, past the door to Room 521, around the corner. She almost panicked when she saw that the corridor ended in a blind wall.

But she forced herself to keep walking. She did not look back. She did not dare. There was a stairwell somewhere. There had to be. Yes—there was.

She almost threw herself against the door. There was a landing with a cement floor, and a heavy metal guardrail. She bolted down the stairs, taking them two or three at a time. Her flat-soled leather shoes clattered against the cement so that she could not hear if someone was following her.

By the time she reached the ground floor she was panting for breath and close to terror. She opened the door and stepped out into the lobby, forcing herself to stop running and walk. She had to look as if nothing had happened.

Apparently her act wasn't too polished, because one or two people turned to stare.

In the lobby she saw Jim coming through the front door. She almost fell into his arms.

"I've seen her," she murmured, pressing her head against his chest. "Angel."

chapter 33

Falling backward into the darkness, one grabs at anything.

It did not take Kinkaid very long to figure out that Frank Rizza, sitting on a packing case with a gun in his pocket, considered himself in as much danger as his prisoner, sitting on the concrete floor in his gym shorts. All that was required was to play upon his fear.

"Do you want me to help you?"

Rizza looked surprised, then suspicious. "Whadaya mean?"

"Give me a dollar."

"What the fuck . . . ?"

"Give me a dollar."

Apparently not knowing what else to do, Rizza took his wallet out and extracted one very crisp bill and handed it to Kinkaid, who thrust it into his shirt pocket without looking at it.

"That was a hundred," Rizza said, in a slightly offended tone. "I can always take it back if I decide to kill you after all."

"I'm now your attorney."

"You're WHAT?"

"You've just given me a retainer and I'm now your attorney. Everything you tell me is covered under the confidentiality of the lawyer-client relationship. So what precisely does Angel Wyman have on you?"

It was one too many for poor Frank. He looked so bewildered that Kinkaid was half tempted to just get up and walk out—he had the distinct feeling that no one would try to stop him.

But it wasn't to be. Kinkaid had also decided that this dumb thug might have his uses.

"Answer the question."

"You outta your mind?" It seemed an honest question. "Why the fuck should I tell *you*?"

"Because I need to know, Frank. Now, once more, what did you do and how can Angel prove it?"

"I'm not gonna tell you, Counsellor."

"Fine. It's your choice. Good luck on Death Row."

"I killed this broad," Rizza answered finally. It was obviously a painful admission. It offended his pride. "I got a little carried away, which ain't to say she didn't have it coming. Angela—Jesus, is that really her name?—she's got the whole thing on film. She's also got the body somewhere."

Kinkaid took a chance and stood up. When Rizza didn't shoot him and his legs didn't collapse out from under him, he ventured to walk around a little. Then he decided he was tired and found his own packing case to sit down on.

Angel had the whole thing on film. *And* the body. Well, why not? He also decided that, if somehow he got out of this alive, nothing would ever surprise him again.

"That's the point. She doesn't have it. Admittedly, I can't say about the body. She might be keeping that in a freezer down in her basement. But the film is in her lawyer's safe."

"So?"

"I can get to her lawyer," Kinkaid said, as if announcing that the firm's number could be found in the telephone book—he thought he was doing pretty well, considering he was making it up as he went along. "His name is Grayson and at the very least he's guilty of misprision of a felony, and when he finds out what his client has been up to he'll do anything necessary to climb out from under. I'll explain to him everything I know and can prove about how Angel Wyman laundered some thirty or forty million dollars and how she couldn't have done it without his knowledge and assistance. Then I'll present him with a simple choice. Believe me, all I have to do is offer him an out and he'll give me the law school diploma off his wall."

"Angela'll have his butt."

"Angela will be in prison, or in a hospital for the criminally insane."

"She'll still have the body."

"The body means nothing without the film, and I'll have the film. The lawyer will deny that he ever knew anything about it. With any luck, they'll add your girlfriend to Angela's felony murder indictment."

Rizza liked that idea. He liked it so much he actually grinned. He couldn't help himself.

There was, of course, one problem. Eventually it had to occur even to Rizza.

"You just said it. Then you'll have the film."

"Frank, what am I going to do with it?" Kinkaid smiled, as if touched by such naïveté in a career criminal. "If I turn it over to the police, you'll have me killed. And even if you don't, I will have destroyed my career. How could I possibly explain how I got it? Believe me, I don't even want to see it. I don't want to know anything about it. If I get it, it's yours."

Rizza thought about the matter, his face rumpling with concentration, and at last he decided.

"Okay, Counsellor, let's say I believe you. But just remember one thing, okay? You cross me, you won't live long enough to get disbarred."

Then the conversation turned to practical considerations. Rizza had to be made to understand that if Angel sensed a trap she would simply disappear—after all, she had done it before. She probably had an escape already planned against just such a contingency. In which case Rizza would be in jail before nightfall.

"I give you the film, then you give me Angel. But until then, you stay away from me. I'm in San Francisco on business, and you've never heard of me. Clear?"

"Yeah yeah—I get it. But you don't get Angel until I get the film."

"Can you deliver?"

"Oh yeah, I know where she lives. She's got a house on the beach—I'll tell you that much for nothin'. And you don't have to worry that I'll welch on you. I just wish I could be there to watch when they put the straightjacket over her head."

Then Kinkaid remembered that he had once loved Angel Wyman, and he felt something that almost amounted to shame.

"You want a lift back to your hotel?" Rizza asked, his attitude by now almost benevolent.

"No thanks. I'll walk."

"You pissed off I had them work you over?"

"No—I understand. Business is business."

"Then why . . . ?"

"Look, it's better we're not seen together. Okay?" Kinkaid attempted a smile, but it wasn't very successful. "Besides, the exercise will keep me from stiffening up."

So he walked back to the Saint Francis. It was a distance of slightly more than two miles, but it took him an hour and a half. And then, almost as soon as he is through the door, Lisa tells him about Angel's visit.

"How do you know it was her?"

"You said she was the most beautiful woman you had ever seen."

It was her. Kinkaid didn't need to be convinced. He discovered he wasn't even particularly surprised.

But it wasn't something they had to stand around discussing in a hotel lobby. "Let's go upstairs and have a look," he said.

The room wasn't disturbed in any noticeable way. The suitcases were shut and locked, and nothing seemed different in the closets and drawers. Nevertheless, Kinkaid took a wastepaper basket and emptied out the medicine cabinet into it.

"It's a good thing you don't use Chanel," he said. "We can afford to replace everything. We'll find a drugstore this afternoon."

"I don't want to spend another night in this room." Lisa was sitting on the edge of the bed the way people who are afraid of the water sit beside a swimming pool. "I know it's silly . . ."

"Sounds like a reasonable precaution. Just let me clean up and I'll phone the front desk and arrange to have us moved. It doesn't solve the larger problem, though."

He didn't elaborate. Instead, he went into the bathroom and started the shower running. Not wanting to be alone in the bedroom, Lisa followed him in and sat down on the toilet seat. It was then that she saw the bruises on his chest and abdomen.

"My God. What happened to you?"

"Some discussions with a client got off to a rocky start. You remember the man in the restaurant? He's a local gangster named Rizza. We had a little misunderstanding, but it's all straightened out now."

Lisa just stared at him as if he were speaking in tongues.

"It looks worse than it feels." Kinkaid pressed the fingers of one hand tentatively against his belly and then decided that perhaps he had gotten it backwards. "Don't worry about it. This is just the way gangsters negotiate—he wanted to be sure he had my full attention, so he had a couple of his associates polish their shoes on me."

"Oh Jesus."

"But we're the best of chums now. Angel keeps threatening to put him in the gas chamber. He's scared to death of her, so we've formed a temporary alliance."

"Oh Jesus."

"I think it's time for you to go home, Lisa." He said it like he meant it, without raising his voice. "Go back to Daddy and let him lock you in his gun closet. Angel doesn't seem to have a fix on you yet—I think you'd better get out of here before she does."

"We've had this discussion before. Besides, if she's been in this room she knows you're not sleeping with just your teddy bear."

"Get on a plane and go home. I've seen the photographs of what she does to the Significant Others. I can face a lot of things, but I couldn't face that."

"That reminds me! Your friend the cop left a message. He'll be flying in this afternoon."

She smiled cheerfully, as if no end of proud of herself for remembering.

"I'm not going home, Jim."

And she meant it too. As far as she was concerned, it wasn't even worth talking about.

The bathroom was gradually filling with steam, so he got under the shower for one of the more excruciating experiences of his life. He had once read somewhere that when people used to be flayed alive the torturer's assistant would stand by pouring water into the wound to intensify the pain. He could believe it.

Afterwards, however, he felt better. And Pratt was coming. Pratt would know how to keep Lisa safe.

"Do you think there's any chance they're still serving breakfast?"

Frank Rizza was in a small coffee shop on Vallejo Street when he took the call.

He had a ten-dollar bet on with the owner, who turned out to be a kid he had gone to grade school with, that Terry Szorza could eat his way straight through the doughnut case. There were forty-seven doughnuts in that case, and Terry only had eight white-frosted coconuts to go, so it looked like his money was safe.

"Frank, it's for you."

George Bellocchio, who used to deal cigarettes in the boys' room at North Beach Elementary and sometimes hired out young Rizza as an enforcer, handed him the phone.

"Yeah, what? I'm busy."

"Mr. Rizza, I think you better get back here pretty quick."

It was Andy Esperanza, sounding as if somebody had a gun muzzle screwed into his ear. Andy was a clerk in the hardware store that Rizza used as a front and, though he was ambitious for a career in the rackets, maybe as a narcotics runner across the Mexican border, he would be selling fry skillets and copper tubing until he died. Somehow you just expected a spic to have more in the way of balls.

"Yeah well, Andy, I got business here. Whatever it is it'll keep. Am I right?"

"I don't think so, Mr. Rizza. There's a lady waiting up in your office—you know the one I mean."

Yeah, he did.

He looked at Terry, who was dunking half a frosted coconut into that filthy stuff he called coffee, and saw his ten bucks waving bye-bye. Then he handed the phone back.

"Game called on account of rain," he said, taking two fives from his wallet. "Tell you what. Next time, double or nothing."

"Maybe not." George Bellocchio took the money and rang up a No Sale on his cash register. "I think that guy could eat through the left side of my dinner menu."

"I think you're right."

Rizza let his gaze wander over the coffee shop, with its counter stools and its five tables and its plateglass windows. The place was a dump.

"When we were kids I always thought you'd be the one to make it big in the rackets. What the hell happened, George?"

George leaned against the counter. The hair on his forearms was going gray. He looked out at Rizza through heavy, pouched eyes.

"You remember Dolores Mancuso?"

"Yeah. Sure."

"We got married."

"That explains everything."

For all the years he had been working out of Felmer's Hardware, Rizza had maintained one hard and fast rule: nobody waited in his office. The door wasn't locked, but it might as well have been—nobody went in there if Rizza didn't invite them.

And not because he was hiding something. He wasn't fool enough to have anything stashed there, and the papers in the filing cabinets all had to do with the hardware business. It was a question of privacy. Privacy and respect.

But none of that mattered to Alicia Prescott, a.k.a. Angel Wyman, the Ice Queen. She had come to the store only one other time, a surprise visit to announce that she had a noose tied tight around Frank Rizza's balls.

"I'll wait in his office," she announced to Jerry Langella, who happened to have the watch that morning.

Jerry, who was a big strong boy and a heavy favorite with

the ladies, had probably found this amusing—women generally amused him; he was that type—and had probably put one of his large, meaty hands on the arm of her white suit jacket and shook his head.

"I don't think so. The boss wouldn't like it."

And the gorgeous Miss Prescott, as he knew her then, had reached back to take a gardening claw off the wall and had shoved all three points straight through poor Jerry's elbow.

"I don't care what he likes," she said. "You find him and let him know he has a visitor."

She had done that and nobody had made her disappear into the sewer system. Rizza had returned to have his conversation with her and then had called her a taxi when she was ready to leave, so she was marked down in everyone's book as privileged. Besides, she was fucking dangerous.

So when Andy said there was a lady waiting in his office, Rizza didn't have to ask himself any questions.

She looked different today. She was wearing a gray suit—it suddenly occurred to Rizza that he had never before seen her in anything except white—and she seemed to have made herself up to hide her impressive beauty as much as possible.

But it was more than that. She was sitting on a heavy wooden chair that looked old enough to have come west tied to the back of a covered wagon. It was a bitch of a chair, with a seat as flat as a skillet bottom. Everybody avoided it. Not her though. There was something about her that suggested she maybe wanted to be uncomfortable.

And she was angry, if "anger" was the right word. Her eyes were restless and just a shade too bright. She was almost human.

"There's a man staying at the Saint Francis Hotel," she said. Rizza felt his heart beginning to pound. "Room 521. His name is James Kinkaid and there is a woman staying with him. I don't know her name, but you can find it out easily enough. I want you to bring her to me, and I want you to do it this afternoon."

It was almost a relief. She didn't know. She wouldn't be demanding something so crazy if she knew.

"You mean you want me to kidnap her?"

"I didn't imagine you'd phone and ask her to tea."

"You can get twenty years for that," Rizza almost bellowed—Kinkaid was right, this broad was a head case.

"Just remember what you can get for murder, Frank." She rose from her chair, as if there wasn't another thing to say. "This afternoon. Phone me when you have her."

And then she did something really strange. She smiled at him.

"You do this for me, Frank, and you're off the hook."

A snatch was a delicate operation. It required research. It required planning. You couldn't just grab somebody, not if you wanted to keep out of the slammer.

Besides, Kinkaid was probably going to look upon kidnapping his girlfriend as not in the spirit of their agreement, in which case maybe he wasn't going to be all that concerned about the lawyer-client relationship.

Not that Angel Wyman cared if maybe your vacation plans didn't include San Quentin. The inconsiderate, crazy bitch.

But Rizza decided he had to look on the bright side. Maybe she really meant it about letting him off the hook, particularly if he was able to pull her into a kidnapping charge. And Kinkaid wasn't all that much of a problem—if things began to get tense, Rizza could always send somebody around to put his lights out.

And he knew more about her than Angel suspected. He knew her name, for one thing. "Lisa Milano," for all that she was registered at the hotel as "Mrs. Kinkaid." The first day they were in town, Rizza had bribed one of the housekeepers to search their room, and that was the name on the luggage label. He also knew what she looked like.

It occurred to Rizza that he would have a lot more leverage with Angel if the snatch ended with the victim dead. Then she would have one on him and he would have one on her. It would be a great pity about the Milano girl, but everyone had to make sacrifices.

So all he had to do was pick her up. It was a good thing he hadn't sent Ralph and Terry home yet. They were great at this sort of work.

"Mrs. Kinkaid." Jesus. The guy was worried about what the desk clerk thought, as if they cared these days. It was just too quaint.

Which gave Rizza an idea. If Kinkaid worried about her reputation maybe he told her things. Maybe he would have told her about what happened this morning.

But the first thing was to get a clear shot at her, away from Kinkaid, who would only complicate things. It would be dangerous to kill Kinkaid now, since Angel was obviously playing some complicated game with him that wouldn't be nearly as much fun if he were dead. Otherwise, why snatch the girl? Why not just pop the guy and let everybody go home? No, Kinkaid had to be out of the frame so he wouldn't be tempted into getting heroic and making a nuisance of himself. And, besides, it would be safer if he didn't immediately figure out that their little arrangement was off.

Fine. Get the girl by herself. But how do we manage that when the lady says "this afternoon" and it already *is* this afternoon?

Rizza thought of himself as a student of military history: he had watched *The Civil War* series all the way through on Channel 9, had seen the movie *Patton* twice and had once read a magazine piece about Napoleon. He knew that a commander sometimes had to be audacious.

So he was going to use himself for bait.

There were risks. He was kind of a celebrity in San Francisco. Passing Frank Rizza on the sidewalk was something you told your wife about. If he went out for dinner the restaurant owner might come over to his table to have a picture taken together. In the Saint Francis they might send the house detective by to ask him to leave. He was somebody people recognized.

He couldn't go into the hotel and meet Lisa Milano in the lobby—as soon as she went missing the police would be all over him. She had to come outside. And Rizza had to figure how to get Kinkaid out of the way for an hour or so.

Except that in the end he didn't have to figure anything.

Rizza's man at the front desk phoned just before twelve-twenty.

"Mr. Kinkaid has ordered a rental car."

"What time?"

"One-thirty."

"Is he checking out?"

"No, but he has requested to be moved to another room. And he's made another reservation. I think he's picking someone up at the airport."

"I want to know when he leaves, and if he's alone."

In the hour he had to think the matter over, Rizza gave serious consideration to the idea of grabbing Kinkaid when he picked up his car. It wasn't as wild as it sounded—"I'll just drive you around to the lot, sir. We just need a couple of signatures." If the girl was with him, there might not be any choice. But the plan he finally settled on was to do it at the airport, in the parking garage. He would have the car tailed and send a couple of teams on ahead. The airport garage was dark and noisy. You could get away with anything in there.

But at 1:30 Kinkaid left the hotel alone. As far as the desk clerk knew "Mrs. Kinkaid" was still in the room.

Rizza figured it was about god damn time he had a piece of luck. He dialed the hotel's main number and asked for Kinkaid's new room number.

"Hello?"

"Could I speak to Jim Kinkaid please."

"You just missed him. Who is this?"

"Is this Mrs. Kinkaid?"

"Close enough. Now, once more, who are you?"

"Mrs. Kinkaid, I'm a sort of a friend of your husband's. We met this morning—maybe he mentioned it to you."

There was a pause, during which Rizza couldn't even hear her breathing. Sure, she knew all about it.

"He told me about it, and I saw the bruises. He said you were some crook."

"I'm a businessman, Mrs. Kinkaid. My name's Rizza. Jim is gonna be my lawyer."

"Fine. What do you want?"

"He asked me to get some information for him. If you could say when he's gonna be back, I'll phone again. I'm in kind of a hurry."

"He'll be back around three-thirty."

"Oh Jeez. That'll be too late. Maybe I can try again tomorrow."

"Leave it at the front desk."

"I can't do that, Mrs. Kinkaid. If you know anything, you know I can't do that. I guess it'll have to wait."

Again the line seemed to die as she thought it over. She was cautious, but not so cautious that she was willing to just say "Fine, let it wait." Like any woman, she just wanted to be tempted a little.

"Listen, Mrs. Kinkaid. Just tell Jim I called and that I'll be in touch. Okay. It was nice talkin' to you."

"No, wait." There was an edge in her voice, somewhere between eagerness and fear. "You can leave it with me."

"Well, I don't know . . . I don't think so. It's a little touchy, Mrs. Kinkaid—I'm not sure Jim'd like me draggin' you in. . . ."

"I've already been dragged in, Mr. Rizza. If it's about Angel Wyman I'm sure Jim will want to hear about it as soon as he comes back."

"Look, I'm not sure . . ."

"Where can we meet, Mr. Rizza?"

With a vast display of reluctance Rizza allowed himself to be persuaded into naming a tobacco shop just two blocks from the hotel. It was a very public place, on the corner of two streets that got a lot of foot traffic. She would feel safe there, the stupid little guinea broad.

Rizza hung up the phone, mightily pleased with himself. The tobacco shop was owned by his wife's cousin's husband, who would be taking the afternoon off. It was perfect.

chapter 35

Lisa knew the shop. She had never been inside, but she had passed it several times over the last week and had noticed it the way women do notice such purely masculine shrines. The windows were plate glass and highly polished, but the interior was dimly lit. It looked expensive. It was a place where men went to buy cigars and pipe tobacco, to hear the latest sexist jokes and to be male together.

Until her father retired from the Marines when she was sixteen, she had spent most of her life on military bases, so she was not unacquainted with the atmosphere and its particular effect on her. The Non-Commissioned Officers' Mess was a place at once immediately familiar and totally alien: the experience of feeling out of place grown more or less habitual.

And it blended perfectly with the sense of disquiet that enveloped her as she prepared to meet the man who, only a few hours before, had probably been intending to murder Jim. But Jim was not there and the opportunity, whatever it was, was not to be missed. So she reminded herself that she was used to feeling apprehensive. She had been more uneasy about lesser things, so it wasn't likely to kill her.

It was a two-minute walk from the hotel, so Lisa was not surprised when she looked through the window and did not see Frank Rizza inside. Rizza would still be on his way. There was only the man behind the counter and one customer, a huge fat man who stood reading a newspaper.

Her entrance was announced by a little bell that hung suspended over the doorway. The man behind the counter turned his head to look at her and then seemed to lose interest. The other man remained concealed behind his newspaper.

She glanced around, as if trying to find some excuse for her presence. The back of the shop was covered with shelves of cardboard cigar boxes and large glass canisters of tobacco. There was a display of humidors and an umbrella stand filled with carved walking sticks, some of them very elaborate. There were several signed photographs on the wall, presumably of famous patrons. Lisa didn't recognize any of them.

"Can I help you, Miss?"

It was the man behind the counter and his question sounded really more like a challenge, giving the impression that he knew she could only have found her way in here by some grotesque accident.

The choice was, lie or tell the truth.

"I'm suppose to meet someone here," she said, which at least had the virtues of simplicity and directness. What was he going to do, ask her to leave?"

"And who might that be, Miss?"

The question only surprised her for an instant. Of course— this was the sort of place where Frank Rizza would be a well-known and probably popular figure. He might have phoned ahead.

The man with the newspaper folded it neatly and dropped it on the counter before turning to leave. Except that he did not leave. He passed out of sight behind her, but the little bell did not ring. He had not opened the door to go back outside.

Lisa felt a sudden impulse to leave, but there was no hope of that. The fat man was between her and the door.

"My husband." She forced herself to smile. "He has a birthday coming up. . . ."

There was a curtained entrance to some back room and now Frank Rizza was standing in it, staring at her with bored, appraising eyes.

"That's her," he said.

Almost at once she felt the fat man slam into her, as if she had accidently backed into a wall. His hands closed over her elbows.

"Quite now," he said. "Don't make a fuss and nobody has to get hurt."

As if on signal, Frank Rizza stepped aside and she was propelled through the curtained doorway.

Even in her surprise and fear, she could not help a certain sneaking admiration for the efficiency of the thing. They had allowed her no time to react. She was in the back room and then out in an alleyway and into a car. She couldn't have described the room, she couldn't have described the car—it all happened too quickly. She was on the backseat with Rizza to her right and the man who had been behind the counter to her left. The car doors slammed shut and the engine throbbed into life and still she had not opened her mouth.

"Spare yourself the trouble, Miss," Rizza was saying to her when the car began to move. "You're not climbing out through the window and if you start screaming nobody'll hear you. All you'll buy yourself is enough pain to shut you up. Be a good girl and maybe we can have you home in time for dinner."

If Lisa had had any doubts about her fate, this was the moment when they disappeared. The hint of strain in Rizza's voice told her everything. Besides, she had seen their faces. She was sitting in the backseat of their car—they weren't even trying to conceal where they were taking her. She was never coming back. They were delivering her to death.

Yet somehow this was just one more factor in the equation. She was surprised herself at her lack of fear, at the quiet that seemed to inhabit her. It was as if this were happening to someone else.

She said nothing. Rizza was right. There was no escape and no point in making a fuss. Besides, if she was quiet they would begin to forget about her as a human being. She would become simply an object they were transporting from one place to another, and they would begin to relax. Then she might learn something, or they might make a mistake. It was her only chance.

The fat man was driving and the car moved out into traffic

with smooth, graceful speed. After a few sharp turns they were heading west.

The man to her left was calm, as if he did this sort of thing every day, but Lisa did not even have to look at Rizza to realize that he was afraid. She could feel it in the tension of his body as he pressed against her on the backseat. What was there in all this to make Frank Rizza afraid?

And then, of course, she knew. And her calm evaporated. She could feel terror fluttering in her chest like a trapped bird.

Angel keeps threatening to put him in the gas chamber. He's scared to death of her. . . . I've seen the photographs of what she does to the Significant Others.

Angel had her reception prepared. Frank had stopped somewhere to phone, just to tell her that they were on their way. She could hear a lot of street traffic in the background, so she knew he was calling from San Francisco, which meant she had about half an hour's warning. She didn't need it.

If only in the mind of its owner, every house has a focus point, some single feature around which its life seems to organize itself, and in Angel's house that point was the fireplace. It was large in itself, but the stonework of which it formed the center took up one entire wall of the living room, which was almost the whole ground floor. It was a baronial fireplace, like something out of a medieval fortress, and on either side, fastened to the wall with bolts that looked like pieces of anchor chain, were two iron rings, each about eight inches in diameter. Beyond their questionable value as decoration, they served no detectable function, but they were the deciding factor in Angel's decision to buy the house. She had looked at several up and down the coast, and the rings clinched it for her.

If she ever needed to restrain someone, she had thought, those rings would do nicely. She had kept Charlie Accardo handcuffed to one for three days while he rubbed his wrists bloody trying to get free. Shackled to that rough stone wall in a house that was anyway as private as a dungeon, he might as well have been in the Bastille. Even he realized it after a time, and he had probably welcomed death.

Charlie had been something of an experiment—not that Angel had had any doubts about the impossibility of escape. She was more curious about his reaction to the hopelessness of the situation, and what forms his despair was likely to take. He had given up surprisingly easily, and hardly struggled at all when she put the plastic bag over his head and sealed it shut around his neck with duct tape—there being so few ways to kill someone without leaving a mess on the carpet. Perhaps women were more tenacious of life. It would be interesting to see.

And she had learned a lot about Frank Rizza in those three days. She had just let Charlie talk—after a while, when he somehow got the idea that he might have something he could trade for his life, it had proved almost impossible to shut him up. Charlie had really understood his boss.

Angel stood in the middle of her living room, gazing at the stone fireplace as if it held the answers to some riddle. But there was no riddle. Everything of importance was known. Everything was ready. She was ready.

The carpet under her bare feet was cool. The whole house was cool, even now, in the middle of the summer. She was wearing a floor-length kimono and the green silk was pleasantly chilly everywhere it touched her skin.

Frank Rizza hated her. She had made him afraid and he was humiliated by his fear, so of course he hated her. And, since he wasn't very good at distinguishing between rage and lust, the best revenge he could imagine was sex. If she offered him the chance to climb on her belly and fuck her to death, he wouldn't be able to resist it. She wouldn't have to be subtle. He wouldn't suspect anything. Rizza wasn't the subtle type.

She could hear the sound of automobile tires on the gravel driveway, so she went to the front door and opened it. The car was a dark blue Ford, two or three years old, and at first she could see only Rizza in the back and an immensely fat man in the driver's seat. Then Rizza opened the back door and got out, and she saw the girl.

She was smaller and not quite as pretty as one might have expected, which was a disappointment. She climbed out of the car as if her joints had gone stiff and then glanced at Angel as if merely confirming an identification. Yes, of course. They had already met once today. She was the one from the hotel corridor, the one who had kept on walking past the door to Jim's room.

Another man, small and thin, opened the car door on the other side and stood speaking quietly to the fat man, who was still behind the wheel. They would be an added complication.

"I hadn't expected you to bring such a crowd," she said to Rizza, letting just the slightest trace of flirtatiousness into her voice. He had the girl by the wrist, but his eyes were following the lines of Angel's body as they were revealed by the green kimono.

"They can wait outside if you like."

"No." She shook her head and smiled. "Let them come in where they can look after their prisoner in comfort."

Then she turned and disappeared back inside the house.

Rizza stood in the middle of the living room, looking around him like a tourist in a cathedral. Their relationship had changed. He had at last been admitted to the center of the shrine. One could so easily read the thoughts passing through his mind—he was really beginning to believe that he was about to break free of the net.

Angel opened the drawer of a small table beside the staircase and took out a pair of handcuffs.

"'Use these," she said, throwing them to Rizza. He caught them in both hands, the way a young boy catches a baseball. "Try the ring by the fireplace."

Then she smiled again, partly for effect and partly out of amusement at the hurry Frank was in to do her bidding.

"There—good. Now she won't get into mischief. Tell your

friends to sit down and relax, Frank. I want to talk to you upstairs."

The staircase wound in a tight little curve and on the landing there were only two doors, one of which was open. Angel didn't hurry. She made Rizza work to keep from crowding into her. He was close enough behind that she could hear his breathing.

Without looking back she passed through into her bedroom. When she turned around Rizza was standing in the open doorway.

"It's right there on the dresser, Frank," she said, pointing to a VCR tape on the black slipcover. "There aren't any copies. Velma was fish food a long time ago."

He just glanced at the tape, as if to confirm its existence, and then seemed to lose interest in it. He had his freedom— now he wanted to punish her for having taken it away.

She climbed up on the bed, near the headboard, and crouched down, her knees wide apart so that the kimono splayed open.

"Is there anything else I can do for you, Frank? Why don't you come over here and sit down?"

He hesitated. For just a second or two, he hesitated. Maybe he had heard something somewhere that made him cautious, but in the end Frank Rizza was not a man to believe permanently that any woman was dangerous. At last he grinned, as if he knew he had won. And then he reached back to pull the door closed behind him.

"Why don't you come over here, Frank, and let me make it up to you.

He didn't sit down immediately. He stood in front of her for a moment, at first very still, and then he put his hand into the opening of her kimono, taking hold of her breast. He wanted to squeeze, to hurt her, but he couldn't quite nerve himself to do it.

She put her hand on his arm and pulled him toward her.

"Let me show you how nice I can be, Frank. Come—sit here next to me."

He sat down. She had positioned herself so that he sat facing away from her, back toward the door. She put her arms around him and kissed him on the neck. Then she began unbuttoning his shirt, at first with both hands and then with just the one. The other caressed his face for a moment and then reached back and slipped under the pillow.

It was so easy. He was so busy enjoying himself that he didn't even see the knife until the blade was at his throat. And then it was too late. By the time he began to pull away she had already cut through the artery. He tried to say something, but the first word died in a wheezy gasp as his windpipe was severed. Angel's hands were becoming slippery with blood as she struggled to hold him down. He was strong for such a little man and broke free, but only to stumble and go down on his hands and knees, the blood now pumping rhythmically from his neck, spattering the bedroom carpet. Then, almost at once, he simply collapsed and rolled over onto his right side. Angel had the impression that he was looking at her face when the light went out in his eyes. He had taken only a few seconds to die.

The ring in the stone wall was about four feet off the floor, which was an awkward height if you happened to be handcuffed to it. The smaller man, whose name seemed to be Ralph, had offered Lisa a chair, but if she was going to die she wanted to see it coming and the alternative to facing the wall would have been to sit with her arms folded back over her shoulders so that her elbows pointed almost straight up. On the whole she preferred to stand, thank you very much.

Once she was safely fettered, Rizza's two thugs seemed to forget she was even there—perhaps they regarded her as already dead.

"Jesus, did you see the tits on that broad?" the fat man said as he sat down at one end of a white sofa and lit a cigarette.

He was not five feet away from Lisa, but he never even glanced at her. That was fine. She figured it was probably safer to be ignored.

"No, and neither did you."

"Maybe, but she wasn't leaving much to the imagination. What a piece of work. I think she's wasted on Frank."

"Show her your leg iron and you could be next."

They both laughed at this, so apparently it was an established joke between them.

"Maybe I should tell his wife," the fat one said, and they laughed again.

A few minutes later they could hear water running upstairs.

"Well, that was quick." Ralph looked at his watch, as if he had been timing them. "I guess Frank doesn't go in for a lot of foreplay."

"No, listen," the fat one said, pointing at the ceiling. "It's the shower. She's washing his back for him."

They both listened, in perfect silence. After a while the sound of the water ceased.

"Now they'll get busy."

"Don't get excited, Two-Gun."

"Excited, hell . . . I just wish I was up there instead of Frank."

So they were both surprised when they saw Angel coming down the staircase. First they saw her legs, with the green silk trailing slightly behind, then the rest of her. She hadn't troubled to tie the belt of the kimono.

"Holy shit . . ."

The fat man began to push himself up out of his seat, apparently out of respect for the sight of her naked body, but he had hardly made it to a crouch when the room seemed to explode.

Except that it was only the fat man's head. The back part of his skull came off in what seemed like one big piece, filling the air with a pink haze. The second shot must have caught him in the chest, because he pitched forward as if he had had the wind knocked out of him.

Ralph never got out of his chair. He was still struggling to free the gun from his shoulder holster when the third shot tore his neck open.

Lisa hadn't been aware she was screaming until the sound of gunfire died away and she could hear herself. She stopped at once. She stood staring in mute horror as Angel walked over to where Ralph was still half sitting half lying in the chair, calmly put the muzzle of her enormous revolver to his temple and pulled the trigger. His face just blew apart, leaving nothing but a bloody crater, and the force of the blast made him collapse to the floor.

Without any show of hurry, Angel knelt down and reached inside Ralph's coat, pulling out a flat automatic pistol which she then threw to the other side of the room. The fat man was harder to manage, but at last she found a gun in his belt and it joined the other. Only then, when she had satisfied herself about the two dead hoodlums, did she seem to remember Lisa. She looked at her for a moment and then smiled.

"It's a mess, isn't it?" she said. "My cleaning woman will probably quit after this."

The room smelled of gunpowder and blood, and Lisa's ears were still ringing from the concussion of the explosions.

"What about Rizza?" she asked.

Angel smiled again, a smile at once beautiful and frightening. "Frank is taking a nap. He won't be coming down."

Then she pulled the front of her kimono back together and tied the belt, since apparently the distraction had served its purpose. She sat down at the other end of the sofa, her foot almost touching the fat man's shattered head.

"Now that we're alone we can talk." She dropped her revolver on the coffee table the way another woman might have put down her handbag. "Tell me about Jim."

chapter 36

Warren Pratt was hungry when he landed in San Francisco. He couldn't touch solid food on planes, not even the peanuts that came with his obligatory double vodka, and the half-hour layover in St. Louis had been consumed by the jog trot from one end of the terminal to the other in order to squeak aboard his connecting flight.

Kinkaid was sympathetic, but only to the point of buying him a hotdog to eat while they walked back to the parking lot.

"I'll make it up to you at dinner," he said. "I want to get back."

"You worried about your girlfriend? I don't blame you. So why didn't you bring her with you?"

"I figure she's safer at the hotel than she is with me. It's been an eventful morning."

Then he told Pratt everything that had happened.

"And she's sure it was Angel?"

"She's sure."

"That doesn't mean she's right."

Kinkaid didn't answer, which meant that he believed that Angel Wyman had been pawing through his shaving bag, which meant that she probably had.

"What about this gangster? Can you make good on your deal?"

"Probably not."

"Then I'll send a nice wreath to your funeral. Guys like that generally don't much care for being screwed over, you know. They don't feel it's good for their standing in the community."

Kinkaid stood beside the door of his rented car, fumbling with the key. He had a psychotic ex-sweetheart on his ass, and now some local *capo* who was trying to keep off Death Row. He probably didn't need reminding that things didn't look too good.

"You can have him put away any time you like," Pratt said gently. "Don't worry about him. His little escapade with you this morning amounts to kidnapping with bodily harm, which is a capital offense in this state."

"I can't do that, Warren." Kinkaid glanced at him over the roof of the car and then smiled the way he always did when he seemed to have reached the end of his tether. "I need him—he can lead me to Angel. And if I touch him she'll go to ground. She'll just fade away. I can't kid myself that I'm not on her list, and I can't live the rest of my life waiting for her to turn up again."

By then he had the door open, and for a while he could retreat into the details of getting the car started and out of its parking space. He didn't speak again until they had turned onto the freeway.

"How are we with the FBI?"

"I phoned them after I talked to you," Pratt answered, who was carefully reading the billboards as they drove north. "They're looking for a judge to sign an arrest warrant for interstate flight, and as soon as they find one it'll be faxed to every Bureau office in the country."

"Did you tell them what I told you?"

"Yes. The San Francisco office is primed. Just don't be under any illusions that they're going to kill themselves looking to find her, though. They'll wait until we've found her and then they'll make the collar. As far as I'm concerned, they're welcome to it."

Kinkaid glanced at him inquisitively and then, perhaps a bit ostentatiously, returned to his driving.

"The Bureau has something called the National Center for the Analysis of Violent Crimes," Pratt explained, in the tone of a man conveying unwelcome news. "And their guru on serial killers put together a crash profile of our Angel. The verdict is there's no way she'll let herself be taken alive. If she goes down she'll stage it as *Götterdämmerung*. Best not to be part of the supporting cast."

When they got to the hotel, Pratt collected his room key while Kinkaid inquired if his room had been switched yet. The answer was no, not yet. He tried to call his lady friend on the house phone, but there was no answer.

"Mrs. Kinkaid went out a little more than an hour ago," the desk clerk told him.

"Then there isn't much point in going up," Kinkaid said, with an indifference that was just a little too studied.

"Relax, Jim. It's Sunday afternoon. She probably decided on a little therapeutic shopping."

"I promised you lunch, didn't I."

"Yes, you did."

He left a message that, if "Mrs. Kinkaid" came back, or if there were any calls, he could be found in the Redwood Room. Then they left Pratt's suitcase in the bellman's closet.

The Redwood Room had something of the atmosphere of a gentleman's club. The decoration was spare and the white tablecloths immense. Their waiter seemed to resent the intrusion, which at that hour was not unreasonable.

"I can recommend the fish," Kinkaid said, once they had been seated and offered something to drink. "Try the abalone."

"What the hell is that?"

"It's like a huge barnacle. The foot is considered a local delicacy."

"I'll pass, thanks. Besides, you're always recommending the fish."

It had been intended as the lightest banter, but Pratt could have saved himself the trouble. No one was listening. From one second to the next, Kinkaid had simply switched off.

"I wonder if you'd excuse me for a moment," he said,

checking his watch for the third or fourth time since they had sat down. "I'll just go up to the room and see if she left a message."

When he was alone, Pratt took the liberty of being amused by the romantic nature that apparently boiled within his well-bred client. He booked his honey into hotels as "Mrs. Kinkaid" and got the fidgets if she took herself off for a couple of hours. Ah, love.

Pratt was not romantic. He had been divorced for twelve years and his teenage daughters were in Cleveland, being raised by someone else. But he wished Kinkaid all the luck there was, figuring that after Angel Wyman he probably deserved it.

What the hell, maybe he would try the abalone after all.

"There's nothing," Kinkaid said, easing back into his chair as if afraid someone might catch him at it. "After this morning, I don't like it."

"Maybe she didn't fancy sitting alone in a hotel room. She's probably safer out in public anyway."

"If she had intended to be gone for any length of time she would have left me a note. I think she went out assuming that she'd be back before we returned."

Pratt examined the cover of his menu with poignant regret, because he realized that lunch was a lost cause.

"Maybe we'd better go up and have a look together," he said.

In his professional life Pratt had become a connoisseur of hotel rooms, and his general rule of thumb was that you get what you pay for—the higher the per diem the better the forensic yield. He hated a call to some downtown flophouse where the carpet was a worn, dirty fuzz and the corpse was face down on a bedsheet that looked as if it hadn't been changed since the Truman administration. He always maintained in such circumstances that, unless his perpetrator was a complete idiot and had left his prints on a half-empty water glass in the bathroom, the only useful evidence he was likely to find might be some blood and tissue samples recovered from underneath the victim's fingernails. A cheap hotel room was as anonymous as a bus terminal and a good deal more private. Unfortunately, homicide being a great respecter of class barriers, the vast majority of murders occurred in precisely such places.

This room, on the other hand, would have made an ideal crime scene. The maid service was obviously excellent, which meant that a lot of the irrelevant hair and fiber traces from previous occupants had already been vacuumed away, and all those polished surfaces, the marble tabletops and the ornamental brass of the chairs, had the potential for giving up some really clear and useful fingerprints. It was almost a pity there was no dead body.

Doubtless Kinkaid didn't see it that way. He stood in the center of the room, his hands clasped behind his back, looking almost as helpless as surely he felt.

"When you came back this morning and found out you'd had a visitor, did you straighten things up?"

"I didn't, but it appears that Lisa did," he answered, glancing around as if a little astonished to find himself in such a place. "It's natural . . ."

Natural yes, but unfortunate. Pratt would have liked to see the room right after Angel tossed it, if only to know what she was interested in finding out.

Nevertheless, he went through the drill. The bed was still unmade, which meant that the housekeeper hadn't gotten this far in her rounds yet—a small but significant plus. He checked the wastepaper baskets and found nothing except a toothpaste carton and a laddered stocking. He ran the side of a pencil lead over the message pad next to the telephone and came up with nothing.

In the bathroom he did find a half-ounce spray bottle of perfume, the kind women usually carried in their handbags, left on the sink. It had been there long enough that he knew the fragrance without having to check the label. Sandalwood.

"I assume this is Lisa's."

"Yes."

"Then we can forget about my shopping theory. No woman is in such a hurry to look at dresses that she leaves her perfume behind."

The suitcases were on their racks.

"Are they locked?"

"Yes, I think so. Most of my things are in the dresser, so I haven't checked in some time."

Kinkaid took out his keycase and then was surprised to discover that the latches on his brown Samsonite popped open at a touch. Inside was one of Lisa's nighties, a black see-through babydoll that had probably looked very sexy before someone spoiled the effect by tearing the front open from neckline to hem.

Pratt took it out of his hand and only had to glance at the tear to see what had happened.

"She just took it in both hands and ripped it apart," he said. "She found out you've got yourself another playmate and she's letting you know she isn't happy about it."

At that precise moment the phone rang.

Girl talk. Comparing notes, a few shared confidences—that sort of thing. Except for the handcuffs and one or two other details, it might have been a high-school slumber party.

Angel seemed to regard the two dead bodies soundlessly bleeding into her living room carpet like old stains on the furniture. They no longer even annoyed her. She had stopping noticing them. They weren't interesting. She wanted to hear about Jim. More than that, she wanted to tell Lisa about Jim.

"I don't think he'd ever been with a woman when I knew him," she said. "I was a little forward. I think I frightened him."

"He's not the only one."

Lisa was having a tough time. Tears of the purest terror were coursing down her face, and her knees kept threatening to fold under her. She had to hang on to the ring in the wall to keep from falling down. And on top of everything else she felt an almost overwhelming desire to pee.

If she even heard, Angel gave no sign of it. She had her legs drawn up under her on the sofa, exactly where the fat thug had been sitting not ten minutes before. She could have used his corpse for a footrest.

"Is he still shy? Or has he gotten over that?"

When there was no answer her brilliant blue eyes began to darken, creating the impression that her surface calm was just that, and at any second a terrible rage might break through it.

Keep her talking, Lisa thought to herself. She was on the edge of panic, but her mind was clear enough to perceive that that rage could end everything before the next breath.

She was insane. This woman was out of her fucking mind. And the fact that she was so flawlessly beautiful only made her all the more terrifying.

Keep her talking. Or she may just decide to kill you right here and now.

"He's shy." The words were dry in Lisa's mouth, so that she almost had to spit them out. "He just needs . . ."

Needs what? What in God's name was she talking about? She couldn't remember. . . .

But it didn't make any difference, because Angel had picked up the thread and was busy weaving it into some fantasy of her own.

"Some encouragement."

She seemed wholly satisfied with her own answer. She knew just exactly what Jim needed. She knew what everybody needed. And deserved. You could see it in her face.

"He could be anything," she went on, as if drifting into some sort of trance. "He has the brains. He just needs someone to give him confidence in himself. With the Wyman family backing he could be governor one of these days. Or senator. Anything. His father shouldn't have interfered."

"Did he interfere?"

Keep her talking. It was a strategy to stay alive. And to fight the fear. *Do something. Make her think you've taken her side.* And yet mixed with the fear and the longing for life was a strange kind of curiosity. Jim had never talked very much about his father.

So the question was not entirely innocent.

Angel glanced up at her face, fixing her with the intensity of that glance. And in that instant Lisa was granted an inkling of the power this woman must have over men—perhaps only another woman would see that there was something not quite human in the expression of those brilliant blue eyes.

"Yes." There was a coldness in the word, a sense of grievance that went beyond anger. "Yes, he did interfere. He said things about me, things he didn't have a right to say."

Because they weren't true? Or because they were? Did it matter to her, or could she even see the difference?

Angel let her gaze wander about the room a bit, until it came to rest on the dead fat man who was curled up just beside her foot. The hole in the back of his skull was as large as a woman's fist and its edges were spattered with a dull, coagulated liquid that no longer even looked like blood. He was so dead that it was difficult to believe he could ever have been alive. But Angel stared at him with passionate hatred, as if she wished she could will him back to life just to have the satisfaction of killing him again.

"I never met him. Jim's father—I never met him."

There was no response. Angel wasn't listening. In the wide world there was only her and the dead man on the floor.

"I want to go home," she said at last. Then she turned her attention back to Lisa and smiled, perhaps a little pityingly. "I lived at Five Miles once, with my Grandmother. If your name is Wyman, it's where you belong."

"It's been sold."

"I know. I bought it. How did you know it's been sold?"

There was a certain edge in the question, suggesting that the wrong answer could lead anywhere, but then Lisa remembered the obvious answer.

"I'm a real-estate broker. A property like that sells, everyone in the business hears about it."

"Oh yes." Angel nodded, apparently satisfied, dismissing the reason as unimportant. "My mother grew up there, and she never wanted to go back. Can you imagine that? She wanted to stay in Paris with her men friends."

She looked down again at the corpse, only this time the hatred had shaded off into contempt.

"Did this animal try to take advantage? No? But he would have gotten around to it eventually. I know the type. The more repulsive they are the more trouble they have keeping their hands to themselves. If he were alive I'd cut his fingers off. A joint at a time. I'd trim him smooth all over."

She stood up again, taking the gun from the coffee table. Then she turned to face Lisa and, without the slightest trace of malice or even irony, she smiled.

"You'll excuse me now. I have to make a telephone call."

When Angel was gone, Lisa simply let go. She crouched by the wall and sobbed, clutching at the great iron ring as if it were her only safety as panic seemed to wash through her in waves.

But at last she was quiet. She felt wrung out, too despairing even to be afraid anymore. Angel was going to kill her—she knew this. She was going to die. But somehow this was less dreadful than the thought that that woman might any second come back into the room. Angel Wyman inspired a fear that was greater even than the fear of death. It was fear that began and ended with itself, abstract and pure.

She almost envied the two dead men who kept her company in the silent room. The little one was partially obscured by the coffee table, just a pair of legs and an arm thrown out at an odd angle, so that he might have been a tailor's dummy rather than a human being, but the other one, with his shattered head pointing toward the staircase, was there for her inspection. She could see his left ear and the puckering of flesh where his shirt collar pulled tight around his fat neck. She could see the watchband on his wrist and the permanent press creases that ran all the way up the backs of his trouser legs. She could see . . .

She had no idea how long she was staring at him before she was conscious of something odd in his appearance. It was his leg—his left one, to be precise. It didn't look right.

She studied the leg for quite a while before she figured out what it was. The material of his trousers didn't hang right. It was as if there was some kind of lump on the inside of his left calf. She couldn't imagine why, under the circumstances, this fact should have the slightest significance for her, but somehow it seemed vitally important.

"I have to go to the bathroom."

Angel had come back into the living room. She was dressed in a pair of white linen trousers and a knitted top of the palest blue, and she was carrying a small brown handbag, which meant that she was going out.

"Please let me go to the bathroom," Lisa said, letting her voice break a little with a desperation she didn't have to fake. "I don't want to make a mess here with these two guys on the floor."

"I doubt if it would matter to them, but I understand."

Once more Angel smiled her terrible smile, the gracious hostess in the House of the Dead, and Lisa saw she had been right. This bitch was an instinctive predator, but give her a chance to play the woman-to-woman game and she got distracted. It was as if the effort of trying to be human for even a few seconds took her full concentration.

And that was fine, because Lisa didn't want her to start reading her mind. She didn't want her attention drawn to the odd lump under the fat man's left trouser leg.

Angel took a small silver key from her handbag and held it up for Lisa to see.

"I'll unlock you," she said, her old self again. "I'll even let you have a little privacy in the toilet. And if you act up I'll hurt you. And I mean I'll hurt you. Just now you're more useful to me alive, but I wouldn't presume very much on that if I were you."

Even as one handcuff bracelet sprang open she took Lisa's right hand and bent it at the wrist so there was no choice but to let the elbow lock straight. One twist sent a spasm of pain all the way up into the chest.

"That's just a taste," Angel murmured into her ear. "If you want me to cripple you, all you have to do is give me a reason."

Without releasing her hold, she half walked half dragged Lisa down a short corridor and opened the door to a tiny, windowless room containing nothing but a sink and a toilet. There she snapped the bracelet to the towel bar.

"I'll give you two minutes."

Two minutes. And you're dying to pee, so you do that first. How much time does that leave you? How much time do you need in a room almost as bare as when the builder finished with it. Aside from a small circular rug on the floor and a roll of toilet paper in the wall niche, there was nothing. There wasn't even a towel. Lisa ventured a peek in the medicine cabinet, but of course it was empty.

She thought about the toilet tank, but she knew she couldn't get the lid off one-handed without making a noise that would bring Angel right straight back in through the door. She checked the underside of the rug—maybe it was coming unraveled and she could steal a few feet of thread. No such luck.

Then she remembered the toilet paper. Or, more accurately, she remembered the rod that was holding it in the wall niche. Those things were usually two tubes of metal, one of which slipped into the other, and there was a spring inside to maintain the tension. The spring might be worth having.

She got it out easily enough, and managed to put the toilet paper back on the rod, and the rod pulled out enough that it would stay in its two little holes provided nobody touched it. But then where was she going to hide the spring?

Well hell, it didn't have to stay a spring. She pulled the wire as straight as she could and then looped it a couple of times around her waist, dropping her skirt over it just as Angel gave two quick knocks on the door and then opened it.

There was no conversation. Angel grabbed hold of her free arm, pinned it behind Lisa's back, and then unlocked the handcuff bracelet from the towel bar. In fifteen seconds they were down the corridor again and the handcuff chain went back through the iron ring beside the fireplace.

"I'll be leaving now," Angel said, picking up her handbag from the coffee table. She took out a small black object, just a trifle too large to be a compact, and put it on a narrow stone shelf above the fireplace, where Lisa would be able to reach it.

"When you open that thing you'll find it's a telephone. But don't get your hopes up—it's on receive only. I've disabled the call button."

"Then why . . . ?"

"You'll find that out when somebody gives you a ring."

She seemed ready to laugh, like a teenager talking about a surprise party. *None of this is real to her,* Lisa thought. *It's just some kind of weird game. We all might as well be paper dolls.*

"I'll see you later. Right now I have a date."

chapter 38

"Is it her?"

Covering the mouthpiece of the receiver with his fingers, Kinkaid replied to Pratt's whispered question with the faintest of nods.

"Yes, Angel, I recognized your voice right away," he said, in a tone that almost managed to be chatty. "It's been a long time."

There was a pause, lasting fifteen or twenty seconds, during which the veins in Kinkaid's neck began to stand out like cords.

"Yes—I understand . . . Yes."

Pratt would have given a fair chunk of his pension to listen in on that interesting dialogue. He even checked the bathroom for an extension, but it appeared the Saint Francis had not as yet yielded to that particular luxury. So he was forced to go back and read the progress of the conversation as it registered in Kinkaid's face.

"Angel, let me talk to her. I want . . . Yes. Okay. Yes, if . . ."

At the outside the call lasted four minutes, but it seemed to go on forever. And the accumulating strain on Kinkaid, as he sat on the edge of the bed listening to that maniac, was something you could almost measure.

And then, all at once, it was over. Without a word Kinkaid replaced the receiver and leaned forward, his elbows resting on his knees as he stared at nothing over his folded hands. He was wound so tight it was at least an even bet that he was not even breathing.

"She's got Lisa," he said finally. "If I want her back I have to come to her."

"She won't give her back. You know that."

"I know."

In that instant Pratt would have liked to have found some word of hope or encouragement, but there was none. And no place for comforting lies either, because James Kinkaid, Esq., was not the type to take solace in fantasies. His pain, as he contemplated the narrow choices open to him, was almost unbearable to watch.

And then, thank God, the homicide lieutenant from Dayton remembered that he was working a case.

"I want you to tell me, word for word, everything she said."

Kinkaid glanced up at him for a bewildered moment and then seemed to reach for some sort of inner control.

"There isn't time," he answered, without yet rising from the bed.

"Make time, Jim. I need to know."

"Yes—I suppose so." He ground the heel of his hand against his forehead, as if trying to erase something there, and then grew very still. For perhaps as long as ten seconds he seemed perfectly insensible. Then a faint shudder passed over him, and he came back to life.

"She told me to go to the front entrance of the hotel, that a car would be waiting for me there."

"What kind of a car? A taxi? A limousine? Will she pick you up? What?"

"She didn't say." Kinkaid's eyes narrowed, as if he were trying to bring the car into focus. "She wouldn't be fool enough to come herself, so she'll either send a driver or it'll be a rental."

"If it's a rental, how will you know where to drive it?"

" 'I'll be in touch.' That's what she said—'I'll be in touch.' Not 'You'll hear from me,' but 'I'll be in touch.' The car will have a phone."

"It could still be a limousine."

"No—a rental car would be safer. She'll want to keep me isolated as much as possible. A driver would be too big a risk."

Pratt considered the idea for a moment and decided Kinkaid was probably right. A rental could be delivered and the keys left with the doorman. She might even have arranged it through the hotel. A rental was the smart choice and, whatever else she might be, Angel Wyman had so far shown no signs of being stupid.

"Have you got a local map?"

"In the top drawer of the desk. I bought it yesterday when we . . ." He seemed to lose interest in the sentence.

It was a sheet map, folded up to about the size of a Number 10 envelope. Pratt spread it out on the bed.

"She'll want to get you out of the city," he said. "She's broken cover to arrange all this, so it must mean a lot to her. She'll want to talk, to show off—she'll have something to prove. She'll want privacy. What do you get if you take the road south from here?"

"God knows. Suburbs, I guess."

"I like bridges better." Pratt snapped the line tracing of the Bay Bridge with his fingertip, making the paper rustle. "She'll lead you around by the nose for a while, just to satisfy herself you aren't being followed, but the bridges have a lot of advantages for her. She can drop in right behind you without attracting any attention. Wherever you end up, there's a good chance she'll take you across one or the other."

"Why should she imagine I'm being followed? She isn't giving me time to bring in the police, and there's no reason to imagine she knows anything about you."

"She's got Lisa," Pratt reminded him gently. "She's had her for maybe a couple of hours. We have to assume she knows whatever Lisa knows."

"Yes. I see."

Kinkaid stood up and, like a man leaving the house to go to work in the morning, calmly started checking the contents of his pockets. He looked as if he had only one decision left to make in his life, and he had made it.

"I'd better go now," he said. "The car will be waiting."

"You know she may already have killed Lisa by now," Pratt told him, more for form's sake than anything.

"Yes, I know that."

"And she certainly means to kill you—don't imagine she's the sentimental type."

"No. I wasn't imagining that. But she isn't giving me any choice, is she?"

"Then at least take this."

Pratt reached under his coat and took out the .38 police special he had carried for twenty-five years, but Kinkaid only smiled as if at some sad joke and shook his head.

"I've never even held one," he said. "And I don't think I could bring myself to use it. Besides, she'll be looking for something like that."

His briefcase was standing open on the desk. He peered into it for a moment and then extracted a flat, square object about the size of a hip flask. It was a tape recorder.

"But she may not be looking for this." Kinkaid clicked a button and produced a faint whirring sound. "The pocket secretary, every lawyer's friend. You can get about an hour on a tape. I'll hide it under the seat, so if you find the car you might learn something worth knowing."

He slid it into his shirt pocket.

They rode down in the elevator together without exchanging a syllable. As they walked across the vast lobby, almost empty on a Sunday afternoon, Pratt touched the other man on the arm.

"Let me go out first," he said. "Give me ten seconds and then follow, but once through those doors you don't know me. I want to get the car's make and license number and then I'll get on the horn to the Bureau.

"One more thing—if she does send you over a bridge make sure to go through the toll booth on the extreme left side. Maybe, if there's time, I can get a homing device planted on your car."

Kinkaid nodded, as if he hadn't really been listening, and then took Pratt's hand.

"Thanks for everything," he said.

When he came out into the bright summer sunlight, Kinkaid could not quite dismiss the suspicion that all of this was not really happening to him. He found it strangely hard to imagine that Angel Wyman was anything more than a bad memory, that he wasn't on his way to meet Lisa in some tourist trap where the worst fate they could expect was a mediocre dinner. He wasn't the dramatic type, he told himself. He was the type who died in bed, with his insurance premiums fully paid up.

This illusion of safety lasted right up until he saw the short, squat man wearing a bill cap with a *Capital Car Rentals* patch on the brow as he stood next to a chocolate-brown Jaguar with a high gloss polish—apparently Angel thought her old beau's last ride should be a class affair.

"Are you waiting for me?" he asked, smiling pleasantly at the man, who after all didn't know he was officiating at a funeral.

"Mr. Kinkaid? Yes. Could I just see your driver's license?"

Sure enough, the car had a phone. It rang almost as soon as Kinkaid had pulled out into traffic.

"Turn right onto Geary," Angel told him. "And, yes, I'm close enough that you might see me if you turned your head, although I wouldn't advise it. I also wouldn't advise you to make any calls. I'll be dialing your number every fifteen or twenty seconds, and if I ever get a busy signal your little friend wi!l step off into oblivion. Do we understand each other, Jim?"

"No, and I don't think we ever did. But I take your point. I won't be on the phone to anyone except you."

"Good boy. If it rings three times, you pick up. Three rings means I want to talk to you."

And then, abruptly, Kinkaid found himself listening to a dial tone. He put the receiver back on its cradle, where it snapped into place, and surrendered himself to the traffic on Geary Street.

After noting the car's description and license number along with the sticker on the left rear window that declared it the property of Capital Car Rentals, Pratt watched it disappear around the corner, wondering if he would ever see the driver again, alive or dead.

She's playing with us, he thought. She puts Kinkaid in a conspicuous luxury car as if daring anyone to follow. His own private theory was that Angel knew Kinkaid was in contact with the police and didn't give a damn. She had made her plans, and any surveillance they tried to run would turn out to be a waste of time. And the Jaguar was her way of rubbing it in.

This was just a game to her, the clever bitch.

Pratt allowed himself about fifteen seconds to study the traffic, but he didn't see any beautiful blond women in open convertibles rushing in pursuit of their prey. Fat chance. He went back into the hotel and found himself a public telephone.

The switchboard operation at the local Bureau office didn't seem very impressed when he asked to speak to the agent in charge on a matter of extreme urgency.

"Yes ... It's an emergency. ... That's right, a matter of life and death. Tell him it's Warren Pratt, Dayton Homicide. He should have received a fax from Preston Richards in Washington. ... No, I'm not in Dayton, sweetheart. I'm right here in San Francisco."

It took three whole minutes to get the stupid fuck to come to the phone. Jim Kinkaid is riding around town at the whim of a lunatic, and the Bureau wants to make an impression by keeping everyone on hold.

"Special Agent Blandford here," came the response— finally. "What is this in relation to, Mr. Pratt?"

So obviously he hadn't received the fax. So wonderful.

"Agent Blandford, this is in relation to a double homicide that is certain to be committed today, unless we can prevent it. You'll want to get on the wire to Preston Richards at the National Center for the Analysis of Violent Crimes, who knows all about this matter, but in the meantime I need you to get people to the Golden Gate and Bay Bridges. We have to get some sort of homing device into a car."

"Mr. Pratt, perhaps you should be speaking to the local

police, since homicide falls within their jurisdiction. I can give you their phone number . . ."

"Agent Blandford, I know I sound like a mental case, but if you don't want a major disaster on your hands I suggest you call Richards. We have no time on this. I'll be knocking on your office door in five minutes."

Actually, since he got lucky with a cab, and the traffic was light, and the Federal Building wasn't very far away, he made it in about four and a half. By then Special Agent Blandford had apparently spoken to Washington.

"I don't know what the delay was," he said hurriedly, taking Pratt by the hand as if they were fraternity brothers. "We still haven't received our copy, but a federal warrant on a charge of interstate flight was issued this morning against one Angela Wyman. Of course you have our complete cooperation—if you could just bring us up to speed on this . . ."

"Absolutely, but right now we need to get men in toll collector's uniforms out to the bridges. Angela Wyman's next victim is on his way to her right now, and if we can't pick up on him before he gets to where he's going I think we'll almost certainly lose both of them."

It took another ten minutes of fumbling around before agents with the proper equipment were actually out the door and even longer than that before Agent Blandford, who had a map of San Francisco open on his desk and kept drawing what he called "sweep corridors" over it, could be dissuaded from launching a full-scale manhunt, complete with helicopters.

"We put a bird in the air and we'll track down your friend Kinkaid," he said, apparently still under the impression that Jim, if not an actual fugitive, was at least some sort of accomplice. "They find the right make of car, they fall back to get the angle on it, they got lenses up there can read a license plate from four hundred yards like it was the headlines of your morning newspaper. No sweat, we'll find him."

"And then what? You'll just follow along behind until he leads us to the Angel of Death?"

Pratt shook his head, as if he could hardly believe what he was hearing. In police parlance the FBI were called the "suits"—not real cops, but bureaucrats with badges—and this joker Blandford was a perfect example of the type.

"Let's just remember that a helicopter is a fairly noisy and conspicuous object, and our subject is neither deaf, blind nor stupid. Besides, she'll be looking for a tail. This is a very clever nut case we're dealing with here, so let's try not to underestimate her."

This didn't sit very well with Blandford, who kept drumming the eraser end of a pencil against his map. He was a thick, strongly built man with a wide face, and like a lot of the Bureau's supervisory personnel he bore a carefully cultivated resemblance to the late J. Edgar Hoover.

"This fellow Kinkaid goes bumbling in there and we could end up with something very messy," he said, apparently having just made that discovery. And then, as if to himself, "Yes, very messy."

"Kinkaid won't bumble into anything, so don't worry. And we have to wait on him. We don't have any choice."

"He was a damn fool to go out on his own like that, though. He's got about an eighty percent chance of getting himself murdered."

"I think he would consider that an acceptable risk," Pratt answered with a faint, joyless smile.

"Well, let's just hope we can avoid a hostage situation."

"You seem to forget—we have one already."

chapter 39

Angel was gone. There was no doubt of it. She had closed the front door behind her and the sound of her car's engine had faded into the distance. Her house was now quite still. Lisa could feel the silence flowing from room to room, thick as water, like bottom currents around the riblike spars of a sunken ship.

Yet she was not quite alone. The two dead men were there with her for company. Was it her imagination or were they beginning to smell?

The big one, lying so close to her, his right arm hidden beneath his body and what was left of his head pointing into the room, looked as if he had been shot in the act of trying to run away. His left leg was bent slightly at the knee and the trouser cuff on the other was pushed up over the top of his sock, revealing a band of white, hairless flesh about an inch wide. In fact he had only been trying to stand up, more likely from motives of chivalry than fear, when his brains had made their sudden and unanticipated exit. He might simply have collapsed back into his chair, or he might have fallen backwards, but in either case Lisa probably would never have noticed the lump under his left trouser leg.

"Don't get excited, Two-Gun."

She had stared at that lump for a long time before it occurred to her what it might be. *"Show her your leg iron and you could be next."*

As chances go it wasn't much, but when the alternative was ending up on the floor with a couple of dead gangsters you tried everything.

The sole of the fat man's shoe was about five feet from the

wall to which Lisa was handcuffed. With her maximum reach, supporting herself on the fireplace ring and stretching herself as far into the room as she could go, she could not quite touch him. But she could reach his chair, so she settled for that.

It was a heavy, deeply upholstered chair, designed for comfort and stability, and the only place Lisa could get a purchase on it was one of its short, square-cut legs, the corners of which cut into her feet. Dragging it to the wall was not a pleasant business.

But by standing on it she could bring her hands down to her waist and unwrap the coil of wire she had stolen from the toilet paper dispenser. The wire, when pulled as straight as it would go, was only about five feet long, Unfortunately, if she held the wire in her hands, that was about two and a half feet short feet short of what she needed.

So it was back up onto the chair to try to wriggle out of her pantyhose, no small feat with your hands chained to the wall. She managed to work the pantyhose down to her crotch, but that was it. Even standing on the balls of her feet she just couldn't reach any lower.

She went through about five minutes of the most terrible desperation before she noticed that the armrest of the chair upon which she was standing had about an inch and a half of lip. If she squatted down very low, and was very careful not to fall, she might be able to snag the waistband on that lip and pull them the rest of the way down.

After several tries it worked, after a fashion. She got them down to her knees, after which it was a simple matter to work her way out of them.

This meant that her feet were bare.

She made a tight loop at one end of the wire and bent the other end so she could hold it loosely with her toes. It was clumsy, but it would give her something with which to grapple.

She moved the chair around so its back was to the wall and then sat down on the edge of the seat. Her arms were stretched painfully back over her head, but it gave her a secure position from which to go fishing up the dead man's trouser leg.

With the first try she was sure she had guessed right. Held between the toes of her right foot, the wire was almost like an extension of her body. Through it she could feel a smooth, hard object about three inches wide at the top and tapering toward the bottom. When she tapped at it, the sound she as much felt as heard was crisp but without any metallic ring.

It was leather—stiff, heavy, molded leather. It was a holster.

And a holster implied a gun.

Two-Gun. Of course. Angel had missed it when she frisked the corpse. She had found a pistol in the man's waistband and she had stopped looking.

It was likely to be a flat, small-caliber automatic, or perhaps something like a derringer. Nothing extraordinary in the way of firepower, but perhaps good enough at close range. Lisa's father, the ex-Marine gun nut, had always said no pistol was worth much except maybe across the room.

Anyway it was better than nothing.

Or would be, if she could figure out some way to get it. The god damned thing was doubtless strapped in at the top to keep it from falling out every time the fat man took a walk. How the hell she was going to slip it out she had no idea.

She needed to get the trouser leg up so she could see how the holster worked and see what she was doing. The wire was plenty long enough, but it was way too flexible to push back the heavy fabric, especially with the weight of the dead man's leg holding it in place.

It seemed she was all through.

Lisa knew she was very close to coming unstuck. Her arms ached and the handcuffs dug cruelly into her wrists. Her nerves were ravaged by the constant fear. She was exhausted. And now it looked as if her last, best chance of saving herself had eluded her by about half a yard. Terror, the numbing, immobilizing terror that abandons all hope, the final surrender to death seemed ready to engulf her the way the sea engulfs a drowning swimmer as he slips below the surface.

But there was something inside her, some small central core of will that would not let her give up. She was just not ready to die.

Despair can sometimes bring with it a wonderful clarity of purpose. Lisa's eyes, bright with unspent tears, searched the room for anything, anything that would give her those extra fifteen or twenty inches. She was no longer herself, but a ruthlessly efficient machine with no purpose but its own survival. Her mind, chilled with fear, searched for some possibility of life.

She found it in the fireplace screen.

It was the usual thing, coils of brass wire linked together to form a curtain that could be pulled aside by a small cord. Around the top, concealing the rod that held the screen in place, was a strip of brass trim apparently bolted to the wall at either side of the fireplace.

The rod was at least four feet long. Each end fitted into a small hole in the trim, but whatever held it in place couldn't amount to more than a couple of screws. A good yank and the whole curtain should come down.

She had to balance herself on the arm of the chair and grip the curtain with her feet. It was clumsy, but a couple of tries and the whole thing gave way and fell to the floor in a heap.

The rod simply slipped out. It was just about a quarter of an inch thick. Perfect.

Back on the edge of the chair seat, only this time using the rod, she managed to get one end hooked into the cuff of the fat man's trouser leg. Then, pushing the other end with her feet, she raised his shoe off the carpet. It took her about twenty minutes to work the trouser leg up high enough to let her see the gun butt.

The holster was held in place by two straps, above and below the bulge of the calf muscle. The pistol was a nickle-plated automatic with pearl grips, the sort of thing a woman might carry in her purse, and the snap that kept it from falling out was at the top of the curved stock. It was the work of a few seconds to pop open the snap and then to slip the tip of the rod through the exposed trigger guard and pull it free.

Lisa slipped her instep under the rod to tilt it so that the pistol slid down its length until it came to rest against her foot. Then she kicked it over closer to the wall and stood up. The backs of her legs were stiff and her arms were killing her. She tried picking up the pistol with her toes, but the experiment was not a success. Finally she gave up and used the wire, bending the loop at the end into a hook.

When she was able to examine the pistol, she wondered why a professional criminal had troubled to carry around such a toy. It was .22 caliber, which didn't say a lot for its stopping power, and it would only be accurate to within about squirt-gun range. She pulled the clip, which slipped out of the butt, and found only four bullets. They were the ordinary solid-point type. With hollow-point bullets you could do some real damage, but the fat man clearly hadn't taken this weapon very seriously. Still, it was better than nothing.

Or maybe not.

The real question was how she was going to use it with her hands chained to a wall four feet from the floor. From that position how could she aim the thing? And she had nowhere she could hide it, not where she could get at it without a major production, and she could hardly stand there holding it, waiting for Angel to come back. The front door was at least forty feet away. Angel would come in, take one look, and go right back out. Even if there was time for a shot Lisa knew she was in no danger of hitting anything, not at that distance, and then it was all over. Angel could take all the time she wanted finishing her off.

The only possibility was surprise. At short range, pull the gun out of nowhere and hold nothing back. Four shots, just like using a fire hose—maybe that would be enough. Maybe.

Except it wasn't going to happen that way.

With a surge of hopelessness that was almost physically painful, Lisa shoved the clip home. The pistol, which had taken so much effort to retrieve, was actually a liability. It would get her killed if Angel caught her with it. Yet the thought of parting with it was bitter.

She would try to hide it, she decided. Hide it and hope for a chance to use it. The chair was the only place within reach— she used her foot to lever up the cushion and then she threw the gun underneath.

The next thing was to get the fat man's trouser leg back down to conceal the holster. Then she had to wriggle back into her pantyhose—she didn't want Angel wondering why she had gone to the trouble of taking them off—and at last she pushed the chair back into its original position.

All that was left was the fireplace screen. She would have to provide Angel with a plausible explanation of why she had pulled it down, so she put the rod through the ring to which she was handcuffed and bent it double. Angel could think she had tried to pull the ring out of the wall. Angel would expect her to be dumb enough to believe that might work.

After that there was nothing to do except to wait. To wait, and to let the silence of the house once more close around her like the waters of some deep and lightless sea.

chapter 40

Warren Pratt, whose great-great-grandfather had been a saddlemaker in Essex, nursed an abiding prejudice against policemen with Anglo-Saxon names. Righteous cops had names like "Kowalski" or "Glickman" or "Salazar." If you were black you might get away with "Adamson" or "Jones," but a white man with a name out of an Edith Wharton novel was probably a lost cause.

Special Agent Blandford—whose first name turned out to be Frank—was a case in point. He knew nothing about the street. He put his faith in gadgets and organizational technique, and there was nothing in his experience or his temperament that allowed him to understand a woman who could shoot holes through the tops of children's heads while they slept. He worked on the assumption that criminals were morons—which, granted, was usually the case—and he didn't grasp that he was dealing with a monster who operated without the restraints of either pity or fear and who was at least as clever as he was. How do you explain to the Frank Blandfords of this world that this was Angel Wyman's game and they had to play by her rules?

"Leave the local cops out of it," Pratt told him. "What's the point of tailing Kinkaid? It isn't Kinkaid you want."

"But Kinkaid will lead us to your suspect," Blandford countered, tucking his chin under a little as if this were the unanswerable argument.

"Not if he's in front of a parade. Trust me, she'll spot it. And if she does she'll disappear and pull the hole in after her. Right now she thinks she's got him all to herself. Let her go on thinking that."

But he couldn't be convinced. The cruisers will have their orders, he said—if they spot Kinkaid's car they will merely report. They will not attempt to follow. They will remain inconspicuous.

Sure. Pratt knew all about patrol cops—they hear the calls over the radio and they can't resist a drive-by. It would be a fucking posse.

"We can't take the chance of just losing him," Blandford said, as if this was the one incontrovertible fact of the case. "We have to stay in control of this operation."

"You just get those tracking devices out to the bridges."

"Don't worry about it, Mr. Pratt. My men know what to look for. All of that is well in hand."

Except that it wasn't.

But Jim Kinkaid never had any illusions about being rescued. As he drove around the Sunset district, haphazardly wandering until he was ordered to switch directions, he knew that Angel had anticipated that he would somehow involve the police. Sometimes he would go far enough west that he was able to look down the thin strips of shimmering asphalt and see how they seemed to drop straight off into the Pacific Ocean, and then with a few abrupt turns he would find himself in a wilderness of tract houses.

And always, although he never had a glimpse of her, she seemed to know his exact position—"Turn left onto Taraval, which will be the next light." It was as if she already held him caught in the netlike pattern of the streets.

But the intention was clear. She wanted to satisfy herself that he had not allowed himself to be followed. From whatever vantage she was watching, she wanted to be sure that none of the cars behind him had grown too familiar. She was being cautious and wary. She would keep him circling until she was sure he was alone.

And it didn't help Kinkaid's state of mind to have the phone suddenly start bleating very fifteen or twenty or thirty seconds, the intervals just irregular enough that he couldn't anticipate them. Once, twice—he would pick up on the third ring, if it ever came. You never knew. And you never knew what it might mean when it did come. Probably that was part of the fun. Driving around like that, going nowhere, was like having one's nerve fibers drawn out with a pair of tweezers.

Once, twice. This time he got in the middle of the third ring. He didn't speak. He just held the handset to his ear and listened.

"Stop the car, Jim."

She always called him "Jim," and she always spoke in the same calm almost reassuring voice, as if she were sitting beside him, giving directions from a map she had spread out over her lap.

"Anywhere—it doesn't matter. Just pull over. There. Good. Now, you see the diner across the street? There's parking in the back. Leave the Jag where it is and walk over to the lot. Don't worry, Jim. I'll let you know which car when you get there. The keys will be under the floor mat."

He was on Judah Street, heading east. A light rain spattered the windshield as he picked up the tape recorder from the seat beside him and put it in his jacket pocket. He took nothing else, not even the car keys. When he opened the door he was surprised by the force of the wind coming off the ocean.

The rain had come up suddenly, just in the last few seconds. On the sidewalk opposite a woman and a little girl were still laughing as they scurried along, clutching each other, on their way to some safe, dry place. They were dressed for warm weather. The wind caught at the hems of their weightless dresses.

Kinkaid walked across the street, his hands thrust into his pockets, at least partly to disguise the lump made by the tape recorder. He did not hurry. The rain was startlingly cold on his face, as if to remind him he was alive.

The parking lot behind the diner had spaces for about twenty cars, but that late in the afternoon there were only four. One of them was a Chevy Cavalier, dark blue, with the front window on the driver's side rolled halfway down. Almost as soon as Kinkaid noticed the window he heard a phone ringing. He opened the car door and climbed in. He let the phone ring several times before he picked it up.

"I noticed a couple of police cars slow when they saw you, Jim. But maybe they were just admiring your Jag. I don't think they'll pay any attention now, do you?"

He didn't answer. Instead he reached into his jacket pocket and took out the tape recorder, snicking it on as he hid it under the seat while he took the keys from under the floor mat. The tape would run for an hour. He had the feeling that would be more than enough.

"Where's your sense of humor, Jim? Mad at me?"

"Where do you want me to go?" he said, his voice heavy, as if he were half asleep.

"Very well—if you're going to pout. Drive up to Nineteenth Avenue and turn right."

"Nineteenth and turn right," he repeated, once he had hung up the phone. The volume control on the tape recorder was turned up as high as it would go.

When he reached Nineteenth Avenue he knew at once that they had stopped playing hide-and-seek. It was the approach to the Presidio, and beyond that the Golden Gate Bridge.

He was on his way through the Park when she called again.

"If you look in your ashtray you'll find three dollars for the toll. Isn't that thoughtful of me?"

"I notice you haven't made provision for a return trip."

"Now, Jim, you mustn't jump to conclusions. As it happens they don't charge in the other direction."

"There's only about a quarter of a tank of gas in this car."

"Don't worry. You won't have far to go."

"Angel, pretty quick I'm going to have to hear from Lisa again, or all bets are off."

"It's all arranged, darling."

Darling. She'd never called him that before, not even when they were kids.

"I want so much to see you, Jim. I really do."

Then the line began to hum again and he hung up. Kinkaid found himself wondering if she imagined they were still lovers, that nothing in between mattered—not Lisa, not all those murders, nothing. Probably she was just playing with him, teasing him before the kill, but both were possibilities. Perhaps that was what it was to be insane, the capacity to feel conflicting emotions and to know that they conflict.

Perhaps he would find out. Doubtless he would find out a lot of things in the next few hours, and then he could carry it all into the oblivion that Angel had prepared for him. It never occurred to him to doubt that she meant to kill him.

In the beginning he had felt so safe. A list of names, bad boys who had climbed Mrs. Wyman's wall to fool around with her granddaughter—kids, whose only offense had been to answer the call of their adolescent hormones. He had climbed that wall too, but he had been too shy to take advantage of what was so plainly offered. That, he had thought, set him apart. He had loved Angel Wyman, who after all was only sixteen, and he had wanted to do the right thing.

But apparently Angel hadn't seen it that way, because now he was going to join the others and suffer whatever humiliating death she had picked out for him.

But the thought of that death left him strangely unmoved. It only takes a second to die, and the embellishments that came after wouldn't matter to him then. He could accept dying if he could trade his life for Lisa's—and maybe, while he was at it, put a stop to Angel.

And he had an idea how he might do that. If he was reading her right, there was just a chance.

Beyond the park the city seemed to fall away. There was a golf course, although the rain, which was picking up, seemed to have driven everyone inside. Then there was a short tunnel, and then the direct approach to the bridge.

The car phone, which had been silent for five whole minutes, suddenly bleeted into life again. Kinkaid didn't wait for the third ring before picking up the receiver.

"Just a thought, Jim. On the off chance you had something in mind. When you get to the toll plaza, choose the third booth from the right. I don't suppose the police can have a man in all of them, do you?"

Clever girl, he whispered to himself, so the tape recorder wouldn't pick it up. Clever little Angel. Once more she had anticipated him.

The toll lines were mercifully long that Sunday afternoon, so he had a few seconds to rummage through the car. What he found, in the glove compartment, was the rental agreement, made out to one Agnes Wycott, initials A. W., in case anyone needed a hint.

Doubtless Angel had a whole library of phony identities, so Agnes Wycott would remain a dead end for the police. But the agreement did contain a description of the car and the license number. Maybe Pratt would be able to make something out of that.

Kinkaid folded the agreement until he could wrap a twenty dollar bill around it. Then, when he finally made it up to the tollbooth window, he passed them both to the clerk.

"Call the FBI and tell them you've spoken to Kinkaid," he told the man, who seemed on the verge of handing his money back to him. "This isn't a joke. Wait five minutes and then call the FBI. Remember 'Kinkaid'—and keep the change."

Then he rolled up the window and drove through, before there was any chance of a reply. He knew that, considering the circumstances, the sense of triumph he experienced was absurd.

chapter 41

It was on the bridge itself that Kinkaid first caught sight of her. He glanced in his rearview mirror and saw that the car behind him was coming up fast—it even flashed its headlights once to attract his attention.

The rain was becoming intense, and up there on the bridge the wind from the ocean was strong enough that you really had to steer to keep from drifting over into the next lane. But there she was, maybe fifteen feet behind him at sixty miles an hour. She was wearing sunglasses, but she took them off so he could see her face.

He had no more than a glimpse of her before she fell back and switched to another lane, effectively losing herself in the flow of traffic.

The phone rang just as he got off the bridge.

"You had a long conversation with the toll collector, Jim. Did you give him the rental slip I left in the glove compartment for you? Did you read it? It's for another car, Jim. Same make and year, but gray. And of course different plates. It ought to keep the police amused for a few hours."

Check and mate. Kinkaid put down the receiver without having uttered a word. What the hell was there to say? He was playing Angel's game and, predictably, she was winning.

And why not? What else did she do but play this game? She was clever, and she had years of experience. By comparison, he was an amateur.

You don't win by letting opposing counsel define what the case is about, as one of his law professors had been fond of saying. You win by insisting on your own definition.

The initiative was all with Angel. Somehow he had to take

it away from her. He was a lawyer, not a criminal or a conspirator. He had to think like a lawyer.

He had to take Angel where she had never gone before.

"There's a turnoff about two miles ahead. After that I'll give you directions. We need to talk, Jim."

The road was narrow and apparently deserted. It seemed to go on forever. Then there was a bit of cleared ground and an abandoned building that looked as if it might once have been some sort of store. There was a car parked in front, a metallic green Plymouth he suddenly realized he had seen half a dozen times that afternoon without really noticing it.

Angel was waiting for him on the porch that occupied the front of the deserted building. He sat in his car for a moment, watching her from behind the swish of his windshield wipers as she stared out at him.

She was wearing a dark raincoat and there was a scarf over her hair. The rusted screens that ran around the porch on three sides obscured her face just enough that for that sliver of time she was not the person he had known, much less the monster which had slowly taken shape in his mind, but simply a small, sad-looking woman, all alone, taking shelter from the storm.

And he knew, if by some miracle he survived this terrible day, if he lived another fifty years, that in a part of his mind she would always remain this fragile, forlorn little creature, that he would never be certain if in this moment he had not glimpsed the secret of her soul.

And then she raised her arm and gestured for him to come to her, and the spell was broken.

The rain was coming down hard now, and there were gusts of wind that seemed to blow it sideways then all at once swirled it around so there was no escaping. The soft ground fairly smoked with dampness. Kinkaid hurried to the screen door, which slammed shut behind him with a sound like a whip cracking.

And there she was. In her right hand was a small pistol, a snubnose revolver, which she held pointed down at the board floor, but with her left she reached up to pull away the scarf that covered her hair while she looked at him a little questioningly, as if trying to measure the effect.

"Oh, Jim—I've waited so long for this. I can hardly believe it."

And, yes, it was a kind of miracle. Ten years had gone by, she had passed from sixteen to twenty-six, but the change from schoolgirl to woman seemed no more substantial than a shift of mood, as if the one could step back into the other almost at will.

She was more polished now, more expensive looking. She wore her hair shorter, and she was better dressed. There was about her now a certain exquisiteness of surface that had been missing in the girl to whom he had brought a glass of lemonade on the rear porch of his father's house, but that girl had shown him a worldliness which now had simply found a different expression.

Yet in herself she seemed not to have changed at all. Angel at sixteen had looked older than she was. Now she looked younger.

And as he stood there, staring at her, he experienced a kind of awe that was so close to what he had once thought of as love that he could hardly find a way to distinguish them. It frightened him. It frightened him precisely because it could not dispel the horror of what he now knew her to be. She was a monster. She had killed at least eight people and probably more. And yet in that moment he was back on his father's porch, unable to turn his eyes from her, as if the sight of her alone was the promise of paradise.

She took a step toward him, then another, then one more.

"I can't," she said, her voice husky with emotion. "I can't resist . . ."

And then, when they were only a few feet apart, she raised the pistol and let the muzzle come to rest just an inch below his rib cage. The pressure was faint but unmistakable, like the warning. *I will kill you,* it said, *if you make me.*

But with her left hand she reached up and touched his face, letting the tips of her fingers slide over his eye and cheek. She seemed to want to reassure herself of his reality.

"I'm here," he answered gently. "I'm here because you wanted it. Now you have to tell me what else you want."

She snatched her hand away as if she had burned it. Then she stepped back. The pistol muzzle remained against his side.

"Why are you so cruel to me? How can you speak to me like that after all this time?"

"There's only one thing you can do with a gun, Angel. Do you intend to do it?"

A flash of surprise registered in her eyes.

"You aren't afraid then?" she asked—apparently a serious question. "You don't think I'd do it?"

"Kill me? Maybe." His voice seemed to come from within some impenetrable calm. "I guess I'll find out, either now or later. But if not now, then put the gun away."

It was a direct challenge, not so much to her advantage over him as to her sense of theater. She had to make good on the implied threat or back down.

So she stepped back a few paces, until she was well outside his reach, and then lowered the pistol.

"You have something I want, Angel. I'm willing to trade for it, but I mean to have it back."

"You mean the girl?" She allowed herself a brief, almost voiceless syllable of laughter. "Is she really so important to you?"

He didn't answer, because he didn't need to. She had known the answer when she kidnapped Lisa.

And she seemed to realize at once that attempting to diminish her hostage was a tactical error.

"I'm not sure it's possible for you to have her back. . . ."

This time it was his turn to laugh.

"Anything is possible for you, Angel. You can rise from the grave—don't I have your death certificate in my desk drawer?"

"Then you know about that?"

"Yes, I know about that. I also know about your grand-mother's money-laundering schemes. I know about how your mother's boyfriend beat her to death. And I know about Sherman's Crest. I'm the family lawyer, remember?"

All the time he was speaking she watched him with an oddly speculative light in her eyes, and Kinkaid didn't have to guess what she was thinking. Everything he had told her she knew he could have figured out from an intelligent inspection of her grandmother's check stubs, and none of it was particularly damning. She was wondering what he didn't know—or might suspect.

Kinkaid had a friend who had gone straight from Yale Law School to become an assistant district attorney in New Haven, and who had made quite a name for herself prosecuting domestic violence cases. She had once told him that the worst and most brutal criminals are the most credulous optimists, that the guy who beats his wife and four-year-old daughter to death with a nine-iron will confess to everything, will supply you with a precisely circumstantial account of how he did it and give you everything you need to put him away for life plus twenty, if you just stand aside for a little and allow him to talk himself into the idea that the fact that he had been roasting his brain all day with cocaine somehow constitutes a mitigating circumstance.

They are all looking for The Out, she had said. They all want that little open window through which they are going to crawl to freedom and another chance to victimize the world. And the deeper the dungeon their crimes have prepared for them the more fervently they believe they can see its light.

So Kinkaid, with his carefully edited summary of the evidence, was hoping that Angel was hoping that somehow, in spite of appearances to the contrary, she was in the clear. People are never so reckless as when they think they have nothing to lose, so if she believed that after all there was a chance she might still be going home to Five Miles it could make her just a little more cautious about spilling blood.

"She put me there," Angel said finally, her eyes hardening at the injustice of it. "My own grandmother put me in that gentrified madhouse, just because I was inconvenient."

"And then she thought better of it and got you out again."

"Yes. She got me out."

"And gave you a new identity and a new life, and all the money."

"Yes."

"Did she supply the corpse? The girl who's buried up there, in your grave?"

"I never knew anything about that." She said it as if the Jaws of Hell had just opened to receive her—the scene really was remarkably well played. "Jim, you've got to believe me. I never knew anything about that."

"Then it was the perfect crime. She's beyond the law's reach, your grandmother. She got away with it."

For a moment they stood there without speaking, as if listening to the rain, which banged loudly on the tin roof over their heads. The rusted screens around three sides of the porch shivered in the wind, which seemed constantly to be changing direction.

"Put the gun away, Angel," he said at last. "You don't need it and I'm sick of the sight of it. Put it away."

She seemed to consider the request for a moment, and then she did something extraordinary. She walked over to her handbag, a leather sack that was lying open in the middle of the floor, and dropped the gun into it. For the moment, at least, she had surrendered her claim to his life.

It was a wonderfully persuasive gesture. If he hadn't known about the Billinger family, he would have believed her.

He looked away for a moment, simply because the sight of her was too painful to bear. He stared at the rain, wishing he could be out there in it, letting it wash his mind blank.

Then suddenly, when he turned around, Angel was directly behind him, so close that he almost brushed against her.

She stood there, her shoulders a little hunched, the palms of her hands resting carelessly against her hips. Her eyes were half closed. She had lifted her face, as if she expected him to kiss her.

He could not deny to himself that he wanted to kiss her.

"There's something else we still need to talk about," he said, perhaps more harshly than he intended. "You have Lisa."

She slapped him. It might have been a sudden burst of anger—certainly that was what it was meant to seem—except it wasn't. It had come just half an instant too soon. She had planned to strike him, to appear hurt and angry and jealous. She had planned it the way she planned everything.

She walked away a few steps, turning her back on him.

"You can have her if you love her so much," she answered, with a tiny throb in her voice.

"Yes. I do."

"As much as you used to love me?"

"I can't remember."

And, at that moment, he couldn't. That he had loved her he remembered as an objective fact, the way he remembered his Social Security number, but the memory carried nothing with it. They might as well have been other people. Adam and Eve, Edward and Mrs. Simpson. Anyone. He couldn't remember what it had felt like.

It was like being let out of prison.

"You don't remember." She turned around and faced him, her arms folded together as if the cold rain outside had soaked her through. "It wasn't so very long ago."

"I was somebody else then," he said, and stopped himself just in time from adding, *"and so were you."*

"I want to know what you've done with Lisa," he went on instead. "I want to know that she's all right."

"Do you think I'd hurt her?"

"You've got her—how the hell do I know what you might do with her? This game stops now, Angel."

"Whatever you say, Jim."

Her handbag was still lying on the floor. With a quick crouch she picked it up and slung the strap across her shoulder. She let her hand drop inside.

"You can use the phone in my car."

"I'll use the one in mine, thanks."

"What's the matter? Are you afraid of running up my bill?"

"I'm not getting into your car until I know that Lisa is safe. Then we'll go and find her, together."

She managed the faintest of shrugs, followed by an equally faint smile.

"Sure."

He had parked not fifteen feet from the door, but the wind was so strong it was blowing the rain sideways. All you could do was put your head down and push through it.

In the car he took out his pocket handkerchief and offered it to Angel. It was just a reflex, something he did without thinking, but as she took it her fingertips brushed against the back of his hand.

He picked up the phone. "Give me the number," he said.

"I can dial it for you. . . ."

"Just give me the number, Angel. I'll manage."

And she did. First three digits, then four. And as he punched them in he repeated them aloud, as if he wanted to make sure he had them right.

The first ring seemed to go on forever.

"Hello?"

Hello. The most conventional answer in the world, but filled with dread. What in God's name had the last few hours been like for her?

"Lisa, it's Jim. I'm coming to get you. . . ."

"Jim, are you with her? Get away from her—she's fucking crazy. . . ."

"Lisa, it's going to be all right," he said, emphasizing each word. "I'm coming to get you."

"Oh God, Jim, don't come here! Get away from her. She'll kill you! She's killed three people already to—"

The line went dead. For a second or two Kinkaid didn't realize what had happened, then he saw Angel withdrawing her hand from the phone console. She had cut him off.

"You've heard enough," she said calmly, with perhaps just a touch of mocking pleasure. "Next time she can pour out her troubles in person."

Kinkaid snatched her wrist, pulling it toward him as if he meant to break her arm. In that moment he didn't care about the gun. He was almost as angry as he seemed.

"Get out of the car, Angel."

"Absolutely. We'll take mine. That way we can be together."

He let her go, pushing her violently away.

"I swear, if you've hurt her I'll . . ."

"What will you do, sweetie? Kill me? Have you got it in you?"

"I'll worse than kill you, Angel. Now get out of the car."

He was shouting now, seething with rage. To keep himself from striking her, he reached across, opened the door latch, and pushed her hard enough that she had to catch herself to keep from falling out into the mud.

And for the very first time she seemed genuinely afraid. She scrambled out of the car, slamming the door behind her. For just a moment she stood there in the rain, glancing about as if looking which way to run.

And that moment was all he needed. He set the phone receiver back on its cradle without pressing it back into place.

In a few minutes it would begin beeping to let whoever was within earshot know it was off the hook. It would be like a homing device for the car if Pratt and his Bureau friends had just a little imagination.

He got out and started towards Angel's car, not looking

back. All he wanted was to get her away from there as quickly as possible.

She was waiting for him. And her alarm, if that was what it had been, had left her. She threw him a set of keys.

"I'll let you drive," she said. "Men always like that."

chapter 42

It took the San Francisco Police Department exactly half an hour to find the Jaguar. They dutifully called in their report to the FBI and then, ten minutes later, rang up again to report further that the vehicle seemed to be deserted. Officers at the scene were awaiting instructions.

That was about as much as Pratt could stand. After doing everything short of threatening Special Agent Blandford with his service revolver, he managed to get a ride over to the scene, which by the time he arrived was swarming with Bureau technicians, who, naturally, had found nothing.

"We've lifted some usable prints from the steering wheel and the telephone handset, Sir, but otherwise the interior's as clean as a whistle. In this rain there won't be anything on the outside."

Standing on the sidewalk while the wind drove water into his trenchcoat like nails through a board, Pratt could believe it. A hundred yards away the spray from the waves was visible over the beach wall. The ocean looked like it was going crazy.

The Jaguar had been a setup. Now either Kinkaid was with Angel or she had made him switch cars, so he could be anywhere driving anything.

The clever girl.

"You didn't by any chance find a tape recorder, did you?"

"A what?"

"A tape recorder. A little one, about this big."

He tried to suggest the size by forming a bracket between his middle finger and thumb, but the Bureau lab donkey shook his head.

"No, Sir. Nothing like that."

Then Kinkaid had taken it with him, which meant, since he wouldn't have risked keeping it on his person, that he probably didn't leave with Angel.

"How long do you think the car has been here?"

"Less than half an hour. The engine block was still warm when we arrived."

And in this rain it would cool fast.

"Mr. Pratt?"

It was the nice young man assigned to him as a driver, leaning out of the window of his perfectly nondescript FBI car, shouting back at him through the storm.

"Mr. Pratt, there's news."

Oh, it was news all right. One of the toll clerks on the Golden Gate Bridge had spoken to Jim Kinkaid.

"One of our people had arrived there just five minutes before," the nice young man told him as with lights flashing they sped toward the bridge. "But the personnel in the booths hadn't been briefed. Kinkaid drove through, gave the toll clerk the rental sheet from the car and told him to phone in. The guy claims he told him to wait five minutes before he made the call, but it sounds like he's providing himself with an excuse. Anyway, all chance of organizing a pursuit was lost."

And maybe it was just as well, although Pratt wasn't going to be crude enough to say so. Odds were the Bureau would have fucked it up.

He stared down at his feet and decided that his shoes were irretrievably ruined.

The little parking lot outside the bridge's headquarters building was so crammed with official-looking cars that Pratt's driver had to park fifty feet away. Thank God they were sheltered a little from the wind, which was blowing in from the ocean, but the walk to the door didn't improve his disposition.

Inside, someone handed him a styrofoam cup of coffee. It was Blandford.

"We have a SWAT team on the way," he said. "And we notified the Highway Patrol in Marin County to be on the lookout for a gray Ford Taurus."

"Then let's hope he isn't obliged to double back on us. I notice there aren't any toll booths in the other direction, so he won't be able to drop us any more love notes."

"We have the bridge covered. He won't get past us."

As if to prove his point, Blandford handed him a pink sheet of paper, apparently the one Kinkaid had passed to the toll clerk, and, sure enough, the words "Taurus" and "gray" were spelled out in block letters in the upper right-hand corner. There was even a license plate number.

The signature at the bottom was a woman's. Agnes Wycott. The suits were probably already busy chasing it down, but Angel Wyman was too smart to get caught that way.

"Do you suppose I might be allowed to talk to the toll clerk?"

The poor guy was sitting on a wooden chair in the center of a room filled with policemen who stood around ignoring him. He didn't look comfortable. He was probably around thirty, a latter-day flower child with a drooping mustache and a ponytail. Maybe he had been through scenes like this before.

"How are you?"

Pratt found another wooden chair and reversed it so he could sit with his arms crossed over the backrest. It was easier than way to push his face into the other man's, and it was astonishing how intimidated people got when you crowded into their air space.

"You a cop too?"

"No, I'm a tourist. Tell me about your friend in the car."

The toll clerk shrugged. His uniform looked a trifle small on him, as if it belonged to another life. Maybe it did.

"What's to tell? He comes through, he hands me a piece of paper and tells me to call the FBI. Says his name is Kinkaid."

"Did he pay his toll?"

"Sure he did."

"How? Exact change?"

"Sure. Three bucks."

"Three singles?"

"Yeah." The toll clerk smiled, which meant he was starting to worry.

"I bet he gave you a ten-spot and you kept it."

"No—no he didn't."

"Yes he did. I know him, and he's the type. Maybe it was even a fifty."

"No it wasn't."

"Then how much was it? Listen, nobody gives a shit. I just want to know."

"He told me to keep the change. . . ."

"Fine. Then it's yours. How much was it?"

"It was a twenty."

"That's my pal Jim."

Pratt smiled. Now the barriers were down. Now the poor slob wouldn't lie on reflex.

"So what did he tell you?"

"What I said." The clerk seemed almost angry. "That I should wait five minutes and phone the FBI, and that his name was Kinkaid. He said it wasn't a joke."

"That's it?"

"That's it. Oh yeah, and something about how he'd stay on the line."

"One more thing. What kind of car was he driving?"

"You kiddin' me?" The clerk reached back and smoothed down his ponytail, as if to be reassured it was still there. "You know how many cars I see in a day? In this job, a car is a car."

"You remember the color?"

"I don't know. . . . Blue, green—something like that."

"Gray?"

"No, I don't think so. Hey, anyway, who was the guy?"

"Just another tourist."

Outside, Pratt looked at his watch. It had been at least half an hour since Kinkaid had stopped at the toll plaza. He could be anywhere.

But he said he'd stay on the line.

"Get on to Ma Bell," he told Blandford. "Tell them to listen for anything unusual, particularly anything involving mobile phones."

"Like what?"

"Like how the hell should I know? Anything. Kinkaid will have to use his imagination.

"One other thing—don't put at lot of faith in that gray Ford Taurus."

There was nothing to do except to wait. The Highway Patrol had already found fifteen gray Ford Tauruses, but none of them had the right license plates and none of them turned out to be rental cars. It was close to an hour since anyone had heard from Jim Kinkaid.

"If she's got him, he's probably dead by now," Blandford announced with a certain dismal satisfaction. "Or he probably wishes he was."

Pratt only glared at him.

"Sir, the phone company thinks they may have something." The agent who took the call put his hand over the receiver's mouthpiece as he spoke. "They have a phone off the hook and they're hearing it as a radio frequency, which means it's either a cellular or a car phone."

"Can they find the source?" Pratt asked.

Blandford's boy glanced first at his boss, who nodded, before he answered. "Yes, Sir. They can triangulate on the signal. They want to know whether they should send their trucks out."

Stupid question.

Everybody was in the parking lot within fifteen seconds. This time Blandford invited Pratt to come along with him. His driver knew the area.

Within ten minutes the phone company reported an approximate location, and within fifteen a fleet of Bureau cars had converged on the spot—a wide place in the road featuring a derelict building.

And it was a Chevy, not a Ford. And dark blue, not gray.

"I want our explosives people to check it out first," Blandford said, as soon as they had come to a stop. "We don't even know if it's the right one, but if it is she may have booby-trapped it."

"There's no time for that."

Pratt didn't wait to debate the point. In an instant he was out in the slanting rain, running across the muddy ground toward what he knew by instinct was Kinkaid's abandoned car. He threw the driver's side door open. There was no bang.

The phone was making an awful racket. He began searching under the seat, and almost immediately his hand touched the pocket tape recorder.

"Good man," he whispered to himself. "You delivered the mail."

They could only hear Kinkaid's side of his telephone conversations with Angel Wyman, and the overlay of the engine noises rendered those difficult to understand. Then the car stopped and there was a long pause, long enough to raise the suspicion that perhaps they had transferred to another car and driven away.

Then there was the sound of a door slamming, and then another.

"She's in the car with him," Blandford pointed out, quite unnecessarily.

"Give me the number."

"I can dial it for you."

It was the first time Pratt had ever heard her voice—his first real trace of her as a person. She didn't sound like a monster.

"Just give me the number, Angel. I'll manage."

"Eight-Four-Eight, Seven-Three-Five-One."

Then Kinkaid's voice, repeating it. *"Eight-Four-Eight, Seven-Three-Five-One."*

"Have you got that?" Blandford asked, stabbing a finger at his driver. In the closed car he seemed to be shouting. "Get on the horn to the phone people. Tell them I want an address twenty minutes ago."

The driver scuttled off through the rain toward one of the Bell Pacific trucks that was parked a few yards away, and they went on listening to the tape.

Even though they could only hear Kinkaid's voice, the brief conversation with Lisa Milano was harrowing. Apparently Angel didn't like it either.

"You've heard enough. Next time she can pour out her troubles in person."

"Get out of the car, Angel."

"Absolutely. We'll take mine. That way we can be together."

"I swear, if you've hurt her I'll . . ."

"What will you do, sweetie? Kill me? Have you got it in you?"

That was when Kinkaid seemed to go ballistic. He was shouting like a maniac. And then the indistinct sounds of a struggle as a car door opened and closed. Then nothing.

A few minutes later the tape ran out.

"Sounds like he really lost it," Blandford said. "Doesn't he know what he's dealing with? His lady friend might have offed him right there."

"He knows what he's dealing with—he probably knows better than anybody. And he didn't lose it. He had to get her out of that car to set the phone signal, so that's what he did."

They waited through a few minutes of silence, listening to the rain on the car roof. Outside, Bureau agents were combing the area, looking for clues, ruining their shoes in the mud. It was standard procedure, useless but probably necessary.

The FBI, with its computerized search patterning and all its other wonderful toys, wasn't going to catch the Angel of Death. It wasn't even their fault. They had method and analysis, which was usually more than enough to put the run-of-the-mill sociopath in the bag, but Angel Wyman just wasn't human enough for all of that to do them any good. She was prey to none of the usual frailties, no more than a fire running through dry grass.

In fact, the only hint of weakness Pratt had ever seen in her was the fact that Jim Kinkaid had lived long enough to leave this place with her. Her other victims had probably never guessed that that was what they were, not until the last few seconds of their lives, but she had arranged things so that Kinkaid came to her freely, through his conscious choice. She wanted something more from him than simply his death, some more complete revenge, which meant that she could not keep the game in her perfect control.

Kinkaid had been in love with her once—might, in some remote corner of his soul, still love her. Only fools and songwriters thought that love was understanding, but maybe he knew something about Angel Wyman no one else had ever guessed. Maybe it would even be enough to keep him alive.

Maybe.

chapter 43

Somehow Kinkaid had known the house would be like this.

They left the road and traveled downward on a long driveway walled in with eucalyptus trees the branches of which twisted painfully in the storm, shedding dagger-shaped leaves and strips of bark. The rain was coming in rhythmic sheets, so that between beats of the windshield wipers you couldn't see them all.

And then, there it was. The driveway ended in a circle around a patch of bare grass. Another car was parked in front of the house.

It looked like it belonged there. The dark wood was its own natural color and no light came from the large picture windows. The house was beautiful and modern but forbidding, as if it had been designed for some purpose that had nothing to do with human comfort.

The car had belonged to Frank Rizza's two henchmen. Kinkaid had seen it outside the pier that same morning. He did not allow himself to form any comforting expectations, because it was obvious that neither Rizza nor his goons were going to rescue anyone. One way or the other, Angel would have all of that well in hand.

Still, he would be curious to find out what the car was doing there.

"Let me invite you in," Angel said, her smile faint and mischievous. Her bag was on her lap and her right hand was inside it, doubtless closed around the gun he had not seen since he told her to put it away. "I'm afraid you'll find the place a terrible mess. I don't do much entertaining, you see."

"Is Lisa inside?"

"Yes."

"And is she safe?"

"She's all right. As far as her safety goes, I'll let you be the judge."

He started to say something and then thought better of it. She was enjoying this too much.

So he just got out of the car. He pulled the lapels of his coat tight around his throat and braced himself against the rain and waited for her to follow.

"Go ahead," she shouted over the wind. "The door is open."

His eyes took a moment to adjust, but the first object he picked out of the darkness was Lisa, huddled by a stone wall.

She didn't speak. She merely stared at him, and then slumped against the wall as if abandoning her last hope. She looked dreadful.

"What has she done to you?" Kinkaid was at last able to speak. "Lisa, has she hurt you?"

He began to run to her, but he was stopped halfway by the sight of a man lying on the floor. At first he was merely surprised, and then he saw that the man was dead.

There was another one, lying a few feet away. He knew these two—they belonged to the car outside. They belonged to Rizza.

Which raised an interesting question. Where was Rizza?

It took him only a split second to consider all this, and then to decide, more or less simultaneously, that he didn't care. He didn't give a damn if the whole house was carpeted in dead bodies. What mattered was that Lisa was in handcuffs. She was chained to the god damned wall.

"It's okay, Baby," he said, his voice somewhere between a murmur and a sob as he took her in his arms. "I'm here now. I'll get you out. It's okay."

But Lisa didn't seem to hear him. She raised her hands so that he could see the cuffs on her wrists—the flesh was rubbed raw—and whispered something he didn't hear. Then she shook her head and repeated it.

"Make her unlock me."

But before he could answer the lights came on with a faint shudder of fluorescent bulbs.

"Get away from her."

Angel was standing about fifteen feet from the door. She had taken the pistol out of her bag and aimed it at both of them.

"Get away from her, Jim. Or I promise you I'll blow her fucking head off, just for old times' sake."

It was not a situation which admitted of any uncertainty. The threat was perfectly believable. Kinkaid disengaged himself from Lisa, who, in spite of the handcuffs, tried to put her arms around his neck so that he had to push her away. He stepped back from her and then glanced at Angel.

"A little further, if you don't mind. Over there will be fine. We can't have you stepping on poor What's-His-Name."

She gestured him back with the muzzle of her gun until he was almost precisely in the center of the room.

Behind her, the front door had been left standing open. It was raining in on the stone floor of the entranceway. Even from where he was standing Kinkaid could feel the wind. He found himself wondering why a door left open struck him as somehow important, as if a vital decorum had been breached, and why it seemed to matter so little to Angel.

Because, of course, it meant she was finished with this place. The rain on the carpet didn't matter because she knew the next time she passed through that open door she was never coming back.

"Who will you be when you're done here, Angel?"

The question was like light flooding a darkened corner—for an instant it startled her, but only because she did not immediately perceive its source. Then she smiled, a smile that might have seemed beautiful had you just met this woman for the first time. To Kinkaid it seemed inhuman.

"Another variation on the theme," she said, as if she had to choose that moment. "Another little rich girl, sprung full-grown out of the head of Zeus. Why? Does it matter?"

"I suspect it won't to me."

Her face puckered a trifle, in what might, in someone else, have been disapproval.

"Or was I mistaken?" he went on, trying hard not even to glance at Lisa, trying to seem detached and invulnerable, as if nothing held him to this life except a certain idle curiosity. "Isn't that part of the plan? You kill me as part of the molting process, and then you can reinvent yourself as anything you want. I'd really hate to spoil it for you."

"And how would you do that, Jim?"

"By insisting on having things my own way."

She cradled her right hand in her left and locked her arms straight. The gun muzzle steadied on him, so that he was quite sure that, had she pulled the trigger, the bullet would have gone straight through the middle of his forehead.

"Beg me, Jim."

He said nothing. He hardly even saw the gun, although he was looking right at her. His whole attention was on her—on her, and on his determined effort not to care that he might die before he took his next breath.

After perhaps fifteen seconds she made a quick, impatient movement and swung the pistol around so that it pointed at Lisa.

"Beg me," she repeated.

Crouching against the wall, Lisa stared at him with huge, terrified eyes, as if she had been emptied of everything but fear, and Kinkaid forced himself to dismiss that silent plea. He had to. If he was going to save her life he had to forget that he loved her. This had to be strictly between Angel and himself.

"That won't work either, Angel."

"No."

"No, it won't. And for the same reason. Shoot her and I'll make you kill me too. Right now. On my own terms. I don't think you're quite prepared to let me off as lightly as that."

"I might be, Jim. After all, I might be the sentimental type."

"This is where we find out."

For a moment anything seemed possible. One quick twitch, a few ounces of pressure on the trigger and Lisa's head would simply explode, but Angel might have been made of stone. She seemed frozen in an instant of cold, murderous anger.

"If I kill her, Jim, will you cry?"

"I won't have time."

She glanced at him as if astonished at the sound of his voice.

"Pull the trigger, Angel, and I'm all over you. It isn't much of a distance, remember. You'll have probably less than a second to turn, take aim and fire, and if you don't stop me dead with the first shot I'll roll over you like a logging truck. Believe me, if I get close enough to put my hands on you I'll break your neck, even if it's with my dying breath."

Maybe she believed him. The pistol suddenly swung back to take aim at Kinkaid.

Would she do it? Would she kill him right there, simply because he had as good as dared her to? There was something about the way she held herself that suggested she hadn't made up her mind.

"You know, Jim," she said at last, her voice perfectly conversational even as her face was half hidden behind her clenched hands. "There's one thing I've always been curious about—I thought I'd made more of an impression. What made it so easy for you to throw me over?"

He didn't allow himself to be surprised. It was a tactic, he thought. She was trying to break his concentration.

"Does it make a difference now?" he asked.

"It seems to."

"Then I have another question. What makes you think I threw you over?"

It was a long story—at least, it seemed a long story to tell with a pistol pointed at your head. But he managed to get the general outline across.

Angel lowered the gun. She appeared stricken, her eyes unnaturally bright. She stared down at the floor. She seemed to be looking for something.

"It was because of my mother," she said, almost as if to herself. "Family Tramp Two. Grandmother was getting even."

"Perhaps she thought she was protecting me."

"Don't bet on it. Grandmother never did anything for anyone whose name wasn't Wyman." With an effort that was almost painful to watch, she lifted her gaze to Kinkaid's face. "Would you have minded about the others?"

"I was twenty. Yes, I would have minded. Whether I could have gotten past that is something I can't honestly say. Maybe. I'd never been in love before."

"Then there's a chance it's all been for nothing."

"Either way, it's all been for nothing."

She looked away. For a long moment she was silent. She didn't move. She appeared not even to know he was there. And then the gun came up again and pointed at his head.

"So I've lost it all," she said. "Five Miles, my name, you—everything. Just don't expect I won't want something back."

"You want to settle the account? Fine—then settle it with me. Because it's between the two of us, Angel. We're the only ones left. It doesn't have anything to do with Lisa."

For an instant she looked as if she had been stung with a lash. Then the pain turned to a cold, deliberate anger.

"You said you would trade for her. It's funny, but I don't think you've got much to offer."

"I've got what I had before. I have the power to choose the time of my death. If it suits you to kill me now, then go ahead. Otherwise, let her go. This is not about her."

For perhaps twenty minutes he had not taken his eyes from Angel's face. He had allowed himself to see nothing else in the room but her. The temptation to look away now was almost overpowering, but he knew that if he did she would shoot him in the leg and then his bargaining power was at an end. While he was waiting for it, balanced on the balls of his feet, ready to weave and dodge the instant she lowered her gun, she wouldn't risk it. But if his attention wandered it was over.

"You're right. She doesn't matter." Bringing her left hand down, she reached into a pocket concealed in the waistband of her trousers and brought out something small and silver. She threw it to Kinkaid. "Go ahead. You can take the cuffs off her."

It was a set of keys. Kinkaid didn't even glance at them. He simply heard them drop to the carpet beside his foot. She was making it too easy.

There was a peculiar light in Angel's eyes, a hard glassy quality that reminded him of a predatory animal.

"Let me guess," he said. "I reach down to pick up the keys and you blow my foot off—that should slow me down. Then you have everything your way."

She allowed herself a quick laugh. "Good guess. I must say, Jim, you're making this more fun than I thought it would be."

"So I don't pick them up, and we're back to where we were. I might even be a point ahead because you don't have the keys anymore."

"Go ahead. Pick them up. I promise I'll be good. See?"

She raised the pistol until it pointed straight up at the ceiling.

"What more do you want, Jim? Go ahead. Risk it."

He didn't allow himself to think. Before she had even finished speaking he dropped to a crouch, snatched the keys, and came back up. His little dance step to one side was unnecessary. She did not bring the pistol back down until he was perfectly still again.

"See, Jim? You have to learn to trust me."

Then he understood what she wanted. He would take the keys over to Lisa, begin to unlock the handcuffs, and Angel would blow her head off. She wanted him to be close to Lisa when she killed her. She wanted him to stand there, covered with blood and brains, too shocked even to scream. Then she would have him.

No thanks.

The storm outside was getting worse. The rain on the roof fell like hammer blows. Through the open front door you could hear the sound the wind made in the trees. It was like the agony of God.

"Lisa," he called, without looking at her. "Can you catch this? You get one chance."

Then he threw them. He waited for the faint clink of metal against stone, but it didn't come.

"She's got them, Jim. Nicely played."

Of course it didn't make any difference. He was glad that Lisa was no longer chained up like a galley slave, but the basic situation was unchanged. Angel still had the gun and Lisa was too exhausted and frightened to be a threat to her. As soon as she had the handcuffs off she sank into a nearby chair. She put her hands down between her knees and began sobbing.

"The offer is still the same, Angel. You let her walk out of here and it's strictly between you and me. Otherwise, I'll make you kill me, and then the party's over."

"I think you're bluffing, Jim. In my experience, nobody dies for love—what if I call your bluff?"

At first he couldn't identify the sound. It was so faint, like a bird chirping in the next room. Then he knew what it was.

"Your phone's ringing, Angel."

It was as if he had unconsciously given the signal everyone was waiting for, because suddenly everything happened very fast. Angel swung the gun around toward Lisa, whom Kinkaid could see out of the corner of his eye as she stood up and turned toward Angel—it was impossible to know which of them had moved first. For some reason Lisa was holding her arms out in front of her.

Kinkaid didn't wait. Even before he heard the sound of

shooting he burst into a run, digging in hard so that no matter what happened his momentum would carry him forward.

He wasn't sure how many shots he heard. It could have been three or even four. He didn't know. He had no more than a second or two, and the only thing in his mind was reaching Angel.

She turned, looking at him with blank astonishment. Her gun was raised, pointing back at him. He felt the impact of something hitting, but he never saw a flash.

Then he slammed into her, flat out. She let out a little scream and they went over. They were on the floor, fighting each other like animals. She still had the gun. Kinkaid felt a stab of pain, like a hot knife cutting into him, as he climbed up her arm to get it. He got it. He heard something snap as he pulled it loose from her hand.

Then he rolled away from her, wrapping himself around the gun. He had no thought except to keep it away from her.

It was then, when he tried to take a breath, that he realized he had been shot.

"Are you bad, Jim? Oh God—oh God, I'm sorry."

It was Lisa. She wasn't dead. She was kneeling beside him, very much alive. He tried to speak her name, but all he could manage was a sob of gratitude.

"If he dies, I swear I'll kill you, you bitch."

Until then he hadn't noticed the pistol she held in her hand. Where had she got it? It looked small enough to be a toy.

He turned his head. Angel was only a few feet away, just beginning to get to her feet. Her face and blouse were smeared with blood and she was holding her right hand, the first finger of which was bent at a peculiar angle, against her shoulder. She didn't look frightened, or even angry. She seemed amused. She was ready to laugh at them.

And she didn't have her gun anymore. Kinkaid had it.

The phone was still ringing, faint but insistent.

"Answer it," he said. "Find the stupid thing and answer it."

Kinkaid's wound was really beginning to hurt now. As far as

he could determine he had been shot once, somewhere on the right side of his chest. He couldn't find any bleeding, and for some reason he had more pain in his back than anywhere else.

He pulled himself up to a sitting position.

"I'm not going to die," he said. "At least not anytime soon. And nobody is going to kill anybody."

He looked at Angel's gun, which he was still cradling in his arms like a baby. As far as he remembered, it was the first time he had ever even held one. He pointed it at Angel, who by then was standing some ten or twelve feet away.

The ringing had never stopped.

"Lisa, go answer the phone. It's driving me nuts."

She didn't want to leave him. She put her arms around him and touched his face with her hands. Never, he thought, never had he loved her as much as he did that moment.

"Go on. Really, I'll be fine."

"It's on the floor over there," Angel said. She smiled, as if she had said something funny. "Remember? Right where you left it. Aren't you going to ask if I'm hurt, Jim?"

"Go get the phone, Lisa. We're going to call the cops."

She brought him the phone, a cellular about the size of his wallet. The operator wanted to know if their service had been interrupted by the storm.

"No, but if you'll give your headset to the nice policeman who is doubtless standing right beside you I'd be glad to talk to him."

It was someone from the Marin County Sheriff's Department.

"We could use an ambulance," Kinkaid told him. "No, I don't know the address. You'll have to figure that out for yourself."

Suddenly he felt very tired, so he handed the phone back to Lisa.

"They'll be here as fast as they can," he said.

"So what happens next? I mean, to me."

Angel was still smiling her odd, taunting smile, but Kinkaid shook his head.

"I wish for your sake you were in that grave back at Sherman's Crest."

"I think you mean it," Angel said.

"I do."

He raised his hand and, without taking his eyes from Angel's face, touched Lisa on the cheek. It was a gesture that told the absolute truth, that his heart was no longer divided, that the last claim Angel Wyman could make on him was to his pity.

She looked away.

"Prison or the loony bin," she said. "Will they send me to the gas chamber, do you think?"

"No."

"Too crazy? You're probably right. Just the same, I think it's time I took a swim."

"I don't think so." Lisa was aiming at Angel's head, but her hands were shaking badly.

"I'll take my chances," Angel said. And then, with the odd, crablike gait of someone in pain, she started toward the open front door, through which the rain was slanting in to beat against the stone floor.

There was the sound of a shot, but it didn't hit anything. Probably it went straight out into the darkness.

"Oh shit." Lisa knelt down and began to sob.

"Angel, don't do this," Kinkaid said.

Just at the door she turned around, and smiled once again. Then she was gone, out into the night and the storm.

chapter 44

It took the Marin County Sheriff's Department exactly six minutes to have officers and an ambulance at the house. And that was just as well, because by then Jim Kinkaid was in a pretty bad way.

He and Lisa were already gone when Pratt arrived, on their way to the closest emergency room. On the scene the FBI and the Sheriff's Department quickly became embroiled in a jurisdictional dispute, but to Pratt's intense satisfaction the Sheriff's Department had the better claim—a murder investigation with three bodies *in situ* will always take pride of place over an interstate flight warrant.

It was probably academic anyway, because nobody seemed to know where to find the chief suspect.

It was half an hour before a version of events came back from the hospital—Lisa, one gathered, had not been wonderfully patient with the FBI special agent who tried to take a statement from her while the surgeons were patching the hole in Jim's right lung. But at last a clear picture began to shape itself.

"She shot him in the back," Blandford announced after he closed up his cellular phone.

"Who? Angel?"

"No. His girlfriend. The slug they just pulled out of Kinkaid was a .22 caliber. Angel's gun was a .32. Apparently he got caught in the cross fire when he rushed Angel. He's got balls—I'll give him that. I don't think I'd care to charge a loaded gun."

"It's probably a good thing he did," Pratt replied. The forensic techs were busy circling bullet holes in the floors and walls. So far they had found two near the front door. "I'll bet both of them turn out to be .22s."

"So the first two shots went wild, then she hit Angel, then she missed and hit Kinkaid. Then she realized what she had done and stopped shooting—which accounts for the one round left chambered when we found the gun."

"It's a theory."

"Yeah." Blandford didn't seem entirely satisfied. "What I like is a theory about where our Miss Wyman has taken herself off to."

They didn't have to wait long.

There were still two cars parked in front of the house, and a third was discovered in a garage around back. If Angel had attempted to flee she was probably on foot, and in any case there were roadblocks up all over Marin County—she wouldn't get very far that way.

Besides, they had found her shoes.

There was a patio down by the ocean. There was a glass-topped table and a few chairs—on nice days it was probably a reasonably pleasant spot, but in this storm the waves came all the way up steep, ten-foot-high rock walls to wash the flagstones. Maybe that was why Angel had left her shoes on the table.

Pratt borrowed a rain slicker and he and Blandford went down to have a look for themselves. The shoes were neatly placed together and about three-quarters full of rainwater.

"If she took a header off of here she's fish food," Blandford said, having to shout over the wind. "Nobody can swim in that water, not in a storm like this, and she'd be beaten to pulp against the rocks. Remember, she's wounded."

Pratt wasn't arguing. She had come down here after leaving the house—the next day Lisa would identify the shoes as the ones Angel had been wearing—and it was reasonable to assume she would take them off before jumping into the water. If the search parties didn't find her by morning, there was nowhere else she could have gone except into the drink.

And why now, under the circumstances? She was shot, she knew she was cornered, and the best hope she had after capture was some locked ward in a mental hospital. Besides, there was no way Angel Wyman was going to allow herself to be taken alive.

They never found another trace of her. She was gone, swallowed up. The verdict was suicide.

They went back to the house, where many interesting items were being discovered.

The two dead guys in the living room were old news. They were local hoods, known by sight to half the plainclothesmen in the Bay Area. Upstairs the Sheriff's boys found Frank Rizza, lying across the bed with his throat cut. That was a little more interesting. Everyone agreed it couldn't have happened to a nicer guy.

But the real treasures, the stuff the Bureau's deep thinkers back in Virginia were going to just love, were at the other end of the upstairs hall, in a little room which apparently had served Angel as a study.

Miss Wyman, it became obvious, had approached her victims with the meticulous care of a paleontologist unearthing a dinosaur bone. There was a file on each of them, complete with newspaper clippings of the police investigations.

Among them was one labeled "Stephen Billinger."

"This will clear a lot of homicide investigations," Blandford said. "She wasn't very bright to keep all this junk—we could have put her away for about twenty thousand years. It's funny how they never expect to be caught."

"We didn't catch her."

Pratt picked up a handful of photographs that were lying on the desk. They had been taken with a good camera, probably from some distance, and almost certainly during an interval of no more than a few seconds. They showed a man in work clothes standing in a doorway, leaning against the frame.

"I know this guy," he said.

"Who is he?"

"His name is Flaxman. He runs a gas station in the little town where Jim Kinkaid lives. He's the sort that always comes to a bad end."

"Looks like he missed it this time. You think perhaps he should be told how close he came?"

"What's the point?"

The bullet that entered Kinkaid's back had taken only a small chunk out of his lung, but it was a month before his doctors would trust him on a plane. The day after he and Lisa returned to New Gilead he took her by the arm and walked her down to town hall to apply for a wedding license.

"Is this my punishment for shooting you?" she asked.

"No. That was my own fault for getting in the way. Probably it would have been better if I'd simply left you to it."

"Yes—I'm such a wonderful shot."

"At least you tried."

A faint suggestion of something like regret came into his expression, and she knew what he was thinking.

"You couldn't have stopped her," she told him, not for the first time. "The only way to do that would have been to kill her, and you couldn't kill anybody. That's one of the reasons I love you."

It was the trailing end of August and, while the weather was still warm, already there was something in the air that suggested summer was played out. Kinkaid found himself hoping the winter would come early. He liked winter. He liked to look down from his bedroom window and watch the snow pile up in the backyard. The cold seemed to clarify everything.

He was getting tired. It was not even half a mile to town hall and already he knew that once he got there he would need to call a taxi to get home again. The doctors had warned him that he would probably be several months recovering. He needed a long, cold winter to pull himself together again. He needed time to remember how not to be afraid.

And all he had to do was glance at Lisa to realize he was not the only one who carried scars.

"Maybe it would be a good idea if we tried not to talk about her," he said. "She's dead now. I'd like to bury her."

"Okay."

It was another two months before he was able to put in a full day at the office. He resigned his connection with Karskadon and Henderson, not only because he wasn't up to the work load but out of a vague feeling that somehow they had betrayed him. He decided he would have to content himself with a small-town law practice.

To give his mind something to do while he convalesced he began to work on an article analyzing some recent High Court decisions on copyright infringement cases. He finished it the last week in October and sent it off. Three weeks later he got a letter of acceptance from the *Yale Law Review*.

"Maybe I could be a law professor," he said to Lisa.

"Would you like that?"

"Yes, I would. There's no money in it, but you can have a practice on the side and I had a lot of fun in law school."

That evening he began mapping out another article.

A week before Christmas they got a card from Warren Pratt. He was down in Florida bonefishing.

"I'll have to write him—tell him about the baby."

Kinkaid smiled, the way he always did when he thought about the little being that had been assembling itself for the last two months inside Lisa's womb.

There was snow in the backyard and he had started running again. He felt great.

"If he's a boy I guess he'll be James Kinkaid V," Lisa answered, as if the part about Warren Pratt hadn't even registered.

"Maybe he'll be a girl."

"Don't be silly. Julia told me there hasn't been a girl born into this family in four generations."

"Then we're due for one."

"But if it's a boy. . . ?"

"Four Jameses are enough. What do you think of Mike?"

It was January and the dowagers in dark glasses and straw hats like truck tires sat on benches along the beachfront, staring up at the sun as if trying to remember what it was. Everyone was either very old or very young—retired people, mostly women, and teenagers on roller blades. Across the street were stucco apartment houses painted pink and pale blue.

Angel kept to the shade. She burned easily and, besides, she didn't like to be out in the open. Even though she knew no one was looking for her, either here in Florida or anywhere else, she could not quite shake the habit of thinking of herself as a fugitive.

The manhunt had been a lot of fun for two or three days—she watched the whole thing on television from her apartment in Mill Valley—and for a week she was national news. The San Francisco papers had kept up with the story for more than a month, but they had no suspect sitting in jail, not even a photograph to put on the front page, so they got bored. In California, where there are so many to choose from, they tend to be a little jaded about mass-murder cases. It was all forgotten now.

In the end she was saved by the policeman's instinct for finding the easy way out. First they thought she was wounded and then they thought she was dead, so they weren't prepared for the possibility that she might just walk away, two hours straight through the woods at a fast pace. The rain washed out her tracks, so they couldn't even use dogs. She had ended the night with nothing worse than a dislocated finger and a bad head cold.

The suicide theory was so convenient. Poor Jim—he had seen her covered in blood, never thinking that it was all his own, that he had bled all over her wrestling her gun away. He had taken the bullet with her name on it and then had provided her with the perfect out. She was shot and the police were coming, so of course she would throw herself into the ocean rather than endure capture. Once or twice in the days since, she had wondered if leaving the shoes behind hadn't been overplaying it just a trifle.

It was a rule of the game that you always gave yourself a choice of holes to disappear into, so she had kept an apartment in San Francisco and the one in Mill Valley, where all she had to do was to wait them out. After two weeks she got on a bus going north. From Seattle she flew to Miami. She had had to leave a lot of money behind, but there was still plenty.

The hardest thing was abandoning the idea that she could ever go home. She would never live at Five Miles again. She would never be Angel Wyman of the Connecticut Wymans. That door was closed forever.

But she didn't blame Jim. She couldn't really bring herself to blame him for anything—not even for Miss What's-Her-Name. Miss What's-Her-Name didn't count. If Grandmother hadn't lied, everything would have worked out and they would be at Five Miles this minute.

And Grandmother had, in fact, lied. There was no doubt about it. In the last few months Angel had relived that night a thousand times, and it always came out the same. Jim would never have thrown her over, even if he had known about the others—Grandmother had lied. One could only guess at her motives, but she had lied.

Jim had never betrayed her. He deserved to be left in peace.

The same, however, could not be said of Charlie Flaxman.

He was down here, in a motel not five miles away. He was under the impression he had won a family vacation from Publishers' Sweepstakes, two weeks' accommodation and round-trip airfare for himself and his disgusting family. Nobody ever looks too close when it's free.

They had landed the day before yesterday, and already Charlie was beginning to show signs of restlessness. Excursions to the boardwalk with the wife and kids was clearly not his idea of a wonderful time. He was ready for a little diversion.

There was one snag. Unlikely as it sounded, Charlie seemed to have struck up an acquaintance, a drinking buddy. Yesterday afternoon and then today, they had had a couple of beers together at an outdoor cafe near the Flaxmans' motel.

But it wasn't anything that need seriously get in the way. Charlie was a fun-loving boy and eventually he would get bored and want livelier company.

As for the old man, he was harmless. Angel had followed him to his hotel and then asked a few questions. He was nobody, a middle-aged tourist down for the fishing. His name was Warren Pratt.